REVE

G000026250

Andrew Frediani

About *Revenge*

Caesar is dead. Revenge has armed his hand. His name is Octavian.

Despite his young age, Octavian is already a consul. His position is not yet consolidated enough for him to carry out his plans of revenge upon the murderers of his beloved adoptive father Julius Caesar, though - and no courtroom can quench his thirst for justice.

He makes powerful allies in Mark Antony and Lepidus, with whom he forms a triumvirate, and unleashes upon the streets of Rome a reign of terror, turning the screws until the tension is such that it can find release only upon the battlefield. And he doesn't have to wait long: soon two great armies, led by four renowned commanders, stand ready to clash in Macedonia, far from the city of Rome and its corruption. One on side, Brutus and Cassius – on the other, Octavian and Mark Antony. It is the battle of Philippi, one of the most famous in Roman history. Is this where Caesar's murder will finally be avenged?

I

Assassin. It might almost sound like an honourable profession if you were doing it for the winning side. You could delude yourself that you were killing for a just cause, and that there was no great difference between stabbing a man in the back and confronting him face to face on the battlefield. Ortwin stood staring at the great river which separated him from the land where he'd spent his childhood and shook his head. When he was still living in Germany – back before he had encountered the Romans and fought alongside Julius Caesar and his young heir – he would have despised any man who did what he was now doing.

He used to dream of cavalry charges and battles, and though he had eventually fulfilled these ambitions, it had been very different to the way he imagined them. But life had dealt him more than his fair share of bad luck, and he had to start again from scratch, taking directions he never dreamed he would have to.

Assassin. The word tasted less bitter since he returned from the East and found his leader at the very pinnacle of power – a consul no less, in charge of almost as many legions as Caesar himself had once commanded. He had hoped that the young Octavian would have rewarded him, for successfully concluding the mission he'd assigned him, by allowing him to ride at his side in the civil war he was preparing to fight, an honour which he granted to the other soldiers of the Sect of Mars Ultor. Octavian, however, had dispatched him on another dirty job, sending him off across the borders of Italy, and almost beyond those of Gaul.

In the distance he could make out the country he'd already been forced to abandon twice. And just as in the East, he was once again coming as an executioner.

"Do you want to go over to the other side?" It was not a question. It was a test. One that it seemed natural to set his companion.

Veleda looked at him for a long time before answering. Remembering must have been painful for her. "No, not now," she said finally. "Not without any means of defending ourselves. We don't know what to expect on the other side."

A wise answer. The test was passed. If only he'd reasoned like that after the battle of Munda two years earlier they'd be warriors now, not killers. And with their own people, not with the Romans.

Maybe they'd even have become royalty, just as she had always dreamed.

But Ortwin said nothing. He didn't complain. He'd never complained since she'd persuaded him to abandon Caesar and assist her in her fruitless attempt to retake her father Ariovistus's throne. He'd never blamed her for their inevitable failure, which had left them begging the Romans for work as bodyguards – work which only Octavian had deigned to grant them.

And even then only on condition that they kill Julius Caesar's assassins.

And now here they were on the Rhine, on the very edge of the Roman world, within spitting distance of what could have been their kingdom, on a mission to execute another of the men who'd betrayed Caesar's trust – Decimus

Brutus Albinus.

Ortwin wasn't sorry, though. His destiny could have held worse surprises in store than having to avenge the best commander he'd ever served under. Of course, he'd rather have done it on the battlefield alongside Octavian, Agrippa, Salvidienus Rufus, Maecenas and Gaius Chaerea, the other warriors of the Sect of Mars Ultor, the group into which he had been accepted – that would have been more honourable for a warrior like him. But he was certain that his job wouldn't lessen the pleasure of sinking his blade into the throat of that swine, a man Caesar had promoted to exalted positions, first as his right hand man, then as Proconsul of Gaul, only to be repaid by being stabbed to death. Ortwin was proud of having meted out the same punishment to Trebonius only a few months earlier in Asia.

And now it was Decimus Brutus's turn. They had once fought side by side in Gaul during Caesar's proconsulship more than a decade ago. But that coward had been on the run for months now, fleeing the net that Mark Antony and Lepidus had tightened around him after the siege of Modena. A strange war that. Ortwin, who had been in the East at the time, had only heard tell of it, and wasn't at all sure he understood what had happened. Decimus Brutus had gone to Gaul, which had been assigned to him by the man he later killed, but Mark Antony, who wanted the province for himself, attacked and besieged him at Modena. In response, the Senate dispatched the two new consuls, Hirtius and Pansa, later joined by Octavian, to take on Antony. After a series of battles, they had forced Antony to flee, but Hirtius and Pansa were both killed in battle, and in a strange twist of fate Decimus Brutus ended up being saved by the very man who had most wanted him dead – Octavian. It was a short-lived reprieve, though, and as soon as young Octavian was appointed consul, he declared Decimus Brutus an enemy of the state, along with all the others who had participated in Caesar's murder. Mistrustful of Antony, he had set his best assassin onto Brutus's trail, keen to ensure that his revenge was carried out.

"Are you sure that's Bauto's village?" Veleda's question brought him back to their more immediate concerns. It wasn't like when he was Caesar's chief bodyguard. Now he was a mere executioner and had to act, not think.

"Yes, that's what the woodcutter told me yesterday," he replied, trying to look more confident than he felt, especially in front of the men Octavian had assigned him. "He said it was the only settlement we would find on this part of the Rhine. Bauto considers himself a king around here, and won't let anyone build near his palace."

"Palace?" snorted Veleda, tilting her chin at the humble wood and mud house set between several surrounding huts. The shapes of the buildings were blurred by the morning mist, which lay thickly on the banks of the mighty river. "If that's a palace, my father must have lived in an imperial mansion!" she quipped.

Ortwin smiled, and urged his horse on towards the village. Over time, Veleda had lost her sense of proportion: the residence of her father, the supreme leader of the Suebi, hadn't been much more refined, not even when he'd taken control of several Gallic tribes. "The truth is that you've become accustomed to Roman houses, or at least those of the richest Gauls," he said cautiously, knowing how much the subject annoyed her, "and we both know that a Roman

4

plebeian allows himself more luxuries than a German nobleman."

The woman kept quiet, and Ortwin knew why. She would never have openly admitted that the Romans, the very people responsible for destroying her father and her dreams of glory, were superior to the barbarians. This was a simple truth he'd learned through experience, but for her it was a reality she refused to accept.

There were no sentries at the entrance to the village, which had no moat but was roughly circled by a low fence. Evidently Bauto wasn't worried about anyone from the area threatening his authority. Or perhaps he was just unprepared. In any case, they were strangers and it didn't seem right to barge into the village unannounced. Ortwin stopped about two hundred yards from the fence and ordered one of the Celtic troops from Octavian's guard to enter the village and ask, on his behalf, for an interview with the chief. He looked on as his man entered the open gateway, noticing movement inside as he did so. He continued watching and saw his envoy speak quietly to a soldier. Shortly afterwards, a group of men gathered and his man disappeared from sight, only to re-appear on foot surrounded by a knot of men. They gestured to Ortwin to move forward and stop a few paces from the gate. His soldier came over and joined him. "Bauto is that one there," he said, pointing to a man of fairly advanced age in a rough tunic and trousers who looked fat rather than well-built. "He says that you can come in, but alone."

Ortwin looked at Veleda, who nodded. They'd been through worse: after he'd had dealings with people like Ariovistus, Caesar, Antony, Octavian, Cleopatra, Vercingetorix and Pompey the Great, he certainly wasn't going to worry about a buffoon who liked to pass himself off as a great king.

He dismounted and, escorted by his trooper, entered the village and walked purposefully towards Bauto who stood waiting for him, fists on his hips, studying him warily.

He held out his hand. "My name is Ortwin," he began, trying to adopt a cordial tone, even though he didn't like the look of the man in front of him. "From my lord, the Roman Consul Gaius Julius Caesar Octavian, I bring you greetings, as well as gifts."

"And can't Rome send me anyone better than a one-eyed barbarian?" replied Bauto, contemptuously.

No, he didn't like him at all. But despite the goading reference to his one remaining eye, he forced himself to keep his composure. "Clearly, I have managed to earn Rome's trust," he said, "and that is why I'm here on such a delicate matter. I know you have a guest – a man the Senate has declared an enemy of the State."

"And what if I do?" replied the man. "The authority of Rome counts for nothing here on the Rhine. I can put up anyone I like if there's something in it for me."

"It might be worth your while to hand your guest over to me."

"I doubt it. *If* I had any guests, it would only be because it was worth my while... I don't usually have much time for strangers."

"But you don't know how much you could earn. I'm not here to impose Rome's authority on you, if that's what's bothering you, but to make you rich."

Bauto gave a deep belly laugh. "So you could say that what you're asking me isn't exactly legal, right?"

"That's up to you to decide," replied Ortwin, coolly. "You're harbouring a criminal. By rights you should hand him over to the emissary of a consul of Rome without any conditions. But Octavian would like to reward you personally. He would consider it... a personal favour."

"I don't think Octavian could pay me more than Mark Antony... Especially if you also take into account the generosity of my guest, who is willing to reward me handsomely for his stay. I'm already rich, my friend."

Ortwin had to hide his astonishment. He wasn't surprised that Decimus Brutus was willing to pay, perhaps using money from his fellow conspirators. No – what struck him was that Mark Antony too, was willing to pay just to get his hands on Decimus Brutus. Octavian was right to be wary of the former consul. Until then, Antony had shown no signs of wanting to avenge Caesar's death, so why had he decided to get hold of Decimus Brutus now, if not to execute him just as the Sect of Mars Ultor planned to?

The answer seemed clear: Antony wanted to protect Brutus from Caesar's son, perhaps to use him against Octavian. Perhaps Antony, who knew he'd have to deal with Caesar's heir in the very near future, had thought to limit his power by saving Caesar's killers rather than attempting to pursue them seriously.

All the more reason, then, to eliminate Decimus Brutus.

He heard the village gate close behind him.

"But I could make even more by handing you over to Antony and keeping your money," said Bauto, motioning for his men to surround Ortwin. Then he turned to the Celtic trooper. "Tell your soldiers out there to put down their weapons and bring me the money if they ever want to see their leader in one piece again."

At that moment, a Roman emerged from the nearest hut. He gave Ortwin a wry smile, turned away with ostentatious indifference, and disappeared.

Decimus Brutus Albinus had always been contemptible, said Ortwin, cursing himself for having misread the situation.

*

What a strange feeling, being on the verge of bringing a new life into the world whilst simultaneously being about to take one, thought Etain to herself as she watched Lucius Minucius Basilus stroking his wife's hair. She had just styled it with a *calmistrum*, a red-hot iron.

"Don't I look better with straight hair, dear husband?" said the woman, pleased with the work of her new slave.

Basilus looked at Etain casually, before noticing that several strands of his wife's hair hung from the slave's hand. A cruel gleam appeared in his eyes, and his free hand shot out towards the girl, striking her violently on the temple. Etain shuddered but didn't make a sound: she was used to it.

"You damn fool! Do you want to make her bald?" shouted Caesar's killer, stepping forward as though he intended to continue beating her, without any regard for her pregnancy.

But his wife rose from her chair and stepped between him and Etain. "It's normal that the hot iron makes some hair fall out, Basilus," she protested. "It always does, no matter which slave does it. In fact, she's more careful than the others…"

Basilus stopped, trembling visibly. He looked at Etain and then at his wife, shook his head, and left the *domina's* room.

"Don't be afraid," the woman said to Etain tenderly. "He's very irritable at the moment and gets worked up over the smallest thing. But it's not we women who should be afraid of his anger in this house," she re-assured her, indicating for her to take the kohl from the bowl on the dressing table shelf and continue applying her make-up.

Etain knew exactly what she meant. Her *domina* Octavia had taught her well, before dispatching her to kill Minucius Basilus for his role in the Ides of March conspiracy the year before – the very conspiracy which had cost Octavia's great-uncle Julius Caesar his life. At first, she'd taken it badly. It had been a chaotic time and she'd been shaken by the behaviour of the person she considered her man: Salvidienus Rufus, who had abandoned her after learning she was pregnant. But that had turned out to be the least of her problems. Within less than a year, she had been raped, found out that her first lover, Agrippa, was sleeping with Fulvia, one of Rome's most captivating and high-ranking matrons, been submitted to Rufus' courtship, discovered she was pregnant and let herself be dragged along by her feelings. And all that only to receive yet another slap in the face. She would have wanted to die had it not been for the life she was carrying inside her. Or for the Sect of Mars Ultor, which had made her swear before the gods to serve the cause of taking revenge on Caesar's murderers whatever the cost.

Whatever the cost. Even if it meant ending up in that madhouse and becoming a killer – she, who had never hurt

9

a fly in her entire life. Even if it meant pretending to be a slave for other people, as well as for her mistress Octavia, despite having been made a freedwoman years before.

These were dangerous people she was dealing with, and she was alone, far from Rome and from Octavia or anyone in the sect who could defend her if things got really bad. They hadn't told her how to kill Basilus, limiting themselves to suggesting that she exploit the discontent that reigned in the house: for the slaves hated their master for his cruelty. The head of the sect, Octavian, had never deigned to talk to her about it, but his sister Octavia had told her that he was especially keen for this one of Caesar's assassins to be killed. Basilus was the only conspirator who had chosen to stay on Italian territory rather than escaping to the provinces or going to stay with one of the other murderers.

From all accounts, Basilus had joined the conspiracy out of frustration. He'd fought with Caesar in Gaul and had received a large sum of money at the end of the civil war instead of a province like many of the others. For this reason, and for this reason alone, he'd continued stabbing Caesar's body on the Ides of March longer than anyone else, even injuring one of his fellow conspirators in his frenzy. At least – Octavia had confided to her – he hadn't wrapped his actions up in ideological motives, like most of his associates, who had claimed to be freeing Rome from a tyrant when all they were really doing was taking out their frustrations and jealousies on their benefactor. All those who had wielded their knives in the Curia of Pompey had tried to convince the Roman people that they had done it to free them.

Etain understood nothing about politics. Before

entering the sect, she had simply served her mistress, but since joining her perspective had changed and her horizons had expanded, and thanks to the oath she'd taken, she was now bound more than ever to the fate of the *Julia* family. She even had the chance to influence the course of history, and this might help her forget the terrible romantic disappointments she'd suffered in such a short time. She'd therefore welcomed Octavia's mission when it had come so soon after Rufus's rejection. She had a mission, her first since entering the sect. But her pregnancy still served as a constant reminder of the many injuries she'd received from men... just like Caesar. On the other hand, it was only because she was pregnant that Octavian and Octavia had decided to use her as an assassin. Basilus was the only one of Caesar's murderers to hand, the only one who could be arrested with relative ease. But Octavian had no intention of granting the traitor the privilege of a court trial, with the risk that the killer's supporters in the Senate would simply sentence him to exile. The complex network of patronage and co-operation that Octavian had created with his sect had enabled him to find a front man to sell Etain to Basilus with false ownership papers. And Basilus had thought he'd got a bargain in buying a pregnant young slave girl, two slaves for the price of one.

It had been child's play so far, but the hard part was coming now, the girl said to herself as she applied pigment to her mistress's cheeks. The more she thought about it, the more she realised that she would not be capable of killing him with her bare hands. She was convinced that the best way was to stir up the discontent of the slaves until the most volatile person reacted. And she'd already identified one young slave, with whom she'd entered into

11

confidence. Even though she was pregnant, she'd slept with him and learnt chilling details about the household – things even more horrific than those of which Octavia had warned her. She would have loved to have had even a fraction of the eloquence she'd so often admired in Octavian now, to convince the slave to undertake the task for her.

But she needed a spark to light the fire, so she waited. She'd been waiting for weeks for Basilus to use his dagger again – perhaps the same dagger he'd used to murder Caesar in the brutal and ferocious fashion she'd heard about. And when she heard a piercing scream which made her mistress leap from her chair, and her start so violently that she dropped the make-up brush into the woman's hair, she knew that the time had come. The *domina* ran from the room and she rushed out after her. They followed the sound of the screams to the room of Basilus' eldest son, a young man who had recently started to wear the *toga virilis*, even though he wasn't yet worthy of it. They found him on the bed, naked and in tears, his father standing next to him holding a knife, its blade red with blood which dripped onto the floor. In a corner of the room, a kneeling slave groaned as he squeezed his bloody hands between his thighs.

In a pool of liquid scarlet in front of him, it was just possible to make out his cleanly severed penis.

*

The Curia of Pompey was already packed. Lucius Pinarius noted with satisfaction that virtually no senator had neglected their duty to come and attend the session. That said, with civil war imminent, everyone wanted to have their say, but it would be quite another thing to induce them to vote for the sect's objectives, which were not exactly those they thought they had come to agree to. He watched as his cousin Quintus Pedius settled into the Consul's chair on the stage, and sighed. Yes, he thought, I was actually jealous when Octavian chose him as a fellow consul a few months ago, but I wouldn't change places with him now for anything in the world.

No one could predict what would happen when the senators realised they were being hoodwinked – and they would realise that as soon as Pedius started to introduce the day's agenda. Would they bend to Octavian's will? Or would Cicero's views prevail? It was precisely this that frightened him: if the senators rebelled, how would he and Pedius cope, given that Octavian and the other sect members were already marching towards Gaul? It would be easy for the supporters of Caesar's killers to take them prisoner, along with Octavia and her mother Atia, and use them as hostages to force Octavian to respect the commitments he'd made to the Senate in return for his election as consul. The cohort that had been left in Rome to protect them, commanded by Gaius Chaerea – a member of the sect – would probably be next to useless.

And Pinarius wasn't at all sure that Octavian, unscrupulous and ambitious as he was, as well as madly determined to avenge Caesar's death and to emulate his achievements, would allow himself to be swayed by a threat to his relatives' lives. The men most useful to him in that moment were already with him, and perhaps that was all he needed.

Pedius let the *princeps senatus* declare the session open

as the last senators took their places in the banked seating of the hall which Octavian planned to close, having defined it a *locus sceleratus* after the death of his great-uncle. The consul then covered his head with his toga, offered a prayer to the gods, and placed an offering of food on the brazier which burned on the podium. Pinarius distractedly followed the sacred ritual whilst focusing most of his attention on his colleagues' expressions, trying to work out who might give his cousin trouble.

"Illustrious colleagues, as you know, the young consul Gaius Julius Caesar Octavian is currently nearing Gaul's borders with the legions entrusted to him by the Senate," Pedius began. "He has taken upon himself the immense task of bringing the enemy of the state Decimus Brutus Albinus to justice, and of bringing the rebels Mark Antony and Lepidus back under the authority of the Senate. We should therefore be grateful for the dedication he is showing in protecting Rome and our communal interests."

Pinarius watched the senators, catching sight of the occasional fleeting grimace and laugh – Pedius's words undoubtedly lent themselves to facile mockery.

"But it is a mission full of unknowns," the consul continued. "We do not know how many allies Decimus Brutus will find as he flees. The latest news has him headed towards the Rhine. And we do not know how a pitched battle between Republican troops and those available to Antony and Lepidus would finish. Nor do we know who the provincial governors will side with. During the recent battle in Modena, they behaved in a highly ambiguous way. And you know how many deaths a civil war might cause, how many privations it could force on the very people who have entrusted their fate to we senators."

Here he goes, thought Pinarius, feeling a slight shiver run down his spine – he's preparing the ground to deliver his blow.

"Julius Caesar's heir has always put himself forward as a peacemaker. He has never sought confrontation with anyone, apart from his father's murderers. Ever since he received his inheritance from the dictator, he has always tried to seek consensus, never to impose it, persistently calling for the assistance of Mark Antony and the most distinguished members of this assembly, starting with you, Cicero. Conversely, Mark Antony has never shown himself to be accommodating, but has rather exacerbated the situation, even forcing us senators – we who at first appreciated his approach – to deny him support. Antony is unpredictable. He has his own personal agenda, which is impossible to know, but he holds sway over the soldiers and over Lepidus, and we cannot afford to ignore that. Rome is already engaged in a battle without quarter against Caesar's assassins, who are becoming increasingly powerful in the East. Wearing ourselves out in a conflict against Antony and Lepidus would only play into the hands of people like Marcus Brutus and Cassius Longinus. They are waiting for any chance to launch a counter-offensive and regain control of the city. In short, a civil war against Lepidus and Antony would only benefit Caesar's killers, the very people you have just defined 'enemies of the state'."

These were valid arguments. Pinarius saw that some senators were nodding. But there weren't yet enough of them to constitute a re-assuring block of support. On the other hand, many held that the condemnation of Caesar's killers had been unjust and that it had been forcibly extorted by Octavian and his troops camped outside Rome.

"Therefore, distinguished senators, why should we help our principal enemies by killing one another? Why should we decimate our troops when we could build an invincible army by joining forces with Antony and Lepidus – an army strong enough to destroy any opponent, and to finally put to rest the threat posed by Brutus, Cassius and the rest of them? Why should we give up the very real possibility of regaining control over the East, over the precious provinces of Asia, Syria and Macedonia, that these criminals have stolen from Rome, with the attendant risk of starving it?"

This time there were more signs of agreement from the senators. Some appeared hesitant and muttered to their neighbours whilst others spoke animatedly. Many more, however, and not only those related to Caesar's killers, made sneering faces of superiority or shook their heads.

"I would therefore ask you Senators – you, the principal guardians of Rome's welfare and that of its citizens – to drop your many rightful demands for revenge against Mark Antony. Illustrious fathers, grant my colleague Octavian the opportunity to once again attempt to convince Antony and Lepidus to return to the service of Rome and to place themselves under the authority of the Senate. In return, we will lift any charges laid against them last year and during the war of Modena."

Uproar broke out in the hall, echoing off the high walls. Pinarius thought that Octavian's offer of a Senate amnesty would easily convince Antony and Lepidus to join him in the game for power. His cousin had reached the pinnacle of state power thanks to a play of strength, but he no longer had the means or the authority to stay in the saddle: his position was precarious, and his lucid intelligence wouldn't let him deceive himself. Only by convincing Antony and Lepidus to support him could he become unassailable and thus pursue his vendetta, as well as his plans to reform Rome and give it a stable and lasting empire.

"That's a contemptible proposal! First Octavian gets us to give him a consulship to fight Antony, then he makes an agreement with him."

"You've made fools of us! You've been planning to join Antony all along!"

"Right! And maybe you've always been in league with him – even before you marched on Rome!"

"Of course! Octavian hasn't fought him since the war of Modena!"

Pinarius glanced at his cousin standing on the podium. Pedius, his concern evident, returned his gaze. Only the dissenters were shouting. There were far too many of them, but fortunately there were no prominent figures among them. What counted was what Cicero might have to say, and Cicero had always shown himself to be favourable to Octavian, believing him to be the lesser of the evils in play.

The great orator rose after the protests had quietened down and the Senators' anger had dimmed to a level which allowed him to speak.

"Distinguished colleagues," he began, "you all know how strongly I spoke against Mark Antony both before and during the war of Modena. I now regard him as the worst of Rome's enemies, and my speeches against him will stand as a testimony indelibly etched upon the memory of the Romans. I certainly cannot retract them, even if politics often requires us to retrace our steps for the good of the State. By expressing my views so clearly I undoubtedly earned his everlasting enmity, but I have no regrets, nor fears for the consequences. I am increasingly convinced that this man – the same man who exploited our support to consolidate his own power – is the worst tyrant to have ever befallen Rome. I am convinced that from the very beginning he has sought to become a new Julius Caesar, or worse, given that he is no genius and is not of equal stature. Because I will grant that Caesar had stature, even if he was an autocrat. I would therefore urge you to fight him to the bitter end. Not to protect me but because I think he represents a far greater threat to our Republic than those who acted in good faith and in the name of freedom. Rome would suffer more under Antony than under anyone else!"

Pinarius saw with dismay that senators who had earlier been favourable to Pedius's argument, were now nodding thoughtfully at Cicero's words.

Things were looking bad.

II

"He doesn't really want me to do it," Veleda kept repeating to herself, as she approached the village's home fence. "He *can't* want me to do it. It just wouldn't be like him, not after what we've been through." In the meantime she continued to glance furtively at the men Ortwin had left her after having first assured himself that they were ready to spring into action at her command. When they'd left for Gaul, he had struggled to convince these coarse Celts that in his absence they would have to obey a woman. And now they would find out if he had taught them well.

She was close enough to the Gauls to be able to see the mistrustful expressions of the two warriors who had come to guard the entrance and escort them to their chief. Veleda could read lust for the money Ortwin had promised them in their eyes, which stared fixedly at the wagon. No, he can't really want me to, she continued to say to herself. Bauto and Decimus Brutus would kill them anyway, and even if they didn't, Octavian would never forgive them for their failure and they would once again find themselves without a home or hope. Their earlier success in the East, where they'd killed Trebonius and Dolabella, wouldn't count for anything. She didn't expect any sympathy from Octavian, and was certain that he would abandon them at their first mistake.

Thirty men. Only thirty men against an entire village. And with no weapons, as Bauto had insisted. For all she knew, there might be hundreds of warriors inside the enclosure they were about to enter. It was madness even to think she could do it, but it was clear that Ortwin wanted her to do something. Veleda approached the sentries, who checked that she and the Celtic troopers were carrying no arms, their fingers lingering unnecessarily long on her body. She had to struggle to resist the urge to grab the hands that were groping her and bite off their fingers, but just when she thought she could restrain her impulsive nature no longer, the other sentry motioned for her troops to bring the wagon into the village.

Encouraging. Or was it simply deceptive? Veleda tried to re-assure herself by thinking of the many times that she and Ortwin had been up against it, but she could think of no situation riskier than the one they found themselves in now. She was escorted to the centre of the village, past wretched huts and pack animals, until she could make out the form of her man, against whose chest two warriors stood pressing the tips of their swords. Next to them was another man, wearing a decorated helmet and chain mail, who she took to be Bauto. As she moved forward, she exchanged another quick look with her men to ensure they were positioned closely around the wagon, and studied the situation. The Gaul chief was surrounded by about fifty warriors while many others roamed the area, some armed, some not. About the same number of women also stared at them with hostility, and it was clear that they wouldn't just be spectators if a fight broke out.

It would be impossible to take them all on.

She only had one chance, and she had to use it well. In the eerie silence, with everybody's eyes fixed upon the wagon that the Gauls already considered their booty, Veleda looked at Ortwin, hoping to understand what he expected of her. But he remained impassive. His face gave nothing away, and his eyes bore no message.

Veleda approached the Gaul chief while staying close to the wagon. Bauto inspected her with an expression of contempt and desire, his eyes dwelling upon her mutilated hand.

"This is the first time I've see a woman – and a maimed woman at that – lead a squad of soldiers. Are things so bad for our new consul that he has to make use of half-women?" asked Bauto, derisively. "And who are you, anyway?"

"I am his consort," she said neutrally, pointing at Ortwin, "and he is our leader."

Bauto gave a hoarse laugh. "A one-eye and a cripple! It gets better and better! What a lovely couple!" The other warriors followed their chief's lead, and soon a chorus of laughter echoed around the village.

"An old joke," scowled Veleda. "A sign of little imagination, if not actual stupidity." She'd heard it countless times over the last couple of years, ever since she'd mistaken Ortwin for an enemy and stabbed him in the eye. For his part, years before he'd had to follow Caesar's orders and cut a hand off every one of the defenders of the Gallic stronghold of Uxellodunum, and it was only after he'd put his sword down that he'd recognised her.

The chieftain was suddenly serious. "Woman," he said, "you don't appear to be in any position to make jokes. Unlike me."

"I bring you great riches, my lord," replied Veleda, trying to keep her nerve and not lower her eyes, "which surely earns me some privileges." If these Gauls were like the Germans she'd grown up with, they'd appreciate a proud attitude more than a submissive one.

The chief nodded. "Well, let's see this money, then," he said, signalling for one of his warriors to jump up onto the wagon and open the chest that stood in the middle.

Veleda pretended to believe that he was addressing her, and moved to jump onto the wagon ahead of the man. The Celtic troops closed in imperceptibly on the wagon, and, as they'd agreed earlier, one of them casually took hold of the horse's harness. The woman glanced quickly at Ortwin and thought she saw a flicker of concern in his eyes. She then peered at Bauto, who looked annoyed.

"Leave it to my soldier, woman," the chief said, immediately.

But by now she had climbed up onto the wagon. "The chest has a complicated lock," she muttered. "I wouldn't want you getting angry with me if your man can't open it." The soldier had now climbed up as well and they found themselves facing each other. The Gaul hesitated a moment and stared at his chief, his expression asking whether he should step back. The chief was undecided. He looked at Veleda suspiciously, but gave no order. She leapt towards the large trunk, opening the lid easily and grabbing the swords she'd placed inside earlier then throwing them quickly to her men. Before the Gaul next to her, who had recovered from his surprise, had time to throw himself at her, she seized the one remaining sword and ran it through his stomach.

In the meantime, her men, exploiting the element of surprise, managed to surround Bauto, who suddenly found himself with at least three blades at his throat before the Gauls had time to react. They immobilised the soldiers holding Ortwin, and unhitched the horse from the wagon.

Veleda climbed down from it and approached the Gaul chief, who was looking at her in bewilderment. All around them were seething warriors and women, desperate to intervene, but the blades pressing into Bauto's body seemed to be a sufficient deterrent.

For the moment, at least.

Ortwin managed to free himself from his guards' grip, taking a sword from one of them and ordering his men to disarm everyone in the immediate surroundings, then he walked over to Veleda, smiled, grasped her stump, and whispered in her ear, "I knew you'd do something, but I didn't think you'd handle it so skilfully. I also thought you might have got us all killed. I'm proud of you."

Veleda's chest swelled with pride. She knew that Ortwin loved her more than anything, but as for respecting her... well, she'd always had her doubts. Because of the bad choices she'd forced him to make, as much as anything. She stepped back to let him take over.

"Well, my lord," said Ortwin to Bauto in an openly mocking tone, "it would seem that you have no choice but to accept our offer. Hand over Decimus Brutus Albinus or these miserable lands will have a new owner. And naturally you'll come some of the way back with us on our return journey. We wouldn't want your friends here getting any ideas about taking revenge for this little episode."

"If you kill me, none of you will get out of here alive," said Bauto. He was attempting to appear sure of himself, but his voice had lost its tone of ostentatious self-confidence.

"Maybe," admitted Ortwin. "But there will be a

massacre. Before your men can overpower us, we'll kill everyone we've disarmed. And anyway, what would it matter to you – you'd be dead anyway. In fact, you'd be the first to go."

Bauto's face remained grim a moment longer, then he shrugged his broad shoulders, sighed deeply and said, "So be it – take that dandy if you must. I just hope the sum is generous."

Veleda heaved a sigh of relief. They'd done it. Now all they needed was for someone to show them which hut the former Pro-consul, who had kept himself well hidden from view since she'd entered the village, had crept into.

"Kill him if you want. He's no longer the chief." A voice from over near the fence stopped her in her tracks. She turned in the direction from which it had come, and saw a young man, fully armed and with thirty well-equipped warriors and more by his side, moving forward.

Ortwin looked at the lad and then at Bauto in bewilderment.

"Who's that?" he asked the chief.

"My son," said Bauto bitterly. "It would seem he's decided to take advantage of the situation to bring forward the succession. I'd say we're in trouble."

*

"Do you want to end up the same way?"

Etain stared at the slave she'd started sleeping with, sneaking into his bed in the dead of night while the Basilus household slept. She didn't especially like the lad, and she found it tiresome making love whilst pregnant, but she was working for the sect. "I love playing with this thing,"

24

she said, smiling, as she stroked his member, now limp after he had climaxed earlier, "and I wouldn't know what to do with you if they cut it off. Spending time cuddling isn't exactly my idea of making love…" She was amazed to hear herself talking like this. Only a month before, when Rufus had left her after discovering that she was pregnant, she'd still had a romantic view of love and sex. Agrippa and Rufus were the only men she'd ever been with, apart from the criminals who had raped her, and she had never imagined she would have gone looking for lovers. Now, though, she had begun to use her body as a tool, and men as a means to achieve her ends. She was becoming a corrupt woman, like that Fulvia – and she didn't at all mind the feeling of power it gave her. That poor frightened slave was putty in her hands, as she could see clearly now, and would do anything to remain close to her.

"The young master hasn't forced me to do anything so far…" the slave objected, but with little conviction.

Etain rose from the pillow and sat up, flaunting her beautifully sculpted breasts, and a spark of desire re-ignited in the boy's eye.

"*So far*, as you rightly say," she replied. "But you don't know how long that will last. How many house slaves have been castrated since that boy started having sexual urges? Three? Four?"

"Five…" he replied, swallowing, and caressing her breast.

"That's right. You do know that when he turns to you, you won't be able to refuse his attentions? You'll finish up like all the others. Every slave he chooses is forced to go along with him in the hope that they'll get away with the lesser evil, as long as Basilus doesn't find out. But Basilus

25

always finds out, sooner or later..."

"Maybe... maybe his father will finally manage to get him to like women."

"There are some impulses that can't be suppressed. He'll always be attracted to men, starting with the easiest ones to lust after: his slaves. The only thing left for you is to decide how to die. Either way, you lose me," she said, colder than she'd ever imagined she could be. But then, she cared nothing for the young man. She had a life growing inside her, and all that mattered was protecting her own future and that of the child she would be raising. Once she'd completed the sect's mission, she would quickly return to Octavia, the best mistress anyone could hope to have. Because, if Basilus didn't die, her child would have to grow up in the horrible atmosphere of that house.

"What do you think I should do?" the young man replied, burying his face between her breasts like a child looking for protection.

Etain hugged him, then caressed his back and ran her hands down his body. She drew his head to her nipples, prompting him to suck them, and held his penis, making him shudder with pleasure. "I'll explain," she whispered in his ear, then bent down between his legs to demonstrate what he'd miss if he didn't take action.

Within two days, the boy said he was ready. She knew that no matter what steps he might take to hide his tracks, it would be extremely difficult for him to get away undetected. It was quite probable that every male slave in the house would be executed as punishment for the master's death, but she didn't care. Their death would be a small price to pay for achieving the sect's main objectives, as well as a kind of revenge for everything that men had inflicted on her.

It was the dead of night again. He had come to her room carrying a dagger in his hand. They had made love, and she had used every sensual trick she knew, all those that Agrippa and Rufus had taught her as well as any others that came to mind. She had put aside every last trace of modesty to convince him to overcome his fears and refuse to become the object of a spoiled boy's pleasure and the cruelty of a traitor like Basilus.

"Just think: when you've killed the master, I'll be yours forever. And when I've given birth, you'll be the father of my child and won't have to see me with this big ugly belly..." she told him as she lay beneath him, caressing him. Her voice didn't even tremble: by now she had learned how to lie.

In the end she had to practically push him out of bed: the slave continued tossing and turning under the sheets, stroking her naked body and trying to put off the moment of action. But it would be dawn shortly and they would have lost the perfect opportunity. He had to do it that night, and make it look like suicide. In that way, the slave naively hoped, the household staff wouldn't suffer the family's reprisals. Eventually the boy went, silent and hunched under the weight of responsibility and fear for the consequences. He threw one last hopeful look at her.

She blew him a kiss of encouragement and remained in bed, waiting for the events she had instigated to unfold. She strained her ears but the house lay cloaked in silence. Gradually, as the minutes passed, she realised that she was breathing more heavily, that her heart was beating faster, and that her stomach felt like it was being squeezed in an ever-tightening vice. Just then, the door opened, and the

27

man who had left her bed what seemed like an eternity ago dived under the sheets, sweating and breathless.

"Have you done it?" she asked, trying not to reveal the turmoil she was feeling.

"Y-yes," he stammered, hugging her and kissing her all over.

Irritated, she pushed him away. She knew that she should comfort him, but first she had to know. "What happened?" she urged.

He was hurt. He was more fragile than ever at that moment.

"Er... I think it went well. He was sleeping when I went into his room. Without thinking, I stabbed him in the chest with all my strength, and he just shuddered slightly. I saw blood pouring from his mouth, and his eyes widen and stay like that."

"So you're sure he's dead?"

"As sure as I am that you're here with me, in my arms," replied the young man, holding her and searching for her mouth.

"And then?" she insisted, turning her face away.

"And then... I put his hands on the weapon as though he had stabbed himself, and came back here to you. I'm sure no one noticed anything. We'll just have to wait until someone finds the body. They'll put two and two together."

"Let's hope so," sighed Etain, finally conceding the man a reward but without actively participating herself. Her mind was focused on the coming dawn when the whole household would wake up and discover the crime. She would then have to wait for the news to reach Rome. At which point Octavia would immediately set about buying her back, enabling her to escape this place full of madness.

The scream came shortly after sunrise. Etain recognized the voice of the slave responsible for waking the master, and then, suddenly, a great clamour broke out, shaking the walls of the building. The two lovers had to pretend to be curious about the commotion and so they also left their room – some people saw them rushing out of the cubicle together. It was perfect, just as she'd hoped: that way the young man had the alibi of having spent the night with her. Etain was comforted by the chaos into which the house had been plunged as it meant that the slave really had carried out his task – another of Caesar's murderers was dead, and yet another step had been taken along the path of revenge in the name of Mars Ultor.

She saw the despairing *domina* embracing her son – the very person who had indirectly sparked off the uproar. The young boy cried like a little girl, but the slaves were terrified by the thought that they were the obvious suspects. Before long, the city's decurion appeared. He immediately ordered the four gladiators of his escort to search the house. The magistrate, a clumsy, greasy, middle-aged man, began to question the servants one by one. The questions were the customary ones: "did you seen any strangers enter the house?", "did anyone here have any reason to hold grievances against the master?" This last question, in particular, elicited embarrassed responses from everyone.

Clearly, the magistrate was trying to examine every possibility and determine if it really was suicide: if Basilus had decided to settle in that obscure part of Apulia, it was obvious that he had been able to count on the support of the city authorities. Perhaps the decurion was a friend of his, or Basilus had paid him handsomely? In any case, the decurion felt duty bound to check the circumstances of his death in far more detail than the duties of his position actually called for. After all, Basilus had been a declared enemy of the Roman Senate, and he shouldn't really have tolerated his presence in the city. For a magistrate loyal to the institutions, Basilus's death should have been good news, something he didn't need to worry about.

However, he was not a magistrate loyal to the institutions, though, but a client of Caesar's killers. And when it emerged that the master had castrated several slaves, his murderer began to tremble. Etain feared that it might give him away and elbowed him to urge him to keep control. He had yet to be questioned, and in his condition would almost certainly break down.

The decurion began to check the slaves and got someone to point out who had been castrated. There were only three of them left – the other two had already died following their mutilation. The unfortunate slaves were interrogated, harassed and pressured to confess to a crime they hadn't committed. They screamed, protested their innocence, and knelt in supplication, but the magistrate remained unmoved. Then a gladiator took him by the arm and whispered in his ear. The decurion nodded, thought a moment, and went to confide something to the sobbing widow. The woman opened her eyes wide and looked at the three castrated slaves before passing a gaze full of hatred over each of the household slaves.

The magistrate cleared his throat and declared: "I don't think there is any point continuing this questioning. One of my bodyguards found bloody footprints by Senator Minucius Basilus' bed. The murderer was so stupid that he didn't even notice he'd stepped in the blood dripping from the bed... understandable given that he acted in total darkness. In any case, we now have evidence that this wasn't suicide. And I don't care which of you is the killer. As is the custom, every slave in the house will be put to death."

Etain had reckoned that it might go like that. She didn't even bother to cast a look of understanding at the boy she'd driven to kill. She didn't care about the slave's fate, nor about that of the rest of the staff.

"I hope the authorities will refund the cost of all the new slaves I'll have to buy," said the sobbing *domina*. "To add insult to injury we risk becoming penniless if we're forced to make such an expensive purchase. With *all* the confiscations we've suffered during Octavian's regime, our financial situation is far from rosy."

"We'll see what can be done," the decurion assured her. "In any case, you'll have to buy new female slaves as well. Custom dictates that all the slaves are executed to set a clear example. If not, we risk having a second Spartacus revolt sooner or later."

Etain felt her stomach tighten. This was something she hadn't foreseen.

*

"I can have no doubts about who to side with in a conflict!" re-iterated Cicero, as a growing number of senators tried to have their say. "Could I ever give my trust to someone who has already betrayed it? Could I ever agree to collaborate with a man who has made a mockery of the Republic on several occasions, ignoring the deliberations of the Senate just as Caesar did before he crossed the Rubicon? Could I ever choose the dissolute Antony – a drunk and a womaniser who prefers to spend his time revelling rather than governing the State – as a political ally? A man even Caesar no longer trusted, going so far as to punish him upon discovering the trouble he'd caused when he'd been left to govern Italy while Caesar was in Egypt? How could I ever accept the Senate collaborating with him, when I can debate with gentlemen like Marcus Brutus and Cassius Longinus? Why should I ever be content to ally myself with such an unpleasant, treacherous individual when doing so would lead to the elimination of people I love and respect?"

Not many people were still listening to him at this point. Quintus Pedius, seated on his curule chair, was one of the few, but he was also trying to gauge the mood of the senators whose increasingly noisy shouting was drowning out the illustrious orator's words. Many disagreed with Cicero's views, but many others showed support. The old man didn't realise – or perhaps realised all too well – that speaking about Caesar's murderers in such complimentary terms de-legitimised Octavian's work. Having praised the young consul and publicly supported him in the face of his colleagues' scepticism only to then continue doing all he could for his enemies was either a sign of bad faith or of senility. And the fact that so many would follow him proved that there were still those who supported the conspirators. Only force and the threat of a military regime in Rome had silenced them, but they were still out there, ready to rise up at any moment.

"...As smart as he is, Octavian is still young and naive. If he tries to make an agreement with Antony, that old fox will twist him around his little finger: he's completely without scruples or morals."

"But we can't entrust the destiny of Rome to a child! Antony has broader shoulders. They must join forces, and then they'll keep each other in check. Hasn't that always been the essence of the Republican system? Two consuls, two supreme magistrates who keep each other in line. If we had two tyrants who detested each other, it would be like not even having one. The problem is when they get along."

This last sentence made Pedius's ears prick up. He decided to let Octavian know as soon as possible that he could push for more than a simple back-room deal with Antony: certain senators would actually be happy to be officially led by such a partnership in the conviction that the two parties would cancel each other out.

"But how can we trust a boy who first convinces us to give him supreme power by promising to fight a man who betrayed us, and then proposes to make an agreement with him? If you don't trust Antony, I don't see why you should trust someone who wants to be his accomplice!"

"We've had plenty of proof that the so-called 'liberators' will never do anything against the Senate. If anything, they will support it. Why should we contribute to their downfall, and by so doing arm our worst enemies?"

"As long as it remains a case of maintaining the equilibrium between the liberators, the young Octavian and Antony, count me in. But if the situation changes to their advantage, this will no longer be a Republic! Nor a democracy! And at that point it will no longer be in the Senate's best interests."

"Of course! Let's remember that consuls, magistrates

and dictators come and go, but the Senate remains! It's the Senate that's the beating heart of Rome and its true leader, and we must do all we can to preserve its integrity!"

Pedius had heard enough. There were still many who defended the insular position of an institution which was no longer capable of deciding anything. Just as Octavian had always said, it was no longer a question of freedom or tyranny but one of making the state function, and the Senate was too weak to do that. The time had come to entrust the state to less cumbersome systems and to fresher men – men concerned with the interests of the common good rather than of a single political class. The Senate was willing to accept a civil war between Octavian and Antony, or Octavian and Caesar's assassins, in order to continue serving as the balance of power and retain its increasingly flimsy influence. But it too was a tyranny, albeit one that championed freedom.

Pedius gestured to his assistant to proceed. He had hoped that it wouldn't come to this, but at the same time he had no illusions. With so many cooks in the kitchen, the broth would never boil: it was time for someone to shut them up and get the meal cooked. He didn't respond to those who asked him to call for order, nor did he try to speak: there were those who would do that for him. He waited for his assistant to open the heavy chamber doors, the noise attracting the attention of many senators and silencing them instantly. Some, perhaps, even guessed what was about to happen. Moments later, the unmistakable form of a fully-armed centurion came into view. The heavy footsteps of Gaius Chaerea, the trusted officer of the Sect of Mars Ultor, resounded through the suddenly silent hall. The creaking of his breastplate echoed through the ranks of speechless senators. In the distance the sound of hobnailed boots approaching could be heard growing louder, announcing the arrival of more soldiers. *Many soldiers.* The entire praetorian cohort that Octavian had left in Rome to defend his regime and protect his family.

The legionnaires filed out in two rows at the base of the tiers where the senators sat, and, with menacing expressions visible between their helmets' cheek-guards, stared threateningly at the frightened senators. Only then did the consul take the trouble to speak.

"Distinguished colleagues," Quintus Pedius said, his tone of voice far more authoritative than when he'd opened the sitting. "In a state of emergency such as this, we are forced to take drastic measures. Debate is a luxury we cannot afford at this perilous time, with the homeland threatened from every side. The populace look to us for safety and stability, and the only way we can provide them with that is to bring Antony back under institutional authority and forestall the danger of an invasion or blockade from the East. By virtue of the authority invested in me as senior Consul, I hereby establish martial law, and authorise a vote to mandate Octavian to seek a truce with Mark Antony and Lepidus, or better still, peace, for the good of the State and the salvation of the Republic. As is customary, all those in favour move to the right."

The soldiers all moved towards the left flank of the two blocks of tiered seating, pointing their lances forward, right under the noses of the senators sitting on the lower benches.

At least half of the senators moved unhesitatingly towards the opposite side of the hall.

In dribs and drabs, the others followed.

But within a few moments, they were all there. Cicero included.

III

Ortwin reflected. The situation had turned full circle: he was now holding hostage a chief who was no longer a chief and so of no use to him. Unless he could find a way to make him chief again.

Bauto's son continued to stare at him threateningly, certain that whatever happened he was now king of that small community on the edge of the world. In fact, if Ortwin surrendered, he would claim his inheritance from a man divested of authority, a man who'd stupidly allowed himself to be fooled by a handful of troops. If the German killed Bauto, he would be doing him a favour, and he would be able overpower Ortwin easily, given the numerical superiority of his soldiers.

Unless…

"No, we're not really in trouble," Ortwin said finally to Bauto, "not if you decide your son isn't worthy to succeed you". And he glanced meaningfully at the weapons he'd taken from the old chief's warriors, leaving him to understand that he would be willing to give them back.

Bauto understood. He was disconcerted for a moment, then nodded.

"… And if you're a man of your word," the German whispered to him, still nursing some doubts about trusting a man who'd already tried to trick him.

"I'm ruthless with my enemies, me, but generous to those who help me," Bauto said softly, and Ortwin realised he had no choice but to trust him. And hope that he really did want to make his son pay for his volte-face.

He gestured to Veleda, who had heard the exchange and understood instantly, indicating the weapons piled on the ground in front of her. She immediately rushed over to them and began throwing them to Bauto's men. Ortwin went back to staring at the chief's son, who looked confused and stood immobile at the edge of the village whilst his men exchanged anxious looks.

Once Bauto's sword was returned, the men with him turned in unison towards the small army. Ortwin joined the chief, tightening his grip on his weapon, and said with a wry smile, "It looks like there's a small civil war going on here..."

"Let's just say it's a settling of scores," Bauto replied curtly, as he started to move forward, immediately followed by his men. Ortwin exhorted his men to form a line too: if he was to have any chance of getting through this, he couldn't just stand back and think. He gave Veleda an intense look, knowing full well that it was useless to insist she keep out of the fray. She advanced as far forward as him and positioned herself on the opposite side, her one remaining hand firmly gripping her sword. However, none of their men had shields, and only a few of their unlikely allies were carrying them, whilst their opponents were fully armed. By uniting their forces Ortwin and Bauto had numerical superiority, but it still wasn't going to be a walkover.

After marching a few steps, the old chief roared savagely and broke into a run, and his men followed suit. His son's men had the fence behind them and couldn't retreat, so they too moved forward to avoid being knocked over by the force of the charge, and hurriedly tried to create a wall with their shields before the impact. Thanks to their greater momentum, Ortwin and his companions managed to dent the barrier, but not to break through it. The German started to rain down blows on the man hiding behind his shield in front of him, forcing him back on the defensive. In the meantime, he couldn't help but glance over to his right to see how Veleda was doing. He had told her a thousand times that he couldn't help but worry about her during a battle, and that sooner or later this would distract him and probably get him killed, and it was only after much insistence that he'd managed to convince her to stay away from hand to hand combat. This time, though, he hadn't had time to, and that little skirmish was about to become even more dangerous for him.

Fortunately, the small army fought with no great conviction. Perhaps they were already regretting their decision to back the young man, and they probably hadn't expected to actually have to engage in combat. Ortwin rid himself easily of his opponent, breaking the man's shield in his fury to strike him and running him through from behind as he tried to escape. He switched to the next man, but realised that the fighting had already moved to the edge of the village. His opponents were massing along the embankment that ran round the village – not a smooth, regular one like those the Romans set up around their marching camps, but a simple mound of roughly piled-up soil topped by a few sharpened stakes.

Once again, he turned towards Veleda and thought he could discern her long blonde hair flying loose over the heads of the other warriors. His eyes widened when he realised that she'd jumped onto the back of an enemy soldier and had her legs wrapped around him, clutching him to her chest with her maimed hand and cutting his throat with her sword. A shattering blow to his left shoulder brought him back to the task in hand. A warrior had hurled himself against him, but, fortunately, he'd thrust forward with his shield arm rather than his sword. Unbalanced, Ortwin took a few steps back. His adversary pursued him, launching a powerful downward strike that landed a hand's breadth from him. The German regained his balance, lowered his head and charged before the man could get another blow in, and this time, it was the Gaul who staggered. Ortwin seized his chance and stabbed him in the throat.

He withdrew his blade in a fountain of blood, saw that there were no other enemies close by and glanced towards Veleda. He caught another glimpse of her hair above the soldiers' helmets, but this time it was she who was in the grip of an adversary. An enemy warrior had disarmed her and was holding her tightly to him, using her as a shield against the hail of blows raining down upon him. Ortwin immediately realised that he was the chief's son.

The coward! Incensed, he raced over towards them, ploughing his way through the two sides and hacking furiously to left and right to clear his way. He roared, shoved and ran until he stood in front of his woman, gasping for breath as he stared down his adversary. Bauto's men stood back, even they were intimidated by his savage expression.

The chief's son seemed hesitant, afraid. He pointed his sword at Veleda's throat as she continued to kick and thrash about, stopping only when the blade began to prick her neck. "If I really have to die, I'll take her with me, you ugly one-eyed German!" the young man cried, pressing the tip of the sword harder against the woman's skin. Ortwin could see that he was on the verge of panicking and might sink his sword in whatever happened. He looked into Veleda's eyes, begging for her co-operation, and she understood. In the meantime, the battle had ground to a halt and a tacit truce had broken out between the two ranks of soldiers as they found themselves unable to resist watching the duel.

Veleda gathered her thoughts, then suddenly jerked her head to one side to avoid contact with the blade for an instant. Ortwin had to exploit that instant to attack. With no time to prepare he just hurled his sword, which he'd been holding tightly by his side at hip height. Hundreds of eyes followed its trajectory and the warriors held their breath despite their fatigue.

Ortwin hadn't been able to get enough force into his throw to keep the sword straight, but it still hit home. The young man was struck by the flat of the blade, and Veleda took advantage of the momentary distraction to break free of his clutches and escape. A Celtic warrior threw Ortwin a second sword and he immediately launched himself back into the fray, managing to get it under the chin of Bauto's son just as he was about to regain his balance. The young man realised that the rampart behind him impeded any escape and prepared to fight back.

"Leave him to me."

Bauto's voice resounded through the village. Ortwin turned and saw the chief moving closer, shoving his way through the mass of soldiers just as Ortwin himself had done a few minutes earlier. Only this time the soldiers stepped aside deferentially to let him pass. By the time he arrived in front of his son, the young man had lost all his remaining bravado.

"So, you want to be king?" Bauto asked him dismissively, as he stepped forward brandishing his sword. "Well, now you have the chance to earn the title fairly."

Ortwin glanced at Veleda, who was now by his side. Apparently, the chief had decided to jeopardise an almost certain victory. All they could hope was that he knew his son well enough to be certain there was no real risk involved.

*

"I... I'd never have let them kill you, father... I was just playing for time. I knew they wouldn't kill you," mumbled the lad, his voice thick with fear. Yes, Ortwin thought, Bauto knew his son well: he wasn't risking anything. In fact, he was using the occasion to assert his authority over the village.

"But now you've got to kill me if you don't want to be killed yourself," Bauto replied flatly, moving forward another step, his sword thrust forward.

Wide-eyed with terror, the young man raised his sword, but his father was quicker and struck first. The son managed to block the blade but the blow was so powerful that his sword fell from his hand, and he found himself helpless. Disorientated, he looked at his father, who moved forward a pace, before reaching down to retrieve his weapon. Bauto didn't hesitate and struck again, the blow landing on his son's neck just as he was leaning forward to retrieve his sword. A second later, his head rolled onto the beaten earth of the battlefield.

A cry of triumph arose. Not from the victor, but from the whole community as they hailed the return of their undisputed leader.

At that point, Ortwin realised he was at Bauto's mercy. The Gaul's position was such that he wouldn't have to comply with the agreement now that he had regained his authority over the village, had the situation in hand and numerical superiority. He looked at Veleda, realising she was thinking the same thing, then at Bauto who stared long and hard at him before speaking.

"The person you're looking for is in that hut there," he said, pointing to a house at the edge of the village, "guarded by my men. So he certainly won't have escaped during all this confusion. Help yourself, but leave someone here to take me to where you keep the gold. In the meantime, I have a few accounts to settle here," he concluded, turning to the warriors who had backed his son's attempted coup.

Ortwin breathed a sigh of relief. He motioned for one of the men who had remained with Veleda to hand over the money, and, together with his men, walked towards the hut.

Behind him, he heard the screams of the first warriors being executed.

*

Gaius Chaerea returned to his barracks accompanied by a vague sense of dissatisfaction. For the second time in his life, he had personally imposed his will – the Sect of Mars Ultor's will – on the Senate. He, a humble centurion, had enjoyed the privilege of overpowering the most important men in Rome. Yet it had given him none of the pleasure he'd felt on the previous occasion when he'd virtually forced the civic fathers to accept Octavian as consul. He couldn't feel any sense of triumph, unlike his colleague Popilius Laenas who had gone with him to the Curia of Pompey. Laenas, unable to contain his excitement, was talking incessantly and, knowing that Gaius was a member of Octavian's General Staff, was continually asking him to pass on his praises to the consul and to tell him how much he wanted to be a part of his circle of collaborators.

If Laenas had only known it was a sect he would have done anything to join: he had been an unbridled admirer of Caesar and was now ready to follow his son to the ends of the earth. In fact, he was fantasising about what the young man could achieve once he'd come to an agreement with Antony and the vendettas he could put into action under his patronage.

Chaerea realised that he should have been the first to be thinking like that. And yet, he merely nodded unenthusiastically at his colleague's hyperbolic talk, which to him seemed puerile and unfounded. Yes, he too felt an instinctive need to take revenge upon the murderers of Caesar, a man he'd admired and respected as a commander, but he also felt that he shouldn't have to dedicate his life solely to revenge and ambition, as he'd vowed to do when he joined the Sect of Mars Ultor.

He had another goal in life, and he was finding it increasingly difficult to reconcile that with what he'd sworn to do. Even then, he didn't want to return to the barracks, but to go home to his woman and son in the Suburra. He felt the need for the tenderness only they knew how to give him, and which nothing could replace. And even if army life – which actually suited his nature – *was* partly compatible with having a family, being a member of the sect made it difficult.

Because Octavia was a member too.

As soon as he set foot in the barracks, his *optio* told him that Octavia had herself requested that he go straight to her home. His stomach tightened: seeing her was a severe test of his composure, especially as he'd decided a few weeks earlier to put aside all his feelings for her and devote himself exclusively to the woman raising his son.

Octavia's son.

No, he couldn't risk being alone with her. He asked Laenas to accompany him, and the centurion agreed, enthusiastic at the prospect of being introduced to his idol's sister. Gaius walked thoughtfully to the house on the Aventine where Octavia lived with her husband, Marcus Claudius Marcellus, and daughter, Marcella, wondering what she wanted from him. He had made it clear to her that he could no longer indulge the feelings that had bound them in the past and that she had recently attempted to re-ignite. The torment he still felt at having taken advantage of her when she was a young girl had never left him, even though she'd never harboured any rancour towards him – and, indeed, had shown herself willing to renew their relationship.

It was too late, and it wasn't proper, he reminded himself, ignoring the rhetoric of glory Laenas kept inflicting on him. Octavia had been forced by her family to get rid of the child she'd had during their fleeting relationship, and he'd taken responsibility for it, finding in his current woman the ideal companion and mother for the baby boy. Nothing a relationship with the high-ranking Octavia, one of Rome's most high profile matrons, could give him would replace the love and warmth that enveloped him when he went home and played with little Marcus and gave himself up to sweet Fabia's ministrations.

When he reached the door of Marcellus's *domus*, it occurred to him that Octavia might have summoned him for matters pertaining to the sect and that Laenas shouldn't therefore be present at their meeting, at least not initially. He had the custodian announce him, then said to his colleague: "Wait here, Popilius. She called me, and it might annoy her to find a stranger in the house without anyone having informed her." The centurion nodded vigorously with the zealous attitude that irritated Chaerea enormously. "Of course, of course. I understand... she might have a message from the consul reserved for his general staff. No need to tell me more. But please, the only thing I ask is that you tell her my name and, if possible, introduce me."

Gaius forced himself not to raise his eyes to the sky, waited to be called, then entered and followed the custodian, who led him to Marcellus' *tablinum*. He had only been waiting a few minutes when Octavia appeared in the doorway. The two looked at each other in silence. She had made an effort to look beautiful for him, as was obvious from her carefully applied make-up and elaborate hairdo, both of which were unusual for that time of night. She wasn't beautiful, but her grace gave her a certain charm, which always reminded him of the sweet and fearful little girl she'd been a few years before.

"Minucius Basilus is dead," she began with a strained voice, keeping her distance.

Gaius wasn't expecting that. "Thank you for telling me, ma'am," he replied formally. "Obviously, I cannot help but rejoice. I... uh... I came with a colleague who's very keen to work for your brother's cause. He is a great admirer of Octavian, and he's waiting to..."

She took a step closer. "I didn't call you here only to tell you of Basilus's death."

There was a moment's pause and the silence returned. Gaius feared he would resume their relationship. Now that he saw her, he wanted to hold her in his arms, and he desperately hoped she wouldn't give him the chance. He, for his part, would not take the initiative.

"I called you because you must go to get Etain. As you know, it was she who administered justice, just like Ortwin was sent after Decimus Brutus Albinus. But now it seems that all Basilus's house slaves are to be executed. You must hurry to Apulia to save her: you know how much I care about her."

He too cared about Etain. She had been Octavia's eyes and ears in the years when the matron hadn't been able to see her son grow up. She had kept her mistress informed of Marcus's progress and had regularly given his father money so the boy would want for nothing and the family could live comfortably in a suitably dignified house. And it had been with Etain that Gaius had communicated in the years when he and Octavia hadn't been in touch, before the events that followed the Ides of March – Octavian's rise and the birth of the Sect of Mars Ultor – had brought them back together.

He would have liked to save the girl, but... "But your brother's orders were very clear, ma'am," he said finally. "He said I should immediately go to his camp on the Po to tell him about the events in the Senate, and join him for the meeting with Antony and Lepidus…"

Octavia nodded, puzzled. Then she said, "Well, why don't you send your colleague, then? You said he was anxious to be useful… I want it to be you who goes to Apulia. You're the only one I trust." She narrowed her eyes as she spoke. Was she trying to seduce him? "But… Octavian doesn't know Popilius Laenas… my colleague, that is," he objected. He knew that Octavia didn't like it when her instructions were disobeyed. "Besides, Laenas is a soldier, you can't just move him around like that…"

"I'll prepare a request for my cousin Pedius" Octavia said. "When it's the consul dispatching him to my brother, none of his commanders will have any objections. And as regards Octavian… well, your Laenas will take a letter to him in which I'll explain why I've entrusted you with another assignment. He'll understand: Etain is a member of the sect and so should be defended at all costs." She immediately went over to a writing desk, picked up a wax tablet and stylus, and began to write. Gaius waited silently until she'd finished. Octavia didn't look up until she'd signed the message, then she put the tablet in a bag, got up and handed it to him. Only then did she look into his eyes.

Intensely.

"Tell your friend he has to depart tomorrow at dawn," she murmured, moving even closer. Gaius smelled the essence she had sprinkled on her body and the pleasant breath that accompanied her words. Then he realised that she was taking his hand. "Don't… don't you want to meet Popilius Laenas? He was very keen to be introduced," he said, swallowing. He even found the strength to pull his hand away.

Octavia stiffened. "Call him then, if you must," she replied, moving brusquely away.

Gaius sighed. Had he hurt her? He made as if to speak, then bowed his head and left the *tablinum* to find Laenas.

*

Upon arriving at the door of the hut where Decimus Brutus Albinus – one of Julius Caesar's top lieutenants during the Gallic pro-consulship, victor of the naval battle of Sinus Veneticus, pro-consul designate of Cisalpine Gaul and future consul... but the dictator's killer – was being held captive, Ortwin trembled with emotion. And that hadn't happened often lately. The sentries stood aside to let him enter, but the German paused in the doorway for a moment to think things through. Only a few months earlier he'd killed Gaius Trebonius in a campaign that had been even more dangerous than the one which had brought him face to face with his latest victim, and he had to admit to himself that it had been one of the greatest satisfactions of his life. He had fought alongside those commanders, proud of being under Caesar's command, and his disgust at their betrayal had only been matched by the pleasure he'd taken in being used as an instrument of revenge and justice.

He'd begun to get a taste for it, and he hoped that he'd be able to get rid of many more of the cowardly traitors who had eliminated their benefactor, not to mention one of the greatest men in history.

He looked at Veleda: her expression was inscrutable and she indicated that he should enter without her. He understood, ordered two men to accompany him, and went through the door. He found Decimus Brutus sitting at a makeshift desk, busy writing on a tablet. The Roman lifted his head slightly when he heard him enter, resumed writing, then looked up again and stared intently at him. It took him a moment, due to the eye missing from Ortwin's face, but he finally recognised him.

"So it's you, Ortwin, Octavian's servant come to take me to Rome... I thought you died at Munda."

The barbarian was determined to enjoy every wound he would inflict with his words before running him through with his sword. "Not to take you, Decimus Brutus, but to kill you. If anything, the only part of you that will reach Rome is your head," he said, measuring out every syllable.

Decimus Brutus began to fidget in his chair. Beads of sweat started to drip from his forehead. "You can't. I'm a magistrate appointed by the Senate. There has to be a trial. And I'm writing my defence."

"Maybe some people think that. Perhaps Antony himself does. But that's why Octavian wants you out of the way right now." Decimus Brutus could no longer mask his terror. He glanced over at his equipment, piled in a corner of the hut, and Ortwin immediately positioned one of his men between the Roman and his weapons. In an instant, Brutus found himself surrounded, with a wall behind him. "I know where to find a pile of money... all for you, Ortwin," he said, in a trembling voice, his hands clutching the edge of the table.

Ortwin smiled contemptuously. "I'd pay to execute *you*, you revolting traitor, so you can imagine how much I care about your money! But I'd like to know why you did it. I didn't get the chance to ask Trebonius before I cut his throat like the dog he was."

"You'd have done it too if you'd have been a Roman of high birth, instead of a loutish barbarian with no pride," snapped Brutus, irritably. "We could no longer tolerate a man setting himself above everyone else – a man so sure of his own superiority that he was convinced no one would dare kill him. And yet everyone wanted to, everyone! We did it, the twenty of us, but others would have willingly participated had they dared, so they limited themselves to backing us. I didn't want to. I didn't hate him that much... I would have been happy to strip him of his power, but I also knew that he would never have agreed to stand aside. And Cassius and Trebonius made me feel like a coward. They convinced me that I would be a tyrant's servant, and so I was forced to join the conspiracy. If I could, I'd go back, I swear on my Lares, and..."

He didn't finish the sentence. Ortwin could stand no more of his whining litany, and struck him in the head with his sword. Only after he'd seen it split in two, brains splattering the table top, did he realise that he'd lost the chance to take irrefutable and intact proof to Octavian that he'd carried out his mission. But the sense of gratification the act gave him was, for the moment, worth it.

"Cut the head off and patch it up as best you can," he ordered one of his men, "we'll take it with us." He walked out of the hut and, catching Veleda's eye, smiled conspiratorially at her and took her hand, and together they walked towards Bauto. The chief was dipping his hands into a series of bags of gold hanging from horses' saddles in the midst of an expanse of dead bodies.

"So Bauto?" he asked. "Are you satisfied?"

"I'd say so, yes. And you?"

"Immensely."

"Good. So this business is concluded profitably for both of us."

"Well, you lost a son…"

Bauto shrugged. "Better to lose a son like that than find one. And anyway I've got two other younger sons. Too young to be a threat. I shouldn't have to worry for a few years yet…" He smiled. "You're free to go, my friend."

"There's one more thing that the consul Octavian wants from you in exchange for all that money," Ortwin added, as he signalled for his men to move off.

Bauto looked at him suspiciously. "What, by Toutatis?"

"He needs it to look as though this traitor," and he pointed to the bag, still dripping blood, that the man who'd just joined him was carrying, "was killed on behalf of Mark Antony. So I'd be grateful if you would tell that to anyone who asks."

The Celtic chief maintained his superior manner. "As you wish. After all, it's he who's paying me now, not Antony…"

"Right – be sure to remember it," Ortwin reminded him. "It would be in your best interests to keep him as a friend: he's young and already very powerful, and one day he'll be more important than Caesar."

He saw Bauto swallow: the warning had had an effect. Yes, he'd keep quiet. And, as Octavian had wanted, it would look as though Antony had one of the conspirators brutally killed. It was the best way to separate Antony's cause from that of Caesar's killers and force him over to Octavian's side.

Executed. Etain hadn't thought that could happen. And, what was probably worse was that her mentors, her mistress and the head of the sect, hadn't considered it either. Or perhaps they had taken it into account but hadn't cared much about it: she was one of the group's expendable pawns, after all.

Their goal had been achieved: another of Caesar's killers was dead. What might happen now was irrelevant when compared to their aims of revenge and power. That she might lose her life was of no concern to anyone, not even to Rufus, who would also lose his unwanted child, or to Agrippa, who had probably returned to Fulvia's arms by now.

It didn't even matter to her any more. Ever since the sect had become part of her life, after an initial moment of happiness she had only ever known bitterness and disappointment. And were it not for the child who would never see the light of day, she wouldn't care about dying. She had begged the mistress to delay killing her until the baby was born: that creature was completely blameless. If nothing else, the mistress would have gained a slave without spending a sestertius.

But the woman had proved herself heartless and had been adamant. She'd been so in thrall to the magistrate that she hadn't wanted to hear reason. She'd barely even managed to tolerate waiting the three days it took the decurion to complete his investigation and clear up any doubts.

And soon it would be her turn. Rather, their turn. She felt a shiver run down her spine when she heard yet another muffled cry from the *tablinum*. And she saw that the slaves winced too as they sat awaiting their turn in the atrium with her. The decurion's soldiers were carrying out the sentence in the study, executing the house slaves one by one. Those still alive were forced to drag the bodies away and load them onto carts parked in front of the domus' entrance from where they were taken off and burned, together and without any funeral rites, as if they'd never existed. Every time the study door opened, two grim-looking slaves would appear, dragging a freshly strangled slave whose face was still contorted into the grimace typical of suffocation. Etain imagined herself the same way, her beautiful face showing the signs of its agonising end, and her baby dying an even slower death, perhaps suffocating in a body no longer capable of sustaining it.

And to think that she wasn't even a slave. But she was in no position to shout from the rooftops that she was a freed woman and had the right to a trial. She might save herself, but she would reveal the intrigues that had brought her to the house, and expose Octavian's family to public disapproval. And they would have made her pay: once you joined the sect, you had to be ready to die for it. And she'd known that – or at least she had before she got pregnant. Now she had another reason to live.

The two slaves charged with moving the bodies returned. This time they were carrying the body of the man who'd been her lover: the real assassin, although the decurion hadn't thought it necessary to proceed any further with his enquiries and ascertain who had really killed the *dominus*. The slaves' lives counted for nothing in the eyes of free men. She decided she would at least have the satisfaction, a moment before being strangled, of screaming in the mistress's face that the slave had only been a tool, and that it had been she who had despatched him.

She saw the two slaves disappear into the vestibule, and immediately the tense, bleak silence of the wait descended again. As usual, the few remaining slaves began to wonder who would be next. And when Etain saw them re-appear, she realised it was her turn even before they fixed their eyes upon her. She was tempted to remain sitting and start shouting, to force them to lift and drag her into the killing room, but, absurdly, it occurred to her that it would agitate the baby and make it suffer. She therefore got up meekly and surrendered to her executioners, who escorted her into the *tablinum*. In the study she saw five soldiers, the decurion, a chair in the centre of the room, and, sitting at a desk, a grim expression on her face, the mistress of the house and her frightened, distraught son. It was clear that the lady was forcing the fragile youth to watch the spectacle, perhaps hoping to make him feel guilty for being the indirect cause of the tragedy. Etain almost managed to smile: if the young man ever had any hope of growing up with a modicum of mental stability, what his mother was putting him through now would negate it.

A soldier pointed to the chair and, after a moment's hesitation, she sat down. Only then did she notice that one of the soldiers was holding a noose, and that he was approaching her. When she felt the rope tighten round her neck, she spontaneously began to think of Agrippa. She hadn't intended to, but images of their happiest moments filled her mind. At that point she realised that something inside her was urging her to go out surrounded by positive thoughts, and her time with Agrippa had undoubtedly been the happiest of her short life. She'd loved him more than she ever thought herself capable, and had deluded herself that her love had been reciprocated. The young man had then exposed himself to all sorts of dangers to avenge her and had even got himself expelled from the sect to show her how much he loved her, but she'd refused to give him another chance. Perhaps she'd been wrong, but how could she ever have trusted him again?

Yet she should have done, she said to herself, a moment before seeing the decurion nod his assent to the executioner, who immediately began to tighten the noose.

Within a few moments, her vision became blurred and the noises around her became louder as she began to struggle for breath. Her temples throbbed and her stomach clenched in a grip as tight as the rope around her neck. She was slow to realise that someone had knocked at the door. She felt the noose loosen and saw indistinct figures enter the room. When she was able to focus on them she recognised the massive form of Gaius Chaerea, the sect's centurion.

It took her several seconds to understand the words being exchanged between the various people present.

"…You are not authorised to proceed. The consul forbids it. I have come from Rome to remove the suspects. The Senate will conduct the investigation," Chaerea said.

"You can't do that," protested the decurion, "custom dictates that all the slaves are killed."

"You, Decurion, are relieved of your duties and charged with sheltering a criminal. You'll come with me to Rome, where you'll be judged by a court."

"But that's not possible!" cried the woman. "These people killed my husband."

"Ma'am, I'd urge you to remain quiet unless you want to lose what little there will be left to you after the confiscations the Senate has already sanctioned against your husband," the centurion said coldly.

Chaerea's words and his authoritative tone had the effect of quashing any other attempted protest. The officer took a few steps towards Etain, extended his arm and offered her his hand.

With the sweetest smile anyone had given her since Agrippa.

IV

Gaius Julius Caesar Octavian felt omnipotent. It seemed to him that the gods really had chosen him for great things, as he'd been telling people for months in an attempt to impress them. He tightened his grip on the knife and plunged it into the neck of the bull that had been stunned in preparation for the sacrifice and now stood meekly, ready for his blade. Blood spurted onto his face, veiled by a white toga which instantly turned scarlet. The bull collapsed to the ground and the young man dragged his knife through its stomach, ripping it open and releasing the streaming entrails. His three ministers prayed to Mars Ultor and their cries echoed around the small clearing, surrounded by a screen of densely packed trees in the Po Valley. A cordon of soldiers positioned at a suitable distance kept prying eyes away.

Not even he could resist the impulse to voice his excitement by shouting the name of the god to whom he'd dedicated the sect, but a deep roar came out, a noise which no one would have thought could have come from such a slight, sickly body. He marvelled at the sound which seemed to come straight from the underworld, as though he had been invested with the strength of Mars. And he too, started to believe that he was the *chosen one*. The one to whom the gods had assigned the task of saving Rome, completing what his father Caesar had only started.

Only a year and a half earlier he'd been a boy of nineteen, with no political or military experience, a physique unsuited to hard work, a family threatened by factions on all sides, an inheritance that seemed unrealisable, seemingly unassailable enemies and a vendetta to carry out with no prospect of success. Now he was a consul of Rome at the head of a fifty thousand strong army; he had the Senate in his pocket and he was able to impose terms on the most powerful men in the *Urbe*. Above all, though, he had made progress with his vendetta, if the latest news from Apulia and the farthest reaches of Gaul were anything to go by.

"Mars Ultor, you who have protected, favoured and blessed my undertakings," he declaimed, raising his arms and holding up the entrails of the sacrificed animal, "accept these entrails in place of those of the murderers who have just paid for their crime. The road of revenge is still long, but with your support and help, Mars the Avenger, dispenser of Justice, in time, my ministers and I will be able to rid the earth of the foul pack of traitors and cowards who raised their fetid hands against my divine father, killing him with a ferocity worthy of barbarians, they who more than anyone else had benefitted from his magnanimity with titles and positions which they still hold close to their chests."

He glanced at his three ministers, the three men without whom he would have been able to do little in that eventful year and a half. So great had their impact been that he even wondered if Mars himself hadn't put them in his way at various points in his short existence: Marcus Vipsanius Agrippa in his childhood, Salvidienus Rufus just before Caesar was killed, and Gaius Cilnius Maecenas shortly after the fateful Ides of March. His three friends nodded with conviction, as absorbed as he was in the rite celebrating the sect's latest double success.

He kept his arms raised, despite the blood seeping out of the bull's entrails which continued to drip onto his head and trickle from his hands down his arms. He spoke again. "Five months ago I sacrificed another bull, Mars Ultor, to offer you the death of the first two of Caesar's killers, Pontius Aquila, killed by the minister and brother Marcus Vipsanius Agrippa, and Gaius Trebonius, executed by the sect member Ortwin. You guided their movements and ensured them success in extremely difficult circumstances: Agrippa in a battle in which he shouldn't even have taken part but during which he saved my life, and Ortwin with a skilful attack in the midst of a horde of enemies. Our German follower also killed a man whose elimination had become necessary given the nature of the society we created in your name: Dolabella, who Caesar promoted to the rank of consul but who later boasted of participating in the conspiracy to kill him, thinking that it would win him greater popularity. For this reason, I felt we had to add him to the list of people who should atone for my father's murder.

"And now... now I rejoice with your ministers because justice has been done again. Our disciple Etain has put an end to Minucius Basilus, and the valuable Ortwin has managed to eliminate the vile Decimus Brutus Albinus! We have managed four in a year and a half! And here, now, in your presence, and in front of your ministers, I swear to execute as many again by the end of next year! Give me the strength to assemble all the forces of Rome against Marcus Brutus and Cassius Longinus, and I will make war upon them and destroy them in a single battle! Give me the chance to convert Mark Antony into an instrument of our vengeance and justice, as he has hitherto always refused to be, and we will have an army so powerful that none will be able to oppose it. And Rome will be cleansed of the filth of those men who committed the most appalling murder it is possible to commit, that of the greatest man who ever lived – a man, like Romulus, destined to become an immortal god."

Once again, his ministers prayed to Mars Ultor, without assistants and without the audience of soldiers that usually preceded a battle. It was just the four of them, four men who would change the world and lead everyone else – junior disciples, external allies who knew nothing of the existence of the sect, even rivals and enemies – to shape history according to their plans. Because what Octavian hadn't said as he'd called his ministers to him was that now he felt had the support of the gods, he too wanted to be remembered as one of the greatest men that had ever lived, worthy of standing in the Pantheon alongside his divine father.

He didn't have Caesar's strength and endurance and would never be a great general, but he had his lucid intelligence and, as he was discovering, his ruthlessness. Everything else he could get from the three men who watched as he dipped his hands and arms into the animal's butchered stomach and smeared blood and bodily fluids over himself whilst praying to Mars. When he saw them in the dim and flickering light of the brazier which burned next to him, stained red like himself, he pierced the bull's entrails with a poker and hung them over the fire, turning them until he judged them properly cooked. All the while, he reflected on the mission with which he felt he had been charged and how best to accomplish it.

He wanted to bring peace to Rome – a peace that had

been missing for almost half a century – and to make Rome the largest, most powerful and enduring empire that had ever existed. He wanted every citizen to be proud of being a Roman, for them to be aware that they were privileged, and for even the poorest and most wretched of the Quirites to know that they always had more resources than a foreigner. He wanted the borders to be solid, consistent, and secure, and for the barbarians absorbed into the city's domain to feel no desire to leave. He wanted it to be possible to travel quickly from one end of the empire to the other in safety, for trade and supplies to be guaranteed throughout the year, for justice to be fair, and for the soldiers to maintain a large, professional army. And for Rome primarily, but also other important centres, to be able to boast of great monuments and efficient services capable of satisfying every need and providing every convenience. Finally, he wanted the religion of their ancestors to be scrupulously adhered to in public and private, for customs and traditions to be restored, and for institutions and their representatives to be respected.

And he wanted to be the one to accomplish all of this.

He placed the cooked entrails on the tree trunk he'd chosen as an improvised altar, pulled them off the poker with a knife and cut them into four pieces, which he distributed to the three ministers, saying, "Blood brothers, eat this as though it were the heart of my father's murderers. Take nourishment from their spirit and strength to continue our arduous mission. Revenge is just the first step on a path that will lead us to change the world, to make it more just, to glorify the power of Rome and save it from the inevitable decline to which it has been condemned by civil war."

Agrippa, Rufus and Maecenas waited for him to take the first bite. He speared his piece with a sword and bit into the intestines – and his palate was assailed by the unpleasant contrast between bits that had been burned to a crisp and others that were still raw. He got it down hastily, swallowing with difficulty. Tears came to his eyes, but he immediately opened his mouth and took another bite, and the others promptly followed suit in silence. Their eyes, wild in the light of the brazier, glowed in their scarlet faces, like those of victors riding their chariots to the Capitoline Hill on the day of their triumphal ceremony.

It was *their* triumph. They had won a new, personal battle, defeating yet more enemies, and they deserved it. They were already beginning to change the world: their decisions and their actions were influencing events, and had already profoundly changed the course of Rome's history in that year and a half. But they had only just started. Up until that point, the foreign wars had shown themselves to be nothing more than a means for favouring and enriching certain political allies, and not a way of consolidating Rome's supremacy. The civil wars, however, had simply created exasperation between factions, rival generals, and parties, rather than a new, more rational, solid and coherent system of government as Caesar had intended. Soon everything would change.

If more blood still had to be spilled to achieve peace, so be it, the young consul said to himself as he looked at his friends, covered from head to foot in the stuff. But this time no blood would be wasted: the blood of Caesar's killers, and of all those opposed to a new order would be the sacrifice, the tribute to the gods, for the survival of the

Urbe.

"Mars Ultor, I offer you human victims so you will allow me to save Rome from certain death!" he said in his mind, without opening his mouth.

*

"They're coming!"

Salvidienus Rufus burst into the *praetorium* pavilion, startling all present. He was well aware he was bringing bad news and he'd spent the whole journey from the outpost on the Po to the camp wondering how best to deliver it. Eventually, he'd concluded that the quicker he gave it to them, the quicker they'd think of a way to confront the dramatic situation.

The young tribune read the shock in his friends' expressions. *Too soon.* Antony and Lepidus had arrived too soon: the consul hadn't yet got the Senate's blessing to negotiate with them, and it wouldn't be a good idea to come to an agreement with people the civic fathers had defined as 'public enemies'. At least not until Quintus Pedius had changed the illustrious assembly's mind...

"How many legions do they have?" Agrippa asked. He was always the most practical one.

"More than we do. And that's all you need to know," Rufus replied, venomously, immediately hating himself for being unable to conceal the hostility he felt towards him. He blamed himself, because he was well aware that his hatred was fuelled by envy, and he would have liked to have been a better man. But he couldn't manage it. Fortunately, he told himself, the others hadn't noticed, and even Agrippa was too upright a type to suspect that a sect member, a man he considered a friend, harboured such a grudge. "Then it's a real problem," said Maecenas, rising from the chair he was sitting on at a table next to the sect's leader, and pacing back and forth in the tent. "We need to find a way to play for time until news arrives from Rome."

"The problem is if *they* don't play for time," Octavian intervened. "Antony and Lepidus know that it's in their interests to make an agreement with me. But it would be even more advantageous for them to destroy me, offer my head to the Senate, and re-propose an amnesty for Caesar's killers. Those old windbags like Cicero would be more than happy to sacrifice me to save their friends Brutus and Cassius. They'd even be willing to hold their noses and put up with someone like Antony... Cicero, who has said and written every imaginable awful thing about him, would accept him if he returned, just to protect Brutus and Cassius. That's why I wanted it to look like Decimus Brutus was killed on Antony's orders: perhaps that will make it more difficult for him to reach terms with those traitors."

"Right," Agrippa agreed, "even more so given that the senators know full well Antony's ambitions can be reined in by Caesar's killers, while with Antony at your side and your father's murderers in Hades, you would be uncontrollable."

"I hate to say it, but this time we must act absolutely legally," Octavian said gravely. "We need the Senate's damned consent, otherwise we might find ourselves up against the whole lot of them: those old windbags, Caesar's murderers and Antony and Lepidus. Even all the provincial governors, people like Munatius Plancus and Pollio who are still waiting to see which way the tide turns.

It didn't take long for Antony to make an agreement with Caesar's assassins after the Ides of March, and he wouldn't hesitate to do it again – even more so if his political survival depended on it."

"But if they attack us, we're done for," Rufus objected. "At this point, the only hope is to attack first – the Senate's consent might not reach us in time."

"These are frenetic times," Maecenas said, continuing to pace up and down. Rufus was annoyed by his pacing, but as no one else dared take him by the arm and sit him down, he didn't feel he could either. "It takes very little to disrupt an equilibrium and alter the make up of opposing blocks, as we've seen in the year and a half since Caesar's death. We must always keep in mind that we need to be working to create a united front against Caesar's killers. That's what we need to do to complete our revenge and consolidate our rise to power. But it would only take one false step on our part for everyone to unite against us, as Octavian has just postulated. And to attack now would undoubtedly be a false step. If we want to change the world, we'll have to control it first if we want to avoid being hindered by circumstance."

"Nice words," Rufus said, irked by the implied reprimand. "But for us mere mortals, how do you translate that into action?"

Maecenas gave no sign of wishing to fuel Rufus' rancour. "Don't forget that Antony and Lepidus are tempted by the prospect of reaching an agreement with us. In theory, they're here because Octavian has been trying to meet them for months, and has shown that he doesn't want a war. And that, *despite* the fact that the only reason the Senate gave him the praetorship and then the consulship was to fight them. Maybe it's less advantageous for those two to ally themselves with us rather than destroying us, but it's certainly less strenuous and less risky. And, fundamentally, Antony is lazy: he prefers to gain a little with minimal effort rather than work hard for a result that may not be achievable. And let's not forget, he'd struggle to find common ground with a Senate under the sway of Cicero. And, as Octavian noted, Caesar's killers won't go along with him since, officially, it was he who executed Decimus Brutus."

The others remained silent. He was arriving at a conclusion that all were now keen to hear.

"So I say that we should take our time and keep them hanging on until we know that the Senate, willingly or not, is officially on our side."

"I couldn't ask for more," Octavian said. "But I still can't see how we can stop Antony attacking us if that's what he decides to do." Rufus was pleased that his friend had pointed out to Maecenas the inconsistency of his reasoning. He didn't like always being the only one to be taken for a killjoy, the one who always soured the idyllic atmosphere of mutual respect that bound the sect's leader and its ministers. As ever, Maecenas kept his calm. He always seemed to know what he was talking about. "Simple," he said. "We have a powerful weapon, and we should use it. It is..." A cry of alarm from outside cut him off.

The four ran out of the tent almost in unison, and immediately saw soldiers rushing to the side of the fortified camp which looked out over the river. Rufus grabbed a legionary and asked what was going on. The soldier, noticing their rank, stood to attention and said, "I don't know much, Tribune... it seems that Antony and Lepidus's men are on the other side of the river and..."

Rufus left him, exchanged a knowing glance with the three friends and together they started walking to the northern fortification. When they reached the embankment, they saw the soldiers massed on the terraces. They continued through the crowds, the men hurriedly moving aside to let them pass when they recognised the consul. They peered over the sharp tips of the poles at the surrounding countryside. Over on the other side of the Po, stretching as far as the eye could see, was Antony and Lepidus's immense army. Soldiers continued to emerge from the woods in the background in a never-ending flow, forming ever deeper ranks.

"Well, if Anthony wanted to impress us, he's succeeded..." said Octavian, sounding a little discouraged.

"Look!" Agrippa pointed to a boat in the middle of the river. There were five legionaries on it, one with no equipment and two manning the oars. The vessel proceeded towards them, but before reaching the southern shore, one of the legionaries pushed the unarmed soldier into the water. He thrashed about in the waves trying to swim to the shore, but the current was too strong and he was quickly swept away, disappearing from Rufus's view. Shortly afterwards the boat reached land and the four men walked up to the rampart.

When they were within earshot, they stopped and one of them shouted: "Soldiers of Rome! The man you saw disappear in the river was one of your comrades in arms. He was in one of your reconnaissance patrols." Then he stopped to let his words take effect on the legionaries on the terraces, without even asking to speak to those in command.

Amid cries of outrage, Octavian turned to Rufus. "Was that the patrol you were with?"

"Um, I think so," replied an embarrassed Rufus. "When we returned I sent them back out to check on the movements of Antony's army. They must have got too close…"

"…Or the enemy got too far forward," Agrippa suggested, perhaps with a hint of malice. Rufus felt obliged to justify himself. "When we left them it looked like they'd made camp. They didn't look like they had any intention of moving forward."

In the meantime, the envoy had started talking again, and it was clear that he had no interest in addressing the consul. "We have captured twenty of your men. Every day, we will throw one in the river. If they're very lucky and the water is calm, they might just survive. If not, you'll never see them again. And this is the message that Antony sends to you, soldiers of Rome," the man continued. "Most of you were under his command and he has no wish to fight you. But if it comes to it, you will die because you are outnumbered and your commanders have no military experience, unlike him. Stop resisting and arrest your leaders, who forcefully extorted their positions from the Senate, and we'll once again be comrades in arms, able to conquer the entire world, and with it rich spoils and a fair reward for our service."

The soldiers on the terraces began to mutter among themselves, some in an increasingly agitated way, while others glanced towards the four young commanders, and their expressions were far from re-assuring.

"Antony wants to open negotiations from a position of

strength, that's all," Maecenas commented immediately. "He wants to show us that he has a certain authority over the soldiers. Over *all* the soldiers."

"Well then, maybe the time has come for you to tell us what your idea was, my friend," Octavian said. Maecenas was silent for a moment as he looked around him, noticing, like the other three, that no one had raised a dissenting voice against the envoy's proposals. Then he shook his head. "Unfortunately, my idea was precisely that: to use the soldiers to put pressure on him. But he's beaten us to it…"

*

"There are more and more of them out there," Maecenas said, on returning from an inspection tour with Salvidienus Rufus. "And at the head of the line is a delegation of centurions who insist on speaking to you. They say they represent at least four legions, but I doubt they're speaking for all forty of the constituent cohorts…" he added. Octavian was bent forward, staring at the walls of the *praetorium* with one hand in his hair and the other resting on the table.

"Have you spoken to them?" he asked, without moving either his face or his eyes. He had just had one of his coughing fits. He was not in bed, but he was blue in the face and it was better that no one outside the sect saw him like that: it might adversely affect his influence over the troops, assuming he still had any. No soldier was willing to be led into battle by a sickly commander.

"I told them the truth: that you're waiting for news from Rome," the Etruscan explained. "And not just to gain time: it must be made very clear that we are the ones acting within the law, not Antony or Lepidus. They have to be frightened of becoming outlaws."

"That's not such a great offence these days," commented Octavian bitterly, accompanying his words with a fit of coughing. "Since Caesar's death, almost every player on the political stage has been an outlaw at some point or other, myself included, and without it causing them any serious disadvantage, I'd say. Today's outlaw may be tomorrow's consul, and they know it…"

Maecenas appreciated his friend's clear-headedness. To an acquaintance he might have seemed gloomy, but the Etruscan already knew him well enough to realise that he had absolutely no intention of giving up and surrendering to Antony. "Always remember that they've had enough of civil wars," he commented, "and they want you and Antony to agree so that you can avenge Caesar and finish all this once and for all, and they're willing to support the strongest one to make a union happen. It all depends on you showing them that you're the strongest."

"Unfortunately, at the moment it seems that he's the strongest," Octavian admitted. "I should give thanks to the gods that Antony almost wiped out two legions when he was in Brindisi. At least those soldiers will never be willing to put themselves under his command and accept that I should submit to him. Have you ensured that their defensive perimeter is in order?"

"Don't worry. All twenty cohorts of the Marcia and the IVth are taking turns to guard the *praetorium*. If, by any absurd stretch of the imagination, Antony convinced the others to open the camp's gates, he'd find it difficult to break through their barricade."

"That's exactly what I'm frightened of," the young consul confirmed. "Anyone could let an enemy patrol in, even at night, and allow them to open the gates."

"That's true," Maecenas re-assured him, "but if Antony had wanted to attack, he'd have done so as soon as he got here three days ago. He just wants you to relinquish operational command to him and become his subordinate."

Octavian coughed again, pressing his palm over his mouth and staring at the blood that appeared on it. His doctor Glycon – who was always by his side during these attacks, even mild ones like this – hurried to soak a cloth in a bowl of water and press it gently to his face. "But if the soldiers rebelled and arrested me," the consul said, having cleared his throat, "I don't think he'd turn it down. People have short memories, you know. Seeing me in difficulty, the legionaries would quickly forget that I've done infinitely more for them than Antony has recently.

"And above all that you've paid them more than he has," the Etruscan specified, before stopping to listen to the sound of a fracas outside. He looked out and saw Rufus, who had preferred to wait outside the tent and keep an eye on the increasingly tense situation, pushing back an insistent centurion. The officer was shouting that he wanted to talk to Octavian at all costs, while behind him others were trying to push him through the Martia legion's barricade of soldiers.

And they were all armed.

Rufus had to pull out his sword and point it at the centurion's throat. The man froze, but only for an instant, then he took a few steps back, turned to his men and began to bemoan the consul's behaviour. Maecenas saw that

Rufus was agitated and feared that he might lose control: he knew that the young man was hot-headed and had none of Agrippa's poise. In fact, a moment later, Rufus shouted at the centurion to shut up and dealt him a heavy blow between the shoulder blades with the pommel of his sword, and the officer fell to the ground gasping while the young tribune set about kicking him viciously.

None of the soldiers who made up the cordon dared interfere with a superior, so Maecenas felt duty bound to intervene. He walked over to Rufus and grabbed his arm in an attempt to restrain him, but Rufus was much stronger than he, and easily shook him off, forcing him to repeat the gesture. The Etruscan called him by name, but the younger man was blinded by rage and continued to kick the centurion without heeding his words. The subordinates of the man on the floor had by now unsheathed their swords and were making it clear that they wanted to intervene to protect their superior, but the men of the Martia tightened their barricade and the *praetorium's* defenders turned their swords on their comrades.

"Someone's going to die here," Maecenas thought, "and that will make everything more difficult. I must make this imbecile see reason." But on his second effort to block him, Rufus not only wriggled free but pushed him back. The Etruscan lost his balance, and found himself lying on the ground, covered in mud, but even then Rufus did not seem to realise what he'd done. He continued to shout and insult the rebels, waving his sword at them and every so often launching a kick at the centurion who was trying to escape his beating by crawling away, probably with several broken ribs. Maecenas tried to get up, but a pair of powerful legs stepped between him and Rufus.

He looked up and saw Agrippa, who had joined them in that precise instant. The young man, who was far stronger than him, grabbed Rufus with both arms and yanked him back. Perhaps not even recognising his friend, Rufus turned around and told Agrippa to leave him alone, trying to free himself with a punch. But Agrippa was faster and grabbed his arm, twisting it behind his back. "Do you want to cause a riot, you fool?" he whispered in his ear, quietly enough to be out of the soldiers' earshot, but loud enough for Maecenas to hear.

A genuine expression of hate appeared on Rufus' face. "Don't you dare humiliate me further in front of my subordinates," the tribune hissed softly. "Get your hands off me."

Agrippa released him instantly, but Maecenas was in no doubt that he did it out of good sense not fear. The young man helped the Etruscan to his feet, then turned to Rufus and Maecenas, indicating a centurion who was with him: "There's no reason for us to quarrel. The news we were waiting for from Rome has come. This is Popilius Laenas," he said, even managing to smile in an effort to ease the tension between them, "who Gaius Chaerea charged with the task that should have been his. And he has plenty of interesting things to tell us…"

*

"Here we go, at last," Agrippa said to himself, as he saw a small group of armed men appear on the opposite bank of the Po, near a boat moored in the reeds. He ordered his oarsmen to put his boat to water and continued to observe the movements of Antony's men. He had to seize the moment, otherwise it would all have been in vain.

Since Popilius Laenas had brought the Senate's official approval for an agreement with Antony and Lepidus, leaving it up to the consul to determine the means, he'd been keen to put an end to the tension that hung over Octavian's legions. He'd even offered to take the news to Antony personally, just to enjoy the look on his face. Maecenas and Octavian had agreed: it would be best to send a prominent envoy over the river so that he could deal directly with Antony, otherwise Antony might not take their proposals seriously. But the Etruscan had suggested waiting until the next day: being a good strategist, he'd decided that they should make a spectacle of the meeting for the benefit of the soldiers.

A large military audience had assembled on both banks of the river. Everyone was curious to see what would happen to Antony's latest victim. And it was legitimate to worry about what might happen in Octavian's camp afterwards, given that the consul and those loyal to him struggled to hold back the soldiers after the first drowning.

The boat left the opposite shore. Agrippa climbed aboard his own and the oarsmen began to row towards the centre of the river in the direction of the first vessel. The young tribune looked at the prisoner, who was behaving in a dignified manner, neither complaining nor fidgeting. The other people in the boat, however, seemed nervous at the arrival of a vessel from the opposite bank. But they continued to perform their duties. The oarsmen rowed and, once the boat had reached the right position, two soldiers cut the ropes around the prisoner's hands with a dagger and pushed him into the water.

The current was strong. Agrippa ordered his oarsmen to head towards the man to intercept him. He calculated that he'd moved slightly too late. They were parallel to him now, but they would lose him at the point where the current grew stronger. He picked up the rope he'd brought for just such an eventuality and tried to attract the legionary's attention so he could throw it to him, but the man was too busy trying to keep afloat to notice. And he wasn't an expert swimmer – in fact, he was just flailing around rather than swimming. Agrippa therefore tied one end of the rope to his waist and, having given the other end to one of his men, dived into the water.

Thanks to his size he was able to reach the soldier and intercept him. He reached out and grabbed his arm, but the terrified man continued to thrash about, and, with his other arm, began to slap and punch at Agrippa's face. Agrippa tried to defend himself by turning away, but by doing that he risked losing his grip. He looked towards his boat and his men began to pull him in while the oarsmen continued to row towards the opposite bank. Keeping his face in the water to protect it from the blows of the man he was saving, Agrippa stretched out his arms and grabbed him by the neck. The soldier tried to pull away but by this point was so weak that he could do little against Agrippa's superior strength, and finally they reached the boat.

Once they'd pulled him on board, a standing ovation broke out on the edge of Octavian's camp. Agrippa felt encouraged: as Maecenas had predicted, the soldiers would have been reminded who protected them and who, in contrast, merely used them for their own ends. In the meantime, his boat reached land. Antony and Lepidus's soldiers looked on in stunned silence, having just witnessed the same scene. Agrippa looked at them carefully, and read admiration, not mistrust nor even hostility, on their faces. It was going well: Maecenas's plan was bearing fruit.

After he'd untied the rope round his waist, he wrung out the edges of his tunic, which were dripping wet, slicked back his hair and ran a hand over his face, then he picked up the armour he'd left in the bottom of the boat and, with the help of one of his men, put it on. He put his hand on the shoulder of the man he'd saved, who, having returned to his senses, looked at him with gratitude. He was about to speak, but Agrippa indicated that there was no need, then picked up the bag with the Senate document in it, told his men to wait for him, and stepped ashore.

He walked towards the woods surrounding the narrow clearing near the river, in the direction of the deployed soldiers, his bearing as proud as his dripping clothes would allow. The legionaries stepped back respectfully to allow him to pass and when he spotted a non-commissioned officer he said, "Take me to Mark Antony, *optio*. I have urgent news for him – *from Rome*." The officer hesitated and looked around for his centurion who, standing a few paces away, signalled for a soldier to escort Agrippa. The man came over and led him through the wood, which turned out to be only a thin line of trees, beyond which extended a much wider plain. On this, there loomed a fortified marching camp, in front of which foragers were at work, engineers were busy building scorpios and ballistas, carpenters worked on boats, and supply patrols went about their business. The presence of wooden planks alongside the boats showed that Antony was planning to erect pontoon bridges to facilitate the passage of his troops over the river and enable them to besiege Octavian's camp. The Senate's authorisation had arrived just in time.

His escort took him through the camp's entrance and led him down the main thoroughfare. Some of the soldiers loitering between the tents recognised him and greeted him, whispering his name to the others who didn't know his face, despite the fact that he had become something of a celebrity amongst the legions since distinguishing himself at the battle of Modena. There were some jibes about him being soaking wet, but once news of what he'd done at the river spread through the camp no one dared to mock him. On the contrary, even the men at the *praetorium* looked at him with respect when he arrived there. One of Antony's bodyguards, who was on sentry duty outside his billet, took Agrippa's weapon, escorted him to the commander's *tablinum*, announced him, and told him to enter.

What he saw surprised him, at least until he remembered who he was dealing with.

"Well look who we have here – a drowned rat," said Antony, sitting at his desk with his wife Fulvia standing next to him, her tunic lowered to her waist. Under the table, a slave girl was busily attending to the intimate parts of both.

"Greetings, Mark Antony," said Agrippa, pretending to have received a respectable welcome and trying to maintain some formal aplomb, despite the state he was in and the scene playing out in front of him. "I bring a message from the Senate, which has been sent to the young consul by the old consul. Given the circumstances, I'd ask you to read it immediately." He couldn't help but catch Fulvia's eye. He'd felt her deep, penetrating glare from the moment he'd entered the room.

Antony didn't put out his hand to take the message and said nothing. Fulvia, however, spoke with that warm, sensual voice that sent shivers down his spine. "It seems that you were quite the hero down at the river, and made my husband look the fool of the situation…"

Agrippa had expected such an objection from Antony and had prepared a response. But he hadn't expected it from Fulvia, whose presence in the camp he'd been unaware of. The woman still had the power to seduce him: he detested her and desired her at the same time, especially as he had now lost Etain. But with Etain it had been something else, something that was more than just sex, while with Fulvia he could lose himself in her perverse lovemaking, and even in his moments of greatest despair – when he had lost Etain and been thrown out of the sect – he couldn't deny to himself that he missed her.

"Erm… I only stopped a brave Roman soldier from dying unnecessarily, ma'am. One more soldier will be useful to both of us when we fight side by side against Rome's external enemies."

"So tell me, young Agrippa," said Antony. "What makes you think we'll be fighting side by side?" As he spoke, he grabbed the slave girl by the back of her neck and pulled her towards his turgid member, while with his other hand he grabbed one of Fulvia's magnificent breasts and began squeezing it between his thumb and forefinger, as though to flaunt her before the eyes of his interlocutor. And she was letting him.

Agrippa swallowed. He couldn't remember ever having been in a more embarrassing situation. "What it says in this message, if you'll deign to read it," he said, trying to make a show of confidence. He felt the breath of Antony's bodyguard behind him.

But Antony ignored his answer. "And, who might these so-called 'external enemies of Rome' that we should fight together, be?" he continued.

"Caesar's murderers, who you yourself began fighting before the Senate even declared them public enemies. Decimus Brutus, for example, who you besieged at Modena. And who you've just had killed," he said.

Antony jumped up, shoving the slave away and moving away from Fulvia. "I didn't have him killed, as you and your young friend know very well," he protested indignantly. "You want to frame me, do you? Well I've already sent a letter to Marcus Brutus and Cassius telling them that it wasn't me."

"They'll never believe you," said Agrippa. "After all, it was you who besieged him all that time at Modena and then pursued him. Maybe now you'll decide to finally pick a side."

"I've already chosen a side. And it's mine, you insolent dog!" he snapped, walking round the table and raising his arm to slap him. The young man raised his arm too, holding out the message from the Senate. Out of the corner of his eye, he noted that Fulvia was smiling, apparently pleased by his behaviour.

Antony relinquished the slap he'd intended to give Agrippa and stared at the letter for a long time before eventually snatching it from his hand. Then he walked back over to his wife, unrolled it, and read it with her. Agrippa saw the slave crawl away while Fulvia, in the meantime, had put her tunic back over her shoulders.

Antony nodded several times then raised his eyes to

Agrippa. After a long silence that not even Fulvia, who obviously wanted to speak, dared interrupt, he said, "So, the Senate has given this pantomime consul the authority to make an agreement with me and Lepidus 'for the good of the Republic' and to form a common front against Caesar's murderers..."

"Exactly, sir," Agrippa confirmed. "And if you've read it all, you'll see that the consul has also been given the authority, in this emergency situation, to appoint you to any public position he deems appropriate for tackling the war and at the same time ensuring that the empire carries out its administrative functions."

"A sort of amnesty if we co-operate, eh?"

"If you want to put it like that... You and Lepidus would certainly no longer have to be looking over your shoulders, and you'd know that you only had one enemy to deal with. Which is why Octavian invites you to talk to him about it: an agreement would be advantageous to both of you and he would like to meet as soon as possible."

Antony didn't hide his anger. "If you think I'll stop watching my back for that serpent Octavian you're very much mistaken, Agrippa. I'll do it anyway because he's the man I trust least in the world. But his offer deserves consideration. Of course, I'll have to talk to Lepidus first: after all, we could crush you in a moment if we wanted to, and none would weep over your death, I'm sure..."

Agrippa nodded and struggled to hold back a smile. Antony and Lepidus had numerical superiority, but that didn't necessarily mean tactical superiority. And it was precisely these unknown factors that were inducing Antony to keep an open mind.

"Very well then," he said. "I'll report to the consul that

you'll give him an answer shortly. Say by sunset tomorrow." Antony nodded thoughtfully and continued to stare at the message, and Agrippa took it as a dismissal and turned to leave, nodding a quick goodbye to Fulvia. But just before exiting the *tablinum*, he heard the woman's voice behind him.

"Wait a moment, you stripling."

He clenched his fists in anger and turned around. "For our safety," Fulvia continued, addressing her husband, "I'd suggest holding Agrippa as a hostage. Octavian cares greatly for him, my husband, and he won't play any dirty tricks on us as long as Agrippa's with us, both during your talks with Lepidus and in any negotiations that might follow."

Antony nodded. "Excellent idea. Guard – arrest him and hold him until further orders," he said, addressing the soldier who had been standing a pace behind Agrippa throughout the entire conversation.

The young man looked in dismay at Fulvia and the expression of triumph on her evil, beautiful face. Had she done it out of revenge or to resume their relationship?

He would soon find out.

V

Octavian tried not to feel overawed by the imposing line-up of forces Antony and Lepidus had assembled on the other side of the small tributary of the Po. Through the thinning early morning mist, the faint light of the rising sun sparkled off the armour of at least twenty-five thousand legionaries, who stood between the trees and the river bank in an eerie silence broken only by the sound of twittering birds, chirping crickets and croaking frogs. On the other hand, Octavian said to himself, his forces were no less significant: five legions deployed in battle formation a few hundred yards from the bank, as had been agreed in the preliminary contacts they'd had in the hours before the painstakingly prepared meeting.

He saw a detachment of Antony's legionaries occupy the end of the bridge nearest the island. He signalled to Rufus, who nodded and, in turn, dispatched a cohort to defend the far part of their river bank. The more distant bridges had already been occupied by both armies to ward off any attempted outflanking manoeuvre by those still perceived as the enemy. Then he waited for Antony to make the next move: it had to be he who made it, because he was a fugitive and an exile. There had been a time, just a year before, when his opponent had demanded deference because he was older and held the post of consul. Well, Octavian was now chief magistrate of the Republic, and the fact that he was the younger counted for very little. This time it was the other man who should be showing deference.

But Antony didn't emerge from the ranks of the five legions deployed on his side. Octavian pictured dramatic scenarios in which the strict procedure agreed upon for the tri-partite meeting fell apart and a battle broke out between the ten legions deployed along the river, gradually drawing in the units which had remained in their respective camps. On the other hand, the fact that the three of them had seen fit to bring fifty thousand men with them spoke volumes about the lack of trust between them.

Who would prevail? Probably, the first side that could establish a bridgehead on the opposite bank. There would be fierce fighting along the banks to establish solid fording points, and that wretched stream would turn red with blood and be choked with corpses. Octavian imagined columns of armed men pouring over the bridges as others arrived from a more distant crossing point to launch a rear attack on troops busy containing an attempted frontal breakthrough. He felt profound despair growing within him: Agrippa was being held prisoner by Antony, he didn't rate Rufus's ability, he himself certainly didn't feel like a leader, and he really couldn't aspire to be Antony's equal as a commander, nor perhaps even Lepidus's. He therefore felt that he had no chance of victory if things took a turn for the worse.

Consequently, he had to make sure things *didn't* take a turn for the worse. He hoped that Rufus would keep control of his soldiers, many of whom would have preferred to cut things short and avoid any negotiations, proceeding directly to the election of a single commander, who could only have been Antony. For his part, he was considering the possibility of setting his pride aside and making the first move. But if he did that, Antony would be convinced he could get anything he wanted out of him, and the meeting would become even more of an uphill struggle for Octavian, the youngest and least skilled of the three participants.

The more time passed, the more willing he felt to make concessions on the ceremony the envoys had agreed upon to preserve the dignity of the three commanders. He didn't want to give Antony any excuse to pick a fight, nor the opportunity to surprise him with some move he hadn't considered. He hoped he'd thought of everything, and it comforted him to know that Maecenas and Rufus had also carefully considered every eventuality. Antony tended to decide everything himself, probably depriving Lepidus of authority even though he was a proconsul and had been *magister equitum*. And if his opponent hadn't been so underhand as to take Agrippa hostage there would have been four minds preparing to forestall any possible risk instead of three.

But he couldn't press too hard: Agrippa's imprisonment gave Antony an advantage and limited his scope of action. Octavian had several times wondered if he'd be willing to lose his friend, or even just risk his life, to achieve his objectives, and had always answered himself that he wouldn't. No matter how great his desire to avenge Caesar, reform Rome and become the most important Roman ever, he would do everything he could to avoid sacrificing Agrippa on the altar of his unrestrained ambition. It wasn't just his friendship he had at heart: Agrippa had everything he lacked – military aptitude and courage in battle. Qualities without which he was sure he would never be able to attain his objectives.

The thought of his friend finally spurred him to make

the first move. It would be even more difficult to obtain concessions from Antony if he realised just how much he cared about Agrippa, but never mind: nothing had been easy since he'd learned he was to be Caesar's heir. He raised his arm to signal his bodyguards to move forward, but in that precise instant saw Antony's plumed helmet emerge from the ranks, along with an escort of three hundred men. Breathing a sigh of relief, Octavian lowered his arm and stood and watched as Antony walked to the edge of the water. Only then did he raise his arm again and walk with his men to the river bank, where he, in turn, stopped near a small boat that had been prepared to carry him over to the islet.

At this point he expected to see Lepidus appear. In fact, the pro-consul emerged from the ranks straight afterwards, recognizable by his plumed helmet and large scarlet cloak, and climbed into a boat moored in the reeds, accompanied by his two bodyguards. It had been agreed that he would go to the island first to inspect it for any traps laid by the other two participants. The river wasn't very deep at that point, and he could have walked across, but it was undignified for a general to wade through waist high water, so the use of boats had been agreed upon.

After a few oar strokes, Lepidus reached the isle. He walked up and down it – which, given its size, took only a few moments – and checked the top and even the underside of the table that the servants had placed there before dawn, as well as the three chairs they'd set around it. Next, he pulled several wax tablets and styluses out of his shoulder bag and told his bodyguards to position themselves to the side of one of the three chairs, then he turned towards the shore and signalled for Antony and

Octavian to join him.

It was time. The young consul looked around him, searching in vain for a comforting look from his ministers. But none were in sight. And besides, they had precise tasks to carry out to ensure that this difficult transition in their lives, as well as that of the Sect of Mars Ultor and Rome's history, went as they hoped.

In that moment, and for as long as the meeting with Antony and Lepidus lasted, each member of the secret society had to give their all. Even Agrippa, although a prisoner, was aware of the need to turn his current situation to his advantage. Their every act, their every decision – *everything* would influence the way events developed. *Had to* influence the course of events. Even he, Octavian, must play his part, as Maecenas had reminded him. As he got into the boat that would carry him to within a hair's breadth of Antony, after months of trading insults at a distance, he felt his legs tremble.

He was less than half their age, and if he wanted any chance of surviving he would have to prove himself more cunning and skilled than them in a negotiation that promised to be gruelling. He had to remind himself that if Caesar had chosen him to continue his work it was because he had seen in him something extraordinary, and it was this thought which gave him the courage to climb over the edge of the boat and set foot on the islet, walk up the short slope to the top, and take his place at the table. He stared into the eyes of Lepidus and Antony, who had arrived just a few moments before him.

*

Maecenas disembarked from the boat that had carried him over the river dividing Octavian's army from that of Antony and Lepidus, and approached the camp where he assumed he'd find Agrippa. His friend wasn't the only reason for his mission: pleading for his release was just a pretext for approaching the enemy troops. "Funny," the Etruscan thought as he began to make out the shape of the rampart Antony's legionaries had built: despite being a military tribune, he didn't really know his men – men with whom he'd only occasionally exchanged a few words on this campaign and the previous one in Modena – and yet now he was there to try and gain the confidence of soldiers from another army.

He was sure that his subalterns didn't think much of him, even though they ought to at least respect him for being one of the consul's closest confidants. On the other hand, he hadn't proved himself particularly skilful and brave in the one campaign he'd participated in. But he wasn't the first – and he wouldn't be the last – of the many military tribunes to hold office for purely political reasons. The soldiers would understand, even if they continued to regard him as arrogant and distant, for he didn't partake in the camaraderie and endure the hardships of the troops as Agrippa did – and as Rufus and Octavian did too, to a certain extent, though the latter simply to show himself worthy of Caesar.

In general, he didn't like the close proximity of others or being subjected to the stench of sweaty, drunken people with rotten teeth and foul breath. He loved to drench himself in perfume and dreaded the idea of smelling bad. But the truth was that he kept away from the troops because he was scared of them. Or rather, he was afraid of himself and his reactions. And now, as he approached the sentries guarding the camp's gate, he asked himself whether he would be able to curb the impulses to which he gave free rein with his young slaves, as he tried to attract the attention of Antony's soldiers. He would never want to reveal what emotions a muscular, well-sculpted body caused in him, as to do so would only earn him the contempt of the soldiery: certain rumours were quick to spread...

He told the guard to announce him to the highest-ranking commander in the camp in the absence of Antony and Lepidus, then waited at the front gate, under the wary eye of the other sentry and the guard patrolling the ramparts. He knew that, despite being a military tribune, he didn't have a particularly martial bearing, and he was slightly ashamed of the fact. Like Octavian, he just wasn't cut out for war or physical exertion. His head was his best weapon. Had it not been for the sect's highest goals he would never have allowed himself to be involved in these military campaigns.

The guard returned and invited Maecenas to follow him. Once inside the camp, Maecenas carefully scanned his surroundings, and immediately sensed the lax atmosphere that prevailed. The habits of the supreme commander, an unkempt pleasure-seeker, were reflected in his soldiers, many of whom wandered lazily between the tents, laughing and joking instead of dedicating themselves to physical exercise and daily training, as was good practice in every legion, including Octavian's. It would seem that Antony demanded obedience, not discipline, from his troops, and his was the only Roman army where the two did not go hand in hand. For this reason, he was occasionally forced to resort to extreme solutions, like the decimation at Brindisi.

Consequently, there was fertile terrain for propaganda, as Maecenas had expected.

They took him before a *laticlavius* tribune who observed him with a surly, inquisitive look. Maecenas didn't take much notice: he was used to the contempt of other officers. "What do you want, Tribune?" his colleague asked, without preamble.

"Just to make sure that Marcus Vipsanius Agrippa, who is being held in this camp, is in good health," he replied, in a mellifluous tone.

The tribune's expression became openly contemptuous. "Of course he's in good health!" he replied indignantly. "Probably *too* good! What do you think, that we're barbarians? We wouldn't hurt one of your men when we're in the middle of negotiations…"

Maecenas remained calm. "I do not doubt it. But I'd rather hear it from his lips, if you wouldn't mind."

"I don't see why I should do as you ask," the tribune replied, obstinately. It was clear that he was slow-witted, and perhaps even mercenary, Maecenas concluded, if it turned out that he couldn't persuade him with legitimate arguments.

"Because, as you yourself said, we're currently negotiating. And you wouldn't want to antagonise a potential ally, especially since, as you're holding captive a dear friend of his, you're now in the wrong. We are not holding any of your men at the moment. Indeed, over the past few months we've returned several officers captured at Modena as a sign of good will. Furthermore, I doubt Antony would consider letting me see Agrippa dangerous

– though he might find your behaviour regrettable. Just think: we could be allies by tonight, and then your conduct might be adjudged inappropriate," he suggested. The tribune looked confused. After a few moments he nodded. "Very well. But only for a few minutes. You don't need to hang around long." He called a guard over and ordered him to take the visitor to the tent where the captive was being held. Maecenas nodded his thanks, and followed the soldier. As he went, he calculated that by now news of his visit must have spread throughout the camp.

"Never mind, soldier. I'll take charge of our visitor," he heard someone say behind him. He turned around, and there before him was the person he'd been hoping to see: one of the officers who'd been released after the Modena campaign.

The legionary gave his superior a puzzled look, then bowed his head and obeyed. He moved away promptly, happy to return to his game of dice with his fellow layabouts.

"Hail, Tribune," the man greeted him, "was I fast enough?" Good, he wanted to appear zealous. He wasn't a member of the sect, just someone who had joined the cause to earn some money. But that was fine.

Maecenas nodded with satisfaction. "We expected nothing less when we told you to keep yourself available" he replied. "We have little time, so I'll give you your instructions immediately. Take me to Agrippa, but then let me evaluate the mood of the soldiers. I want to walk around the tents and explain why they all stand to gain if they support an alliance between Antony and Octavian. Then, when I've gone, you should discreetly continue the task of persuading them until the agreement is made. If everything goes as we hope, there'll be a further, substantial reward for you."

"I'm counting on it, Tribune. And you can tell the consul that he can rely on me," the officer said, gesturing to the Etruscan to follow him. They quickly reached a tent guarded by two sentries, to whom the officer signalled to be let through. They pushed aside the leather flap over the entrance and the officer went to enter, but Maecenas gave him a telling look, which was enough to make him stop by the entrance with a nod of assent.

The Etruscan entered a space dimly illuminated by two oil lamps and immediately saw the massive form of Agrippa lying on a couch in the corner. "Still in bed, eh?" he said, with a smile. "Do you think you're here on holiday?"

His friend sat up, rubbing his face. His beard was unkempt and his tunic unfastened. "It's about time you got here... I'm getting bored, and there's nothing to do but sleep. And, if I'm not much mistaken, it's just after dawn..." he said, standing up and going to shake his hand.

"Well then, my arrival can only be welcome," Maecenas replied. "I must give you a little work to do."

"Work? Aren't you going to take me with you? This lot here might do something nasty to me. Plus, you know that Fulvia's around, and I'm worried about what a woman like her might be capable of after being scorned... If you'd seen her face when I met them, her and Antony... I'm expecting her to visit today, and I don't imagine it will be like her visit of a few months back..." He walked over to a chair and invited Maecenas to sit down in front of him.

But the Etruscan shook his head. "There's no time. I've got other things to do in the camp. And don't worry, you're not running any risks: not with an agreement in sight. I'm just here to tell you that her visit *should* actually be like that of a few months ago. And you should do everything you can to make it so," he declared, to an open-mouthed Agrippa.

*

"I want to pick up where Caesar was forced to leave off. I want to reform the State and make it more powerful. And to do that, I need to hold the same office as he: dictator. Not for life, but for at least five years." After some unfriendly small talk, Octavian had decided to put his cards on the table, as Maecenas had suggested. It was possible that Antony and Lepidus might just get up and leave, but if they really wanted to benefit from the meeting it was more likely that they would negotiate. According to the Etruscan, manoeuvring them to where the sect wanted them would require playing for high stakes.

Antony screwed his face into a grimace of contempt, and Lepidus assumed an expression of shock. They were two men in their prime: the former highly vigorous and very good looking, albeit slightly overweight, and the latter decidedly corpulent, but charming – just beginning to go bald but without it ageing him much, and with the sort of elegant demeanour that came from belonging to one of Rome's oldest and most illustrious dynasties, the *Aemilia*. And yet, as far as Octavian was concerned, it was time for them to step aside: they were old because they represented the past. They were the personification of the ills which had plagued the Republic and caused it to decline. Personal ambition, debauchery, the inability to look far and think big. They were mediocre politicians, and the causes of a state's ruin always lay in the mediocrity of its ruling class: those holding the sceptre of command could make all the excuses they wanted and blame everyone but themselves, but the truth was that responsibility for the decline was theirs alone.

"Dictator? It was *I* who made them abolish the dictatorship! You're the same little shit as always! Isn't it enough that you've managed to extort the title of consul from the Senate!" exclaimed Antony, pounding his fist on the table so forcefully that the entire surface vibrated.

"Why? How did *you* get the title of consul, by regular elections?" Octavian answered promptly. "Caesar had it given to you, and so far you have not shown sufficient gratitude to him. Even if, thanks to me, people will now know that you've decided to execute at least one of his murderers..." He didn't give him time to reply and pressed on. "In any case, what Rome needs is order and prosperity, and I cannot provide those as a consul: there are too many constraints, too many opponents, too much institutional bureaucracy and the tenures are too short... Things will stay the same unless we change them. And you have to help me change them, if you care about Rome and not just yourselves."

"Just listen to him!" Lepidus interrupted, sarcastically. "Now setting yourself above everyone else means doing what's best for Rome."

"Discovering you were Caesar's heir has really gone to your head!" put in Antony. "You're not half the man he was, and never will be!"

Octavian had convinced himself that he could not only match his father, at least in some respects, but that he could even surpass him. But he was careful not to say so. Now that he was aiming so high, he could allow himself to flatter them and be humble. "There are many who think that I am. *Especially among the soldiers,* if you've noticed," he pointed out. "And you know very well that if you keep attacking me, you will not win their support. If you're here, it's because you too have finally realised that it's in your interests to co-operate. I've been trying to come to terms with you since the Ides of March, but you've constantly slammed the door in my face. How exactly did that help you, given that you're now a fugitive and an exile?" He deliberately ignored Lepidus, as it was clear that he simply followed Antony's lead. Antony was the one to convince. However, with Lepidus in a secondary position, he hoped to pique his sense of rivalry and encourage him to make proposals which would play into the sect's hands, albeit unwittingly. Or at least, that's how Maecenas hoped things would go.

Antony snorted. He couldn't deny anything that Octavian had said and it annoyed him. "Assuming I'm resigned to the idea of collaborating with a snake like you, I'd rather die than put myself under your command."

Octavian was silent. It was now that he needed Lepidus's co-operation. He looked at him, giving him his full attention for the first time since the discussion had started. And Lepidus felt compelled to speak.

"Young Octavian, it seems clear to me that we are currently the three most powerful men in Rome. It would be useless to deny that, and foolish to belittle one another out of pure vexation," he said with his familiar, affable tone. Lepidus was someone who tried to get on with everybody. "That's why I do not think it would work to have one of the three of us rule over the others. If, however, we could find a way to hold positions and powers of equal importance and power..."

This was precisely what Octavian had hoped to hear him say, and he could barely conceal his satisfaction. He was ready to raise his bid. "You mean like the triumvirate of Caesar, Pompey and Crassus?" he exclaimed, immediately.

"Why not?" Lepidus insisted. "After all, for as long as they got on with each other, for as long as Caesar and Pompey were related and everyone had what they wanted – Caesar in Gaul, Pompey in Italy and Crassus in the East – Rome benefited and there was a certain degree of political stability."

Octavian deliberately looked impressed by Lepidus's intuition. He looked at Antony and saw that he was thinking about it. Of course, the idea appealed to him: it would facilitate an instant return to the institutional fold and would give him power and influence, both of which had become increasingly precarious since he'd moved against the Senate. However, the young consul didn't want to appear too compliant, having earlier expressed ambitions of a far greater magnitude. "Hmm ... I am not sure that we share the same vision of what Rome needs. The risk would be that we would end up arguing all the time, and I'd feel as though my hands were tied..."

"All three of us have Rome's welfare at heart, don't we?" Lepidus continued. "So what's the problem? If those three, who couldn't stand each other, managed, why shouldn't we?"

Octavian had to keep putting up opposition for a little while longer. "For example, we don't see eye to eye about

Caesar's killers. I don't think that administering justice is one of your priorities. And yet you haven't lacked for opportunity. And with Caesar's killers at large, a triumvirate would be seen by those fanatics as an attack on democracy and we would never be left in peace. Whatever happens, they must be taken out of circulation. In a word, it's a case of us or them."

"Enough of this!" snapped Antony. "I did what had to be done at the time to avoid bloodshed! They had so many powerful supporters that they would have started a civil war and all Caesar's men would have been killed. I even saved you, you stupid little idiot! And I sometimes wish I hadn't!"

"And what about me? What could I have done with so few means at my disposal? But I've never intended to let those traitors get away with it!" said Lepidus – he, who in the days after the Ides of March, had slipped off to wait and see how events played out, probably with the intention of backing the party that eventually prevailed.

"Then prove once and for all that you want to avenge Caesar!" said Octavian, attempting to shame them. "Thanks to your inaction, his killers have become even stronger: they've managed to take over Roman territories with impunity, governing them as they wish without answering to anyone. They've stripped cities of their resources and put together vast armies which will force us to embark on a difficult and expensive war if we really want to see justice done! Do you know that Brutus and Cassius have at least twenty legions, thanks to their possession of Syria and Macedonia? And that Cassius is trying to get his hands on Egypt? We don't know how long Cleopatra will be able to resist the pressure: she's already lost four of the legions allocated to her."

"I know that very well…" Antony interrupted testily.

Octavian didn't allow himself to be intimidated. "And do you know that Cassius's nephew has killed Ariobarzanes of Cappadocia and seized his country's immense wealth? And that Marcus Brutus has his sights set on the coast of Cilicia and Rhodes? Not to mention the friendly relations Cassius has with the Parthians: apparently, he's receiving help from their king. If we wait any longer, they'll take over all of Rome's eastern possessions. In practice, half the empire…"

"Alright, alright," Antony cut him off impatiently. "If – and I say 'if' – we form a triumvirate, we'll need to define our roles, responsibilities and spheres of influence. And we should also respect the hierarchies and prestige we've acquired over the years: you are young and inexperienced compared to the two of us, lad. Most importantly, it should be up to me and Lepidus to decide who gets the most important posts. You can take responsibility for building works and the quaestors, if anything. And we should be given control of the major provinces: for example, I was assigned Gaul, and woe betide anyone who tries to touch it."

The discussion was going in the direction Octavian had hoped, so he kept his calm. He'd expected Antony to play the bully, and was even willing to concede him more: the important thing was that they formed a triumvirate, an important step in the sect's ascent to power, as well as his own. "You're talking to someone who became a consul at the age of twenty, and against your wishes, dear Antony," he replied calmly, "so I can't be all that incompetent. I have no intention of playing a junior role in any eventual triumvirate: I wouldn't be able to contribute to Rome in the way I've promised myself out of respect for the memory of my father Caesar. Each of us must receive an equal share, and this is a fundamental prerequisite for these negotiations to continue. Otherwise I'll go back to my initial request for the dictatorship, with or without your support."

Antony was seething with rage. Lepidus tried to keep his cool, but it was clear that he too was annoyed by the young man's attitude. Of course, Octavian said to himself with satisfaction, they hadn't expected such a determined approach. Indeed, they must have thought they would have been able to walk all over this young man who had presumed to negotiate with them as an equal. In short, they'd been caught unprepared, with no alternative strategy to the one they'd studied to crush him and render him harmless.

"Well, we can talk about the details of how to share the duties and provinces later," Antony said finally, without looking him in the eye. "But if we do create an alliance, I don't want you remaining a consul: people will always see you as my superior."

This he could concede him. In Rome, power didn't lie in the office you held but in the following you enjoyed, above all in the army. But he couldn't remain without an office. "Don't fool yourself that I will agree not to hold an institutional office. It could even be that of triumvir, just to prove that I'm willing to meet you half way," he replied. "The agreement between Caesar, Pompey and Crassus was private in nature, without actual defined offices other than those they held as part of their normal *cursus honorum*. We, however, should legally establish a new magistracy –

an institutional triarchy whose duration we should decide, for the protection and preservation of the Republic in these exceptional circumstances. I always work by the rules of the institutions and the Senate, and the people are re-assured by being governed by a legally sanctioned body. This way, we'll have a greater consensus."

They were totally astonished, he could tell. They hadn't been in any way prepared for a proposal like this. And that was precisely what would defeat them: they hadn't prepared for the meeting the way he had with his ministers. He couldn't wait for the day to end so he could tell Maecenas that his strategy had once again proved to be a winner.

VI

She appeared suddenly. Maecenas had only just left, and even if he'd been expecting Fulvia to visit him at some point, he certainly hadn't been expecting her to come so soon after dawn. However, without warning her sinuous and sensual form materialized in the tent and she loomed up silently before him with that provocative expression he knew so well.

And which excited him so much.

Fulvia continued to say nothing, and Agrippa, who had decided to stay sitting at the table where he was eating breakfast, said nothing either. To stand up would have been a sign of deference and respect, and respect was the last thing she wanted...

And besides, she was quite something to look up at: majestic, imposing, proud...

And fierce. He must forget that. For ever. Being around her was like playing with fire: you ran the constant risk of getting burned. Yet even if the sect hadn't ordered him to, Agrippa would have done the same thing: he loved taking risks, whatever form they took.

He restricted himself to pushing aside the bowl of porridge they'd brought for him and wiping his mouth on the back of his hand, as he continued to look her up and down. She liked to be desired, and he desired her – very much. He had never stopped craving her, and had hated himself for it when he'd been trying to save his relationship with Etain. Fulvia was like a disease that he hadn't quite shaken off, and of which he didn't know whether he would ever be free.

He waited a long time, caught up in that psychological duel where the loser was the one who gave in first. For a few moments, Agrippa feared that she might leave like that, without doing or saying anything, having just eyed her prey closely – whether he was useful to Antony alive or dead, Fulvia was crazed enough to go against her husband's orders out of pure vindictiveness. But when she opened her mouth, he knew he'd won: he'd gained the upper hand.

Until the next wrong move, of course.

"You hurt me, Agrippa," she said finally, without moving from where she was.

"I didn't mean to," he replied. "I suffered too, I can assure you."

"I have never suffered because of a man before. If anything, it was me who made them suffer."

"There's always a first time." Never bow your head in front of her, unless you wanted to end up like the many people she enjoyed harming.

"I liked it."

Agrippa jumped. She always managed to surprise him. So he was right; there were no half measures with Fulvia. She either made you suffer or suffered herself, so you always had to attack, and keep the pressure on. You could never lower your guard. Just like in battle.

"But I didn't do it on purpose…" was all he said.

"It doesn't matter. I don't care if you make me suffer – as long as you're mine. If you fall in love with another woman again, I swear by all the gods I'll have her killed. You can fuck whoever you like if you want, with or without me, but woe betide them if I see that you care about them.

And you can't keep it hidden."

The threat was real, he knew only too well. However, Agrippa also knew that he would never love another woman like he'd loved Etain. And Etain was no longer his, so there was no problem: no one would be in danger because of Fulvia.

"For you to control me like that, it will be necessary for Octavian and Antony to get along and work together. Otherwise our paths will inevitably go their separate ways," he said. He must never forget that he was serving the sect.

She moved towards him. Now Agrippa could smell the penetrating scent of her perfume. "Don't worry about that. Antony knows that it's in his best interests to come to an agreement with Octavian, for as long as it suits him. And as long as your friend isn't too arrogant, you'll see that they'll find some common ground."

"If they don't manage to, I hope you'll play your part," Agrippa went on. "If we are to continue seeing each other, such an agreement is necessary. You don't have a daughter you could marry off, do you? Matrimonial alliances are the best..." he added, following Maecenas's suggestion.

Fulvia made a disdainful gesture with her hand. "Just listen to him! If I couldn't see the lust in your eyes, I'd say that you were my lover simply to help your little friend."

Agrippa realised that he must be careful not to overplay his hand. He had to remember that with her you were always dancing on the razor's edge. "Try me, and see for yourself whether I find it a sacrifice," he said, standing and raising his tunic, beneath which his excitement was more than evident. With her you had be bold: it was part of the perpetual challenge in which they were engaged.

Fulvia took a step forward, putting her face close to his and straightaway shoving her hand under his thong. As their lips began to brush together, Agrippa felt her breath upon him, hot and intense, and she suddenly dropped to her knees, seeking his sex. The young man found himself with her face between his legs, her panting breath enveloping him as it reverberated around the tent. He'd thought about her groans and whimpers at least as much as he'd thought about Etain's sweet smile.

When he felt her wet tongue tickle his member, he felt like he was about to burst. He wanted to pick her up, slam her onto the table and have her in that wild, brutish way they both liked. And he was just about to do so, when Fulvia suddenly began to use her teeth instead of her tongue – she gave him a quick but intense bite, gripping his member fiercely before releasing it just in time to avoid Agrippa's reaction – he instinctively lashed out with his arm, striking where he thought her head would be.

The young man looked at his now limp penis, dripping with blood.

"And don't think it's finished here, boy," she said, wiping her red blood-stained lips on the back of her hand. "You've got to earn your forgiveness. See you tomorrow, Agrippa!" she said, turning round and pulling aside the tent flaps before disappearing from sight.

*

"Anyway, irrespective of any other discussion, nothing is more important to me than revenge for my father," Octavian pointed out, when he saw that the negotiations were beginning to run aground over the division of territories under their control. Antony and Lepidus picked at the provisions their bodyguards continued to put on the table every time they saw an empty bowl, seemingly in no hurry to work out the details of the agreement. "It must be clear to you and the people of Rome and the provinces that the ultimate goal of this triumvirate, presuming it's ever formed, will be to return the Republic to a normal state of affairs. But its primary objective will be justice. And if necessary, war, against any of the murderers who aren't yet dead."

"And you ask if there will be war, lad?" snorted Antony. "Of course there will! You said a few minutes ago that they are powerful now, and they certainly won't accept a triumvirate."

Octavian looked deep into his eyes. "I must correct you, Antony," he said in a patient tone that belied his two glacial eyes. "What they don't want doesn't count. They are outlaws, and it is we who will not tolerate their appropriation of entire parts of the empire. Above all, we will not tolerate the fact that there are criminals who have been convicted by the Senate and are still at large. We are the authorities, not them. Don't forget that."

Antony smiled contemptuously, resentful at having being slapped down but also aware that he should not give in to resentment. "It takes money to fight people who command so many legions and control wealthy countries like those in the East," was all he said.

"That's precisely why we need to divide up the provinces" specified Octavian. "Or at least, the ones that we still control, seeing as we can no longer count on those beyond the Adriatic Sea. If Caesar's murderers control theirs and draw resources from them, we'll have to do the same. We can't afford to allow them any advantages."

"Theirs are richer. They've already got the advantage..." said Lepidus, his eyes already shining with greed.

"But they have fewer of them," Octavian replied. "Even Pompey, when he was fighting Caesar, had the eastern provinces. Indeed, his sphere of command stretched much further. And who won in the end?"

"Caesar was a genius..." replied Lepidus, disconsolately.

"And much of the soldiery considers me the same," insisted Octavian. "Even though you may not agree, we should exploit this advantage to instil confidence in the army. You fought for Caesar, and you, Antony, in particular, played an important role in some of his successes. On their side, Decimus Brutus and Trebonius have been eliminated, which means that only Cassius Longinus can boast of any past military glory. Marcus Brutus doesn't count for anything, and you could say much the same about the others: they killed Caesar because he'd never appreciated them, knowing very well that they didn't amount to much."

"That's as maybe," conceded Antony, whose vanity Octavian had tickled, "but what it means is that whoever of us goes to war should have more legions than the one who remains to defend Rome – because someone will have stay and defend the rear. And that means more resources. Which is to say, more provinces, or at least the richer ones."

Octavian had seen that objection coming. Or rather, Maecenas had warned him that it would. And had prepared his counter measures. The ministers of the sect were well aware that what was at stake here wasn't so much the war against Caesar's killers as possible future ones. "I agree. And I think, with all due respect to you, Lepidus, that it should be me and Antony who go to war. Me because I'm a consul and a symbol for the soldiers, and Antony because of his experience and his popularity in the army. The division of the empire should consequently be made on this basis."

Naturally, Lepidus reacted strongly: "Are you joking? It seems more logical to me that Caesar's two lieutenants should go to war against those who killed him, and his young adopted son should stay to protect the centre of the Empire. It's also a question of seniority..."

"I agree," agreed a visibly pleased Antony. "Just think, Octavian, you could have Italy. Doesn't that please you?"

The young man shook his head. But then again, he had expected this.

"Absolutely not," he responded. "I have no intention of staying at home while you two fight my father's murderers." And besides, he didn't want Italy: to procure resources he would be forced into conflict with the interests of the large landowners, who were also members of the Senate. He would make too many enemies and his position would become compromised. You could strip resources with impunity elsewhere, as many provincial governors did, but he and the sect certainly had no intention of behaving like everyone else. In fact, one of their objectives was to make the administration of the Empire more just. But it wouldn't be possible to tread too lightly whilst a civil war was in progress, and Antony and Lepidus were obviously counting on the unpopularity that governing Italy would cause him while they themselves earned glory on the battlefield and returned home in triumph. Not to mention that by staying in Rome, he would be entitled to fewer legions, and so would end up weaker than the other two. Certainly, it was inevitable that one of the three of them would be at a disadvantage, but he had to do everything possible to ensure it wasn't him.

He pushed away a bodyguard who had approached the table to refill empty water glasses. "To win the war you need me," he insisted, "because I'm the consul, and because I'm not convinced you'll conduct it with conviction. You've made agreements with them in the past, and you could do so again: I'll be there to remind everyone, from my fellow commanders to each and every soldier, that we're fighting for justice and to avenge the greatest man Rome has ever seen."

"Of course... and perhaps you also want the most important provinces and the right to appoint consuls and most of the legions. In practice, you want the dictatorship and two *magistri equitums...*" said Antony, as Lepidus nodded vigorously.

"It seems to me that there's little to choose from," insisted Octavian, imperturbably, pretending not to hear. "We have the Gallic and Spanish provinces, Italy, and Africa. Macedonia, Syria and Asia are theirs, at the moment. And unless we act soon, they'll also have several important Mediterranean islands. In fact, Sextus Pompey controls Sicily as well as having many clients in the Iberian Peninsula. The empire is split into two – no, into three – and it's up to us to re-establish unity, even by sub-dividing what nominally remains under Senate authority. Antony, do you want the Gallic provinces? I'll let you have some of them, but certainly not all of them: there are too many.

You would control an immense territory. The Spanish provinces are another matter: Lepidus, you already govern one, and you could administer the others as well. Africa requires substantial resources to control it, and whoever does so might run into difficulties. The Numidian kings are unreliable and you never know who they'll side with. What's more, several of Caesar's killers have found refuge there. As for Italy, joint governance would be best, to share any problems that might arise."

"There are two things that I won't negotiate on," said Antony, decisively. "If this agreement is to be made, I'll take charge of fighting the war and have all of the Gallic provinces. And one of my men will be made consul in your place – Ventidius Bassus, for example. Furthermore, I don't want you around when I face Brutus and Cassius. Lepidus respects hierarchies and knows how to act as vice-commander. You don't, and you'd only get in the way, especially given your weak physical constitution, which means you're unsuited to campaigning. If you don't like it, it will mean war... between us."

Octavian clenched his fists under the table, trying to hide his frustration. He had expected fierce opposition from Antony, and he was well aware that he could only overcome it if Maecenas, Rufus and Agrippa successfully played their parts.

By now, the day was drawing to a close, and they'd reached a stalemate. For the work of the triumvirate to benefit the sect, Antony had to cede on at least something. Instead, he was absolutely inflexible, and Octavian didn't yet have enough leverage to force him into changing his arrogant, intransigent mind.

Soon it would be time for them to retreat to their

respective camps and prepare their strategy for the following day.

He hoped his ministers' work would prove fruitful.

*

"That group there," Maecenas said to the officer escorting him after they'd left Agrippa's tent, indicating a small group of soldiers without armour. The legionaries didn't appear to be doing anything important, just killing time with idle bets on bones and dice, so he reckoned they might be an audience willing to at least listen to him without walking away when confronted with his unmilitary bearing and the fact of his belonging to Octavian's army.

He walked towards them accompanied by the officer who he'd instructed to play along with him. They stood within earshot of the soldiers and Maecenas began addressing his companion, though in reality he was speaking for the benefit of Antony's men. "I tell you it would be in everyone's interests for those three to agree," he said, passionately. "The rewards would be guaranteed, the usual payments and extraordinary gifts, and they wouldn't be subject to the whims of the Senate and the progress of a campaign like they are now. Can't you see how uncertain it all usually is? Every soldier fights for years without any guarantees, and the only thing he can do is trust in the goodness of his commander's heart. And, as if that wasn't bad enough, in his luck."

Out of the corner of his eye, he noticed that some legionaries had stopped their game and, on hearing the word 'reward', had given him their full attention. His interlocutor was quick to reply: "You're quite right. I think the consul, Antony and Lepidus have more reasons to agree than to fight. They all loved Caesar, so why should they play into the hands of his killers?"

"If they strike an agreement," continued Maecenas, as several soldiers began to move closer, "the State will benefit, and when the State prospers soldiers are better off too: resources that would otherwise be wasted on domestic wars would instead go to the legionaries. Octavian is trying to convince Antony and Lepidus that the soldiers will only be satisfied after they've avenged Caesar and received a just reward for their efforts."

"What do you mean by 'just reward'?" interrupted a legionary who'd moved closer than the others.

Maecenas made sure his response could be heard by his comrades, none of whom were concentrating on what they'd been doing before. "Prospects. Octavian wants to give all of you – all of us – solid prospects for the future. And that's what sets him apart from every other general in Rome's recent past. Even Caesar. Or rather, he plans to perfect what Caesar had in mind, but didn't manage to finish before they did for him. To establish an army with a salary and, at the end of the period of service, a pension for every soldier who has conscientiously done his duty."

"I've been waiting years for a just reward!" one of the soldiers shouted.

"Of course, my friend," replied Maecenas, patiently. "And you've never had one because nobody has ever taken care of it and because the particularly dramatic circumstances of recent years haven't allowed for it. Maybe you haven't even had any wages other than the occasional reward. No, Octavian – and I'm sure that in the very near future, Antony and Lepidus too – wants to establish a solid system for everyone who puts their life on the line for the Republic."

"And what does that mean?"

"It means a period of service with a definite, fixed duration, a regular salary, and, above all, a nice homestead on retirement," he said solemnly, remaining to study his attentive audience and see how they'd react.

Many were left open-mouthed. "Yeah, homesteads in the middle of nowhere, most likely…" said a sceptical legionary.

Maecenas smirked to himself and paused for an instant to prepare himself before shooting the sharpest arrow in his quiver. "Not at all, my friend. I'm sure that our three commanders are right now already talking about land in Italy!"

The soldiers' murmuring grew into a noisy clamour, accompanied by expressions of astonishment as well as of scepticism. "In Italy? Yeah right. Those senator pigs will never allow that!" someone cried out.

"Maybe they won't," Maecenas pointed out. "But it's for precisely that reason that our three commanders need to be united. Do you think the senators would object to the demands of generals who commanded such a massive army?"

"Of course! Remember what Caesar managed to do for the veterans of Pompey the Great, when they formed the triumvirate with Crassus?" a legionary said.

"Right! The three of them together managed to do things Pompey had never managed to do on his own!" added another.

"If we carry on fighting between us, we won't see a

sestertius for years, I tell you!" cried another.

"And Caesar won't be avenged! Caesar, the only one who ever really acted in favour of the soldiers!" echoed another.

"Our work is done here," whispered Maecenas to his companion. "They'll speak to their comrades who weren't here, you'll see. In any case, it's up to you to make sure they do. Now take me through the tents before escorting me to the praetorian gate. I want to have a word with a few more soldiers."

"As you wish, Tribune," said the officer, leading the way to the nearest section of common legionaries. The eight-man tents were in disarray, with dirty bedding and equipment scattered all around, and only a few men were busy polishing their weapons or duelling between the tents. Most were playing or talking, or resting on their camp beds. Maecenas couldn't understand how a famous leader like Antony could keep his troops in such a deplorable state: when he wasn't fighting, Caesar's favourite lieutenant neglected the most elementary duties of a commander, starting with that of imposing strict discipline and keeping his men busy. And sooner or later that could cost him dear.

He wandered around the tents, hoping to find a group large enough to make a worthwhile audience. Just one more and he could consider his job done and would no longer have to hang around talking to rough soldiers. But he didn't see any that might suit his purpose, so he resigned himself to the idea of approaching a few people at a time. He just hoped to find men who weren't too awful, and continued to look around for a face that might inspire him.

Finally, his eyes came to rest on two legionaries without armour, sitting on the ground, reading from sheets of papyrus and speaking heatedly between themselves. If they were reading and discussing, they must be people with brains and a modicum of culture, he said to himself, and as such, they were ideal subjects to take in and pass on his message. He moved closer so he could hear the voice of the soldier with the papyri in his lap.

"...The quality of the verse is excellent, dear Plotius, as I told you. But to praise a tyrant like Caesar makes it all puerile, banal. To bring out your talent you should choose less unpleasant subjects for your poems... not conventional stuff like this."

Maecenas stared at the man speaking, and for a moment was overcome by a wave of intense emotion. A moment later he wondered if it was due to the wonder of seeing two soldiers talking about poetry, or to the elegant face and melodious voice of the legionary who was playing the critic. He pushed aside his fear of not seeming manly and decided that, for whatever reason, he had to speak to those two immediately.

And above all to him.

*

"No... I don't agree that the divine Caesar is 'conventional stuff'..." ventured Maecenas, approaching the two soldiers who were discussing poetry, and, in particular, about the composition one had dedicated to Octavian's adopted father. The Etruscan stared at the man who had expressed the criticism: he was about his age, and had an expression that was at once profound and easy-going, which made him appear somehow distant, as though his surroundings didn't concern him.

Terribly beguiling.

The man turned his intelligent eyes onto him, and Maecenas felt a shiver run down his spine. It didn't happen to him often, not with men. It was more likely to happen with young boys, and on a few rare occasions, with equally young girls. For a moment, he put his mission aside.

"It would be hard to be *more* conventional..." the soldier replied, with a superior smile. "It's a very fashionable subject at present, don't you think?"

The other protested before Maecenas could respond. "But I didn't just write it to follow the crowd... It's something I felt growing inside me: I admired him, and I would have liked to have gone with him to conquer the Parthian Empire. For my part, whatever I can do to honour him, I shall. Whilst we wait to fight his murderers, I'll write eulogies for him."

"That seems a laudable intent ... We're all fans of Caesar here... on both sides of the river. And the quicker we realise that, the better it will be for the Republic and for the cause of justice... May I have a look?" Maecenas said, gesturing to him to pass the papyrus over. In the meantime, he shot a fleeting glance at the other soldier who raised his eyes to the sky and said nothing.

The poet hesitated a moment, then handed it to him. The Etruscan unrolled the papyrus with one hand whilst holding the end with the other, and read the verses carefully. They were hexameters, and written with a certain skill too. They needed refining a bit, but there were signs of uncommon talent and passion, the same attributes he always hoped to see in his own compositions but never did. He dwelt on a passage that spoke of 'Caesar's vile death at the hands of his sons,' and thought that Octavian would find it interesting. Yes, there were definitely people in Antony's and Lepidus's legions who loved Caesar and wanted to see him avenged.

"Nice work," he said, handing him the back the rolled papyrus. "What's your name, soldier?"

The man hesitated again.

"When a tribune asks a humble legionary his name, there might be a hidden catch," said Maecenas to himself, and couldn't help but smile. "Don't be afraid," he said reassuringly, "I'm not your direct superior. I'm on Caesar Octavian's General Staff. And I'm interested in poetry. I write myself, but I don't have your talent, and I like bringing out other people's qualities."

The expression on the soldier's face relaxed. "My name is Plotius Tucca, Tribune," he replied, smiling in turn.

"And what's in it for you?" interjected the other man.

"Excuse me?" Maecenas was happy that the second soldier had given him the chance to speak to him, even if he had sounded slightly insolent.

"I said, what do you earn by unearthing other people's talents?" he asked, sceptically.

It certainly wasn't the first time he'd been asked a question like that. Maecenas liked helping people – he'd done so ever since he'd been a boy, using his enormous wealth to help others fulfil their dreams and thus become indebted to him. And when others expressed amazement at this habit of his, which one might consider a character hallmark, he gave up explaining the rest, knowing that they would call him a hypocrite. In reality, the real reason he helped other people was that he liked doing it. He genuinely liked to bring out the potential in people, to help bring out the best in them in the certainty that fulfilled, proud people made the world a better place. But he was a businessman too, and didn't scorn any material gain he could make out of it.

He wanted to make a good impression on the man, so decided not to linger on his whims. Some people tended to find him too eccentric. He cut him short: "There's always something to gain by helping other people. They then remember you," was all he said.

"Bah! You put a lot of faith in other people's gratitude. You must be deluded. When someone takes advantage of you, you've lost them. So it's not worth it," the man said disdainfully, but in a way that was sufficiently light hearted to avoid being offensive.

"I like to think that it's not like that," Maecenas replied. "And so far it's worked out well for me. I've never had reason to regret any of my choices."

"Then you should help him," Plotius said. "He's much better than me, I can assure you. That's why I wanted to show him my work."

"Really?" Maecenas looked at the man with even more interest. "I'd like to read something of yours... soldier. What's your name?"

"First of all, I'm not a soldier but an *optio*. My name is Quintus Horatius Flaccus, and I've no intention of showing you anything," the man replied, and this time he seemed annoyed.

At this point, Maecenas's interest in the man grew exponentially. "And why not?" he asked in an almost desperate tone, fearful of losing the only excuse he had for seeing him again. "When our armies march together – and

I'm sure that will be soon – we'll have many chances to chat and become friends, in the name of our common passion for poetry."

"Simply, because I'm not interested," the sergeant replied. "And because I would never seek the approval of a man who serves the son of a tyrant. If our armies march together, they'll do it without me. I have no intention of fighting the 'liberators': in my opinion, they should be rewarded, not punished."

Plotius put a hand on Horace's forearm, trying to encourage him to be less cutting.

"I doubt the other soldiers share your opinions," replied Maecenas, trying to hide his dismay: Horatius no longer seemed like someone he could establish a relationship with. Of any kind.

The man made a dismissive gesture. "You know how much I care. My misfortune was to have been enlisted in a legion that finished up in Antony's hands. I would much rather be in the East with Cassius and Marcus Brutus. On the other hand, I studied in Athens, and with the times being what they are, I'd happily go back there."

"Maybe you will go back there. We'll be going to those parts when we've sorted out all the institutional issues."

"If that ever happens, I'll be in the ranks of the liberators. And the only way you can help me, Tribune, is to offer me your chest in battle so that I can run you through, along with everyone else who's still fighting in the name of the tyrant."

"Don't mind him, Tribune. He's always like this. He likes to make himself hateful, but he's not a bad person, I assure you," Plotius hastened to put in, fearful that the senior officer might take against them.

But Maecenas took no notice. He turned and joined the officer who had been escorting him. Whatever criticism and insults he received usually had no effect upon him at all: he didn't care what others said about him – for the most part they were people of less intelligence, wealth, knowledge and capacity for enjoying life. But this time, the man had hurt him. There was something about that Horatius that troubled him and made him lose control of the game – the opposite to what happened with everyone else.

More than anything else he wanted to get to the heart of the man's personality and his literary works, and he made a mental note to approach him a second time.

When the two armies had marched together.

VII

Watching the rising sun lose its reddish hue and begin to shine with its usual yellow light on the isle whose soil he was about to tread for the second time, Octavian felt as though a good day was dawning. He was sure that Antony and Lepidus would be less intransigent now that they had had a chance to gauge the mood of the soldiers: all he'd have to do would be to soften his position slightly, so they wouldn't think they'd lose face if they agreed with him. He scrutinised their faces as they approached the isle and felt a surge of satisfaction – the expressions he saw there were far less determined than those of the day before, when they'd come convinced that they would walk all over Rome's consul simply because he was half their age. He read doubts and misgivings on their faces, even discomfort, and this time they were undoubtedly coming to the meeting with respect for him, rather than disdain.

Nevertheless, they shook hands warily, in heavy silence, each studying the others to try and read their thoughts. There was more tension in the atmosphere than the day before, and the bodyguards kept their hands firmly upon the hilts of their sheathed swords. Octavian sat down, and the other two followed suit. He waited: he could afford to wait for them to speak. So far, the only thing they'd decided was to create a five-year triumvirate, to have the Senate ratify it by law, and to assign to this new institutional creation the responsibility for nominating magistrates. The rest was still to discuss.

After many minutes of tense, embarrassed silence,

Lepidus broke the ice. It was obvious that he had been given the role of Antony's legate in every sense, including that of opening the way for him.

"We had some trouble with the soldiers last night and this morning before dawn..." he was forced to admit.

Excellent start.

"Really? I didn't," Octavian said, trying to curb the sarcastic smile forming on his lips.

"That doesn't surprise me," responded a still calm Lepidus, "since it was you who incited them."

"Me? How can you say such a thing?" he replied, assuming the most innocent air in the world, which, with his youthful face, he could do particularly well.

Antony began to look elsewhere. Lepidus replied: "You know perfectly well what I'm talking about. Now, more than ever, the soldiers want you in the war against the self-styled 'liberators'. You've bought them."

Octavian feigned amazement. "Are you joking? Everybody knows, and has for some time, that my priority is justice against those murderers. Those who loved Caesar have always wanted to avenge him under the command of his son and heir," he pointed out. "And I've never hidden the fact that I would like to reward them adequately for their efforts, just as my father promised to do at the end of the Parthian war. Even if there's a civil war, they should still be paid, on top of any booty – which, especially as we're not going off to conquer a foreign country, there might not even be..."

"But you've made a host of promises that you'll never be able to keep." Lepidus raised his voice, but only slightly: unlike Antony, he was a man who knew how to keep his calm. "You've offered veterans plots of land in settlements near major Italian cities, where it's no longer possible to appropriate anything! You've even proposed organising whoever remains in service into a permanent state army! I've heard talk of twenty year periods of service, of wages, of permanent border stations, and of Praetorian cohorts in Rome and surrounding areas with all due benefits! You're buying them, and you've blatantly lied, exploiting their ignorance of the State's accounts. Or maybe you yourself don't know anything about them: what money were you planning to use to pay for a permanent army?"

Octavian kept his calm. "We'll find the money. It will mean the rich pay more: a standing army benefits everybody, it will prevent invasions such as the Cimbri and Teuton offensives of half a century ago and ensure order in the provinces. And given all the turmoil we've seen in Rome over the past few decades, a few soldiers there would be helpful for keeping order. It'll mean we'll have to increase taxes, but we'll improve services as well, so the people will understand they're paying for something useful, not just throwing their money away. And don't forget that a standing army belonging to no one but the State would also prevent civil wars. This one we're preparing to fight, and in which I want to take part at all costs, should be the last one. Even though I see this less as a civil war than as a hunt for some glorified criminals who have become too powerful for simple operations of public order."

"Bollocks!" shouted Antony suddenly. "Absolute bollocks!" Lepidus attempted to calm him down by discreetly gripping his forearm, but with absolutely no effect. "You're behaving like a snake as usual. You always move in the shadows, hatching your convoluted plots like the slimy coward you are! You're not capable of facing your opponents like a man! And not because you're a child – because you're a coward!"

This time Octavian smiled in satisfaction: Antony's anger was an admission of defeat. "Fine," he said, pleased. "And now you've got that off your chest, can we talk about more serious things? I'll go to war because the soldiers know that I've got their interests and desires at heart more than anyone else, and that more than anyone else I'll ensure they get the revenge they've been seeking. And I suppose that I'll go with you. So, Lepidus, I'd suggest you be so kind as to give me and Antony some of your legions, so we can create an army that will guarantee us victory. And I'd suggest dividing Gaul's provinces, Antony. Which would you like to keep?" he concluded, sure that he now had them in the palm of his hand and that he could permit himself to be conciliatory.

"All of them, as I've already told you. If I have to share the campaign against Brutus and Cassius with you, I'll need something to help me swallow the bitter pill. Otherwise, take Lepidus. Though with all due respect, my friend," Antony added, turning to his companion, "I wouldn't bet on your victory."

Despite wanting to explode as Antony had, the young consul remained calm. Antony knew he had something that he could blackmail Octavian with: his worth as a commander, something which the young man had needed ever since he'd appeared on the political scene. He was right: it wouldn't be the same with Lepidus leading the troops. Lepidus would doubtless be more accommodating, and would perhaps even cede supreme command, but he was a much less effective tool than

Antony, who was the best leader around, at least until Agrippa, and possibly Rufus, acquired some experience.

He made a tentative attempt to win him over, but knew Antony wouldn't give in. "Take the Gallic provinces away and there's little left for me and Lepidus to divide. I reckon you should at least give up Cisalpine Gaul…"

Antony looked him in the eyes for a long time, then declared, as though making an official statement, "I get *all* the Gallic provinces, Lepidus gets the Spanish provinces, you get Italy, Sicily, Sardinia and Corsica, and Africa."

The prospect of Mark Antony being free to control all the Gallic provinces, as Caesar had done in his time, was frightening. Octavian had wanted to weaken him, but this way all he was doing was strengthening him, and conversely it was he who was coming out weakened, with the dead wood of a hard-to-govern Italy, a Sicily virtually occupied by Sextus Pompey – who would force him to wage war on two fronts – and a largely useless Africa.

"And what about the legions?" he asked.

"Lepidus will give up seven for the war, but only for the war: four to me and three to you."

This time they had evidently prepared for the meeting. "Why fewer to me? I'm the consul…" he muttered, realising he'd spoken with less assurance in his voice and cursing himself for letting a sense of defeat show.

"You won't be a consul any more, as we've said," Antony replied, his self-confidence, in contrast, growing. "Once this new judicial triumvirate is formalised, you'll resign your position, which Ventidius Bassus will take up. If you want, your cousin can remain a consul until the end of the year."

Octavian's mind began to work. There appeared to be

no way out. It seemed the sect's efforts had enabled him to participate in the war against Caesar's killers and gain more legions, but for the time being, that was as far as he could go. He tried to think of all the potential benefits he could extract from this new situation: after all, these two thought they'd caught him out in spite of his intrigues, and that would make them surer of themselves, meaning they were more likely to let their guard down and leave him free to manoeuvre for the sect's objectives.

In addition, he would still be getting three legions, taking them away from possible future enemies and therefore weakening them. And when the time came to give them back... well, he would find a way of getting out of that. Thanks to Antony's collaboration he had a real chance of destroying Caesar's assassins once and for all, without having to chase them one by one, and as for the loss of the consulship, well that wasn't such a great loss: he could manoeuvre the Senate through Pedius. In any case, the three of them had agreed that each triumvir would have the same powers as a consul. For a while, at least, he wouldn't have to watch out for Antony and Lepidus and all their friends, of which there were still many at large.

But above all, he had ensured himself a pre-eminent position for five years. Over that time he would be able to consolidate his relationship with the army by promoting rewards and reforms in favour of the soldiery, and show that he cared more for the common good and Rome's welfare than the other two. And in the end, tired of the constant bickering between the triumvirs, the Romans would choose him and opt for a monocracy. In the meantime, the Sect of Mars Ultor would be able to further consolidate itself, branch out, and take possession of the nerve centres of Roman society.

"It would seem that we are partners, my friends!" he exclaimed at last, with a genuine smile.

"Very well!" said Antony, standing up and holding out his hand. "What would you say to ratifying the agreement by marrying my stepdaughter, Clodia Pulchra?" he added cheerfully.

Octavian let a few moments pass, just to show a semblance of surprise.

"I'd be honoured," he said finally, pleased to see that Agrippa had done his part.

*

Agrippa woke with a mixture of excitement and fear. Excitement at the prospect of Fulvia's imminent visit, fear for what that terrible woman might do to him. There was no doubt she was determined to make him suffer. He had asked for a physician to treat his injured penis, but none had come: obviously, she had expressly forbidden it. Who knew what else she had in mind: the only guarantee he had was that she still wanted him. Indeed, more than ever. The only thing he was sure of was that she would keep him alive, but that wouldn't save him from further trouble.

Trouble that he realised he actually wanted to suffer.

That woman had bewitched him right from the start, and now that Etain's benign influence was no longer around to counter her perfidiousness, he felt that no other girl could save him from that unhealthy relationship – a relationship he desperately wanted to leave behind him whilst at the same time abandoning himself to completely. It was not love and never would be, at least not on his part, but it was a tie that risked becoming even more binding.

Perhaps it already had, he thought, if he was there waiting anxiously for her instead of focusing on the decisive events which were currently taking place – events in which he had a part to play.

When Fulvia's statuesque figure appeared, bathed in the sunlight that penetrated the thin gap between the tent's leather flaps, his heart began to beat even faster. He'd thought a lot about the position he'd like her to find him in, changing it constantly, and had finally decided to welcome her stretched out on the bed, as though to show her that he was willing to play any game she might have planned for him.

Again Fulvia said nothing. As she slowly moved towards him, his cock began to harden, causing intense pain where her teeth had cut the flesh. She stopped a few paces from his bed, and, with studied movements, took off her cloak and tunic to let him admire her naked body. Agrippa swallowed and began to sweat, then freed himself of his thong, revealing his fully erect penis. Her eyes sparkled at the sight of the wounds she'd caused and the blood that had begun to colour his pubic region.

For a few instants they remained immobile in a state of tense paralysis, that same tension upon which Fulvia seemed to feed. "I'm not like this," Agrippa kept repeating to himself – far from being exciting, the tension was consuming him. And yet, he didn't want to pull out of the game. It was a sort of voluntary, conscious condemnation.

Fulvia continued to move closer and, once by the bed, climbed onto it, placing her feet by Agrippa's sides and raising herself to her full height. He watched as she towered over him, her curvaceous breasts up above, and began to touch her already swollen nipples, swaying voluptuously as she slipped a hand between her legs. Agrippa would have liked to imitate her, but as soon as he touched his increasingly swollen member the pain got worse. He grimaced and Fulvia noticed immediately. With a wicked smile, she lowered herself straight onto his groin, guiding him inside her. She didn't pause for a second and immediately began to move her pelvis frenetically, supporting herself with her feet and hands.

Agrippa cried out in pain, as well as pleasure. He tried to grab her sides to restrain her, but she shot out her hands and grabbed his wrists, then began to move even faster, looking at him with an air of challenge, and he realised that if he complained he would suffer a lot more. So he fell silent, letting out just a few gasps of pleasure.

He let her ride him and hold his arms still. Fulvia's gasping breath was close to his face, but she wouldn't let him crane his neck to kiss her: every time he tried, she pulled his head back, smiling even more perfidiously. Her sighs gradually increased in intensity, until they reached a culmination of pleasure, which made her scream and move on him even more.

The young man thought he was in too much pain to reach orgasm, but the sight of Fulvia sent him into ecstasies, and when soon afterwards he felt that he about to come he made the mistake of telling her – he should have known what Fulvia would do in that sadistic way of hers. An instant after his cry of pleasure, the woman climbed off him and watched as he shouted in what was now only pain.

Agrippa had no doubt that she drew further pleasure from this. He stared at her, and found confirmation in her gratified look. Nevertheless, he would still have liked to pull her to him and embrace her and kiss her. She seemed to detect his desire and immediately got up, picked up her clothes and quickly put them on without saying a word or deigning to look at him again. She then walked towards the tent's entrance, and only when she was in the doorway, once again bathed in early morning sunlight, did she turn towards him and say, "See you this afternoon, Agrippa dear. And make sure you're ready…"

*

Fraternising. It wasn't the best way to make a name for yourself in battle, especially as he had to 'fraternise' with soldiers he'd been fighting until a few months previously, but those were Octavian's orders. Salvidienus Rufus looked across the river, studying Antony's and Lepidus's troops who were guarding the shore opposite, camping out as they anxiously waited for news from the isle.

The task annoyed him a great deal. Octavian was busy in a private meeting with the two most powerful men in Rome, Maecenas was creating clienteles in the camps of the other two commanders, Agrippa … well, Agrippa was probably having a great time with Antony's wife. He, however, had been charged with the most menial, insignificant task: he was to dampen the bellicose spirit of the soldiers of the two armies who were lined up along the opposite banks of the river in order to force Antony and Lepidus up against the wall and get them to back the desire for peace that the majority of the troops felt.

This really wasn't the sort of thing he was good at. Rufus had already turned his mind towards war with

Caesar's murderers, a war in which he hoped to earn enough merit to eclipse Agrippa once and for all and announce himself as one of the best generals of his day. He understood that it was necessary to use Antony's and Lepidus's resources to tackle Brutus and Cassius, but if it had been up to him, he'd have eliminated them directly and taken their troops. He'd even tried to suggest that to the other sect ministers, but they'd looked at him as though he were mad. After all, it wasn't impossible: with a little imagination and willpower, you could come up with a decent enough plan to assassinate those two while they negotiated on the island. By the gods, the Sect of Mars Ultor had bribed dozens and dozens of people, wouldn't it have been possible to do the same with some of Antony or Lepidus's bodyguards? Or perhaps with Lepidus himself, using him against Antony and thus eliminating him too?

Nothing doing: they'd resolutely refused. And not out of any moral scruples: with what was at stake now, it was no longer appropriate to have any. No, out of fear that something would go wrong and threaten the sect's route to success. What nonsense. You couldn't aim for high goals if you didn't have the courage to go all the way, and sooner or later, Rufus was sure, he'd convince Octavian to use even more unscrupulous methods as the stakes continued to rise.

In the meantime, however, they had to use the strange systems that Maecenas concocted in his fertile mind, and he was one who never chose the direct route to obtain a result. Rufus made a gesture of annoyance: he'd become nothing more than the agent of a cowardly, devious little man – and one who'd joined the brotherhood after him at that. And that fucking Etruscan was actually a tribune, just like him, but without having an ounce of his military skill. In reality, he felt as though he'd been demoted, and he was determined to regain favour within the sect. But he certainly wasn't going to be able to do that while he was restricted to handing out spices...

He decided to make the most of his task. He knew that you win soldiers over with valour, as well as with money and loot, and, when the time was right, he intended to show them how courageous he was. Meanwhile, however, he was determined to put his name about so that the legionaries would one day know who was leading them.

"Let's go," he said to the small group of soldiers who were waiting with him on the shore. One of them pushed the boat into the water and they all climbed aboard, loading the gifts. After a few strokes of the oars, Rufus noticed that those on the far shore were already alert and awaited them with drawn swords. If only it had been a military operation... him leading the troops to break through the enemy's defences.

But it was anything but that, and he waved his hand in greeting, trying to ease the tension of the soldiers on the shore. When he realised that they could clearly make out his features, he even forced himself to smile, despite his frame of mind. He arrived on land to be met by the diffident looks of Antony's men, who, under a centurion's orders, had left what they had been doing and lined up on the river bank.

"Relax, friends," he began, raising his arm in greeting and heading towards the nearest officer. "My name is Salvidienus Rufus, I'm a tribune and part of Consul Octavian Caesar's General Staff. We just thought there must be a better way of passing the time while the bigwigs reach an agreement than hanging around our camps wondering how it will all end."

"And what might that be?" the centurion asked, without taking his eyes off him. Rufus had a sword at his side, but he would have been run through by at least ten other swords before he had time to touch the hilt.

The tribune ordered a soldier to give him one of the bags they'd brought with them. "Look, Centurion," he said, opening it and pulling out the contents, "we in the consul's army think of you as brothers. We're all Roman citizens, aren't we? And many of us fought side by side under Caesar's command, right? So I don't see why we should be scowling at each other. I'm only here to talk, and as a sign of good will I thought I'd share with you and the other officers these spices we've been sent from Rome, directly from Arabia. You know, we who are sent by the Senate have less problems with supplies…"

Rufus noticed that the other officers had started to listen more carefully. As had the soldiers. Some had even begun to lower their swords, without waiting for their superiors' command.

"Very generous…" said the centurion, no less on the alert than before. "Come to bribe us, tribune? Get back to where you came from now or I'll have you arrested. I'm loyal to my commander."

Rufus raised his hand in surrender. "Bribe you? Are you joking? With a few spices? I have no wish to separate you from your commander. In any case, we'll all soon be under a single command – Rome's. I told you: it's just a way of making you understand that we're all in the same boat, and that there's no reason to be suspicious of each other. I know my comrades, now I want to start getting to know you as well, so we won't be strangers when we march side by side against Caesar's murderers."

"Come on, Centurion... a few spices won't hurt anyone. We'll put them in tonight's slop, right?" a soldier exclaimed, before an *optio* silenced him with a blow of his baton.

The centurion seemed to hesitate.

"There's plenty more of this stuff," said Rufus, gesturing to the boat. "But I'd like to eat these spices together and have a chat in your tent over a plate of seasoned game – talk about Caesar's exploits, and those we'll have when we avenge his death... What do you say? In the meantime, can I have them distributed to the other officers? Then they can decide whether to give any to their men."

The centurion looked slightly disorientated. Probably the last thing he'd expected from a soldier from the other side, someone he'd fought against a few months before at Modena, was to be invited to lunch. Many of his men were smiling, as were some of the officers. He cracked.

"By the gods!" he exclaimed. "You're right, Tribune! Why should we be wary of each other? We don't have any reason to be. If our commanders are then it's for personal reasons that we don't have to share, unless we're talking about orders. But until they make me fight you – and I hope they don't – you're my comrade and, I'll go as far as saying, my superior, Tribune!"

"Well said! Our only enemies are Caesar's assassins and anyone who chooses to follow them!" Rufus echoed. The other soldiers whistled and cheered, and the tribune's legionaries instantly set about mingling with Antony's men – according to the instructions they'd received – and exchanging opinions on the political and military situation. Rufus nodded in satisfaction and moved towards his interlocutor, putting an arm around his shoulder.

Then, as he climbed the bank with the officer, he raised his other arm. It was the signal: a second boat would now set off, bringing more soldiers and gifts. By evening, the two armies would be 'fraternising' just as Maecenas had wanted.

But soon, he said to himself, very soon, it would be the Etruscan who would be carrying out *his* orders...

*

"Given that you're so committed to the soldiery," said Lepidus, seemingly satisfied with the agreement they'd reached, "and now that we're partners and are in some way bound by your promises, it would be a matter of grave embarrassment if we didn't at least try to fulfil them. What are you actually planning to do?"

Octavian was copying out a draft of the terms of the agreement they'd just concluded, reading what he'd written at each step of the way so the other two triumvirs could confirm the powers that were being ascribed them. They'd agreed that a definitive text should be ready by evening and that it should be delivered to a tribune of people loyal to them for submission for popular approval.

Antony, who was drinking from a jug of water, took advantage of the fact that Octavian was concentrating, to intervene. "Let's be frank – you've dropped us in it. If we don't give the soldiers what you've promised them, we'll lose their support, and we can forget all about the war against the 'liberators'. If we give it to them, we'll be forced to found colonies and confiscate properties from Senate bigwigs and the equestrian class, and if we do that we'll lose their support, which is already pretty lukewarm. But we'll need them if we don't want to be continuously watching our backs while we're at war. I'd rather not even try to be so generous to the soldiers, at least not until we've won. Then we'll see."

Octavian finally raised his eyes and looked at him in amusement. "You've always been a skinflint, Antony," he said. "As I understand it, the soldiers mutinied at Brindisi because you were so much more tight fisted than me. I've kept my promises so far, giving everyone who enrolled before the Modena war everything I offered them when they signed up, and I mean to continue keeping my promises: I have no intention of losing credibility. Credibility is everything in politics, especially in a situation like ours, where even the dimmest voters of the Curiate and Centuriate Assemblies no longer pay any attention to the candidates' promises, knowing that as soon as they're elected, most of them will just serve their own interests. Clienteles, we need to procure clienteles. It comes down to this: people who back us will continue to do so if they know we'll give them what we've promised. We'll need to be like a patron with his clients: always give them something, however small, but constantly show them that you remember them and that you'll look after them. That way you feed their hopes of getting more in the future. And, at this stage of the war, our clients will be the soldiers. The others – all the others – will not be too happy with what we're doing, but given the exceptional circumstances I'd get them to pay a whole year's rent as tax on their rental income, for example. Or I'd get them to maintain the troops in the cities where they winter."

"All right," Lepidus agreed. "I'd suggest we take a note of what measures we can take to try and squeeze a bit of money out of these exhausted lands. Brutus and Cassius can plunder client kingdoms and provinces that haven't been touched by the war and are therefore still prosperous with impunity. Given that, we can't permit ourselves too many scruples: I say let's tax land and slaves. Write that down as well, Octavian."

"If we're not going to have too many scruples," Antony added, "then let's get everyone to pay a tenth of their assets and let them make the estimates. Then we can accuse them of having falsified their estimates and seize the lot! Oh yes, write that too, young man."

Lepidus nodded, but Octavian found the idea abhorrent. "No, that's too much," he muttered. "We're not extortionists…"

Antony moved his face towards him. "Are you forgetting that we're at war? We all know that unless we attack them, sooner or later Cassius and Brutus will try to invade Italy, or at least blockade its supply routes. All we need to do is let these people know that if they don't pay they risk having the war turn up on their doorstep again, causing them even worse privations. You'll see, the Romans will pay to keep the conflict away from their streets."

Octavian decided to give in. Antony had a point: they were at war, by the gods! "So, let's see what taxes have been cut in recent decades and bring them all back…" he said.

"Ah, I see you've got the idea! Just as well that you were the idealist of the group," commented Antony. "You and all your beautiful speeches about reforming the Republic..."

"I am, indeed," Octavian said with conviction. "Once this emergency is over my clientele – indeed, our clientele – will be every single Roman. Everyone will make sacrifices now to be rewarded later. If you only serve the interests of a clique because it supports you, you're simply serving your own interests and those of your friends, but what could be worthier than serving the interests of everybody, even those you don't know? If we manage to benefit everyone, starting with the soldiers, we'll be working for the good of Rome and we'll have fulfilled our objective of helping it become prosperous, peaceful and powerful, just as the gods ordained."

"You've got some big ideas, boy," intervened Lepidus, "but we live in dark times, in which practical needs and personal ambitions are dominant. It's impossible to serve everyone's interests." The conversation had taken a less antagonistic turn, now that the three had reached an agreement and could afford to wind down.

Octavian nodded. And he prepared to fire off his last arrow, curious to see how they would react. "Of course, I'm aware that you can't please everyone. But you can aspire to higher goals if you prevent those who oppose progress from doing any harm..."

Antony's eyes narrowed and he stared at him carefully. His features tensed: in an instant, he was on his guard again. "What do you mean?" he asked.

"Simple. We have to do what Caesar didn't," explained Octavian. "When Quintus Pedius had the law prosecuting Caesar's murderers approved, we trod lightly. In effect, we only struck those who killed Caesar with their own hands.

But they are not the only enemies of the State. We're well aware that they have a strong network of alliances and friends who could take their place at any time. *Rich* and influential friends. Caesar was famous for his clemency too, and he paid for this imprudence with his life. We won't make the same mistake. We're preparing to fight a war which could end all wars, and we don't want any unexpected developments. After his victory at Pharsalus, Caesar had to fight two other wars in Africa and Spain before he managed to best all of Pompey the Great's friends."

"Let me get this straight…" Lepidus interrupted him. "For the good of Rome, we should execute a few more big shots?"

"…And seize the assets we confiscate from them, if I've understood you properly?" Antony added.

"Any big shots who colluded with Caesar's killers, of course," Octavian specified. "If we eliminate the opposition in the Senate then we won't have to look over our shoulders any more. A few selected people, I mean, not some Silla style massacre. I have no intention of bringing back the terror of his proscriptions…" His idea – and that of the sect – was to remove once and for all anyone who might undermine the stability of the State and obstruct the course of justice against Caesar's killers. And to use their assets against those same killers. The assassins would be defeated with money obtained from their executed or exiled friends.

Antony and Lepidus both grew thoughtful, and Octavian could see that the idea had caught their attention. He didn't have to wait long before one of them spoke. It was Antony.

"Silla was able to govern confidently and ensure stability for Rome after his proscriptions..." he whispered, with a malign smile.

"And I certainly know some people who deserve to be wiped off the face of the earth," added Lepidus.

"My uncle Lucius Caesar, for example!" said Antony, bursting into uproarious laughter.

"Why, do you reckon my brother deserves to live?" joined in Lepidus, and he too started to laugh, unable to stop himself. The two triumvirs egged one another on, doubling up with laughter until their eyes watered. Octavian, however, merely twisted his lips into a grimace of faked amusement – just enough to indulge the general state of hilarity which seemed to have spread even to the bodyguards. But the thought that it might get out of hand began to nag at him.

When the laughter died down, the three men looked at each other in silence, and Antony said what the young man had been afraid of hearing. "We should do it, you know?"

"Do what?" he replied. But he already knew the answer.

"Eliminate anyone who might stand in our way. And encourage people to report any potential enemy of the State."

"Making the names of the condemned people public, of course, and offering a reward to anyone who reports where they're hiding or tells us who their closest friends are," Lepidus specified. "Just like with the proscription lists. That way, we'll have all the informers we want."

Octavian bit his lip. Yes, he'd set in motion a perverse mechanism. "But have you got any idea how many people might simply denounce their enemies or people they've argued with?" he objected. "Many innocent people would die..."

"For that matter, some people would quite happily report people they like just to get their hands on a reward," said Antony. "Like I said before, we're at war," he concluded nonchalantly, "and in war a lot of innocent people die."

Octavian felt the need to dig his heels in. There must be a limit even to a lust for power, and he had no intention of turning into a tyrant like Silla. He wanted to be Caesar's equal: hard, but not bloodthirsty. These two, however, didn't seem to pose themselves such problems. If he'd shown himself to be sensitive after he'd done so much to appear strong and determined and to convince them that he was more ruthless even than they, they would quickly walk all over him, and the entire edifice he was painstakingly building, aided by the hard work of his ministers, would collapse. He also had a responsibility to the members of the sect, who had faith in him and had put their destinies in his hands.

He ended up nodding, albeit with his head bowed, and promising himself that once he alone was in power he would give back to the Romans everything that he was taking from them for the war effort. Even though it did occur to him that the lives which would be lost would be impossible to restitute.

"Let's do these proscription lists, then," resumed Antony, announcing his agreement with Lepidus' idea. "But there are a lot of rich and powerful people we shouldn't let escape. I'd get rid of them before making their convictions official. You have excellent assassins, Octavian, judging by what happened to Decimus Brutus, and in at least some cases, you could take care of things."

"Who, specifically, are you referring to?" he asked.

"The first name that comes to mind is Cicero. He must pay for everything he's said and written about me."

Octavian sighed. The old orator had backed him since he first appeared on the Roman stage after the Ides of March. Octavian had used his support as a tool – just like he planned to do with Antony's, although in that case it was far more risky – to make his way in the political arena, playing up to Cicero's vanity and behaving as though he were devoted to him. However, upon meeting him face to face for the first time, the young man had decided to put Cicero on his own personal blacklist and punish him for his moral culpability for Caesar's death. Caesar's assassins had shouted Cicero's name as they killed the dictator, and it was Cicero who had proposed an amnesty for them. There was therefore no way that the vendetta dedicated to Mars Ultor could not involve the celebrated orator. What's more, Cicero was no longer of any use to the cause, and indeed had even begun to hamper it.

The young triumvir nodded again, this time without hesitation.

VIII

Octavia had picked the wrong night to be out and about in Rome. As always, the so-called 'ministers' of the sect had kept her in the dark about any developments in the agreement between Octavian, Lepidus and Antony, and news of this new second triumvirate – after that of Caesar, Pompey and Crassus – had only reached her when she'd already decided to visit her son Marcus. It had been her cousin Lucius Pinarius who'd told her in the late afternoon, just as she was about to go out.

Had it just been for that, a visit to her child would have been a wonderful way of celebrating their success, but her cousin had also mentioned the list of proscriptions that the triumvirs had drawn up on the basis of Silla's model to avoid any risk of their meeting the same end as Caesar, who'd been too soft on his enemies. The lists would soon be put up on walls around the city, but in the meantime the triumvirs had agreed to send assassins to eliminate the most troublesome and dangerous figures. Consequently, it was best to keep a low profile and not be seen around too much for the moment: someone overly anxious to ingratiate themselves with Rome's new masters might easily trigger a manhunt whilst thinking they were doing them a favour. There was a very real danger of rioting on the streets, as had already happened in the city's recent past.

But Pinarius hadn't been authoritative enough. He'd made a suggestion, or at least that's how it had sounded, and that hadn't been enough to make her change her plans

– too long had passed since she'd last seen her son. For days she'd been restless and feeling deeply unhappy. She'd come to the conclusion that she had nothing to be satisfied with: she was part of a sect in which the decisions were all taken by men, she had a dull husband who she didn't love, a son she'd been forced to give up at birth, and her real passion, Gaius Chaerea, was forbidden to her.

No, there really was nothing that made her happy, so she'd therefore decided to console herself by going to see little Marcus, as she sometimes did. She always presented herself as a rich matron who knew about him through the stories her bodyguard Gaius told. This was what she'd agreed with the woman who pretended to be his mother. Octavia had many reasons to envy her, despite the fact that she was from the lower classes and could hardly be considered privileged.

She'd therefore gone to the Suburra, accompanied by Etain and escorted by her slave litter bearers, and she'd immediately felt the tension hanging over the streets. News of the imminent executions must have got around, perhaps mentioned by a soldier to a merchant or courier. But the trip there had gone smoothly, and she'd arrived at Marcus's home without any trouble. She'd spent a couple of hours with the boy, lavishing him with gifts and attention under the watchful and wary eye of his 'mother', all the while secretly hoping that Gaius would return from the barracks to visit his family. She was even prepared to face his anger at her violating his domestic tranquility just to have one look from him, from the man who'd been in her heart ever since she was a little girl.

But Gaius hadn't appeared, and when her hostess discreetly made it clear that she'd overstayed her welcome, she left.

And it was then that she realised she'd done something stupid.

"Shall we take that alley and go the long way back, mistress?" asked one of the slaves, pointing at a side street whose few window torches failed to provide much illumination. At the same time, he nodded towards what was happening on the main street through Rome's most populous district.

Octavia looked around her in dismay. Groups of soldiers were marching from house to house, searching the *insulae* for the condemned men that the triumvirs had decided to eliminate straightaway: certainly, they were all patricians and equites who had backed Caesar's killers but they might have been hiding in these poorer neighbourhoods. And the people tasked with the job by Octavian, Antony and Lepidus were combing the city, albeit without achieving much, other than terrorising the population at large.

It was true that in the first few days after Caesar's death there had been many who had backed the actions of Brutus, Cassius and the other conspirators, at least until the dictator's will had been made public and the Romans had radically changed their way of thinking. Now many had a guilty conscience and were afraid of being included on the proscription lists. Amidst the general coming and going, it wasn't very hard to make out people of rank trying to pass themselves off as plebeian, though they struggled to hide their proud, pompous bearing. Some particularly enterprising folk – anxious, as Pinarius had said, to curry favour with the triumvirs – thought they'd identified them, and people were being assaulted and blackmailed on every street corner. Etain, sitting next to her *domina* in the litter, squeezed her wrist when a man who'd been blocked by a group of thugs a few yards from them was knocked to the ground and savagely kicked. Octavia was about to reply to the bearer when the situation deteriorated, and she couldn't hold back a scream of terror. The thugs had surrounded the man on the ground who had by now become a corpse with a sword in his throat and blood pooling around him as it spurted from his wound.

The sight of the body on the cobblestones was too much for her, and, her nerves already sorely tried by the sadness her visit to Marcus had caused her, she broke down. She didn't reply to the slave and burst into tears, throwing herself into Etain's arms. Etain embraced her tenderly and motioned to the bearer to head into the lane he'd indicated. The luxurious litter began to move, but in that precise moment the men who'd just committed the brutal murder noticed them, and their predatory instincts were re-awakened.

Etain shouted at the slaves to pick up the pace. They entered the alleyway but found the road blocked by another group of unsavoury figures who'd pulled a girl and a man from an insula and were dragging them by their hair. A tongue of flame appeared in the building's doorway. The litter bearers couldn't stop in time and ran into the group, the impact jolting the two women inside, causing one of the slaves to lose his grip and the litter to tilt alarmingly. Octavia fell out, slamming into the cobbles, despite Etain's efforts to hold on to her and pull her back in. The matron found herself face to face with one of the thugs, and the mutilated face of the woman who was the victim of their violence appeared before her eyes. She had a fresh cut running down her right cheek, from which blood flowed copiously.

Octavia felt as if she'd been surrounded by creatures from the underworld and plunged into Hades. She became hysterical and began to wave her arms around to drive the visions away. She felt herself being grabbed by Etain, who shouted at her to calm down whilst a slave began to fight one of the criminals. In the meantime, the man being held hostage by the thugs had got up and, taking advantage of the fact that his captors were distracted, was trying to escape, followed by one of them and the screams of his wife, who was imploring him not to abandon her.

The tongue of fire had by now reduced the doorway of the building to ash and was moving down the street, its heat washing over Octavia and Etain's bodies, and its wicked, flickering light illuminating the scene around them upon which darkness had fallen.

Then Etain began to scream too. Octavia turned and saw that the mob was upon them.

*

Gaius Chaerea was revolted by what he was about to do. But he'd sworn before the gods and couldn't turn back now. Furthermore, he truly wanted to avenge Julius Caesar, and was ready to go to any lengths to do it. But he couldn't see what a task like this had to do with rendering justice to the dictator.

As far as he could make out, this Quintus Asinius Pollio wasn't one of Caesar's actual assassins, unless the triumvirs in Bologna knew differently. In fact, he was the brother of one of Caesar's closest collaborators, among the few who hadn't betrayed him, and he found it hard to understand why he deserved to be summarily executed, without even being able to defend himself in court or even simply justifying himself.

So why then did he find himself in front of the door of Pollio's luxurious home on the Esquiline hill with a squad of legionaries under his command, ready to execute him on the spot?

He had taken an oath. Mars Ultor demanded blood: not just from Caesar's actual assassins, but also from those who'd backed them, and even from those who'd simply approved of their handiwork.

They were all people who could stab Octavian in the back when he and the sect went to defeat the growing forces that Marcus Brutus and Cassius Longinus had gathered in the East, and for those who loved Caesar, the survival of his heir, the man he'd chosen as his son, was essential. He kept telling himself that as he rapped the door knocker until, after an excessive delay, a slave came to open it.

"I am Centurion Gaius Chaerea from the General Staff of the Triumvir Caesar Octavian. I wish to see your master," he said in a deliberately authoritative tone that he hoped would conceal his doubts.

The man looked puzzled. "He... he went out several hours ago, Centurion," he stammered.

"Oh yes? And where did he go?" he urged.

"I don't ... I don't know exactly. He doesn't tell the slaves who stay at home."

He might be telling the truth, but there again he might not. After all, news of the triumvirs' agreement had already reached Rome, and many people had good reason to be on their guard. He pushed the slave out of the way and signalled to his soldiers to follow him as he entered the hall and barged into the atrium. There he found more slaves busy cleaning the *impluvium*, so he continued in the direction he presumed led to the *triclinium*: it was late afternoon, and it was quite possible that the masters of the house had already started dinner.

Sure enough, that was where he found them, lying on the couches. A woman and two children, as well as yet more slaves serving at the table. The matron stared at him, and Gaius saw agitation in her eyes. The children looked at each other, and every so often glanced at the room's other entrance, which gave onto the rear.

It was all perfectly clear.

"Where's your husband, ma'am?" he asked the woman.

"He's gone out. He didn't tell me where he was going," she replied, her voice trembling.

"Of course. And perhaps he went out just a minute ago, as soon as we knocked…"

No answer. But the children continued to glance upwards. Gaius went over to them, squatted beside the couch they were sitting on and said, "Will you tell me where your father went, boys?"

The two looked at their mother, who shook her head. "No," they replied, almost in unison.

Gaius stood up again and approached the lady. "*Domina*, I'm not stupid. Can you tell me where he went without forcing me to resort to unpleasantness? Or I can ask your slaves: someone will talk."

"No one will help you," the woman replied, decisively.

"Centurion, hang one of the kids from the wall and

you'll see how they talk!" said one of his soldiers.

Gaius turned to him, furiously, and snapped "Shut up, you imbecile! In reality, though, he was more furious with himself than with anyone else. He knew perfectly well that a job like this required a much less delicate stomach than he possessed. Anyone else in his place would have done exactly that to get the job done. But he found it too despicable. He was a soldier, not a torturer, and he would not stoop so low.

He stood for a moment in silence, and everyone else in the room was silent with him. He considered every possible way of getting them to reveal where the condemned man was, but they were all foreign to his nature.

"There's a reward for anyone who helps you capture condemned men, right?" A voice caught his attention. A slave behind him.

"Yes. I don't know how much it will be yet, but I know the triumvirs will be generous. And the slaves will be freed," he replied. This wasn't anything official, just information Quintus Pedius had given him, but in that moment he would have paid out of his own pocket to avoid having to resort to extreme methods.

The man hesitated a moment and glanced at the lady of the house, receiving from her a look of contempt. He then replied, pointing at the other door: "He went out there. If you're quick you'll catch him. He was barefoot and only had a tunic on."

Before he'd even finished talking Gaius grabbed him by the arm and dragged him towards the exit, ordering four of his six soldiers to follow him. He found himself in a corridor which led to the garden, in front of a small door which had been left open. He went through it and found himself on the road. At that moment, he heard a woman's scream behind him and was on the point of turning back, but then realised that he couldn't. He preferred to ignore what the soldiers he'd left to guard the house were doing, and looked at the slave, who pointed down the slope to the left of the Cispio hill. "He was going to his clients in the Suburra. At least, that's what he told his wife when he left," the man said, and Gaius immediately broke into a run, urging the others to follow him.

The sun had dropped behind the outline of the housing blocks, leaving Rome wrapped in a soft light which would soon disappear altogether. Gaius continued downhill, skirting the Cispio and passing by the Carinae, the sound of his and his soldiers' boots resounding through the street and echoing off the walls of the buildings. The people they encountered stepped aside, frightened, and wagons stopped and pulled over to the side of the road, some so suddenly that they tipped their loads onto the ground. It occurred to Gaius that his colleague Popillius Laenas would have enjoyed seeing the Romans' terror as he passed, but to him it was just a nuisance, if not actually a source of sorrow: he would have liked to be their defender, not to appear as their persecutor.

"There they are," the slave shouted, with the little breath he had left. When the road flattened, out the number of tenement blocks increased and the narrow lanes multiplied. Gaius slowed down, disorientated, letting himself be caught up by the slave who confidently turned into a gloomy, malodorous alleyway. The gathering darkness hadn't yet made it impossible to see the silhouettes of the men on the streets: shady figures that

Gaius watched closely, wondering who he would soon be executing.

It was the slave who pointed the man out to him. He indicated a man running awkwardly, just visible in the distance, and the centurion increased his pace, despite his equipment beginning to weigh him down. He looked back and saw that the column he was leading was starting to break up, but didn't slow down. The condemned man, for his part, realised that he was being chased and tried to run faster, but in his panic he tripped and rolled onto the cobblestones. He staggered to his feet and continued to race forward, but had lost the speed he had earlier, and his accident had allowed Gaius to make up ground. The centurion was about to catch him up when he disappeared behind the corner of an *insula*.

The panting slave arrived, saying, "That's his client's house. First floor." Gaius nodded and walked round the building until he reached the still open door. He went in, followed by his men, and climbed the stairs under the shocked gaze of the tenants, some of whom hurried to lock themselves inside their homes. When he arrived on the landing, he waited for the slave to reach him. The exhausted slave dragged himself up the stairs to join him, and pointed to a door a few yards away. Gaius knocked authoritatively, without getting a response. He heard raised voices inside, but no one opened the door. With a violent kick, he smashed the door down and broke into the apartment, finding himself in front of the man he had chased, covered in sweat and blood, a woman with a new born baby in her arms, an old man, and three small children.

They were all terrified.

"Come with me, Quintus Asinius Pollio," he said to the condemned man. "You have been found guilty of treason." Meanwhile, the baby was crying uncontrollably as his terrified mother rocked him in an attempt to calm him down. The three children gathered around their father, who was hugging them.

"No. I haven't done anything," replied Asinius Pollio.

Gaius stepped towards him. The man suddenly moved towards the window, grabbing the mother's arm and dragging her into a position between him and the centurion. Gaius knew what he was planning to do: the jump from the first floor wasn't particularly risky and he was counting on getting away with it. Before the man could jump, though, the centurion drew his sword, rushed over to the woman and shoved her aside. In that moment, he jerked his blade forward and ran his quarry through just before he could disappear through the window.

The woman fell, smashing her head against the edge of a table before dropping the baby and collapsing lifeless to the floor, while the newborn screamed along with the rest of the family. The husband ran over to pick him up. The baby was crying and was conscious, but the mother wasn't moving, and a pool of blood was forming around her head. The man, still holding his small son in his arms, knelt sobbing and gently lifted her head. Gaius looked at them: he had been on battlefields, and he could recognise death when he saw it. He pulled his sword out of Asinius Pollio, whose blood mingled on the floor with that of the woman. Gaius looked at his sword, which was dripping with blood. Huddled in the corner of the room he saw three children staring at him in terror.

Not their defender, but their persecutor.

"Now you've got to give me the reward, Centurion. Take me to the triumvir." The informer's voice rang in his ear, as objectionable to him as the scene he was witnessing. He turned and slapped the man with all his strength, and the slave staggered and bumped into the soldiers who had appeared in the apartment's doorway.

No. He wouldn't do this again, he told himself as he walked down to the street, a moment before a fire that had broken out a few dozen yards away attracted his attention.

*

It had to be done, Quintus Pedius told himself as he positioned the town criers he'd decided to bring with him and his escort on the street corners. Stars were just beginning to appear in the sky above the roofs of the city buildings, the first oil lamps were being lit in windows, and torches flickered in the semi-darkness, illuminating small groups of people, their faces contorted with terror.

"They've destroyed my house! Help me, Consul, I beg you!" yelled an old man, his elegant clothes torn and his face swollen, who was trying to approach him until one of his soldiers drove him back. Pedius made an instinctive gesture of irritation and turned away before repenting and lowering his head in embarrassment. After all, as a member of the sect of Mars Ultor who had pushed for the agreement, it was also his fault that the poor fellow had been through the wringer. The leaked news of the agreement in Bologna between the three new triumvirs had plunged Rome into chaos, and many were exploiting the situation to settle old scores and get rid of personal enemies or launch petty vendettas. It was surprising to see how ferocious men could become in the absence of moral or legal constraints.

The forces of order had lost their hold and for the whole afternoon the city had been out of control. Many of those who were linked to Caesar's killers in one way or the other had remained in Rome rather than following them East, in the certain belief that Octavian and Antony would never reach an agreement, but when news arrived of the establishment of the triumvirate, along with that of the imminent proscriptions, all hell had broken loose. He'd been so busy issuing instructions to his assassins about the twelve Senators to be eliminated straightaway that he hadn't realised what was going on – he had remained shut up in the Curia awaiting await news of the executions and hadn't concerned himself with anything else.

Shortly before darkness had fallen, though, he had no longer been able to ignore the violence that had erupted in the city. His men had only reported four summary executions, all people they'd managed to surprise in their homes, when his cousin Lucius Pinarius had told him about the looting and indiscriminate killings. For a long time, Pedius had done nothing as he tried to decide how best to stem the carnage and panic without exposing himself to Octavian's disapproval for failing to comply with his orders. Perhaps the triumvirate hadn't foreseen that by not publishing the proscription lists immediately they would plunge Rome into chaos, or perhaps Octavian actually wanted to sow panic, to serve as a warning and make it clear to the Romans who was in charge. Yet he hadn't specified anything in his letter other than the names of the people to be immediately executed.

"Get out there now with some town criers and declare

publicly who the twelve condemned men are!" Pinarius had urged. "That way we'll put everyone's minds at rest and they won't flee. And anyone wishing to exploit the situation to take revenge upon their enemies will no longer have an excuse for doing so."

"But if I announce the names, the ones we haven't yet found will escape…" he had replied.

"So be it! Do you want to be remembered as the consul who couldn't stop a massacre? Tonight will be wholesale slaughter! What will Octavian think of you?"

"And what will he think of me if I let the people he instructed me to execute escape?"

"How do you know that it was actually he who chose those names? Maybe the other two forced them upon him. Anyway, who cares: we can kill them later, like everyone else."

"That's easy for you to say, you're not the consul! You don't have to take these sort of decisions!" he snapped, closing the discussion and preventing Pinarius from tormenting him further. He was already suffering enough as it was, and in that moment, he wished Octavian had chosen his cousin and not him as senior consul.

More senators had arrived. They'd thrown themselves at his feet and begged him to tell them if they were among the targets. Some had asked him directly to spare them, even though as far as he knew they hadn't been charged with anything. But when he heard talk of fires breaking out in several neighbourhoods he capitulated and, having hurriedly prepared a proclamation, called for an escort and his lictors and went out onto the streets to announce the damned names.

"These people, and only these people, are responsible

for the civil wars," one of the lictors charged with reading declaimed loudly. He'd already listed the condemned men for the umpteenth time to a meagre audience in the hope that he would also have been heard by the people looking out of their windows. "We therefore call on the populace to have no fear for their safety, and we order the immediate cessation of all violence. If that does not happen, the soldiers of Consul Quintus Pedius will act to restore order."

Pedius saw one of the teams of legionaries and troops entrusted with combing the city to flush out the condemned men pass by. He watched as the squad broke into an *insula* a few yards away, followed immediately by the sound of screams of terror coming from the building. He sighed disconsolately, wondering how he could reconcile his proclamation with the actions of the legionaries who were simply following his orders. Yes, it would be a shocking night, he said to himself, as the crier's words rang hollow in his ears.

*

A fire. A fight. Two women on the ground. Gaius Chaerea felt dirty, disgusted: he'd just killed a good man in cold blood and in doing so had also killed an innocent woman. He'd trampled over a mother with a newborn baby in her arms just to kill a man who was no threat to him.

And now, seeing the dramatic scene that was unfolding just a few dozen yards from him, the centurion felt he had the immediate opportunity to, if not redeem himself, then at least to partially cleanse himself for what he'd done. He leapt forward without even checking that his soldiers were following: *he needed to save someone,* desperately, and it didn't occur to him for one moment that he would be better able to do that with the help of his men. In a few seconds, he'd covered the ground that separated him from the scuffle, which from where he was looked as though it was surrounded by a ring of fire.

Flames flickered between him and the desperate people. He saw two men on the ground, covered in blood and apparently dead, and it didn't take his officer's eye long to understand the situation: their two surviving companions were fighting with their bare hands against people armed with knives, trying to defend two women who were hiding inside a litter and who occasionally appeared from behind the curtains. The aggressors could have escaped the fire, but evidently thought they could overpower the surviving slaves and cart off the two women, who were obviously upper class, before the flames got to them. He took off his regulation cloak and used it as a shield to get him through the flames.

The garment ignited as he rushed through them, but it enabled him to reach the other side unscathed. He rid himself of it and drew his sword, positioning himself between an aggressor and a slave with an injured shoulder.

His opponent hadn't noticed his presence and seemed disorientated, so Gaius took the opportunity to land an immediate blow, striking him squarely in the abdomen. The man doubled over with a scream as blood spurted everywhere, even splashing the centurion's face. Chaerea felt a sense of nausea wash over him, and suddenly recalled the earlier scene, when he'd stabbed the condemned man and immediately afterwards seen the dead woman with her despairing baby beneath her. Shaken and dazed, he stumbled and lost hold of his sword: irrationally, he expected to see a corpse and a crying babe appear at his feet, even now.

Too late he realised that a second attacker, who'd just got rid of one slave, had noticed. The man took a few steps towards him, sneering as he brandished a dagger: he couldn't believe he had the chance to kill an unarmed soldier. Gaius looked down and saw his sword on the ground surrounded by flames.

He was unarmed and, because of the fire, couldn't escape his enemy's attack.

The thug gave a cry of triumph and leapt towards him. Gaius heard a woman's voice shout, "No!" then saw his adversary lose his balance and fall forward. A woman had thrown herself against the aggressor, causing him to fall. The man ended up by Gaius's feet, and the centurion instantly kicked him in the nape of the neck with his hobnailed boots. The man's head smashed into the cobblestones and his accomplices fled as the other soldiers arrived. Chaerea went to pick the woman up from the ground, and when he saw her face he froze in astonishment.

Octavia.

"This time... this time I saved you, my love, while you were trying to save me. Can't you see how closely we're tied?" she murmured, without even checking that she was alright, still in shock from what had happened.

Gaius stood there immobile, bewildered not only by the matron's presence and gesture but above all by her words.

My love.

She really did still love him, in spite of everything. Even his apparent disinterest.

IX

Octavian turned to gaze upon the praetorian cohort which followed him. There were also Agrippa, Rufus and Maecenas, flanked by Ortwin and Veleda, and from his saddle, he tried to imagine how the spectacle must look to the hundreds of Romans who were leaning out of windows and lining the sides of the road that passed through the Porta Flaminia Argiletum towards the Forum. He looked with satisfaction at the Servian wall and at the gate, through which the three legions the triumvirate had agreed to bring to the city were passing.

He wondered what his fellow citizens thought of that parade and of the ones which had preceded it. At the very least, he had managed to go from being an outgoing consul to being the last to enter Rome – that way, people would think he was the most important of the triumvirate. It did not matter what they thought of the other two, he was the one with the clearest ideas and the grandest ambitions, and thus he considered himself the association's co-ordinator, just as Caesar had been with Pompey and Crassus before him. And he wanted to make sure that was how the citizens saw things too. More often than not, in politics – as he was beginning to understand all too well – illusions were more powerful than reality.

The agitators he had planted in the crowd didn't have to work too hard to get the public cheering and chanting his name. It was a success, not least because – as he had been informed by his staff – the Romans had not given Lepidus and Mark Antony such an enthusiastic welcome.

The latter would have noticed the difference, and would have hated him even more, but even that treacherous blockhead had now realised he had no choice but to co-operate with him if he wanted to survive politically.

It was extraordinary that they applauded him. Their enthusiasm was a measure of how much he was loved by the mere fact of being the son and heir of Caesar. That would always be his extra weapon, his advantage over his associates and enemies. From what his cousins had told him, things in Rome had been terrible since the news of the agreement and the imminent proscriptions had become known three days previously. They should have hated him for what he had put the city through, without clear dispositions or official decrees. The law now existed, and there was an initial list of outlaws to be affixed to the walls of the city, but in the prevailing uncertainty, all had something to fear.

Which was just what he – and the other two triumvirs – wanted.

And yet they loved him nevertheless. Evidently, they continued to see him as the only bulwark against Mark Antony's tyranny and the anarchy and treason perpetrated by men like Brutus and Cassius, and they were even willing to tolerate a regime of terror as long as he was there to give them the illusion that, sooner or later, institutional stability and peace would return.

It was beneficial and profitable to be illuminated by Caesar's reflection, of course, but Octavian was determined to shine in his own light. He was, he felt sure, Rome's best possible hope.

The parade he led arrived at the Forum, where the senators were deployed near the two basilicas, the Basilica

Aemilia, still being renovated, and the Basilica Julia, which Caesar had rebuilt on the foundations of the Basilica Sempronia but which had not been finished in time for him to inaugurate it. In the middle of the platform, the tribune Publius Titius stood ready, properly coached by the triumvirate to rapidly propose and approve the institution of a five-year judiciary for the re-organisation of the state.

A huge step forward from the private agreement of the first triumvirate. Absolute power enshrined in the Constitution. On the podium with the tribune was the senior consul Quintus Pedius, who to Octavian's eyes seemed to have aged, even though it had only been a few weeks since he had last seen him. He was not cut out for the huge responsibilities which had fallen upon his shoulders, and it was no coincidence that Caesar had used him but little. That was fine, however: he had no desire to stand in the shadow of any member of his family – he and only he must be the undisputed representative of the *gens Julia*.

Awaiting him next to the podium of the Rostra were Lepidus and Mark Antony, to the side of whom stood his wife Fulvia with their daughter Clodia Pulchra – his betrothed. Octavian did not remember having ever paid much attention to the little girl whom he had met briefly at the home of Mark Antony once while Caesar was still alive. She was fourteen years old now, and, looking carefully at her as he approached, he realised that she had become a girl who might live up to the pretentious name her parents had given her. She looked as though she might one day be really beautiful, and perhaps he would be happy that he had taken her as his wife, as Pompey the Great had when he married Julia, Caesar's daughter, only to later fall in love with her.

But it was a fleeting thought, which he dismissed immediately. He had no time for it now, and perhaps did not even really care. He realised that, since he had learned he was Caesar's heir, the female world had not held much interest for him. He had too many important things to think about in the meantime, and too many ambitions had been aroused in him after the dictator's death for him now to feel compelled to waste time seeking futile, carnal satisfaction from women. Along with Agrippa and Rufus he had sought it in the past, but now it was time to think about serious things, and love was not one of them. He felt certain that he could never fall in love. A man like him, upon whose shoulders the fate of an empire rested, could not afford to waste time and energy.

That little girl, then, was simply a bargaining chip and perhaps, when his alliance with Mark Antony was finished, he might even get rid of her. He saw her smile affectionately at him, and felt pity for her. He knew that he had a certain effect on girls, and had no doubt that Clodia Pulchra was already fantasizing about their union.

He dismounted and shook hands with Mark Antony and Lepidus, who looked at him again with that air of superiority which came from their conviction that they had cheated him and managed to exploit his popularity. Poor fools, they didn't realise that it was quite the opposite! Each of the three was hoping to gain leverage from their alliance in order to obtain tyrannical power, but he was the one with the winning dice in his hand. He bowed deferentially at Fulvia, realising immediately that she had eyes only for Agrippa, who stood right behind him, and then nodded politely at Clodia Pulchra, who gave him an embarrassed smile as a lively blush tinged her already rouged face.

He sat next to the two triumvirs and nodded at them. Mark Antony glanced at the senior consul who, in turn, authorized the tribune of the people to initiate the procedure. Publius Titius did not make them wait long – he was a venal man upon whom one could count as long as he was able to live in luxury, and now there was no lack of money to pay him with. Meanwhile, the square of the Forum had filled up. It seemed that all of Rome had gathered there, thanks to the news released by order of the triumvirate: given the emergency there would be the voting for the approval of the law that same day, notwithstanding the constitutional practice which proscribed seventeen days between the proposal and its approval. The pens of the *Saepta* which divided up the citizens according to their tribe and allowed them access to the forum to vote were all ready and well manned by Mark Antony and Lepidus's soldiers. The presence of the legionaries would guarantee, Octavian was sure, some kind of plebiscite in favour of the new judiciary.

The Tribune announced that Octavian would give up the consulate, granted to him only two months ago, to become part of a new judiciary, which was required to address the serious problems facing the State and the civil war. A judiciary, he stated, which also sanctioned the harmony and unity of purpose of the men most able to ensure the stability of the Republic for the common good and against partisan interests. The young man listened patiently to the empty words that they had ordered Titius to say – platitudes and cliches thrown to the crowd to re-assure them. If the will of the people had really been important, they would never have been allowed to express it. Ordinary people were like a mass of children who had to be guided – they lived without being able to provide for themselves, unable to conceive of grand designs, and it was for that reason they needed men like him – men capable of providing for those needs which they themselves were unable to satisfy.

When the tribune finished speaking and gave the order to vote, Octavian felt certain that this was a huge step forward from the acquisition of the consulate two months before. And it was such, despite the need to share power, this time with two very dangerous individuals. He had before him five years of assured dominion.

Another important step towards the invincibility of himself and his sect.

Marcus Aemilius Lepidus, Mark Antony and Caesar Octavian, elected to restore order to the State, hereby establish the following. If the malefactors, once pardoned, had not become first enemies of, and then conspirators against, their benefactor, they would not have killed Caesar, who after having defeated them upon the field of battle had spared them out of mercy, had made friends of them, had bestowed upon them honours and public office and had showered them with gifts, and we, for our part, would not need to resort to these measures against those who attacked us and declared us enemies of the state. But now, as we see with the attacks upon us and the injustice suffered by Caesar, that evil will not allow goodness to triumph, we prefer to strike our enemies first rather than be struck. Let none then consider our actions unjust, cruel or disproportionate, yet remember what Caesar suffered and what we too have suffered. In the midst of the sacred building of the Senate, under the eyes of the gods, they killed with twenty-three dagger wounds Caesar, the dictator and Pontifex Maximus, who had defeated and subjugated the nations most feared by the Romans and was the first among men to cross beyond the Pillars of Hercules into the unsailed sea, discovering unknown lands. These lands, conquered by him in war and then spared, were in part included in his will as the estate of his heirs. And even after this sacrilege, instead of punishing the wicked ones, the others honoured them, and granted them political or military office which the killers used to loot public funds with which they are now raising an army against us even while they request another from the barbarians, those eternal enemies of our empire. They have burned cities subject to Roman rule, and destroyed and razed to the ground those who would not follow them. They have terrorized the others and

incited them against our homeland and
against us.

"You're with Octavian Caesar, aren't you?" The young
man got as close to Maecenas as the Etruscan's
bodyguards permitted and tried to attract his attention
while behind him the crier, just as in many other parts of
the city, read the decree of proscription which was
intended to re-assure the population.

Maecenas was annoyed. He was always annoyed when
someone approached him, unless he had been the first to
make the move, and at that moment he had a great deal on
his mind. He was determined to find Horace and confide in
him his idea of disseminating his work – and above all to
have a pretext for continuing to see him. He had tried to
find him, but so far without luck. Moreover, it was not
easy in this climate of terror: his unit had been ordered by
Mark Antony to oversee the entrances to the city so that
the outlaws, who numbered almost three hundred
senators and Equites, would not be able to escape as soon
as they discovered that their names were on the lists on the
walls.

"Perhaps I am. Why?" he answered, after some
hesitation.

"I saw you with him in the voting for the judiciary
triumvirate today," said the young man. From his clothes
and manners, it was clear that he belonged to a wealthy
family. "I... I want to make a complaint..."

"One of the outlaws who appears in the lists?"

"Not exactly... You see... those lists are incomplete.
There are other men who supported Caesar's assassins
and conspired to overthrow the state."

Maecenas sighed. Predictably, given what had happened with Silla's proscriptions, there were those who attempted to take advantage of the situation to settle their own accounts. "That cannot be established by the common citizen, as you can well understand," he explained patiently. "Proof is needed..." In reality that was what he was required to say: the triumvirate desperately needed money, since Caesar's murderers were procuring it using the most illicit means, but the idea that people who had not been involved in the assassination of Caesar and had not supported his murderers should suffer revolted him. He, at least, demanded evidence of any purported collusion.

"But I've got proof!" said the young man, with conviction. "In the days after the Ides of March, I saw my father Turanius receive the Bucilianus brothers several times at home."

The Etruscan gave a grimace of contempt. The Bucilianus brothers were among those responsible for the twenty-three stab wounds in the Curia of Pompey. "You're accusing your father, then?"

"Certainly," replied the boy, without embarrassment.

Maecenas sighed. This young man would do anything to get his hands on his inheritance. "You know that you will only receive a part of the family property if your father is convicted? A part will be confiscated and will go to the state to support the costs of the civil war."

"I realise that. But even one part is better than what I have now and will have for many years. My father is young."

"Tell me, lad," he asked, "for how long did the conspirators come to your house?"

"How long? I don't remember... A couple of months, I think. Yes, yes – just a couple of months. "

"Disappear now or I'll have you arrested! The Bucilianus brother left Rome as soon as Caesar's will was opened," said Maecenas, turning to walk away and gesturing to his guards to free him from this nuisance.

"But it's true! Perhaps I remember incorrectly, perhaps it was only a week or a few days, but they were there, really they were!" protested the boy, untroubled by the bad impression he had made. "I saw them! And my father is still giving seditious speeches! You must proscribe him!"

A soldier pushed him away, sending him sprawling to the ground, but he continued, "It won't end here! I'll go by the triumvir in person! I'm sure that he will listen to me!"

Maecenas shook his head. He had no doubt that sooner or later that wretched creature would find ears willing to listen to him. His father's fate was sealed, even if all he was guilty of was possessing assets which were coveted by his own son. And if his own son coveted them, he could imagine how much the triumvirate would. If the boy went to Lepidus or Mark Antony – or even the more venal of their lieutenants, so eager to prove themselves efficient – he would be on fertile ground for sure. The same would probably happen if he went to Salvidienus Rufus. He was annoyed to admit it, because he was a minister of the sect, but Rufus was thoroughly unscrupulous, and he had the impression that the proscriptions would bring out the worst in him.

Just then, he saw a citizen run by carrying a still-bleeding head by the hair. He was heading in the direction of the forum, where he probably expected to get his reward.

The proscriptions wouldn't bring out the worst only of Rufus. Maecenas had the impression that they would bring out the worst of the entire city.

> Some have already been punished, and as for the others, you will see that – with the help of the gods – they will now pay for their sins. But though the larger part of the undertakings have already been completed or are nearing completion in Spain, Gaul and here at home, one more remains: that of taking the war to Caesar's assassins across the seas. In preparing to serve your interests by fighting a war far from here, it would seem unwise, both for you and for ourselves, to leave behind us other enemies who might exploit our absence to seize the opportunities offered by circumstance, just as it would to waste valuable time dealing with them in such urgent times, so it is therefore opportune to eliminate all those who undertook the war against us when we were declared enemies of the state.

"I *would* get picked to look after this idiot," said Agrippa to himself while the crier, busy reading the decree of the proscription, walked ahead of him towards the house they were about to enter. The subject in question was Popillius Laenas, the centurion who had come to the camp near Bologna to take Gaius Chaerea's place. The officer had shown himself to be such an enthusiastic supporter of Octavian that his friend had decided to keep him close with an eye to drafting him into the cult of Mars Ultor, and with the beginning of the executions he had seen fit to entrust him with killing the tribune Salvius. A delicate task, since Salvius was not only a magistrate but one with a sacred and inviolable role, and his death might raise a great deal of criticism and protest. Perhaps that was why Octavian did not want one of his own men to get his hands dirty. Agrippa had to be the 'observer'. He had tried to refuse the assignment, but his friend had made it clear that Salvius was one of those Mark Antony wanted rid of, for his having taken Cicero's side during the writing of the *Philippicae*. It was a kind of 'obligatory' favour and it had to be done properly. Popillius Laenas seemed the right person for the job. He wasn't too bright, was devoid of scruples and was sufficiently motivated. And unsurprisingly, he hadn't turned a hair when he was told who he was to execute. Agrippa was merely to be present in disguise, dressed as a legionary, without any authority to intervene unless things turned unpleasant.

The centurion knocked loudly on the front door, which opened almost immediately.

"Come in, gentlemen – you are expected," said the slave at the door, inviting them to enter. Laenas gave Agrippa a confused glance then decided not to show any hesitation and strode into the vestibule, ordering the other soldiers to follow him. Agrippa followed, bringing up the rear, until they entered the triclinium. When they entered, the dining room was full of people lounging on the sofas and staring at them in shock and fear – some dropped the food they were picking at, while others spilled the wine they were drinking.

"Which one of you is the tribune Salvius?" asked Laenas immediately, waving his sword under the noses of more than one of the guests. Another thing Agrippa thought unnecessary.

"I am. And you need not threaten my guests," said the tribune in a firm voice, proudly rising to his feet. "As you can see, I was ready to receive you."

"Good," said Laenas, visibly irritated by the offender's dignity. "You have made my job easier." He approached him. "You are an enemy of the state and I am commissioned to execute you on the spot."

At his announcement, the guests became agitated and began screaming in anger and fear. Evidently they had already been at the table at midday when the lists of proscriptions which had been posted on the walls of the city had been read out. Unlike their host, they had not imagined that Salvius might be a target of the triumvirate. Laenas gestured to his soldiers to position themselves around the tables and sofas, and began to bang his sword on the nearest table, knocking to the ground trays full of rich dishes.

"Silence, all of you!" he shouted, "or you'll all go the same way. You have been found in the house of a traitor to the state! I could consider this a hotbed of sedition, and Salvius might not be the only one to be executed!" And so saying, he pointed his sword at the neck of an old man who was one of those protesting most vehemently. The man shut up immediately and opened his eyes wide, drops of sweat instantly beading his forehead.

He was going completely over the top, so Agrippa tried to attract his attention with a wave of his hand, and motioned with his head to go more gently, but the centurion was behaving like a man possessed and did not seem to notice. Salvius spoke again, inviting his friends to stay calm. "My guests have nothing to do with me nor with my actions, centurion," he said trying to keep his voice calm. "I am here because, after learning of the triumvirate, I quickly realised I could no longer escape the revenge of Mark Antony and, fearing that I might never see them again, I wanted to have dinner with them one last time. Please disturb them no longer and allow them to leave before you do what you must."

Agrippa thought it was a reasonable request, but Laenas scowled. "I don't think so," he snapped. "The condemned must also serve as an example. Let all present see what happens to those who attempt to subvert the state and spread the word. And remember that if they do not toe the line, they will suffer the same fate! Now kneel down and rest your head on the table, quickly!"

Agrippa was increasingly irked by Laenas's intimidating attitude, but he had received clear orders: he was to intervene only in the event that the situation got out of hand. Octavian wanted to see what Laenas was capable of and, for the moment, he still seemed to be in control of the situation, despite his somewhat questionable methods.

Salvius looked at the centurion with pleading eyes and an expression of consternation. "At least let my wife and my mother leave. Please do not make them witness the death of their loved one."

A cruel light appeared in the centurion's eyes when, looking around, he realised who the two women the tribune had named were. "They made the mistake of giving birth to and of marrying a traitor. Witnessing his execution is the least that they deserve!" He took a step towards the man's elderly mother who was still lying on the sofa, his imposing figure towering over her, and whispered, loud enough for Agrippa to hear, "You hear me, you old bitch?" Then he grabbed her by the hair and put his blade to her throat. "So are you going to put your head on the table or not?" he asked the tribune again.

There were cries and screams now, more from the women than from the men. Agrippa quivered with indignation. No, Laenas was not suitable material for the sect: too cruel and sadistic, fanatical to the point of madness and no sharer of the ideals that guided the secret society's aims. It was all he could do not to punch him. "Stop, centurion," he managed to say, breaking the order not to intervene. "Just get it done."

The centurion looked at him and, still caught up in his wrath, was about to reply, before realising that it was not one of his soldiers who spoke. He let go of the woman and walked towards the tribune, who was waiting for him, still standing upright and staring at him. Laenas did not say a word, but simply raised his sword and cut through the neck of the victim horizontally, severing his head with one clean blow. The shouts of those present accompanied the fall of his head onto the table, while his body remained standing for a moment like a fountain from whose neck gushed copious amounts of blood. In an instant the guests in the tribune's triclinium found themselves covered in vermilion liquid while Salvius's head bounced off the table and fell to the ground, rolling towards his wife's feet. The woman fainted, and immediately the others rushed to her aid. Ignoring them, Laenas stepped over her, picked up the tribune's head by its hair and headed for the door. He turned around before crossing the threshold. "Woe to you if you move. Anyone who makes a move now will suffer the same treatment," he said, before leaving, gesturing to the soldiers to follow him.

He waited for Agrippa to join him outside and his face was that of a fanatic, 'Good job, eh? You'll tell the triumvirate, won't you?"

Agrippa looked at the head with a nauseated expression, then stared the centurion in the eye, without concealing his disgust. But Laenas was so pleased with himself that he didn't even notice.

"You can be sure that I will tell him, centurion," was all Agrippa answered.

It was their intention to eliminate, along with us, many thousands of people, without regard to the punishment of the gods or the contempt of men; we do not blame so many, nor indicate as enemies all those who have opposed or have plotted against us, and we care nothing for the riches they enjoyed. Though it is inevitable that three people must have more than one enemy, we will not send to death as many as did another dictator before Caesar and before us, he too engaged in a civil war to restore the state and who, for his achievements, earned the nickname 'Felix'. We will punish only the worst and those who have been the cause of all. Although we could arrest without warning those we have decided to strike, we have preferred to render the list public instead of taking them by surprise; we do this for you, so that the soldiers, in the excitement of their anger, do not allow themselves to take out their excesses upon the innocent, but, possessing the lists of the names of the wanted, abstain, in accordance with their orders, from attacking others.

The more they killed now the fewer they would have to face in the future, thought Rufus as he listened to the crier's decree. The fate of Caesar had proved beyond any reasonable doubt the harmfulness of clemency, amnesties and pardons: all nice ideas that only served to let your enemy escape so he could return later and stab you in the back, or just make your life difficult. He had been the first to congratulate Octavian when his friend had told him that the agreement with Mark Antony and Lepidus also included proscriptions like those introduced by Silla, and precisely because he was the idea's most enthusiastic supporter, he willingly threw himself first hand into the task of finding the proscribed: he was a man of action and would never have stood by idly doing nothing in the palaces of power while civil war against Caesar's murderers raged in Rome.

And so he was even willing to go down into the sewers in order to root out all forms of opposition. Not like Maecenas, who was too busy playing at developing plans and projects with his young slaves, or like Agrippa, who Octavian used only for the most important jobs: he got his hands dirty in every sense, as should all those who possessed a modicum of consistency with the objectives of the sect.

He had been chopping off heads all afternoon, and in the most unlikely places. People had started going into hiding as soon as the lists had been made known. If it had been up to him, he wouldn't have published anything and would have descended upon the outlaws directly in their homes when they least expected it, thus saving a lot of time and energy, but the triumvirate had decided otherwise in order to re-assure the citizens, and now he had to flush out these people from all kinds of places, effectively turning the city upside down – because they were in the city, there was no doubt about that. With a minimum of foresight, the triumvirate had placed checkpoints at each of the city gates, and the identity of all those leaving was checked. But Rome was large, with many places to hide: places that would never even have occurred to a bloodhound like himself had it not been for the slaves, wives and children of the proscribed.

Yes, because there was almost always someone in the family with an interest in getting rid of the condemned relative – a child, greedy for an inheritance, a slave hungry for freedom or simply a wife who had had enough of married life. And when there was no one willing to speak, Rufus had learned by now where to look for the fugitives' hiding places. In one of the houses, a slave had told him that the owner had hidden in the drain, and that was now one of the first places he went to check when there was no trace of the offender in the house. He had also found one man huddled in the attic, and another had lowered himself down a well. These were now all places that he checked carefully. When he was forced to find them without the help of someone in the family, he let his soldiers plunder the house before all the property, annuities and money were confiscated by the triumvirate: it was also a way of buying support and goodwill from the soldiery for when he would eventually lead them.

The stench inside the sewer assaulted his nostrils as soon as he entered. He had a slave to thank for the information that the man's master had sought refuge in the sewer, and now that he saw how disgusting it was down there, he decided that despite the tip-off he would still allow the soldiers to loot the place once he returned upstairs: the family members had to pay for giving them the unpleasant task of hunting their prey in one of the unhealthiest places in the city.

He had to shout at the legionaries to get them to move. Upon entering the sewer, some of them had stopped to pray in the small circular chapel dedicated to Venus Cloacina set just below the entrance at the Basilica Emilia. It did not even enter his head to honour the gods in the midst of that stench, and nor would he have done so before killing someone. Not unless he were about to go into battle, in which case he would seek divine protection. It seemed to him that the only reason the soldiers were doing it was to assuage their guilty consciences.

He took a torch from one of his men and hesitated for a moment before deciding which route to take. Under the Forum, the cloaca branched out into two parallel tunnels to compensate for the reduced height, and he had no way of knowing which one the outlaw had taken, but further ahead the two tunnels re-joined so he split up his squad and sent some men down the other one, hoping that the fugitive had not already reached the mouth of the main duct near the bridges of the Tiber Island.

For a moment, he regretted not having brought along the slave who had suggested he look for his master in the sewers – at the time he had not thought it necessary, as he knew the senator who was to be executed by sight, but perhaps now, in the darkness of the sewer, the servant would have been more familiar with this man and his habits. He led the column of men he had brought with him down a narrow tunnel which was slightly taller than a man, with a vaulted ceiling and walls made of large clay blocks. They walked along a sort of walkway wide enough only for one person at a time. Beside them the mephitic water flowed past, bearing with it the human waste of an entire city. After a few steps, he untied the scarf around his neck and held it over his mouth and nose to protect himself from the pestilent odour that forced its way into his nostrils, and the legionaries followed suit. Water seeped through the roof and drops of gooey liquid occasionally fell on him – he would make the outlaw pay for this as well, he thought.

Suddenly, he thought he heard noises. He signalled for his men to stop and in front of him distinctly heard footsteps echoing down the tunnel. He set off again, faster than before, and soon began to see dim shapes moving in the darkness. "Stop!" he shouted, but this only made them move faster.

He began to run, but after a few steps slipped and fell into the shallow water, twisting his ankle and dropping his torch. He swore, but one of his soldiers picked it up before the water had a chance to extinguish it. Two legionaries helped him to his feet while the others, with considerable zeal, continued to run after the fugitives. Rufus angrily pushed the men next to him out of the way and tried to walk unaided, but realised immediately that he could not count on his injured leg and had to lean against one of his men in order to proceed. A few moments later he heard cries and clanging echoing around the walls of the tunnel.

The cries of men... and of women.

With great effort, Rufus managed to reach the place from whence the sounds of the scuffle came. It was at the confluence of the two parallel tunnels, where he found a civilian lying on the ground, half-submerged by water which was now red with his blood. The soldiers who had overtaken him and those he had sent down the other tunnel stood around him. There was a woman in tears, along with two small children clinging to her. Next to her were two huge wet sacks.

"What happened here?" Rufus asked the legionaries.

"We killed the fugitive, sir," replied one of the soldiers from the other squad. "We blocked his escape by surprising him at the junction of the two tunnels."

Rufus looked at the corpse. "This isn't the condemned man. Who is he?" he asked the woman.

She sobbed again, before finding the strength to look at him and reply. "My husband... Gaius Capitus, he was called..."

Rufus looked at his soldiers, who lowered their eyes guiltily. Then he asked for the list and checked the name. "And what were you doing in here, damn it?" he asked the woman. "Your husband is not an outlaw!"

"It's true... but... we fled because we were certain that a slave of ours we had punished some time ago would seek revenge. When the list came out, he had confided to my maid that he would find a way to denounce us, and she told me. My husband went to implore him to change his mind, he even promised him his freedom, but the man was adamant. So before he could report us, my husband gathered together our most valuable belongings and decided to flee."

"I see. But why did he take his family with him?" asked Rufus, who was rather shocked by the whole affair.

"That slave's so obsessed with his revenge that my husband thought it would be safer to bring us as well – and in any case, I would never have abandoned him. We had counted on getting a boat on the Tiber to take us to the sea. We were going to sail to Apulia, where we have properties…"

Rufus looked at the bags. "So, these are your possessions…"

The woman nodded, but her expression was one of dismay. The tribune reflected for a moment. He felt vaguely guilty. If what she said were true, and he had no reason to doubt that it was, she already had enough trouble. "I am sorry about your husband. In these damn sewers, it is difficult to distinguish friend from foe…" he began. "Come on, let's go. We've done enough harm here," he said to his men, and started limping off along the tunnel.

But no one followed him. Not hearing their footsteps echoing behind him, he turned and saw that they were talking to each other. One legionary approached him, took his arm and whispered, "Um… tribune… I don't know if it's occurred to you, but we've committed a grave error here. If this woman reports us, we're all finished."

Rufus had not thought of that. It could taint his career and his enemies could use it against him. And one day, when he was powerful – a celebrated general and an acclaimed statesman – he would have plenty of enemies.

"And all that nice stuff in the bags," said the soldier. "It's a shame to just leave it there…"

Rufus looked at the legionary, then at the other soldiers, and finally the woman and the children, feeling a knot form in his stomach. He told himself that if he wanted to walk the path of glory, there would be some unpleasantness that he must learn to live with.

"Hurry up, then. And make it a clean job," was all he said, turning around and walking away.

Immediately after, he heard the strangled cry of the woman and the wailing of her children behind him, immediately interrupted by gasps of pain.

> Auspicious therefore is destiny: none must welcome or hide in their house any of those whose names appear, nor accompany them elsewhere, nor allow themselves to be bribed with their money. We will consider any who are found to have saved or helped or been in any way an accomplice to the proscribed as being proscribed themselves, and we will hear no justifications or excuses. Those who kill the proscribed must bring us their heads: for each, a free man will receive 25,000 Attic drachmas, while a slave, in addition to his freedom, will receive 10,000 Attic drachmas as well as citizenship. Equal rewards will be paid to informers. No mention will be made in our records of

those who receive these sums, that their
identities may remain unknown.

A scream of terror rang out along the road, drowning
the words of the crier. Gaius Chaerea rolled over for the
umpteenth time in bed, resigning himself to the fact that he
would not be getting any rest that night. Enjoying the
warmth and the sense of peace that her body gave him, he
clung to his woman, who, unlike him, was fast asleep, but it
only lasted a moment. However pleasant and re-assuring
her company was, his inner torments were too numerous
and too intense for him to be able to appease them for
more than a few moments.

Within a week, the proscriptions had degenerated into
an all-out massacre, and the sect was doing nothing to
stop them. Perhaps Octavian could not intervene because
he was not the only one commanding Rome, or perhaps he
did not want to because it was in his interest to establish a
reign of terror. In any case, every man in the city had
reason to fear for his life now. Not only the proscribed, or
those who had helped them or been seen talking to them
even only once, but those who were rich, or who had old
enemies, lived in constant fear of the appearance of the
soldiers at their front doors. Meanwhile, on the walls of
the buildings, fresh lists were constantly appearing, with
new names being added to those already identified and
executed. You could die on any pretext in those days. The
Forum was full of the outlaws' heads – delivered by their
killers to prove the deed had been done and to receive their
reward – exhibited on the Rostra. The streets were full of
headless corpses, as well as bodies which were intact –
killed by mistake among the indifference of passers-by, or

for personal revenge, or simply to gain an advantage by making them look as though they had been supporters of the condemned.

It was man against man, and the triumvirate did nothing to stop the killings. That was why Chaerea had left. He had feigned a serious illness and it had given him the opportunity to stay quietly at home with his family and to reflect upon belonging to a sect which was not contributing to improving the lives of the Romans – quite the opposite, in fact. But the screams that he heard on the street constantly interrupted his thoughts, and made his days even more tormented.

Nor could he banish from his mind and heart the image of Octavia, who had whispered words of love to him a week earlier in the Suburra. She was still waiting for him, and that made it even more difficult to recover his role in the sect. He knew that it was another problem he would have to deal with when he eventually returned to the ranks. A few months earlier he thought he had resolved it, after having told her of his irrevocable decision to remain with his family, but now he realised that his decision was not so irrevocable after all, if her passionate words were enough to make him have doubts.

He would not be able to stay out of the game too long. He had taken an oath and would soon have to return to work, and then he would have to face his own conscience: as a soldier who obeyed the orders of his commander, as a member of a sect which put revenge above all else, and finally as a man who had to understand his true feelings.

And he was certain that his torment would continue, whatever choice he made.

X

"It's Cicero's turn now. We've kept him alive too long," said Octavian to his followers at the meeting of the sect's general staff in the *tablinum* of his house on the Palatine. "Mark Antony is lobbying to have his head as soon as possible, as well as that of his brother Quintus and his nephew." The meeting, which had lasted for much of the afternoon, served to take stock of the proscriptions and of what was available for the war on Sextus Pompey in Sicily. It was to the island, which was under the control of the son of Pompey the Great, that the outlaws who had managed to escape the sword of the executioner flocked.

"Why doesn't he kill him himself, then?" asked Rufus, who, Quintus Pedius thought, seemed to take great pleasure from finding and executing the condemned.

Octavian made a dismissive gesture with his hand. "You know that it is part of the agreement. He kills ours and we kill his. Never mind that ours are few and that he has allowed himself to get carried away by his lust for revenge. I have to keep him happy."

"So why haven't you given the order, then?"

"Because I know Cicero well enough to know that he's stewing in his own juices. As you are aware, as far as I'm concerned he's just as responsible for the death of Caesar as those who stabbed him, and killing him isn't enough. I've let him think that he is one of Mark Antony's victims, but he is actually one of mine, and while Antony just wants him dead, I want him to suffer. And to delude himself, too: he could go to Brutus in Macedonia, but he is hanging about in his properties near Rome because he is convinced that, in the end, I will decide to spare him."

"So you wanted to make him live in fear for a few more days..." mused Maecenas.

"That's right. This is *my* way of imposing justice. The choice of how to kill him is Mark Antony's. But the execution is our job."

"Shall we send Gaius Chaerea?" asked Pedius, who, as consul, had to arrange the practical details.

"No. Gaius is still unwell," said Octavian. "This is a good opportunity to put Popillius Laenas to the test for one last time. I have decided to let him enter the sect, but I still want to see how he handles it."

Agrippa made a gesture of annoyance. "Caesar, I've already told you that I do not think Laenas suitable – he is too brutal and too ignorant. He almost seems to enjoy killing people. If you give power to such individuals, they will abuse it..." he said, for the benefit of those present, who were unaware of what he had already told his friend after his experience at the house of the tribune Salvius.

"He will not abuse it because we will guide him," said Octavian. "In the proper hands, such a tool can be very useful. We need someone willing to do the sect's dirty work. We have given many such tasks to Ortwin, and now I know why my father relied upon him so much – he is intelligent, and has a noble soul, and I have no wish to lose him or waste him in deeds that are at the limits of the possible. And I do not demand heinous actions and demonstrations from him, because he is not a despicable individual like Laenas. Precisely because it is as you say, Agrippa, I will entrust to him the tasks that no one else has the stomach to carry out – and there will be many, you'll see. There are still many of Caesar's assassins from whom Mars Ultor demands blood."

Agrippa said nothing. As Pedius knew well, when Octavian had an idea, no one could change his mind except, perhaps, Maecenas, whose acumen the young man respected. But Maecenas did not utter a word, so Popillius Laenas would kill Cicero.

"Of course, we won't let him go alone," said Maecenas, finally. "The task is too delicate for there not to be a member of the sect present."

"That is reasonable," agreed Octavian. "Ortwin will go with him, then. Laenas will be the head of the operation, but the barbarian must be assured that this is not a demotion. I have begun to think too much of him not to treat him with the respect he deserves."

Pedius noticed that Rufus appeared annoyed by Octavian's words. He always did whenever the triumvir spoke well of anyone but himself. Not surprisingly, he had also seemed to be in a bad mood during the discussions of the war against Sextus Pompey, which Agrippa had virtually monopolized, his ideas overshadowing all the others. But then, it was no secret that Rufus was envious and jealous of Agrippa: Rufus himself was the only one who seemed not to notice the fact, or at least he did not let it show if he did.

The leader of the sect declared the meeting ended and arranged for another immediately after the death of Cicero where, he said, he would take stock of the situation of the proscriptions: after an initial list of a few hundred people, there had been thousands of victims among the senators and equites. Octavian had, in fact, informed the others of the amount of the confiscations and the split with the other triumvirates which had been agreed upon – it was a question usually handled by Maecenas, who divided up the funds flowing into the coffers of the state controlled by his friend, setting aside a part for the enrolment of recruits for the army and another, almost as large, for the expenditure and investments made by the sect in order to gain the support of people deemed 'useful'.

As he left his cousin's house, Quintus Pedius found the twelve lictors which, as a consul, were his by right, and made his way home. It was evening now, and Lucius Pinarius took the opportunity to go with him for part of the way. At night the streets of Rome were always poorly lit and dangerous, and those who could afford bodyguards didn't think twice about having themselves accompanied. Pedius wished him farewell without revealing his discomfort, not wishing to have to put up with his usual teasing. He had wanted to be in charge of the war against Sextus Pompey – a smaller civil war than that being fought in the East against Brutus and Cassius, but still vital. The blockade the skilled pirate had put in place was attacking all cargo ships bound for Ostia and seriously threatening Rome's supplies. He had wanted to very much, not because he had military ambitions, but to escape the horrors of an increasingly bloody city, many of which he was responsible for.

But he had not even attempted to propose this to Octavian. He knew that as far as the head of the sect was concerned, the soldier among them was Agrippa, with Rufus in second place, and he would certainly entrust the naval campaign, which looked as though it would be far from simple, to his close friend. They had discussed this in the meeting, and Agrippa had proposed many ideas which were brilliant, both from a strategic and technical point of view, demonstrating a real expertise in sea battles that he, Pedius, would never have. Among other things, it was an important test for Octavian: the responsibility for eliminating Sextus Pompey, which the other two triumvirs had delegated to him, perhaps in the hope that he would fail and thus provide them with an excuse for marginalising him or diminishing his importance. Therefore, a good man was needed, and he had never been good enough, – otherwise, as Lucius Pinarius often reminded him, Caesar himself would have given him more important responsibilities. Moreover, he felt absolutely exhausted. The commitments and business of recent days had taken it out of him, and he had made no secret of the fact, having twice been forced to suspend sittings in the Senate due to sudden bouts of illness.

He arrived in front of his house on the top of the Esquiline hill and dismissed the lictors, two of whom remained at the entrance, while his personal slave knocked on the door. The porter opened up and ushered them into the hall. Pedius barely had time to notice how tense he seemed when a man armed with a knife appeared in front of him, coming from the direction of the atrium. He pointed the knife at his throat and pulled him towards the impluvium, where all the family's slaves stood around the pool, bound and held by other thugs like him at sword point. With swords that they should not have had, given that soldiers were the only ones permitted to carry swords in Rome.

His wife, bound and gagged, was on her knees, and one of the intruders was pulling her head up by her hair. This, thought Pedius, excluded any attempt to get the attention of the lictors outside. The man walked over to him and looked at him for a long time without saying a word, seeming to enjoy the tension in the air and the terrified faces the consul could see in the flickering light of the torches set around the walls of the atrium. He was probably less than forty, with a long face framed by a mass of curls. A light of despair and madness shone in his deep-set eyes, and his mouth, which was too wide, was twisted into a grin.

"What do you want?" Pedius asked him, not even trying to control the tremor in his voice.

The man smiled, leaned his face towards his and whispered in his ear, "Only to bring you the greetings of Cassius Longinus and all those friends of his that Octavian is killing..." And he pushed him backwards towards the nearest doorway. Pedius saw him pull the sword from his belt and felt himself rising up and slamming into the wooden door as the blade penetrated his stomach.

A spasm of pain shot through his abdomen, and the last thing he saw before losing consciousness were his own feet, dangling at least a foot above the ground.

*

They had not even taken down his body. The corpse of Quintus Pedius was still hanging on the door of his *tablinum*, impaled upon the sword which had pierced his stomach. Maecenas shook his head and looked at the two lictors who were standing with the slaves, embarrassed looks upon their faces. They were the ones the consul had set to guard his house and it was incredible that they had not noticed anything. Then he saw Octavian, to whom he had sent a message to hurry quickly to his cousin's, arrive. The young Caesar contemplated the consul's body and began to walk up and down the hall, his expression simultaneously shocked and furious.

"Did the slaves tell you?" the Etruscan asked him.

"No. It was his wife, poor thing," said Octavian, ordering the two men closest to take the corpse down from the door. "Whoever did this took her with them so that the slaves wouldn't be able to warn the lictors on guard. And, in fact, they didn't call anyone. Then they dumped her in front of my house and left – but not before giving her a good hiding. I'm late because I asked her a few questions."

"I am sorry. It's a warning, then. And what did she say?"

"Not much. She's in no fit state to speak, and in any case, they apparently didn't identify themselves. There were eight of them, I believe, but they didn't say who they were, who they were acting on behalf of, or for what reason. They gained entrance to the house by pretending to be clients, then they immobilised everyone and waited for Pedius to return. As soon as he did, they slaughtered him like a dog. All just to frighten me..."

"The war doesn't run in only one direction, Octavian. We have killed four of them so far, as well as their associates. They want us to understand that they can hurt us too," said Maecenas. "Which means that it might not be over yet."

"What do you mean?"

"That they will try to strike again. We have to put your family under protection. *All* of your family. And try to find the assassins by way of a thorough investigation. Let's get the slaves and Pedius's wife to give us a description of them."

Octavian nodded. "But I don't want to give Caesar's assassins the impression that I fear them too much. I must always appear strong and undaunted if I'm to make myself respected by the people of Rome and the other two triumvirs. Mark Antony is just waiting for me to make a mistake so that he can push me out of the way," he concluded, bitterly. "I have to keep a watchful eye upon my allies as well as upon my enemies..."

"So let us not disclose that Pedius was killed," suggested Maecenas, after careful consideration.

"What?"

"Yes, that's it! Who actually knows what happened here? Only us, his wife and Pedius's slaves. We must forbid them from revealing what has happened and spread the story that your cousin died of some illness... Everybody knew that he was unwell, he had seemed very tired recently."

"Of course!" cried Octavian, seeming suddenly to snap out of his torpor. "We must not give the impression of being vulnerable. It would be the end. We are invincible, our ascent over this last year and a half has been unremitting, with one political and military success after another. That's why I have so much popular support: the people love to win, just like they loved Caesar, and a winner makes them feel secure – they cling to him, entrusting all their dreams, hopes and illusions to his abilities. But if he takes a single false step... Do you remember how the memory of Caesar was abandoned after he had been killed? One false move and they'll crucify you. Were they to see me overcome by emotion, I would

191

no longer be able to offer them security, they would no longer feel protected and they would abandon me, and that would compromise everything we've done so far. No, we have to hide the way poor Pedius died. But that doesn't mean that I won't do everything in my power to avenge his death…"

"You cannot create a commission of inquiry or entrust the investigation to anyone outside the circle of the sect, though," Maecenas observed. "We have a lot of people on our payroll, but sooner or later someone would speak and word would spread that he was killed…"

"True," agreed Octavian. "We must carry out the investigation ourselves. I will entrust it to Chaerea, as soon as he is well. And he mustn't use anyone, except perhaps Ortwin. Tomorrow morning I will have him sent for and put him immediately to work, even if he is sick. This is no time for laying about in bed. In the meantime, you collect statements from the slaves and I'll see what else I can get out of Pedius's wife."

Maecenas nodded. There was a long night ahead of him. "By the way, if she was badly beaten we cannot let her be seen in public for a few days," he pointed out. "We will say that she was so deeply shaken by the death of her husband that she does not even want to attend the funeral."

"Excellent. And we must also consider how to curb Mark Antony and Lepidus's ambitions regarding the new consul. I managed to convince them to leave Pedius, at least, in office, when I had to give up the consulate, and now they will use this opportunity to put another of their men in. Damn them! I must return home and reflect upon a new strategy!" concluded Octavian, heading towards the vestibule and then towards the front door.

Maecenas looked at the corpse of Pedius which the slaves had placed next to the impluvium, and sighed. His friend had completely forgotten about him, nor had he even really been the subject of their conversation, in fact. Octavian had never particularly valued his cousin, and yet he had thought that the young triumvir felt at least some affection for the man who, after all, had given him his share of Caesar's inheritance and had always supported him, even at the cost of his own life.

But Octavian was like that. He always looked to his ambitions and plans without being influenced by the childish sensations normal human beings felt. Just like Caesar, who, in all probability, had recognised in him a kindred spirit. A great mind and a small heart: that was how you became invincible, and it was for this reason that he was the leader of the sect.

*

Ortwin was torn. He should have intervened and stopped the massacre, but on the other hand, perhaps that had been the only way to reach Cicero in time, before he could leave for the East and his Caesar-murdering friends. Allowing the great orator to escape would have serious repercussions on relations between Octavian and Mark Antony, and risked compromising the agreements they had, not without difficulty, recently concluded. That was a responsibility he had no intention of taking, and therefore he forced himself not to intervene while Popillius Laenas tortured Quintus, the brother of the most prestigious of the proscribed.

"It's up to you how you die, traitor," the centurion was

shouting at the condemned man, who, his hands tied behind his back, was sitting in a chair next to his son, who was in the same position. "Tell us where your brother is without making us waste time by looking for him and I'll make sure your death is a quick one," he said, punching him in the chest, but it was useless – he had asked the same question over and over again, but there had been no answer.

Quintus's slaves were crying, and the other soldiers of the platoon were laughing, but Ortwin didn't find the situation comical. It was sacrosanct that Cicero was eliminated, if it was true that he had protected Caesar's killers, but poor Quintus was not, in his opinion, to blame. He had been a brilliant legate during the Gallic War and had saved the Aduatuca camp after the massacre of a legion at the hands of the rebels. Ortwin had fought at his side more than once during the long conflict and had always considered him a man of substance. His only crime, apparently, was that of being the brother of the man most hated by the triumvirs.

Shortly before leaving for the coast of Lazio, to whence it was said the orator had withdrawn while he decided whether to stay or flee, they had been advised by an informer that Quintus had secretly returned to Rome to collect his personal effects from his house. They had thus ambushed him, not only to cross another name from the list but also to extract information upon the movements of his brother. But Ortwin knew that he would not talk, and had preferred to leave when Laenas had started using more determined methods.

It was useless. The centurion had beaten the former legate bloody, but not a word had he uttered with his battered mouth, apart from the occasional insult to his torturer.

Suddenly, Laenas moved towards Quintus's son, who looked to be even younger than Octavian. He drew his sword from its sheath and grabbed his ear. "Come on, tell me," he hissed, "or I'll chop him into little pieces but keep him alive until only his torso and head are left!"

The man looked desperate, and was about to open his mouth and say something, when his son interrupted him with an unsteady voice: "Say nothing, father. I will be worthy of you, fear not."

"How touching!" cried Laenas, happily. "Let's see if you really are, then!" And he moved towards him. Ortwin had had enough and, without fully realising what he was doing, lunged towards him and pulled the sword from his hand before pushing him away. "That's enough," he exclaimed indignantly. "These are brave men!"

Laenas stood there for a moment, stunned by the German's reaction, then he advanced towards him and tried to punch his face, but his movements were made clumsy and slow by his anger and Ortwin had time to dodge out of his way, sending him flying. The centurion lost his balance and fell to the ground, and only then did the German realise he had made a mistake: one should never give outsiders the impression of a lack of cohesion, nor humiliate a commander in front of his subordinates. Not to mention that it was Laenas who was in charge of the operation, and that Octavian would not have wanted his actions questioned.

And that was not all. When he saw the look of hatred on the officer's face, he realised that he had made an enemy of him. A dangerous enemy, if Octavian thought him worthy enough to consider allowing him into the sect. Maecenas had explained to him that the young Caesar was in no way demoting him by taking away his responsibility for the death of Cicero, but was simply giving Laenas the opportunity to gain membership to the secret society.

"You ugly one-eyed barbarian piece of shit, you'll pay for that!" said the centurion, his words immediately confirming Ortwin's fears. Laenas moved towards him again, this time with a more determined air. At the same time, Ortwin was aware that, though he had no responsibility for the operation, he did have responsibilities towards the sect, and could not risk undermining its cohesion with grudges and disagreements. He held out his hands and declared, "Centurion, I don't know what got into me, forgive me. I fought with this man in the past and..." but Laenas did not let him finish his sentence – the centurion's fist hit him directly on his cheek. Ortwin's experience of combat allowed him to realise the blow was coming an instant before the impact and move his face to the side in order to lessen the blow. His massive body did the rest, letting it absorb the punch with sufficient ease. However he did not want to prolong the battle, and began to stagger, pretending to have been knocked out. To avoid falling over, he swayed towards the wall and leaned against it, acting dazed.

"I am not interested in the excuses of a barbarian piece of shit like you!" raged Laenas. "I demand respect, and you have been disrespectful. Even if you are Caesar Octavian's bodyguard, you are nothing compared to a centurion of Rome!" He walked over to him and grabbed hold of his tunic, then pushed him away contemptuously and, trying to regain his composure, snatched up the sword Ortwin had taken off him and headed back towards Quintus Cicero's son.

"No, I beg you! Mark Tullius Cicero is in Gaeta now!" said one of the slaves present, seeing that Laenas was again making for the boy's ear.

Laenas froze. "Really? And how do I know I can believe you?" he asked, while Quintus Cicero glared at the slave who had spoken.

The mortified slave looked at his master. "Forgive me, *Dominus*," he said, "but I brought up your son, and I cannot bear the idea of him being cut up into pieces like that." He turned to the centurion. "I was with the former consul in Astura when we left him, my master and I, to return to Rome. He told us that he intended to go to his villa in Gaeta, and there would decide if and when to leave. But he was hoping for something to happen that would allow him to remain, he didn't want to face a sea voyage..."

Quintus's expression was eloquent – the former legate was furious, so it was clear that the slave had told the truth. Even as unperceptive a man as Laenas had noticed, thought Ortwin at the sight of the relieved expression on the face of the centurion, who however said, "Listen to me, slave, if we discover that Cicero is not in Gaeta I will do to you what I was about to do to your young master. For this reason, you will be imprisoned until we return. If you are telling the truth, you'll get your freedom and a reward, according to the decree."

"I don't want anything," said the man proudly, "I didn't do it for a reward."

"Everyone in this house everyone has such noble

feelings, I see. Well, that means that you will give your money to me when the time comes," continued Laenas. "And now it's time to end this farce. Execute them and let's get out of here!" he ordered.

"Please, kill me first, centurion!" said Quintus Cicero. "Spare me at least the pain of seeing the death of my son."

But immediately the boy cut in. "Never! I could not witness the death of the best of men. Kill me first, centurion. "

"No, don't listen to him! Kill me!"

"Leave him! Kill me!"

Laenas looked on, amused. He turned to one and then the other, these two men fighting over the right to die first. Suddenly, he raised his hand for silence. "Do not say that I am heartless. I will not refuse your requests – *either of them*. I will make you both happy. You two," he gestured to two of his soldiers, "stand by the condemned men and place your swords on their throats. At my order, kill them."

*

Veleda would never have imagined finding herself in a luxurious *domus* in the heart of Rome, spending her afternoons and evenings in the company of two upper-class matrons and their handmaidens. In her eventful life, she had slept almost everywhere – in huts, legionary's tents, barracks... And when she had been the lover of Pompey the Younger she had also benefited from the services reserved only for people of rank. But never in Rome, in the residence of a senator, like the one in which Octavian had decided to bring together the women of his family immediately after the state funeral of Quintus Pedius.

It was the residence confiscated from one of the first victims of the proscription, and the head of the sect had secretly transferred his mother, Atia, and his sister, Octavia, there, along with Octavia's little daughter, Marcella, while putting about the story that they had gone to the country to recuperate. Their respective husbands, Quintus Marcius Philippus, Octavian's stepfather, and Marcus Claudius Marcellus, had been informed that the death of Pedius had been anything but accidental, and they had been asked not to say a word and to stay in their own homes so as not to arouse suspicion and to confirm the official version. The triumvir had absolutely no intention of giving the impression of being afraid for the safety of his family. He was aware of not being able to conceal his women for long without arousing suspicion, but he hoped to find Pedius's killers in the meantime, and in order to prevent the rumour spreading among the soldiers he had entrusted the responsibility of protecting them to Ortwin's small group of Germans. At that time, Ortwin himself was more useful for the executions of the proscribed. He had suggested that his woman replace him for this task, and thanks to his conviction that she was up to the job, Veleda had won over the ministers of the sect from their initial scepticism. She was given her assignment.

Her first assignment.

More than likely, the matrons she was supposed to protect were less than happy. Because she was a woman, or perhaps because she was a barbarian. Or maybe they just did not like having the house full of grim, smelly Germans, accompanied by an amazon with a stump for a hand.

Veleda had sensed the revulsion the two women felt for her immediately, and had declined to make conversation with them. Although she and Octavia shared membership in the sect – which made them in a sense sisters – their roles remained distinct, and there could never be much familiarity between them.

Etain had noticed the situation and had immediately busied herself in attempts to justify the behaviour of her mistress. Or rather, her employer, given that, as Veleda had been informed upon entering the cult, she was a free woman but preferred to pass herself off as a slave. That was something that she, born to be a queen, just could not understand: she had always refused to be a slave to anyone, even though the vicissitudes of life had more than once forced her to satisfy the demands of others: a Gaul nobleman, Quintus Labienus, a Dalmatian tanner, Pompey the Younger... All the men who had taken her and kept her with them against her will, and who had found it exciting to have a woman with only one hand as a lover. Ortwin was the only one she had chosen to be with, and she was proud of the fact, although Quintus Labienus had remained inside her and she still wondered if she had not consented, at least in part, to his often brutal acts.

"You must excuse the *domina*, Veleda," the free Celt had told her. "She is very upset in this period, and not only over the death of her cousin. She needs familiar faces around her."

"Of course! Faces as wild as ours will not do!" Veleda had replied, dismissively. "Don't worry, we'll stay in our rooms without bothering your *domina* with our presence! Anyway, it is I who does not wish to mix with *you* – I am the daughter of a king, not just some little lady from

Roman high society." And with that she had spoken no more of the matter, despite regretting her words immediately. She had spent her life in the lowest places and positions, and should not have given in to this outburst, which was caused more by her frustration at the defeat of her father Ariovistus and her capture, which had denied her the more auspicious fate and position that was rightfully hers. And that evening she felt especially sad, and knew it was because Ortwin was not was beside her. The enthusiasm of being given her first assignment was long gone, now. The hiding place was secret, and she could not see what danger Atia and Octavia were in, even if the killers of Pedius *were* still in Rome and had not already decamped. The more time she spent without her man, the more she realised that she loved him as she had never had the courage to tell him. In many ways, she had ruined his life, and not simply because of her accidental gouging out of his eye.

But he had never held her errors of judgement against her, nor had he ever criticized her for what might have been. He was an extraordinary man, and would have been a king or a great general had he only been given the chance. Not only did she love him, she admired and esteemed him, and although she had never openly admitted it – the ancient pride of a princess still controlled her feelings – she could no longer live without him. Without him, she felt incomplete and imperfect. And even insecure.

She had wavered in Syria earlier this year when they were following Dolabella and had been besieged by Quintus Labienus himself. The man who had made her a woman against her will, and who had loved her obsessively for years in his perverse, sick way, was still able to disturb her. For a long time, she had thought that his unbridled passion was love, and considered it more worthy than Ortwin's apparent indifference, which only later she had understood to be a form of extreme respect. But when she had to finally choose between the two, she had opted for Ortwin, realising that only he could make her happy.

And if she was not happy, it was her own fault and because of the mistakes she had made, forcing them to live a life that was not theirs. A life, however, that Ortwin still found worthy of living, dedicated as he was to avenging Caesar, a goal to which she was completely indifferent.

Without knocking, a slave walked into the room where Veleda was sitting with her four men, the only ones who had been with her and Ortwin since the flight from Germany.

"You – *domina* Atia wants to see you in her cubicle."

She glared at him. "See that you show a little respect, slave," she replied, getting to her feet. "I am a free woman – unlike you."

The slave shrugged, turned and walked out, without even turning around to check that she was following him. Veleda was too dejected to make a fuss, and followed him obediently. It had been dark for some time now and she had learned the habits of the women she had to protect. Atia went to bed as soon as the sun disappeared behind the silhouettes of the buildings, while Octavia, with her daughter and maid, remained in the *tablinum* to study the financial reports and decrees, so as to keep up to date with all the sect's activities. Etain had told her that, in the hope that her brother would involve her more than he did, Octavia needed to prove herself competent, the fool! She didn't understand that this was and always would be men's business. Although Octavian had brought three women into the secret society, he considered them nothing more than mere labourers.

Accompanied by the slave, who stopped at the door, she entered the room of Atia, who was unaware of the existence of the cult of Mars Ultor. No lamps burned, and no voice welcomed her. As she let her eyes adjust to the darkness which was only slightly mitigated by the dim light filtering through the shutters of the window, she felt herself pushed violently inside, losing her balance and banging into the bed. To stop herself from falling she put her hand out in front of her, and as she heard the door slam her fingers touched a body. With a quick glance, she saw that the door had closed, and the sound of a key turning told her that they had locked her inside.

In the meantime, she had begun to realise just what it was she was touching. She felt the rigidity of a corpse, and when she touched its face and closed its eyes she began to identify the contours – it was Atia.

She had failed to protect her. She had failed. But how had they had done it? Then she wondered why they had locked her in there. And immediately, she had her reply.

So that they could concentrate on Octavia, Marcella and Etain.

XI

"Allow me to make a suggestion, centurion," said Ortwin to Popillius Laenas, as he indicated Cicero's villa in Gaeta. He made sure that the other soldiers would not hear him before speaking. "No brutality, here. Octavian might not like it if you make him suffer: he worked long and hard for his support in the past, and perhaps still has some affection for him."

Laenas scowled. "You forget that Mark Antony wants him dead, barbarian. Much more than Caesar Octavian. *And he wants Cicero to suffer.* He expressly told me so in a letter when he learned that I would be handling the matter personally."

"And who do you obey? Caesar Octavian, the man who has taken a liking to you, or Mark Antony, who sooner or later will end up clashing with Octavian?" said Ortwin, certain that his point would enter even that dense mind.

And in fact, Laenas appeared confused. A very rare sight in a man of such little imagination and such unshakable faith in himself, despite his atrocious temperament. He mumbled something unintelligible and did not answer, then spurred his horse and advanced at a trot towards the building. It was an imposing construction jutting out towards the sea in one of those beautiful places that had always impressed Ortwin, who had grown up in the forests of Germany, and was completely unfamiliar with the ocean. For him, the huge expanses of water remained dark and mysterious – another world that the old shamans of his tribe had always described as populated by mythical and dangerous monsters. He approached it, as always, with suspicion and with reverence.

He would never have wanted to live by the sea, in a place like that villa which loomed up before them as they approached, for fear of being attacked by some supernatural creature, but he could not help being awed by the majesty of a sunset or a sunrise on a horizon which met the sea. Heaven and earth melted together, evoking in him the awareness of a world beyond the endless forests where his destiny would have lain, had he only remained in the service of Ariovistus. A world that he had discovered, at least in part, thanks to Caesar. For that alone, he could never be grateful enough.

When they neared the entrance, the slaves immediately realised why they were there, and stared at them in terror, abandoning their work in the villa courtyard and standing immobile in front of the horsemen. After riding down the driveway leading to the front door of the building, Laenas stopped and from the saddle shouted to the doorman, who was watching him with a bewildered expression, "I am the centurion Popillius Laenas, responsible for carrying out the sentence of proscription on behalf of the triumvirate Caesar Octavian, Mark Antony and Lepidus. Tell your master to show himself immediately."

"My master is not here..." mumbled the slave.

"He is not here?" Laenas dismounted and grabbed the slave by his tunic. "And you expect me to believe that?" he hissed in his face.

"It's... it's the truth!" said the trembling man. "He left for the port an hour ago..."

The centurion turned to Ortwin. "You! Take five men

and go along the coast to the port, while I search the house to see if what that slave says is the truth. If you find Cicero, do nothing to him – lock him up and send someone to tell me. I will kill him personally, to make sure that my orders are carried out! And woe to you if you do it your way, barbarian!" he warned.

All Ortwin could do was to obey, even though he would have preferred to keep an eye on Laenas during the search, which, considering his sadistic nature, was likely to be bloody. In any case, even if Cicero was hiding in the house, he wanted to be present at the moment of his execution. But he resigned himself to it. He had vowed not to create further tension with the centurion, so he chose five companions and rode back down the rough path leading to the shore. Once on the beach, he urged his horse into a gallop, enjoying the pleasant sea breeze whipping his face and bursting into his nostrils, breathing it in and letting himself be lulled by memories of when, more than a decade earlier, he had followed Caesar in his campaigns in Britain, riding just like this on both sides of the channel separating the island from the coast of Gaul.

He had been struck by the magnificence and the glow of the cliffs that rose up along the British coast, their blinding white visible from afar, silhouetted against the grey and gloomy landscape characteristic of the area. But he was equally amazed now as he rode along the beaches – sunny, though it was almost winter – in a landscape of elegant villas perched along a hillside full of vegetation, sand glittering in the sunlight and rugged rocks which came up beyond the shoreline, often forcing them to take a diversion through water which came up to the horse's withers.

He saw Cicero sooner than he had imagined. An elegant litter proceeded along the hillside, and perhaps he would not have even noticed it had not the sparseness of the trees and bushes revealed it. Slaves followed it on a covered wagon, which probably contained his most valuable possessions. Ortwin climbed the slope, urging his horse on over the uneven ground and through a thicket of Mediterranean scrub until he reached the road, heading straight for the convoy. There was no time to lose, and if it was not Cicero, he would just have to immediately go back to searching for him. When they saw him coming, the bearers halted, and a head peeked fleetingly through the curtains, before disappearing back inside.

Ortwin came close to the first litter. He decided not to waste time by asking the slaves who they were carrying. He drew his sword from its sheath and pushed back the curtain with the blade. Inside, huddled in a corner, was an elderly man whom he recognized immediately. He had seen him several times in the few months he had been in Rome with Caesar, between the campaign in Africa and the one in Spain which had been the dictator's last – as well, of course, as the ubiquitous busts of the orator which constantly reminded you of the man's features.

"Senator Cicero, you are under arrest on the basis of the decree of proscription of the triumvirate of Caesar Octavian, Mark Antony and Lepidus," he said, motioning to the bearers to lower the litter to the ground. Cicero looked at him and nodded.

Ortwin ordered one of his men to go and inform Popillius Laenas. Suddenly he felt very small and embarrassed before that titan of Roman politics, and he was glad that it would be Laenas who would be carrying out the execution. Caesar had always spoken ill of Cicero as a coward who had repeatedly attempted to hinder his plans, but the dictator had huge respect for his intelligence, memory and learning, in front of which a barbarous, ignorant man of rudimentary education like himself felt inadequate. He found it unfair that a man like this had to die at the hands of an ignorant killer. Certainly, Laenas had no such qualms and would not hesitate when the time came.

"Will it be you who executes me, barbarian?" asked Cicero. "Or has your master Octavian, who I have helped much in the recent past, decided by chance to show a shred of gratitude?"

With each moment he spent with the great orator, the idea that he would receive such a humiliating death seemed increasingly unjust to Ortwin, and he decided to give him a chance, even at the risk of creating further friction with Laenas. "Caesar Octavian will comply with the provisions, Senator. But..." He dismounted and pushed his face between the curtains. "If you do not have a knife with you, I will gladly give you one myself in order for you to die a dignified death as a Roman..."

Cicero's eyes widened, tired and terrified under a crown of uncombed hair, and Ortwin realised that he would never dare, even before the orator answered him. Caesar was right about his cowardice.

"My friend, I did not have the courage to run away and prevaricated until I was taken – do you really think I have the courage to kill myself? No, do what you want with me. It no longer matters now," concluded Cicero, while Ortwin could already hear the distant cries of Laenas's men urging on their horses.

*

With Atia she had failed, but she had to save the other women even if it cost her own life, thought Veleda as she banged on the locked door of the room where she had found the body of Octavian's mother. Her life would have no value if she was unable to prove at least once that she was deserving of an extraordinary man like Ortwin. She began to peer around her in the dark, trying to work out how she could escape while at the same time asking herself the question that, in the confusion of the moment, had only occurred to her then: why had they put her out of action without killing her? She certainly did not look like the most dangerous of the bodyguards assigned to the women – the other warriors were experienced soldiers, capable of giving anyone a hard time. If anything, it was upon them that the killers should have concentrated.

Apparently, the killers were planning to attack the Germans first, and for some reason had spared her. She gave up trying to understand why she was still alive and focused her attention on what to do. She looked around for something to use to open the door, but realised, after having ransacked the elderly matron's bedroom, that it contained nothing useful, but she took the precaution of pocketing a hairpin that she had found on the nightstand next to Atia's bed. Having left her weapons in her quarters, she had to make a virtue of necessity.

All that was left was the window.

She checked it and found that the shutters were locked from the inside. They hadn't been forced from without. Apparently the killers had overpowered the two men who had been set to guard the entrance, perhaps disguising

209

themselves as Roman citizens so as not to attract attention, and had entered by the main gate of the house. Not only had they been certain of finding them there, in that place which was supposedly secret, but they knew exactly where to go once inside. They had found the room of the most harmless person immediately, killing her while the warriors and her daughter were in another wing.

They knew the floor plan perfectly.

That was something no one could have predicted. Octavian would kill her for failing to protect his mother, but there was really no way of forestalling a plan as perfect as this. In any case, the only way to avoid his retaliation was to save what was left of his family. She opened the shutters and cautiously peered outside. Like almost all the other bedrooms located on the upper floor, the room overlooked the back garden. There didn't seem to be any movement below so she went back inside, picked up the corpse of Atia and laid it on the floor, then quickly tied the sheets into a rope, pushed the heavy bed towards the window and knotted one end of it to one of the bed's legs. She tested its resistance then lowered herself to the ground, using her feet to steady herself against the walls of the building. Once on the ground, she stopped for a moment to reflect upon how to avoid capture, and saw, in the gloom, a body lying near the window. Peering at it in the dim light of the waxing moon, she recognised one of the men who had been on guard, and her suspicions about how things had gone were confirmed.

She tried to work out if any of the killers were still outside, but from where she was she couldn't see beyond the nearest corner. Behind which there might be anything at all. Gingerly she climbed over the balustrade and moved slowly towards the corner, where a low wall covered with bushes separated the garden from the courtyard. She found another body and even before turning him over was in no doubt that it was another German. Using the hairpin, she pushed aside the foliage to reach the wall, though not without scratching herself in several places and tearing her tunic. She barely noticed, and looked over the top of the wall.

There did not appear to be anyone in the courtyard, but she now had to decide which way to go. She tried to work out the safest route to take and where she would find some open shutters, unlikely, considering that it was night time and winter.

Excluding the entrance, which would obviously be guarded by the attackers, she made for the servants' quarters. The building was very large, and she hoped that the killers had not yet reached it. If their priorities were the Germans, they might have gone directly to their rooms, sneaking up the stairs and avoiding a break-in that would attract attention from outside. The slaves were almost all in their rooms now and in all probability no one had noticed them. She walked around the building to the opposite wing, the front part of which was inhabited by the slaves and the rear by the warriors of the escort. She kept to the front and, at that moment, a window opened and a slave shook out a tablecloth. Veleda moved slowly and cautiously towards her and discreetly drew her attention, showing her maimed arm as identification to stop the woman from screaming.

"Have you noticed anything happening here?" she asked, softly.

"What should we have been noticed?" asked the

woman, diffidently.

"Let me in," said Veleda, getting the woman to help her pull herself up. Once inside, she found herself in the laundry. "How many slaves are there in this wing?" she asked.

"Twelve. Five women and seven men, including me. Then there are the handmaidens of the *domina* and the overseers of the sleeping area, who sleep in the other wing, near to the masters..."

"Take me to the kitchen now – hurry!" her peremptory tone meant she had no need to repeat herself. The slave accompanied her and immediately Veleda started rummaging through the cupboards, taking all the knives she could find. She ordered the four slaves she found there to wait and told the slave who had brought her to call the others, who were in the adjacent rooms. She returned with them after a few moments, and looked at them carefully. The five women were useless and only two of the men seemed young and athletic enough to be able to help out.

"This is the situation – listen well because there is no time to repeat it," she began, speaking quietly. "Assassins have entered the house and they seem to be familiar with the layout. They have killed the domina Atia and I am sure that they are now at the back trying to kill my warriors. They will have taken them by surprise and I have no doubt that they will succeed, unfortunately. Now we must save the other masters, a thing I cannot do alone, so therefore, I ask each of you to take one of these knives and help me. You will be risking your lives, but I'm sure that if we are successful, Caesar Octavian will reward you properly for saving at least his sister and his niece."

Almost all the women began to sob and the men looked

at one another, hoping in vain to find the courage to take one of the knives. They were taking too long to make up their minds, and the expressions of dismay on their faces did not leave her much choice. She advanced towards the two younger men and put the knives in their hands. One of them took it but the other shook his head and backed away. Another, much older and with hunched shoulders, walked over to him and grabbed the weapon. In the wake of his example, another stout middle-aged man followed suit. Finally even the slave who had accompanied her took a dagger.

"Better than nothing," thought Veleda, throwing the extra knives to the ground. "One of you go to warn the triumvir Caesar Octavian. Leave through the window of the laundry room and perhaps the guards the killers have placed in front of the entrance will not see you," she said to no one in particular, hoping that at least one of them would have the guts to attempt to escape.

At that moment she heard the muffled sound of a scuffle. In the warriors' quarters at the back a massacre was taking place and in the eyes of the slaves she saw growing fear. She motioned them to follow her as she tried to work out a plan of action. The only hope she had was to surprise the assassins the way they had surprised her. She decided to move nearer to the *tablinum* where Octavia was to be found, so she motioned to the armed slave to follow her, ordering the others to remain locked in the kitchen. She warned them that they would come to a bad end if the killers were successful – professional assassins were not in the habit of leaving witnesses behind them.

Veleda moved cautiously through the shadows of the corridor, which was lit every ten steps by small lamps on pedestals. When she arrived at the *tablinum*, she saw that the door was closed, but inside she could hear the voice of Octavia patiently explaining something to her daughter. She gestured to the slaves to hide in the nearby triclinium and she too went into the dining room, opening the door slightly and crouching behind it. The others positioned themselves immediately at her back, and she could feel their heavy breathing on her neck.

They didn't have to wait long. Shortly afterwards she heard soft footsteps approaching. "As soon I jump out, use your knives on anyone who is in range," she whispered. "We will surprise them from behind, so you will have at least one good chance, and you must make the most of it, because you will not have a second one. Then go for the others, attacking them one at a time, starting with the one nearest to you. There can't be more than eight. Clear?" After what seemed like an eternity, she heard them comply. She, however, had something else in mind.

When the footsteps sounded in front of the room, a shiver ran down her spine. She had not thought that they would go into the triclinium first. She grasped the knife firmly in her hand, hoping that the others would do the same, and prepared for a possible battle, with no other hope than that of taking as many as possible with her. She held her breath when she heard them stop before her, but then she heard a creak from the door at the side.

They were entering the *tablinum*.

She waited only a few moments until they were all inside, then flung the half-closed door open and rushed out. She made for the entrance to the *tablinum* but saw that it was obstructed by bulky shapes, and struck out at the first person she came upon, ramming her knife between the man's shoulder blades. Blood gushed from the wound, splashing her face, and the man slumped to the ground with a gasp, allowing her to see the lamp lit room. From the corner of her eye she saw another had fallen to the floor, stabbed by one of the slaves, but now she wanted to get the first in line, who was presumably the leader, in order to set herself between the killers and Octavia. She saw the domina rise from the table and move instinctively towards her daughter, who was playing intently with her toys. Veleda hurled herself towards the assassin who was farthest away, pushing aside those between them, and leapt on him just as he was turning to see what the scuffle was about.

She put her maimed arm around his throat and pointed the dagger at his chest. "Tell your men to lay down their arms, or you'll be the next to die," she whispered.

The man burst out laughing. "Ah, Veleda... I would have known it was you even if you hadn't spoken. Only you would put think of squeezing a man's neck with a maimed arm," said a voice that she knew all too well.

*

When Popillius Laenas galloped up to where Ortwin had stopped Cicero's litter, the German immediately noticed that his armour was stained with blood. As he had feared, the centurion had taken advantage of the situation to give vent to his usual instincts. Once again he berated himself at having failed to convince Octavian not to let him into the sect, and he stepped aside when his superior, ignoring him, walked towards the litter, where Cicero was thoughtfully and quietly awaiting his destiny.

"Hail, Senator!" exclaimed the centurion cheerfully, pushing aside the curtains. "At last we meet again!"

Cicero leaned forward. "D-do I know you?" he asked, nervously.

"Of course..." Laenas replied, contemptuously, "One as highly placed as yourself could never *possibly* remember one as poor as me. Or at least, as I poor as I *was* when you defended me from an accusation of patricide many years ago..."

The magistrate's face brightened. "Really? Who could remember a thing like that... But you got away with it, I see..."

"That's right... and I just wanted to have the pleasure of telling you myself, great magistrate, that I got away with it even though I was actually guilty."

"By the gods, if I defended you it means that I was convinced of your innocence."

"Which means you were wrong. One of your many mistakes, senator, like repeatedly insulting one of the triumvirs."

A glimmer of hope appeared on Cicero's face. "Then I saved your life," he said, implying that Laenas was in his debt.

"That's right, my friend," replied Laenas, maintaining his jovial tone, so surreal in that dramatic situation that for an instant Ortwin thought that he did not actually intend to kill the speaker. But only for a moment. "I have never thanked you, nor have I complimented you on your skills. You owed a favour to a *laticlavius* tribune, the son of a senator friend of yours by whom I was employed – you never wanted to deal with me directly. Of course not, you do not mix with the common people. I would have told you how my father tortured me as a child, locking me inside a trunk all night for a simple prank, or forcing me to beat my mother when he had hurt his hands by dint of doing so, under the threat of punishing me, and how I cried while I hit her and with every slap, every punch, I swore that I would repay them all to him as soon as I was old enough. Too bad that my mother died from the beatings under my bloody knuckles long before I was able to repay my father for his crimes. How much I wished she were still alive when I beat that evil old man to death."

"You're mad…" muttered Cicero, allowing himself to say – as he was practically already a dead man – what Ortwin had already thought even before he heard the disturbing tale.

"And wouldn't you be too, if you'd had a childhood like mine?" asked Laenas. "But you know what? I like being mad – it means that I don't have to think about logic or morality. For example it would be logical and moral to let you go, because in theory I am indebted to you. After all, who would know that we arrived in time to stop you from sailing away?"

Cicero was silent. Like Ortwin, he knew that Laenas would never do it. "But since I'm mad," confirmed Laenas, "it gives me pleasure to kill you. I like the fact that a nobody like me has the power to put an end to a life as important as your own."

"Can't we stop all this? I only know that I die because of a homeland I have saved many times. You are just a poor wretch – an insignificant tool," Cicero interrupted him with an impatient gesture of his hand, and touched his chin with the other, as was his habit. Ortwin admired his outburst of dignity while thinking that what he had just heard Laenas say proved decisively that the centurion was the person least suited to enter a sect where moral constraints were the basic principle of its existence.

The soldiers around him were just as troubled. Everyone sensed the importance of that moment, and felt awe for a man whose fame and works they could never have equalled in a thousand lifetimes. All, that is, except Laenas, who Ortwin saw was quivering with rage and red-faced with anger. He grabbed the orator's hair and pulled the old man's head, which was poking out of the litter curtains, towards him while with his other hand he drew his sword from its sheath and, holding it like a dagger, thrust it into the nape of Cicero's neck. As soon as they realised what he was doing, the soldiers and porters instinctively covered their faces with their hands.

Ortwin was accustomed to death and did not flinch, although his heart was pained. He watched as Laenas pushed his sword deeper and deeper into the speaker's neck, right up to the hilt, and then, moving the blade from left to right to enlarge the wound, begin to remove the head. Blood spurted everywhere, splashing the open curtains of the litter, the centurion's already blood-spattered chest plate and Cicero's face. Blood spurted from his mouth and his bloodshot eyes were still wide open.

Ortwin had seen far more gruesome things in battle, but few had made such an intense impression on him. Laenas did not call anyone to help him. Amid the general silence of the astonished soldiers and slaves, he continued his work, not severing the head with a clean blow but continuing the slow, grisly detachment of the head from what remained of the mangled neck. Once free, the speaker's head fell to the ground and bounced towards Ortwin's feet. He stepped back in disgust, before realizing that Laenas was repeating his work on Cicero's right wrist. In that case too, the centurion refused to sever it cleanly, as though he got some kind of pleasure from savouring that unpleasant task. Which he probably did, thought the German, as he turned away to avoid having to witness any more of the atrocious spectacle. He noted that a good number of the soldiers had had enough too, and many of them had started crowding around the cart carrying the personal effects of the speaker. One legionary climbed inside, then let out a cry of disappointment. He re-appeared holding some papyri which he threw contemptuously at the feet of his disappointed comrades. He had expected to find something else, obviously.

Laenas called for their attention. "Right, it's time to get back to Rome. I have what I need," he said, holding up Cicero's head, still dripping with blood, in his right hand.

Ortwin too, could not wait to get back to the city. He had to convince Octavian – and everyone else in the sect – of how unsuited that grim figure was to join their ranks.

XII

Veleda looked around her, scarcely able to believe that what was happening around her was real. Near the window she could see Octavia, her daughter and her maid, Etain. Their lives depended on her. To one side of the door, three thugs were busy settling their accounts with the slaves she had forced to follow her, and in a matter of moments they were all on the ground, along with three of the assassins.

Suddenly, the crying of the child resounded in her ears, together with the moans of the dying, laying in pools of their own blood by the threshold.

In the crook of her arm, she held the head of the assassins' leader. A man who had possessed a decisive power over a large part of her life – and who apparently continued to do so, even though she had not seen him for over two years.

Quintus Labienus.

Veleda continued to tighten her grip on the neck of the man who had loved her as much as Ortwin, and she held her dagger at his chest, near that heart which had once beat so much for her. When she had realised his identity, she had thought for a moment that she might faint and had almost released him, but the survival instinct within her had prevented her from doing so and allowed her prevent any reaction to her former lover. In a voice which was slightly fainter than before – and trembled somewhat, to tell the truth – she had once more ordered him and his men to lay down their swords. But Quintus had only chuckled again, and not ordered his soldiers to do anything. After killing the slaves, they were now free to pounce upon Octavia and the others at any time.

And now she had no idea what to do next.

She pushed the tip of the blade against his heart until it sliced through the leather corset the man was wearing. "You must want to die, Quintus," she whispered. "And it is about time."

"No, it's not my time yet," he said, motioning his men in the direction of Octavia with the head she held in her arm, and one of them immediately advanced upon the *domina*. The woman held her daughter, who was crying louder and louder, and stepped back against the window. The man slapped the child, and yanked her away from her mother by her arm until Octavia was forced to let go, then shoved her over to Etain, who quickly picked her up and held her against her pregnant belly. Octavia lashed out at the bully, screaming and hitting him but he just smugly grabbed her by the arm and pointed a knife at her throat. Only then did she calm down, though she continued to sob.

"So you see that I won't be dying today?" said Quintus Labienus. "Though perhaps you will..."

"I'll take you with me, then," she said, regaining her swagger as she remembered that she hated him more than she had ever loved him. She pushed the tip of the knife further into the leather.

"And to think I was planning to take you away with me..." said Labienus. "Just like old times. You're used to changing sides, aren't you? How many times did you go from Caesar to Pompey during the civil war? Of course, you care nothing for we Romans... Except for me, of course – the only Roman you were ever interested in."

She didn't know why she was letting him talk nor why she did not order him to be quiet. Somehow, she realised, she had missed that voice – she had been with him too long and she had depended on him, believing that he was the only man in the world who loved her, to be insensitive to that sound, no matter how unpleasant it was to her ears.

"How did you know I was here?" she asked him, eventually. She had to buy time. If the slave she had sent out had managed to escape they would soon be coming to the rescue, and as long as she had her dagger at Quintus's chest he would not kill Octavia.

"The same way I knew you were all here," he said, talking as if they were gathered around the table. "You can understand my surprise and my joy when I learned that I would meet my Veleda again. That's why I had one of the slaves call you, after threatening to kill his mistress if he let on, and he took you to that room. Meanwhile I disposed of Octavian's mother…"

Veleda quivered with anger but forced herself not to let it show. Octavia was also counting on her staying calm. "Who sent you? Cassius Longinus? You were with him when we saw you at Laodicea, during the siege of the city."

"No need to deny it, if you say you saw me in Syria," admitted Labienus. "But this is a personal initiative of mine, although I do not doubt that it pleases him. I had been sent to Rome solely to make contact with the opposition, and I thought I'd make myself useful now that the dissidents have all been eliminated. You know, I could hardly believe it when I stormed Laodicea and they told me that there had been a couple of barbarians in

Dolabella's service – one with only one eye and the other with half her arm missing. I thought it was too strange to be a coincidence, and I knew that we would meet again sooner or later, as you'd placed yourselves at the service of the enemies of the liberators. It seemed logical, in fact, that Ortwin had sided with Caesar's heir – he always did lick the dictator's arse and will no doubt do likewise with his step son. And to think I thought you were both in Germany... Funny that you didn't manage to persuade him to stay, with him drooling over you like that."

"So did you, for that matter, no?" said Veleda, suddenly finding the strength to argue. Their words echoed in the tense silence of the room, interrupted only by the increasingly tenuous sobs of Marcella.

"But I've always made you do exactly what *I* wanted. Like a *real* man."

Just then another of his henchmen appeared at the door and stood there puzzled for a moment before he understood what was going on. He approached Quintus and Veleda with some embarrassment. "What's the matter? Don't worry, you can speak," Quintus ordered him, casually. "She is a friend of mine." Veleda was beginning to feel tired, but kept her knife pressed against him.

"Err... I killed a slave who had escaped from the house," said the man. "He was probably going for help. But we need to keep an eye on the others, and I see that there are only a few of us left."

"Two will do. Everything is under control here. You, go with him," said Labienus, to one of the surviving soldiers. "Go round the house and kill everyone. I don't think they'll cause any trouble. Then come back to report to me and one of you go out to monitor the situation," he ordered, despite the extremely awkward position he was in.

"But... what about here?" objected the puzzled man.

"Don't worry, I'll manage here," said Quintus. "Ah ah ah, Veleda! Apparently, your plan to get me talking and earn yourselves some time has failed. So what do we do now?"

She did not answer immediately. She had lost her last chance of getting away, nor could she hope that the other slaves would help her: they were destined to be slaughtered in a matter of moments, and in fact a moment later she heard the noise of furniture being overturned and a male voice screaming out in pain. Somewhere in the house a woman screamed and then another, which made Octavia cover her face with her hands and burst into tears.

"What music to my ears, Veleda! And soon you will start singing too," murmured Labienus, mockingly. "Why are you doing this? For these Romans who you hate so much? Throw down your knife and come away with me. I know that you have not forgotten me – I can feel how you tremble, and I know you well enough to know that it is not out of fear..."

It was only then that Veleda realised that she actually was trembling. She was shocked. No. She *couldn't* still feel anything for him. It mustn't be so: it was insane to feel a bond with a man who had treated her so atrociously. She had loved him purely to spite Ortwin – and then only until she had realised that he loved her too.

"I'm shaking because I hate you," she whispered. "And because I would kill you right away, but I cannot without jeopardising the life of the person who was entrusted to me." She was not sure it was true, but she felt better after she had said it, because, for once, Quintus was speechless.

But that did not solve her problem.

*

Even to the bathroom. Fulvia followed him everywhere, even to the bathroom, and Agrippa could not even find a moment's peace in there. Not that he cared, mind: this woman was taking him to places he had never been to with other women – sexually, at least. And he was finding it difficult to manage without her. In reality, he allowed her to guide him, and he was more than happy to explore the limits of intimacy between a man and a woman. Above all now, when the air was full of death and cries of pain and despair echoed along the streets each time someone was taken away from their family or tried and executed on the spot. Sometimes Agrippa felt the need to be alone with his thoughts, reflecting on what he had contributed to creating.

Just a moment before, he had heard one of those cries. It had almost been drowned out by Fulvia's groans of pleasure during yet another orgasm, but he had nevertheless heard it clearly. He jumped out of bed, taking advantage of the momentary disinterest that overcame Fulvia after her pleasure had reached its peak, and rushed into the bathroom. He knew that his mistress would not relax for long and that they would soon resume their sexual experimentation, but in the meantime he needed to breathe – all the shouting, inside and outside the building, had brought strange thoughts to his mind.

While he was here enjoying himself, out there people were suffering. He did not usually dwell overmuch on public events – he was a man of action, who believed in the cause he pursued and was sure of his righteousness – but somehow Fulvia made him feel dirty. Not so much because of what they did in bed, but because of her amorality, her disregard for others and the cynicism that characterised her. She was cruel, to put it bluntly, and sometimes he was ashamed to feel so attracted to – almost dependent upon – someone so wicked. Octavian might seem increasingly cynical to him, but he never seemed cruel. He did what he thought was necessary and flinched from nothing, revealing a lack of scruples that he had not previously possessed. He had really changed, in the year and a half since he had taken up the sceptre of Caesar, but he felt no pleasure in making or seeing others suffer, nor did he lack an interest in the people – on the contrary, he followed his goals not only out of personal ambition, but also in order to provide the Romans with a better life and future, because he really felt that their happiness was important, and he wanted to be the one to make it happen.

Yet, however 'dirty' or guilty Agrippa felt, he couldn't help desiring that woman, and the irritation he felt when she interrupted his thoughts by entering the bathroom completely naked was immediately transformed into pure pleasure as she seated herself on top of him and began to rub her body against his, kissing his neck while she did so.

And they began all over again. With her, Agrippa found that he always possessed incredible energy and they did not need to rest in order to recover their strength. She always made him feel ready again. Fulvia broke away for a moment and dropped to her knees, putting her head between his legs and ramming his sex forcefully into her mouth, almost choking herself in the process. He started

226

to pull her up, but she wanted to continue. As always, it was Fulvia who decided when to stop.

Agrippa did not make her wait. He turned her round and took her again, on the floor this time. Anyone else would have said enough at that point, but not her. She could have gone on forever, and he felt flattered that he was able to satisfy a woman like that.

After both of them had cried out with pleasure almost in unison, she stood up, and only then did Agrippa realise that her knees were bleeding, grazed by contact with the hard marble of the bathroom floor. Yet she had not stopped. That was Fulvia. They returned to the adjacent bedroom and lay down on the bed, and only then did she ask him to blow a little on her wounds to relieve the stinging. But while he did so, she took his hand and guided it between her thighs while she started touching him again, her fingers all over his body.

They heard a knock at the door, and a slave's voice said that the thing the mistress had been waiting for had arrived. Fulvia sat bolt upright as though Agrippa did not exist, rose from the bed and, naked, her hair in disarray and without make-up, walked over to the door and ordered the man to enter. She often even let her servants enter the room while the two of them were making love and was not at all perturbed at being seen unrobed by the staff – indeed, perhaps she even enjoyed the feeling of being desired by men who could never have her. As for the women, Agrippa knew she used them for her own pleasure in the rare moments when she happened to be alone, and sometimes even involved them in their games.

"At last!" said Fulvia, when the slave gave her a sack, which she almost snatched from his hand. She dismissed him and ran over to the bed, where she settled herself down next to Agrippa. Intrigued he asked "What were you awaiting with such trepidation?"

"The best gift that my husband and my future son-in-law could have given me. When he wants to, Mark Antony knows how to make me happy," she said, and for the first time Agrippa heard her speaking in an enthusiastic, childlike voice instead of the hoarse, deep, sensual voice she adopted when playing the role of seductress and sorceress. She put her hand in the bag, rummaged inside for a moment and then pulled out the gift. A severed head which he immediately recognised as that of Cicero.

Agrippa had known that sooner or later the time would come, but he had not known that Fulvia had specifically requested that gruesome trophy. Then she pulled out a hand as well. At his questioning look, she explained. "This was Mark Antony's idea, in truth: he wanted to cut off the right hand with which Cicero wrote those shameful orations against him."

Agrippa had read the *Philippicae*, and had not found them so awful: they contained many truths, but he could hardly say that in front of the wife of the sect's principal ally.

The young man stared at the two macabre relics, his eyes on Cicero's embittered expression – no doubt the one that had been on his face in the moment of his death – and suddenly felt that he wanted to be as far away from there as possible. It was true that one of the men upon whom Octavian had been seeking revenge was dead, and that he should be happy, but the pleasure it gave his mistress bothered him. He saw her snatch up the hairpin which had slipped from her hair before they had begun making love.

Fulvia placed Cicero's head between her legs, adjusting it until she found a position in which she could hold it firmly, then forced the tip of the pin into his mouth and, using her other hand for leverage, forced it open. When she had succeeded, she fumbled about between his teeth and pulled out his tongue, which she immediately began stabbing frantically with the pin. Within a few moments, it was reduced to an unrecognisable pulp, but she continued to attack it. "There, damn you! A stab for every wicked word you dared to say against me in public!" she cried, her eyes burning fiercely. "Now you will never speak again! Never!"

Agrippa was overcome by a wave of nausea and felt as though he was about to vomit. Suddenly, he was seized by a powerful nostalgia for Etain. He had always missed her gentleness and kindness, which had provided a necessary counterpoint to the harshness around him, and now he felt that he needed her more than ever. Overcome with disgust, he longed to see her again – he knew where she was hiding with her mistress, and visiting Octavia to check up on how she was would be a good excuse for visiting her. He could not predict the welcome Etain would give him, but he knew all too well how Fulvia would react if she was to find out. However, it was worth a try and in any case at that moment in time he would rather have been anywhere than beside that bloody woman.

He sprang out of bed, flung on his tunic and robe hurriedly without even washing himself and walked towards the door, saying, "The death of Cicero requires me to meet with Caesar Octavian. We will meet again soon."

She continued to stab what was left of the orator's

tongue.

She did not even answer him.

*

"Kill her."

Veleda was desperately trying to think of a way out of this seemingly hopeless impasse, and Quintus Labienus's order to the man holding Octavia filled her with despair. How could he say that with a dagger pointed at his chest?

She pushed the tip of the dagger in further, digging a deeper furrow in the man's corset. His henchman, meanwhile, hesitated, probably asking himself the same question.

"You have decided to die then, Quintus?" she asked, trying not to betray the emotion in her voice.

"I will not die. You will not kill me because you cannot. It was you who convinced Ortwin to spare me, remember?"

"And I have never regretted it enough," she said. At least, not until then.

"Kill her, I said," repeated Labienus, but the man still hesitated, clearly baffled. Meanwhile, a new cry rang out from another room in the house, Quintus's two men were still killing the slaves.

Veleda pushed the tip of her dagger even further, piercing the leather. When she realised that she had sliced his tunic and was now touching his skin, she pushed just a little more in order to cut him. But Quintus did not flinch. She wondered if she had the courage to go all the way, but then Veleda realised that was not the point – killing him would do no good if Octavia were dead too. The *domina*

230

was her priority. She carefully watched the moves of the man who was holding her and decided to take a gamble. She focused her thoughts, ignoring Quintus, who was now screaming at his man to obey him. She would only have one attempt and she tried to remember how, after her hand had been severed, she had trained constantly to compensate for her disability with her great skill in the use of weapons, both as a thrower and as a swordswoman.

It all happened in an instant. She realised that the man was about to carry out his order. With Quintus's voice resounding in her ears, she pulled the knife from his chest, aimed it at the face of his henchman – which by now was about a foot away from that of Octavia – and threw.

The woman screamed. The weapon hit the man in the eye, and he staggered back, his hands to his face, giving a wild scream. Before Quintus had the chance to realise the dagger was no longer pointed at his heart, Veleda cracked him in the face with her maimed arm and with the other she elbowed him in the sternum, which took his breath away and made him double over. This gave her time to throw herself towards Octavia, retrieve the dagger from the man she had killed, who was now slumped along the wall under the window, and put herself between the woman and the other armed men.

Immediately after that, exactly what she had hoped for happened. Etain, eluding the other intruder, rushed over to her with the baby in her arms and stood beside Octavia, between Veleda and the window.

At that moment, the two thugs Quintus had sent to scour the building returned. Now Veleda found herself forced to defend two women against four men.

Well, she thought, I have only put off the inevitable, as

Quintus reminded her as soon as he had managed to get up and get his breath back. "Well done. Beautiful performance," he said, picking up his dagger. "Better than I remembered. Lads, you start with the little girl. I'll deal with her myself."

It was over. The four men advanced towards the women at the same time, making it impossible for Veleda to defend herself against Quintus and protect the other three. The child's screams in her ears, she positioned herself in front of them, but then realised that Octavia was alongside her. The domina took off her gown and wrapped it around her left arm to give it some protection. Soon after, Veleda saw Etain on the opposite side copying her mistress.

"If I must die," said Octavia, with unusual determination in her voice, "I will fight, as would my brother."

Veleda nodded and stared into Quintus's eyes with an expression of defiance. He smiled back at her. "All right, we'll start with the big bellied one," he said, gesturing to one of his men to focus on Etain.

"No, let's start with you, instead!" boomed out a voice from behind Quintus – a man in the shadows outside the door, his head covered by the hood of a cloak. Veleda did not have time to see who it was, for he had already moved forward and pounced upon one of the thugs. He grabbed the man's arm and plunged his knife into his stomach, pulling it out immediately and hurling his victim to the ground before leaping over to the one closest to him and swinging his blade through the man's ankle, nearly severing his foot. A geyser of blood erupted from the stump while the man slumped to the ground screaming.

"Agrippa!" cried Etain. Could it really be him? And

what was he doing there? However, she felt sure that it was him, despite the speed of his movements, the cloak and the shadows. He jumped up to his feet and only then did the hood slip down onto his neck, revealing his identity. Etain was right. He rushed towards the only one of Labienus's men left, while Labienus attacked Veleda. Quintus was no longer trying to be funny, and upon his face there was the fierce expression she knew all too well. Veleda dodged nimbly out of the way of his blade, then swung her own at him, attempting to take advantage of his momentary unsteadiness, but her swing connected with thin air.

For an instant, Quintus came face to face with Octavia. He stared at her for a moment, undecided as to whether or not to take the opportunity to kill her, but the *domina* had enough presence of mind to raise her arm and punch him in the face. The impact sent him staggering back a step, and Veleda, finding him within striking distance, prepared to stab him, but at that moment the man threw himself to the floor and rolled out of her reach, getting to his feet on the other side of the room.

A moment later, he was ready to attack her again. Veleda just had time to look around her, and saw that the remaining killer had pushed Etain to the floor and grabbed Marcella, while Octavia was busy defending herself against Labienus, who was using her as a shield to defend himself against Agrippa. Etain, her swollen belly impeding her movements, stood up with difficulty, then looked around her and picked up a knife one of the dead men had dropped before making for the man who was holding the little girl hostage. Agrippa tried to push her out of the way, but she stayed doggedly by his side.

Veleda noticed that no one was paying much attention

to Octavia, now.

Meanwhile, Labienus was once again advancing upon her. He swung his sword twice, a forehand and a backhand swing, both of which missed. A third swing came closer, but she managed to block it with her own blade at a hand's width from her face.

"How's the one-eyed man, Veleda?" he mocked. "Still alive?"

"More alive than you, that's for sure," she couldn't help answering.

"Why? He's an assassin himself, isn't he? Do you think I don't know what he did to Trebonius in Smyrna? Anyway, Cassius has promised to give me an army... I don't think Octavian will be as generous with your one-eyed man. You've chosen yourself a loser."

"I'd say he beat you when you fought face to face... I'd say that the loser is you!" She too, was beginning to enjoy herself in that perverse game. And with Labienus, every game eventually became perverse.

The reference to his defeat in the duel at Munda seemed to annoy him, and he resumed his attack on her. She dodged him, and again glanced over at what was happening around her. From the corner of her eye she saw Octavia kneeling down and grasping the ankle of the man who was holding her daughter, pulling him off balance. The man fell over and, almost crushing Marcella at the same time, Agrippa leapt on him with all his might and tore his throat open like red fire. They all fell to the ground. Veleda looked back at Labienus and saw that he too had stopped to watch the scene. She was about to take advantage of his distraction, but for some reason continued to gaze at him.

234

Suddenly, the man with the severed ankle threw himself at Agrippa who, still on his knees, was passing Marcella to her mother. The man's knife was aimed for his back and Veleda cried out in warning, but the blade was now close to the young man's shoulders. Etain cried out too, and threw herself between Agrippa's back and the dagger.

The blade caught her in the chest, just above her heart.

Agrippa turned, following Etain's body with his eyes as it collapsed to the floor. His attacker pulled back his weapon in order to strike him too, but Agrippa was faster. In an instant, he slid the knife into the man's chin, slicing his face open lengthways from the bottom up to the top of his head.

Horrified, Veleda turned back towards Quintus, just in time to see him dart out of the room. She took a few steps towards the door, but he was already gone. She heard his hurried footsteps echoing down the hall and then beyond. She had no chance of stopping him. She went back inside to see if Agrippa could help her, although there was now no one left to fight against.

She found him in tears, bent over the lifeless body of Etain, and she decided to respect his pain.

XIII

She had died trying to save him. She had still loved him, then. More than the baby she had been carrying inside herself and which would now never be born. Agrippa continued to stare at Etain's corpse, hating himself for not having done enough to win her back. He paid no attention at all to the hustle and bustle around him. Under the strict control of the sect, people were coming and going and bodies were being dragged into the *tablinum*, evidence of the massacre that had taken place in the building before and after his arrival. He thought only of all the things he wished he had said to the only woman he had ever loved – loved so much that, out of respect for her pain, he had left her in peace. If only he had been less respectful and had tried harder, perhaps they could have been together again... and she would not have been forced to sacrifice her life to prove her love.

He thought of all the opportunities that he had thrown away in those last few months, when they could have been happy while he was busy amusing himself with Fulvia, and cursed himself for his shallowness. But when he heard that Octavian had arrived, he roused himself from his stupor, pulled himself together and ran immediately to Atia's room, ready to comfort him – after all, his friend had suffered the loss of his mother and the near death of his sister, and would be in an even worse state than he, despite being better at disguising his feelings.

"My friend, I grieve with you – she was like a mother to me, you know," he said, when he entered the room, placing

236

his hand on the shoulder of his friend, who was bent over Atia's corpse.

He embraced him, but looking into Octavian's eyes noticed that they were not wet. He saw not desperate pain but grim determination, the same determination that had moved him to avenge Caesar's death. His friend never gave in and Agrippa tried to force himself to think in operational terms, putting aside the devastation he felt at the death of Etain.

"We need to find whoever did this," began Octavian. "It is evidently the same person who killed Pedius. I want him at all costs. As soon as they know that we are vulnerable, it will be the end."

"Then I suggest you talk to Veleda," said Agrippa. "It seems that he was an old acquaintance of hers."

Octavian stiffened. "Her... She was not able to protect them. I was wrong to entrust this task to a woman. But she will pay for this, you can be sure of that..." he murmured, a flash of hatred in his eyes.

"I don't think that's how things went, actually..." Agrippa ventured to say, but his friend had already left the room, rushing into the *tablinum*.

The room housed the corpses of the slaves and the assassins, as well as that of Etain. Octavian, lucid and full of foresight even after he had been informed of the assault, had brought with him slaves and not his lictors so as to keep the affair secret. Octavia had had Marcella taken away from the massacre and was talking to Veleda. The leader of the sect walked over to the German and grabbed her by the shoulder, spinning her round. He stared at her with those that icy intimidating eyes of his and hissed, "You *knew* the killers?"

But Veleda was not one to be cowed easily, and she held his gaze as few people could. "Their leader was Quintus Labienus, the son of Titus Labienus. You know him well, Octavian Caesar."

"Quintus Labienus? Of course, that makes sense. What would you expect from the son of that damn traitor?" mused Octavian. "What else do you know?"

"As you may recall, I had already seen him in Laodicea, when he replaced Cassius Longinus in the siege that preceded the death of Dolabella," explained the barbarian. "He's in Cassius's service. He confirmed that today, but told me that this was his own personal initiative. If he spoke true, Cassius sent him to Rome simply to make contact with the enemy."

"Unlikely," said Octavian, shaking his head. "And perhaps he also told you how he knew where my mother and my sister were hidden..."

"No. I've wondered that myself. They knew their way around. They knew the layout of the rooms. They went straight to your mother's bedroom. They knew where it was and even that she was already in bed."

Octavian approached her menacingly. "All you're doing is trying to excuse your own ineptitude. It is thanks to you that my mother was killed..."

At that point, Octavia intervened. "She saved me and Marcella."

"It was Agrippa who saved you...."

"No, Octavian," said his friend. "I had come here to... to see Etain. I noticed that there were no guards at the entrance, and it seemed strange to me, so I looked for an open window and entered by stealth. I saw the bodies of the slaves and then I went around the house until I got to the *tablinum*, where Veleda had a dagger at Quintus Labienus's throat to stop his men from killing Octavia. The rest we did together. This woman knows her job, just like Ortwin," he concluded, earning a look of gratitude from the German.

"She did everything possible, Octavian, I assure you," his sister confirmed. "If she had not played for time, we would all have died well before Agrippa's arrival. It was too late for our mother, there was nothing we could have done. Veleda is right – whoever did this knew the house and entered secretly, knowing exactly where they were going. We didn't notice anything until they barged their way into this room."

Octavian grimaced. He looked fleetingly at Veleda, unable to find the strength to change his opinion, then beckoned for Agrippa to follow him out of the room.

"Someone in the sect told Labienus," said Octavian gravely.

"That much seems clear," confirmed Agrippa.

"It's unheard of. They took an oath... *They took an oath before the gods,* damn it!" said Octavian.

"And now they have joined the assassins of Julius Caesar."

"Before you call the others to inform them of this, let us take a moment to reflect," said the head of the sect. "You are the only one I can trust – you've risked your life for them, and for a thousand other things too."

"So has Veleda, I would say," stated Agrippa. He had seen her fight like a tiger.

"So she has, yes," admitted Octavian.

"And so Ortwin is trustworthy too."

"Yes. If she is, so is he. To say nothing of Octavia, of

course, and poor Etain, who lost her life," added Octavian gently. "I will never forget that it is thanks to her that we were able to punish Minucius Basilus."

There was silence. The two friends were thinking.

"Only resentment can force someone to take a similar course of action," Octavian went on, "so we must work out who has grievances…"

"…we haven't seen much of Gaius Chaerea for a while," said Agrippa, cautiously.

"Yes. Yes, he has seemed indifferent for some time now," admitted Octavian. "But even though he knew where we kept them hidden, he's never been in this house, so I don't see how he could have described its layout to Labienus."

"And Maecenas? He's been here, but he would have no reason to betray us – he has done so much for you and saved our skin countless times," said Agrippa. "I owe him a lot. It was he who got me back into the sect."

"All this is true. But then none of us really knows why he came looking for me and offered me his help in the first place. Who can say they really know the reasons why he has done so much?"

"Lucius Pinarius too has done much for the sect. He even donated his share of his inheritance, without being forced to. He genuinely admires and believes in you…" continued Agrippa.

"But he wasn't happy with the fact that I chose Pedius as consul over him. I was following the principle of seniority, but he didn't seem to take it well. He might have resented that."

"But he would only have had to wait – you would have made him a consul soon enough. He must have known

240

that, mustn't he? In fact, now he will have to replace Pedius."

"All the more reason to eliminate him and take revenge on me," said Octavian thoughtfully.

Agrippa knew that there was another name he must now mention, but he could not bring himself to be the one to do it. Rufus had made his woman pregnant and then, apparently, had abandoned her – he had good reason to dislike Rufus, and therefore was unwilling to make allegations against him.

"Rufus is eaten up with ambition," said Octavian.

"As are we all, right?" Agrippa said.

"He often appears to me to be unhappy. Very unhappy. He feels superior to everyone. Even to the head of the sect."

Agrippa was silent. He knew that Octavian was right. His friend had noticed everything and was painting a lucid portrait that Agrippa had only guessed at.

"Anyway, it seems that no one is above suspicion," he admitted. "But can we exclude the fact that it was perhaps some slave or soldier?"

"Of the soldiers, I knew only the escort, and they were all killed. As for the slaves, they were all people who had been with us for years. I think that Octavia would swear to their loyalty," said Octavian. "Not to mention that they were all killed."

"Nobody else had been in the house?"

"My stepfather and Octavia's husband," he admitted. "But Marcius Philippus was sincerely devoted to my mother. I don't think he would have betrayed her like this, although I cannot exclude it entirely. I would be less certain of Claudius Marcellus. It is true that he would never have killed his wife and daughter, but we know that he hated Caesar and that he sympathises with the murderers. Even though, at the end of the day, he's not the type who likes taking sides…"

They fell silent once more. "What do you intend to do now?" asked Agrippa.

"First of all, not to let this murder confound us like Pedius's did," said Octavian. "I will say that my mother died of natural causes whilst she was in the country. It might seem strange that it has happened to two people from the same family in a matter of days, but people generally believe the official version of things. Let's hope that the other triumvirs believe it too. As a second step, we must hunt down this Labienus. I doubt he'll want to try again. I rather think he will try to get away from Rome now, and it will be hard to find him. Obviously he goes on the list of our primary objectives. He will die like Cassius, Brutus and the others, and since Ortwin is the only one I trust at the moment, he will lead the investigation. And anyway, he is the only one of us to know this Labienus well, right?"

"And what about the traitor among us?"

Octavian grimaced. "That's the third step, and for the moment the only solution that comes to mind is to keep our ears and eyes open… We will say that one of the slaves had been corrupted by Labienus and we'll see how the real culprit reacts once he feels safe."

Agrippa had no better solution to offer him, but realised that not knowing who to trust was the quickest way of destroying the sect and their aspirations.

*

There had been better times, Maecenas said to himself. He wanted to organize the next moves against Sextus Pompey in Sicily and against the assassins of Julius Caesar in the East with Octavian and the other ministers of the sect. He wanted to create and promote a pool of talented writers with whom to surround himself. He wanted the terror the proscription had caused to be over. And he wanted, finally, to chat amiably with Horace, to whom he felt irresistibly attracted. But none of his aspirations were becoming a reality, despite the fact that only a short time ago none of these things would have seemed so impossible.

The tension within the sect had become almost unbearable since the day of the massacre in which Atia and Octavia's handmaiden had been killed. Meetings between ministers had become less frequent, and their leader seemed to trust only Agrippa, who had saved his sister's life. His single concern was that of finding Quintus Labienius, who Veleda had named as one of the killers, and he seemed to be so obsessed by this that he was forgetting the sect's other objectives.

At the same time, *his* plan to become the patron of a literary circle, which had begun as a pretext for arousing Horace's interest and drawing him into his orbit, was not taking shape at all. This was not a good time for people to be writing poems nor works of history – one might all too easily inadvertently provoke the resentment of someone powerful by neglecting to mention him, or by speaking unflatteringly of his ancestors. Without a clear, unambiguous political situation, the risks were too high for people to wish to be seen with a representative of the institutions like him. One might end up an outlaw for nothing at all.

And Horace wasn't interested. He had refused him an interview and denied him access to the camp when he announced a visit. Plotius Tucca, the soldier Maecenas had met near Bologna, kept telling him what a superior talent he possessed, which only exacerbated his curiosity and increased his desire to know the man better to the point of it becoming almost an obsession.

Plotius was pleasant company, and he might now consider him a good friend had he not so many secrets to hide from him about the sect. But now that things had grown tense, the legionary was the only one to offer him the intellectual stimulation he needed and he often visited him in his legion's camp, which had been set up outside the walls of Rome to provide immediate support for Mark Antony in the case of riots.

Hoping in vain to find some interesting and inspiring poem among those he was examining with his friend, he lay on a triclinium next to a table set with a lavish banquet in the pavilion that an *angusticlavius* tribune had placed at Maecenas's disposal for his visits.

"This is absolutely ridiculous!" said Plotius, throwing a papyrus he had been reading to the ground, while picking at some olives. "It's not even worth you reading it. It was written by the *magister* of the son of a prostitute I visit from time to time. Trash. Oozing flattery in every line and inadvertently ridiculing the object of its praise, your commander. Listen to this – he talks about 'youth, climbing the highest peaks to reach his father and all the other gods.' He writes as though Caesar Octavian is already dead and deified without even realising he's doing it! And then, 'Frail and weak, his body grows, turning him into a giant in the face of his enemies, a new titan before

Zeus.' This person should be proscribed in an instant without even realising why, so stupid is he!"

Maecenas knew he should smile, but he had no desire to. He felt discouraged. He usually took pleasure from the minds of others. "I've had enough, Plotius. Maybe there's no place for my idea of reviving culture at this moment in time."

"You might be right, you know. There is too much politics about at the moment for anyone to produce inspired and sincere art that might actually provoke real emotion," said Plotius. "Everything is calculated and based upon survival and personal benefit. We want people who care nothing for the consequences of what they write, but then we risk losing them immediately afterwards... or rather, we risk seeing their heads hanging from the Rostra. I swear, Horace will come to the same end. It would be a waste of an unimaginable talent. In more suitable times, one like him would vastly ennoble our culture."

'Well I've tried to get him out of his shell, but he really doesn't want to know anything about me, or about fame," admitted Maecenas, bitterly.

"What can you do?" asked Plotius, spreading his hands in resignation. "He is so enraged by the political developments of the moment that he has no great desire to devote himself to his art... Sometimes I think he should join Julius Caesar's assassins in the East, but perhaps he's not too fond of them either. I know he had some dealings with an emissary of theirs a few days ago, but he quarrelled with him too. Just imagine, it was the son of Caesar's traitor. Do you remember Titus Labienus?"

Maecenas blinked. "Are you saying that Quintus Labienus was here?"

"Certainly. I know that he's proscribed, and I would have reported him had I known his identity," said Plotius. "Horace only told me after he had gone when I asked him who he had been arguing with so animatedly, and now I'm telling you because I know that you will never report him – after all, our friend the poet was only approached by that traitor, he didn't give him refuge, and if I'm not mistaken the decree does not punish people simply for having been contacted by one of the outlaws against their will. On the other hand, the fact that he chased him away absolves him of any guilt…"

Maecenas was already on his feet and heard Plotius's final words while he was opening the tent flap to rush out. "Incredible!" he kept saying to himself, as he began rushing about the camp, followed with difficulty by his young slave, in search of a high-ranking officer who could show him where Horace was. Ortwin was hunting for Labienus in Rome and the surrounding area, and the murderer had actually been in the camp of Mark Antony's legion and was perhaps even a friend of Horace's. It would be a bad business when the German found out. That charming *optio* had made no secret of hating Julius Caesar and anyone who wished to emulate him, but Maecenas would never have thought he would actually have colluded with the murderers.

He hurried to the *primus pilus* centurion and asked for Horace, and was directed to the stables. He marched straight there and burst in. The sentries, intimidated by his rank, made no attempt to stop him, and he peered about in the torch lit gloom until, amongst the horses, he saw Horace's elegant profile intent on offering one of the animals some oats. "Strange duties for an infantry officer," he said to himself, then walked over with determination, the *optio* only noticing his presence when he was standing right beside him.

"Stand aside, tribune, you are frightening my horse," was all he said, not looking into the Etruscan's face.

Maecenas was already tense and ready to explode, and he knocked the oats out of Horace's hand. "We need to talk, urgently. Come outside, right away, optio!" he shouted, suddenly realising that the eyes of all the grooms and soldiers were on him.

Only then did Horace look at Maecenas, and he made no attempt to hide his contemptuous displeasure. "Are you ordering me as my superior or demanding that I do so as the pest that you are?" he asked, softly.

Maecenas felt a blaze of anger. Despite his interest in the *optio*, he had promised himself that he would never put any pressure on the young man nor use his influence to force Horace to spend time with him. He thought he had been discreet and now he heard himself being called a pest!

The man was intolerable. So why was he there, taking such an interest in him?

"I am ordering you as a tribune and as a representative of the triumvirate. Come outside, *optio*, immediately," he hissed, hoping that his face had looked grim enough to scare him. But apart from his resigned look, Horace did not appear to be particularly cowed as he dutifully followed him outside. When they were far enough away from the building and the tents, the Etruscan stopped and said, "I know that you met Quintus Labienus."

Horace hesitated. "So...?"

"He's an outlaw."

"He came looking for me."

"Why?"

Horace was silent.

"I asked you why," insisted Maecenas.

"He was trying... trying to incite the army against the triumvirate."

"Is that all?"

"What else would it be?"

"Perhaps he was looking for collaborators to try and topple the triumvirate."

He remained silent again, and Maecenas took his silence for admission.

"Just as I imagined," he said. "But why you?"

"Someone had told him that I was displeased with the state of affairs," Horace admitted.

"But you refused, didn't you? I know that you had an argument..."

"I did not like the man, that's all. He was irritating and arrogant. Exactly the kind of person I can't stand. I would never trust someone like him. He had the manners of a madman."

"But he is a close associate of Cassius Longinus."

Horace held out his hands in exasperation. "And what can I do about that?"

"It means that he is a very dangerous individual. He is wanted, now that we know he is in Rome. Always assuming he still is. To get to him, the triumvirate's men will surely come to you – and you know what happens to those who have had dealings with the outlaws..."

"But *you're* one of the triumvirate's men, aren't you?" said Horace, with a bitter smile. "And you've found me..."

"And it's a lucky thing for you that I have!" burst out Maecenas, hoping that he wouldn't regret what he was about to say. "Soon others will come, so get out of here, quickly. Get away from Rome, leave it immediately and go and reach your heroes, the 'liberators' in the East." The *optio* stared at him in amazement, then was lost in thought for a moment. Finally he nodded, turned and started to leave, but he suddenly turned back and asked, "Why are you doing this for me?"

Maecenas hesitated. "It grieves me to see talent go to waste," he said.

"But you don't even know how I write…"

This time the Etruscan had no answer. He shook his head, and it was he who turned and left.

*

Octavian ripped the innards from the sacrificial ram and lifted them up, solemnly, then gave them to the two slaves to lay on the brazier a few feet away, and said, "Repeat after me, Popillius Laenas: I swear to Mars Ultor, upon the lives of those I love most and my children today as well as those I have in the future, that I will do everything in my power to fulfil the objectives of the Sect of Mars Ultor."

"I swear to Mars Ultor, upon the lives of those I love most and my children today as well as those I have in the future, that I will do everything in my power to fulfil the objectives of the Sect of Mars Ultor."

"I swear to Mars Ultor that I will not rest until I have ensured that all the murderers of Julius Caesar have been punished: Gaius Cassius Longinus, Marcus Junius Brutus, Decimus Brutus Albinus, Gaius Trebonius, Servilius Casca Longus, Publius Servilius Casca Longus, Lucius Tullius Cimber, Publius Sextilius Naso, Quintus Ligarius,

Minucius Basilus, Rubrius Ruga, Lucius Pontius Aquila, Marcus Spurius, Caecilius Bucolianus the elder and Bucolianus Caecilius the younger, Pacuvius Antistius Labeo, Gaius Cassius Parmensis, Petronius, Publius Decimus Turullius and Servius Sulpicius Galba, and their associates, beginning with Pompey and Quintus Labienus. May they face the same end as those already punished by Mars Ultor: Gaius Trebonius, Decimus Brutus Albinus, Lucius Pontius Aquila and Minucius Basilus."

Octavian reeled off the names one by one and waited for the new recruit to repeat them before continuing.

"I swear to Mars Ultor that I will do everything in my power and I will adopt all necessary weapons and resources to bring peace to Rome and transform it into a lasting, prosperous empire, just as Caesar had intended."

"I swear to Mars Ultor that I will do everything in my power and I will adopt all necessary weapons and resources to bring peace to Rome and transform it into a lasting, prosperous empire, just as Caesar had intended," Laenas repeated.

"And finally, I swear before Mars Ultor that I will never betray my friends nor betray this brotherhood, to which I consider it a privilege to belong to. May Mars Ultor turn his arrows upon me if I do not keep my oath."

"And finally, I swear before Mars Ultor that I will never betray my friends nor betray this brotherhood, to which I consider it a privilege to belong. May Mars Ultor turn his arrows upon me if I do not keep my oath," echoed the centurion.

"Now you too are a son of Caesar!" said Octavian. He turned to the others present. "Let us all share the food to sanction our pact and consecrate ourselves to Mars

Ultor." He motioned to them to approach the altar, then to the slaves to pass around the half-cooked entrails of the ram, which he himself distributed to the followers, beginning with the initiate Popillius Laenas, who looked less than enthusiastic.

Gaius Chaerea had been given a cool reception upon his return to the sect, unlike like the initiation ceremony which had taken place several months before, when Octavian – who at the time had been neither consul, nor Caesar, nor triumvir – had consecrated them all together to the avenging God: even poor Quintus Pedius and Etain, the first victims of a struggle which had grown more difficult than ever.

And now, in the first initiation ceremony since that one, it was Popillius Laenas's turn. He certainly wouldn't replace what they had lost, and Chaerea saw that he was not the only one who thought so when Ortwin approached him, shaking his head resignedly. As they ate, several groups formed: Octavian was talking to Maecenas, Agrippa and Rufus, increasingly distant from the armed wing of the sect, while Laenas clung to their togas like a dog waiting for a pat on the head even though no one took the trouble to welcome him to the sect. Octavia was conversing with her cousin Lucius Pinarius and Veleda. Ortwin came up to him just as he was approaching Octavia to ask her about the massacre where Atia and Etain had died. A massacre for which Gaius felt partially responsible. If he hadn't pretended to be sick, maybe they would have sent him to protect them instead of Veleda, and things might have turned out differently.

"Not a good addition, this one," said the German.

"I agree," replied Gaius.

"I accompanied him on a couple of executions and he made a terrible impression on me," Ortwin continued. "He is unbalanced, as well as cruel. I did everything I could to make that clear to the rest of them, but Octavian believes that someone like him can be useful to the sect."

"We are all useful to the sect, I would say – or rather, to him in particular – but no one is indispensable," said Gaius, bitterly. "Lately I have been feeling expendable myself, and I have seen the objectives of justice and peace we set ourselves at the beginning giving way to those of supreme power…"

Ortwin peered at him intently with his one eye. "Those are pretty dangerous things to say…"

"Yes, yes… Ignore me – I just want peace and quiet and to be with my family. I've had enough of all this bloodshed."

"That's rather a strange way for a soldier to think."

"What can I do? Perhaps deep down I'm not cut out for war. I already feel like a veteran who wants to get his pension and retire with his family to some beautiful farm."

Ortwin put his arm round Chaerea's shoulder. "Listen, Gaius, I served Caesar and I watched his methods became less and less orthodox over the years. But he was the best, and I chose to serve him until I decided I had other priorities. He simply did what the times called for, that was all. Obviously, that was not enough, because he was killed by those he had pardoned, but I am convinced that Octavian is the best too. And he must do what the times call for. He must build upon Caesar's successes and avoid repeating his mistakes and show his own clemency. It is necessary to go through all this, however distasteful it may seem, to reach the peace you long for. And the more we do now, the more ruthless we are, the sooner that will arrive. I too have goals to pursue and I can only pursue them once we have completed the task of the sect…"

"I deserve a chance! I am older than him and I have more experience. It's my turn first!" Ortwin stopped at the words of Rufus, who had suddenly raised his voice to the other ministers. Gaius saw Octavian lay a hand on his arm and, with that icy stare which reminded him so much of Caesar, command him to calm down.

Ortwin smiled half-heartedly. "I knew that sooner or later this problem would emerge…"

"What is Rufus talking about?" asked Gaius.

"The war against Sextus Pompey. You have been out of things for a while now, so perhaps you are unaware of the latest developments. As you know, we must defeat him before going to the East – all the more so now that he has taken Sicily from it's governor Bitinicus and is building a stronghold against the triumvirate. The outlaws know this and are fleeing there along with refugees from the cities of Italy whose lands were promised as a colony for veterans. The island is becoming the headquarters of those of Caesar's assassins who are against us, and if we wait much longer, Sextus will be too powerful to defeat. He is proving to be as great an admiral as his father, and many experienced sailors and navarchs are rushing under his banner, especially from Spain, where his family has always had a large following. He has a respectable fleet now, and he can intercept the grain from Africa and starve Rome, attacking us from behind as we head towards Macedonia, or invading Italy with a pincer movement together with Caesar's assassins, or even on his own… In short, defeating him is no less important than killing Julius

Caesar's assassins."

"And Rufus wants supreme command..."

"Exactly. In my opinion, Agrippa is by far the more capable, but if he and Octavian were not such close friends the position would have gone to Rufus, both for seniority and experience. His protests are understandable."

"Rufus has been resentful towards him for quite a while now, and if there isn't already open conflict between them it is because Agrippa is careful not to provoke him," admitted Gaius. He had been aware for some time of Rufus's discontent – he had been the only one who had been happy at Agrippa's expulsion from the sect before the war of Modena. "It seems absurd, but right on the eve of the most difficult of battles, we are no longer so united. And I must confess that what with all this internal dissent, I myself no longer feel as motivated as I once did."

"Hold out, Gaius, or you will have even more reasons for feeling demotivated," insisted Ortwin. "If the sect doesn't attain its goals, there will be no peace for the empire, not even for you. Octavian will not give up, even if it means carrying on alone, and nor will Mark Antony, you can be sure. And neither will Julius Caesar's assassins, now that they are convinced that they represent the only chance of saving Rome. You think our methods are questionable – what about those of Brutus and Cassius? Did you know that Cassius conquered Rhodes with two naval battles and then plundered the city of all its wealth, even that which belonged to private individuals, putting to death any who had hidden their riches in wells or in graves? And that the magistrates of Tarsus sold free citizens to find the money to pay the tribute? If we wait a little longer, Cassius will take Egypt as well, even if Queen Cleopatra *is* with us. Did you know that the citizens of Xanthus committed suicide en masse when Brutus conquered them?"

Gaius glanced over at the ministers, who, in hushed tones, were deep in discussion. There was tension in the air, although Rufus was trying to control himself. Popillius Laenas, now ignored by the others, walked over and put an arm around him, jovially, "So, comrade," he began. "We are like brothers now. And I am a brother of this barbarian, too," he added, looking warily at Ortwin with a forced smile. "Even if he has pissed me off more than once and I'm not the type of man who forgets a slight. But there are other people we need to get rid of, right? We're at war, and we're all on the same side. The three of us might be a kind of little triumvirate, eh? Laenas, Chaerea and Ortwin, united by necessity and not by love... Lovely, isn't it?"

Without saying a word and without changing his expression, Chaerea looked at him, and realised that Ortwin was doing the same. There would be plenty of friction between those two in addition to the animosity which already existed between Rufus and Agrippa. And the animosity which Octavian, now increasingly obsessed with the demands of his responsibilities, seemed to feel for all of them. It was increasingly difficult to remain part of that sect, which had become a sort of mirror of the internal struggles to which Rome had fallen prey since Caesar had died.

He turned in the direction of Octavia, instinctively seeking comfort from the love he knew he could find in her eyes, and when she noticed, she gave him an expectant look which redoubled his feelings of guilt towards his own woman.

He knew then that this rekindled passion would bring him nothing but trouble.

XIV

Octavian stared at those present. All the cult members were there apart from Ortwin, who would be arriving shortly with Titus Labienus's head. Agrippa, Maecenas, Rufus, Lucius Pinarius, the newly returned Gaius Chaerea, Octavia, Veleda, and the new recruit, Popillius Laenas.

He had called them to his *tablinum* for a secret meeting about the tasks and roles assigned to them with regard to the civil war, which needed to be fought on two fronts. After that, there would be the meeting with his staff to discuss purely military matters, and then another with Mark Antony to decide upon the strategy to be adopted. But this was the meeting that mattered most, because here he could speak of the sect's objectives and bring them into focus before facing Caesar's assassins.

And because he was going to find out who the traitor was.

If Ortwin brought Labienus to him alive, he would happily torture him in front of all those present in order to extort the name of the person who had helped him. He needed to know who it was before the campaign began so that he wouldn't have the spy under his feet when he needed to take even more delicate decisions. And if there was one person who could solve the problem, it was Ortwin. Labienus was an old enemy of his, and moreover had threatened his woman, so he had no doubt that the German would use all his skill to try and get the name out of him.

But meanwhile, the others were waiting for the meeting

to begin.

He could feel the tension in the air and there was no need to prolong it. "Dear friends," he began, aware of how false his words rang in that moment, "the crucial challenge is approaching and Mark Antony is already marching towards Brindisi to board and join the eight legions in Macedonia. Before reaching him, however, there are two things we must do. Two delicate tasks, upon which the success of the campaign against the assassins of Julius Caesar depends…"

"I am ready for any task you wish to assign me, my lord!" cried Laenas. The others cast disapproving glances at him, but he didn't even notice, so fervently was he staring at Octavian in expectation of an answer. For a moment, the young leader of the sect was taken aback, but he tried to hide his annoyance at the interruption and gave the man a forced smile and a nod. "As I was saying," he continued, "*two delicate tasks*. I asked Mark Antony to put back the start of the campaign in the East a month, but he pointed out that Brutus and Cassius are growing stronger and that time is in their favour. I have to admit that he is right, and so the war must begin, but if we immediately concentrate our forces against Sextus Pompey, I am convinced that, even if we do not defeat him altogether, we will be able to at least take Sicily from him. I trust that Agrippa, in whom I have complete confidence, will soon solve that problem. He will leave with the fleet and I will join him by land to invade the island and place a garrison there."

"I disagree," announced Rufus bluntly.

This time Octavian did not try to conceal his annoyance. He glared at him, saying, "Again, Rufus? In any case, I have decided."

But Rufus seemed determined to make his case. "I should have been given that task. I have more experience and I am perfectly capable of handling it."

"I need you for the other task, Rufus," said Octavian, trying to adopt a reasonable tone. "The assassins of Julius Caesar have had Staius Murcus position himself along the coast near Brindisi, and he is impeding the transport of troops to the sea beyond. Our convoys have already suffered more than one ambush. I need you to go there and help them, at least until we have all moved to Epirus."

"That's a job even that milksop Maecenas could do!" protested Rufus, approaching the table menacingly. "Send Agrippa to do it, and give me the war against Pompey!" Visibly annoyed, Maecenas shook his head.

Octavian jumped up, and his icy glare had the desired effect – Rufus stopped where he was, half way between the chairs arranged in a semi-circle and the table.

"If you wish, Caesar, send me to fight against Staius Murcus!" interjected Laenas, his foot in his mouth as always. "I will not let you down!"

Octavian waved his hand for silence, a disdainful expression on his face. Laenas was definitely an imbecile – he hoped that he would at least be useful. As for Rufus... "Agrippa has excellent, innovative ideas for the naval war," he explained. He did not want to give the others the impression that he had preferences, so he forced himself to be patient. "You are an experienced soldier, that goes without saying, but on land, and as such I intend to use you for the benefit of the sect."

"But you haven't even heard any of my ideas about how to defeat Pompey!" complained Rufus.

Agrippa intervened, nodding to Octavian. "Let's hear them, then," he said in a conciliatory tone. "You've never even talked to me about them, my friend. How would you fight him?"

Octavian looked gratefully at Agrippa, who was attempting to nip the quarrel in the bud and at the same time save him the mortification of having to go back on a decision already taken. He was truly the best friend a man could have.

Rufus, meanwhile, did not need to be asked twice. "Simply put, I would draw Pompey to the Straits and tear him to pieces. We have enough quadriremes and quinqueremes to blockade him in that narrow stretch of sea. We will encircle him with a fleet of ships larger than his own."

"Forgive me," objected Agrippa, "but acting with large ships in that narrow space would probably mean sharing the same fate as the Persians at Salamis – there's no room to manoeuvre there, and we have triremes we can set against Pompey's more manoeuvrable ships…"

"We won't have to manoeuvre!" cried Rufus. "Once we have lured Pompey's ships into the Strait, we'll force them to surrender – and if they refuse, so much the better: I'll send my men aboard and we'll massacre them."

"It's more likely that they will attack us – the larger ships will get stuck, or will get in one another's way, and end up at the mercy of the enemy," said Agrippa. "And have you forgotten that Pompey has experienced sailors? All we have is infantry that we will be forcing to fight on the decks of ships, and we'll probably have to resort to something like the boarding bridges used in the Punic wars to make them feel comfortable about doing it.

Personally, I would…"

"Are you joking? A legionary is *infinitely* superior to a marine in hand-to-hand combat! If they had to board, Pompey's men wouldn't stand a chance!"

"It's one thing fighting on land and another fighting on a deck that's rocking from side to side… I've seen plenty of legionaries unable to fight because they were suffering from seasickness."

"They'll fight perfectly well if you know how to command them!" snapped Rufus, who then turned to Octavian, almost pleading. "I *need* this opportunity! I need it so that I have a position in this sect. I'm sick of feeling like some damn hanger-on!"

Octavian thought for a moment. The enthusiasm with which Rufus threw himself into their cause would seem to exclude him from the list of possible traitors, but continuing to deny him an opportunity and openly favouring Agrippa might mean ending up losing him anyway. The request put him in a difficult position with his other friend, though, whom he held in equal esteem but whose military skills he respected more. He looked for a moment at Agrippa, who nodded and said, "I have no objections. I consider tackling Staius Murcus in the Adriatic an equally delicate task."

Octavian knew that the task was not one which appealed to Agrippa, who was eager to implement his ideas about ramming enemy ships and had planned his actions in detail. Giving up that battle was a large sacrifice for him, especially coming after the death of Etain. He needed to focus on something important.

Octavian felt Rufus's eyes on him. He did not want to give him the job, but it seemed he had no choice. At that moment, however, a slave came to announce Ortwin's arrival and his attention turned immediately to the German. He gave the slave instructions to bring Ortwin to his study and waited impatiently for him to appear, no longer caring about the quarrel between Agrippa and Rufus.

*

He cared nothing for the other outlaws. He was interested only in Quintus Labienus, and would do anything to capture him.

Even make a deal with the traitor.

Ortwin had been forced to cough up plenty of the sect's money to get the information, but it had allowed him to be on the pier at the port of Ostia that night, a few steps away from the ship upon which, at any moment, his rival was about to sail. Over the course of the investigations, during which he had barely rested for days, he had interrogated all the outlaws he had found until he found one who knew of Quintus Labienus and had been willing to speak in exchange for being set free. The man had told him when and where Labienus would be leaving, and he was now ready to take advantage of the situation.

But he wanted to do it alone. He did not want an escort, and the men who were there with him had orders to intervene only if things got out of hand. For Ortwin, Labienus was not simply a supporter of the assassins of Julius Caesar and an outlaw, but also and above all the man for whom the heart of his woman had once beat – and perhaps still did, despite how much he had made her suffer. Ortwin had defeated him in a duel before her, and she had persuaded him to spare Labienus's life. That was how he had won her over, but apparently it had not been enough. He needed to defeat him again but without making a martyr of him, and that was why he wanted to do it without the help of others, humiliating Labienus in a one-on-one fight and proving himself the better man. Only in that way, perhaps, would he banish him from Veleda's heart forever.

At least, that was what he told himself when he began to approach the moored ship, crouching low to avoid being seen from the deck by the crew. He crawled towards the stern, then lowered himself into the water from the dock, swam a short distance, found a hand hold and hoisted himself up until he was able to peer over the side. He looked around the deck and saw two men talking, but neither seemed to be Labienus, so he waited for them to turn away and then climbed over the bulwark, took his dagger in his hand and set off in search of his prey, hunched over and wondering if Labienus had other henchmen with him – according to Veleda, Agrippa had killed them all, but you could never be sure. Yet he was certain that his rival would not avoid another direct confrontation with him, so he was not particularly worried. Labienus too, was anxious to prove himself the better of the two men.

Some might have said it was a feud between them, the German thought, almost with amusement. They would not have been wrong. He was driven by his barbaric pride, and Labienus... well Labienus was more barbaric than any Roman he had ever known.

He stepped through the hatch and went down the steps, preparing himself to fight with the man he hated most in the world. In the soft light of the torches, he saw a crowd of people in the centre of the hold between the benches of rowers. Apparently, then, they were all awake. He saw no more reason to move secretly and announced himself, declaring that he had been sent by the triumvir Octavian Caesar. Nearly everyone turned towards him and stared at him, some with scepticism, others with suspicion, and a few with fear. He continued to descend until a man approached him with a firm step.

"I am the captain," he said. "What do you want?"

"This ship is carrying outlaws. You are under arrest. And in case you think I'm joking, there is a platoon of soldiers outside ready to intervene."

The captain looked at him, suspicious but mainly surprised. "Outlaws?" he said. "I know nothing about that. Unless you mean that man lying there on the ground…" He turned and pointed towards the crowd of people, which parted to allow Ortwin to see the man who had informed him of Labienus's whereabouts lying on a bench with a dagger sticking out of his chest.

"I do not know who this one here and his partner are. They paid well, and I took them aboard, that is all. Then tonight, when everyone was asleep, we heard a muffled scream and found him like this. His friend has disappeared. Perhaps this note he wrote, which we found next to the corpse—" explained the captain, offering him a blood-stained papyrus, which Ortwin snatched from his hand.

> My dear old companion of many battles.
> We who have fought side by side, or on
> opposite sides. I arrived late at Laodicea,

but the one who has arrived late this time is you. It seems that we can never meet. But I did manage to meet Veleda, who held herself against me at length, which I am sure she enjoyed. If I were you, I would not be too sure of her feelings. When we meet again – and it will happen, you can be sure of that – things will perhaps be different from last time. Perhaps I will be victorious, and she will ask me to spare you. But I will refuse – I will kill you and I will take her, my Veleda. And I can assure you that in time she will admire me for showing more determination than you.

Ortwin trembled with frustration and threw the sheet of paper to the ground. This time, Labienus had won.

And once again, his words had managed to hurt Ortwin.

*

"He'll have sailed by now. He killed my contact, too," said the barbarian, approaching the desk. The distress on his face showed how much effort he had put into the futile search. Octavian saw him staring disconsolately at Veleda, who – distressed too – lowered her head.

The others noticed, and Rufus took advantage of the situation to broach the subject again. "Perhaps Labienus has reached Sextus Pompey. Let me leave immediately, Octavian, and I'll fix him!"

"Calm yourself, Rufus!" snapped Maecenas, who had

never made a secret of his preference for Agrippa. "Octavian has not decided that it will be you who conducts the war in Sicily!"

"But Agrippa himself has pulled out!" protested Rufus. "At least one member of this sect has some common sense!"

"I do not approve. If my opinion still counts for anything, it is Agrippa who should be in charge of the naval warfare," said Maecenas. "Every man must be able to develop his talents and be used on the basis of them, and to deal with a pirate as capable as Pompey we need someone like him, someone with ideas......"

"Ah, so I don't I have these ideas, you're saying?"

"You are an executor, Rufus, while Agrippa is a born leader, with imagination and generosity. But you are an *excellent* executor..." conceded Maecenas.

Octavian did not listen to Rufus's indignant reaction. He was thinking that he would do absolutely anything to stop the traitor from hearing the rest of the meeting. He could not afford to let the enemy know his plans. But nor could he remain alone with the people he was sure of. He resolved to immediately send away the one, over the previous days, he had deemed the most likely suspect. He was about to speak to him when he himself stood up and came towards him.

"Octavian, can I take this moment to ask you why you and the other triumvirs did not include me among the next batch of consuls?" asked Lucius Pinarius.

"Mark Antony has vetoed the consulate to other members of my family," Octavian answered promptly. "I could not oppose him." It was the truth, though he was aware that if he had insisted he could probably have got round it, but in reality he preferred to get on with things he considered more important. He did not exclude thinking about it again, however. At the end of the day, making Pinarius happy would neutralize him and allow Octavian to control him better, and even give him an excuse for assigning him institutional responsibilities when he did not want him to participate in sect meetings. "Your time will come, fear not. But for now I wanted to ask you to go and see Lepidus. He has yet to give me the list of the officers of the three legions he has given me and I urgently require it."

"But... now?" asked Pinarius, looking puzzled.

"Now."

"I'd like to wait until the end of the meeting, if you don't mind," Pinarius insisted.

Was I right to be suspicious of him? wondered Octavian, while Maecenas and Rufus continued to argue and Agrippa tried to act as peacemaker.

"What is wrong with you all today," he exclaimed impatiently, "that you all dare question me?"

This little outburst, accompanied by his usual icy stare, seemed to paralyse Pinarius.

But only for a moment. "I would ask you to write me a letter for Lepidus in which you expressly ask for me to be made consul, then." said Pinarius, finally. "I will deliver it to him personally and I will talk to him. It is not right that I have no significant position when I have done so much for the sect."

Octavian threw open his arms in resignation. Just then Gaius Chaerea approached him. He looked embarrassed and stopped just behind Pinarius, waiting for his turn, but Octavian was grateful to have an opportunity to cut his cousin short. "That's enough. Go to Lepidus now, I don't want to hear another word!" he exclaimed, beckoning to Chaerea to approach him. Offended, Pinarius turned and walked away, and Octavian wondered for a moment what he should do with him. Kill him? Out of the question – a third family member dying in such a short space of time would certainly destroy his strength and credibility, and he was not even sure that Pinarius was the traitor.

"Caesar Octavian... I have to tell you that I no longer wish to be part of this sect." Gaius Chaerea's words brought him sharply back to reality.

"What do you mean, centurion?" he replied sarcastically, feeling his anger growing inside him. "You've only just returned and you want to leave already?"

"All this is not for me, I see that now. I would no longer be useful to you. It is not that I don't want to avenge Caesar, but I can do that by being one of the many – the many soldiers you lead to war."

"What nonsense is this? You have always carried out the tasks assigned to you in the best possible way, and often did even more! Would you insult Mars Ultor so much?" He felt his insides churning and a burning feeling rising in his throat. He knew what that meant.

"Well, now I've had enough," insisted Chaerea. "The work has become too much for me. I'm just a soldier, nothing more. When I'm not fighting, I want to be with my family."

To Octavian, his words started to become indistinct and his outline grew blurred. The young man started to cough, and everything around him began to spin. He was wracked by sudden chills and sweat dripped from his forehead. He seemed to hear the voice of Octavia, who had approached him immediately after she had seen Gaius depart. "Brother, I have risked my life for the sect, and I have done my part. I want to become a minister, like Maecenas, Agrippa and Rufus, and have a voice in the important decisions. I'm your sister and the great-grand-daughter of Caesar, and it is unfair of you to put me aside and limit yourself to using me... I even sacrificed my handmaiden for the sect, and I demand respect!"

His coughing grew worse, and he began to drip with sweat. The voices around him became confused, and his vision was clouded by the tears that welled up in his eyes. The burning in his throat was unbearable. His temples throbbed wildly. He was having one of his attacks, and it promised to be one of the most violent yet. After another coughing fit, he saw Chaerea's face, which had suddenly appeared before him, splattered with blood. The centurion took him by the arms, just a moment before his strength left him. Octavia, who knew all too well what to do when this happened, ordered the centurion to keep him on his feet so that he didn't choke on his own blood. The others arrived, with Laenas elbowing everyone out of the way in order to be at the front. Octavian felt the breath of all present upon him – they were crowding him, not leaving him enough air to breathe, he could not stop coughing and the fire that was burning within him grew hotter and hotter. He felt as though he were suffocating until he saw Agrippa hurl Laenas aside before moving the others back a little less violently.

By now he was weak, and no longer had the strength to keep his eyes open. The sect was disintegrating, he managed to think in the instant before he passed out.

And the fault could only be his. He absolutely must do something to unite them once more.

XV

Pure white clouds, driven by the wind, scurried across the otherwise clear sky over the straits between Italy and Sicily. This would be the setting of the first real battle in a civil war which promised to be bloody and merciless. The coastline – the toe of the peninsular's boot – loomed dark and inaccessible, and the rough seas broke into foaming waves, dancing in anticipation of the great and devastating spectacle to come.

Between Scilla and Charybdis. Yes, he was luring them right where he wanted them, into the straits from which he would ensure there was no escape, pressing them until they were smashed upon the headland of the peninsular's coast. Or targeted by Octavian's men, stationed with scorpios and catapults on the ramparts of the ancient fort overlooking the sea.

Seated on the curule chair of the turret platform in the bow of the quadrireme, Rufus contentedly watched Sextus Pompey's fleet of triremes and liburnas enter the Strait in pursuit of the bait he had sent. He raised his arm and the men on the bridge began fanning the fire burning in the stern, sending up a column of smoke – the signal to close the pincer. He did not have to wait long before the quadriremes appeared from behind the promontory of Scilla. Their massive shapes rose up like hills in the background behind the small boats of Pompey, who continued to advance into the Straits. Right towards him. Horns sounded, and the vessels next to the flagship began to spread out slowly, extending the front until the far wing girded the stretch of sea towards Charybdis, along the side of Pompey's fleet. Rufus rubbed his hands. Soon the enemy would find themselves with the mainland on the left, him in front of them and other ships to the right and the rear. He pictured the image of a quadrilateral fort, exactly like the camps built in stone along the borders. Impassable walls, much higher than the sides of the small enemy ships, would surround Pompey's fleet, blocking them in that sector of the sea, at his and Octavian's mercy.

What an idiot Pompey was! He was nothing like his father. Or rather, he resembled that great man in the declining phase of his career, when he had lost against Caesar at Pharsalus despite outnumbering him. And to think that Sextus had become the bogeyman of the seas, feared even by Brutus and Cassius. With his piracy he had managed to alter the trade routes in the Mediterranean – and even to block some of them altogether, threatening to starve Rome. But at the end of the day he was just a bandit, not a strategist or a tactician. He was only able to attack defenceless merchant convoys, and before an enemy military formation in a real battle he betrayed all his limitations.

He imagined the expression on Octavian's face as he stood on the ramparts of the fortress overlooking the straits above him as he watched the perfect formation of Rufus's ships and expressed his satisfaction to the other officers at having chosen him instead of Agrippa. But above all he imagined his rival's face when he learned of his victory and the tactics he had used to achieve it. From that day on it would be Agrippa who was envious of him – and perhaps Octavian would decide, once and for all, to make him head of the sect's military operations.

Some of Pompey's ships seemed to falter, but then resumed their course, rallied by the trumpets on the flagship, which was heading straight towards Rufus and the quadriremes he had deployed there to block their passage. From where he was, he could hear the sound of drums, which dictated an increasingly urgent rhythm to the oarsmen of the enemy vessels. Before the thrust of the advancing triremes the sea opened up and actually trembled, like the ground under the hooves of a cavalry charge. That was a more familiar image though – this was the first time he had seen a fleet attack, and it was an impressive sight. He was almost sorry that he was fighting defensively, and pictured himself leading a naval attack, the sea opening up at his passage. He imagined himself leading a legion to charge, shouting to the soldiers to follow him and breaking through the enemy lines.

He liked the idea of victory by sea and by land. He saw himself in the victor's chariot, his face painted with vermilion, a laurel wreath held over his head by a slave, and wearing a gown studded with stars, passing between rejoicing crowds praising his name.

Sextus Pompey showed no signs of slowing down and seemed to have no intention of withdrawing from the battle, though there was still time: in that confined space, the powerful swell of the sea was hindering the ships on his flank and allowing him to slip off towards Charybdis. Instead, he continued to advance. What was he thinking? That he could break through a line of quadriremes which were taller and larger than his own? Each of Rufus's vessels was at least twenty paces longer than Pompey's and his men could target the enemy from up on their decks. Many of the enemy ships possessed neither towers nor scorpios, so in the inevitable clashes, the small liburnas would inevitably get the worst of it, smashed against the quadriremes and the rocks of the nearby promontory, their rams capable of little more than scratching the larger ships' armour.

They were unevenly matched. And yet Pompey seemed to be trying to break through. Perhaps he had realised that he was done for and had decided to die fighting, making them pay as high a price for his defeat as he was able to, rather than surrendering. Or perhaps he was simply insane, thought Rufus. So much the better. He would cut him to pieces right before Octavian's eyes and then all he would have to do would be to round up a few survivors.

He turned to look at the defensive barrier behind him, and suddenly realised that there was none. Fascinated by the spectacle in front of him, he had not been paying attention to the deployment of his own vessels, and they were not where he wanted them. The rough sea prevented the ships from advancing together and maintaining their position, so the quadriremes were spread out and some had even turned sideways on, exposing themselves to the enemy rams.

Pompey's triremes continued to advance at great speed, intensifying the roll of the sea and preventing the men on the decks from standing upright. To the left, Rufus was alone and isolated, while to the right, his ship was almost struck by an enemy vessel. He heard a crash and realised that some of the two ships' oars had smashed into one another and been broken before the two separated again. Pompey's ships were now just a stone's throw from land.

Apparently, they would have to fight a battle on equal terms.

"That's all we need," said Octavian, as he left the stronghold atop the promontory of Scilla to meet the delegation from the citizens of Reggio. He should have been in the battlements to watch the naval battle and support Rufus, but instead he had to listen to a protest from the civilians of the nearby town. At first, when Ortwin had told him that there were people outside the walls who were determined to talk to him, he had ordered the German to tell them to go to hell. There could not have been a more inopportune moment, what with his ships deployed right there and those of Pompey approaching them. But Ortwin had told him that it was not just a question of a few people outside who had come to beg an audience. Outside the gates, in addition to a small legation, there were hundreds, perhaps thousands, of civilians armed with sickles and sticks determined to defend their rights.

Nothing that the legionaries in the battlements couldn't handle, of course, but earning himself a reputation as an exterminator of civilians was not how he intended to go down in history, so he felt compelled to hear them out even though he would have much preferred to see the destruction of Sextus Pompey's ships and participate in the battle – safely and from a distance, as Maecenas always suggested. The front line was for the expendable, not for supreme commanders.

"Do you not see that there is a battle underway?" he began, as soon as he crossed the threshold of the fort, surrounded and protected by his bodyguards, led by Ortwin and Veleda. The arrows of the archers in the battlements trained upon them, the three delegates had been permitted to come as far as the walls of the fortress but a hundred paces further back stood their fellow citizens.

"Forgive us, Caesar Octavian, but it is during this battle that we must decide which side to take," said the chief. A sort of indirect threat, then. "I must inform you that if you confiscate the territories and give them to veterans, Reggio is ready to rebel and provide all possible help to Sextus Pompey and to Sicily."

Octavian raised his eyebrows "Do you dare go against the supreme magistracy of the State? This was a decision of the triumvirate, signed by the Senate of Rome," he said, looking the man in the eyes.

"It is an unfair decision, if you will allow me to say so," replied the man. "We live on the Straits, the last strip of Italy, and many people pass through here, to whom we rent plots of land and property. If you take our possessions from us we will become poor, because they are our only livelihood, and this true also of the citizens of Vibo."

Octavian did not answer immediately. He thought that confiscating lands in those parts was stupid – you had to keep the inhabitants satisfied if you wanted them to support the regime and allow free passage to Sicily and Africa. But Lepidus had demanded that those two cities be included in the list of places where the veterans were to settle and now Octavian understood why – the other two triumvirs had wanted to make trouble for him because he was responsible for Italy.

Well, he would not be tricked in this way.

"I understand your distress, friends. Unfortunately,

Lepidus demanded you be included in the list because of certain disagreements he had with some of your fellow citizens in the past. In short, a vendetta, if you follow me…" Obviously, this was a fabrication, but wasn't that what you did in politics? He could not directly accuse Mark Antony, but he could at least try with Lepidus. The other triumvir would find it difficult to disprove and the inhabitants would be convinced that Lepidus had cheated them, so eventually, to persuade them of the contrary, he would have to exempt them from the confiscations.

"But that does not solve our problem," protested the man. "Indeed, it makes it worse."

"I think not," said Octavian. "Since taking up the legacy of Caesar I have also made it my duty to provide for the welfare of the empire's population, and in particular the Italian population, just as my father did when he defended it from the oppression of the powerful. Let me win this battle, friend, and I guarantee you that I will work on behalf of your cities, which undoubtedly do not deserve to suffer this confiscation."

"Do I have your word, Triumvir?" insisted the man.

A cry rang out from the stands. Ortwin ran to the wall to talk to the soldiers on the battlements, then returned to him. "You must return, sir," he said.

Octavian looked at the delegate. "You have my word. Now leave me to my duties. We are fighting a rebel," he said, before turning away, whilst the other man did nothing more than bow his head as a sign of respect and gratitude.

The triumvir ran back up to the battlements and looked out at the sea. In his absence, he discovered, it had become a battlefield. When he had left, Rufus was about to encircle Pompey, deploying his ships on the opposite side of the headland and from behind, but now he was witnessing a free-for-all. An all-out battle from which he was excluded. He could not use the artillery without risking hitting his own ships. Rufus had missed his chance of blockading the enemy, and now the fight was on equal terms. Or, even worse, if Agrippa was right, his men were actually at a disadvantage. His crews were less accustomed to the rough sea, and the quadriremes were less manoeuvrable than the triremes, with little space available to move.

His men shouted encouragement to their fellow soldiers on the decks, but he remained silent as he watched the awful spectacle unfolding before him, the like of which he had never seen before. From up there he could see everything and he realised that his uncertain health would never have allowed him to participate directly in such a battle – a land battle would have been bad enough, but a naval battle would have brought out his maladies as soon as he set foot on deck.

Rufus's ships moved so slowly that they seemed to be practically sinking into the water, and they hindered each other, piling up one next to the other. However those of Pompey, seemed almost to ride the waves, as graceful as dancers and as rapid and lethal as darts. His eye was drawn to a quadrireme being rammed by two galleys, who both struck it on the same side towards the stern. He saw the bow of the massive ship rear out of the water whilst the stern disappeared beneath the surface and the mast snapped and collapsed upon the men trying to crawl up the tilted deck, crashing onto the turret and smashing it into a thousand pieces. Panicking crew threw themselves into the sea while others simply lost their balance and fell overboard. Oarsmen stretched their arms through the holes from which the oars would normally have protruded in a desperate attempt to attract attention.

As soon as Octavian realised that the ship's fate was sealed, he shifted his gaze to another quadrireme which was under heavy attack. Two triremes and a liburna had surrounded it, but the latter had committed the error of trying to tackle it head on, finding itself with the quadrireme's ram in its side. The small ship had split in two, and as the crew were in the water or trapped between the wrecked beams, there was no need to board her. Meanwhile, however, both triremes had flanked the bulwarks of the quadrireme and, although ramming had not had the desired effect, their men had climbed up the sides and boarded the ship, launching into a battle which they seemed to be winning.

He considered the fate of that ship inevitable too, and ran his eyes over the entire Straits. The *naumachia* with which Caesar had celebrated his triumph two years previously, and which he had witnessed, had not prepared him for this hellish scenario. The sea was covered with vessels as far as the eye could see, and seething with foam and blood. The decks were teeming with armed men swarming from one ship to the next, from stem to stern, climbing the rigging to escape from the enemy. Projectiles filled the air above the masts and sails, mainly falling into the water and sending up huge splashes but sometimes indiscriminately smashing masts and oars or slicing through ropes, ripping sails, crashing through the planking and drowning the crews.

Then, suddenly, the first fire began blazing, followed

immediately by others, and that accursed stretch of sea became the Styx.

*

Octavian was counting on him. Mark Antony was counting on him. All those who wanted to avenge Caesar were counting on him, and he would not let them down. Agrippa, still protected by the rugged coastline of Apulia, watched Staius Murcus's small fleet stationed just offshore, waiting to intercept the convoy of cargo ships leaving Brindisi with Antony and some of his legions. Antony, in fact, had no warships because Italy's defence was Octavian's responsibility. If Murcus managed to prevent the passage of weapons and soldiers to Macedonia, Mark Antony could put the blame for the failure of the campaign on the younger triumvir, and perhaps he would actually be willing to sacrifice some of his troops to damage Octavian's credibility.

For this reason, Agrippa could afford no mistakes. He had decided to concede the conduct of the war against Sextus Pompey to Rufus because he was aware that in Apulia an equally important task awaited him. A defeat in the Straits could be remedied, but the loss of the men destined for the Macedonian front could not. For this reason, he had left nothing to chance, splitting his forces and deploying one at sea, to come between Murcus and Mark Antony's convoy, and the other on land, ready to attack the enemy's base, weakening him and forcing him to pull back.

A courier on horseback was arriving. Agrippa already knew what that meant: Mark Antony had taken to the sea.

When the soldier gave him the agreed upon signal, Agrippa gave orders to the navarch to raise anchor and start rowing. The orders rang out in the bay and after a few moments his trireme began to move, immediately followed by the others, towards the open water. Presumably, another courier had simultaneously reported the same news to Murcus, so he needed to move fast enough for the enemy not to notice his presence, in fact, the young commander had stationed himself at a point farther away from Brindisi.

This move had been planned in detail. On the beach nearby were piled up all the materials Agrippa had deemed superfluous, in the interests of moving as fast as possible, and, as he had commanded, the captains had unfurled the sails to take advantage of the wind, which was blowing straight out of the bay where the rugged headlands surrounding them protected the ships from the elements. Agrippa had even ordered that the men were to be freed of their heavy armour and were to fight in light armour using small shields and javelins. He had crammed the ships full of archers and experienced sailors and had the wooden turrets removed, refusing even to board the throwing machines. He'd had the boarding bridges removed as well, along with the heavy ram. He had no intention of getting involved in a real battle, but only of escorting Mark Antony's ships to open sea.

The risks were high. If Murcus managed to stop him and force him to fight, he would have no chance of winning, for he was counting on the extreme lightness of his small fleet to complete his mission.

After emerging from the harbour, he proceeded towards the open water. He could not sail along the coast of the mainland without risking being headed off by Murcus, so he had to surprise him by going round, even though that meant making a long horseshoe shaped detour. When he had decided that he had gone far enough, he ordered the captain to head south. The ships finally found favour in the wind and gathered speed. Agrippa had been at sea several times before, even on warships, but had never gone as fast as he was going now. He was almost overcome with the heady feeling of omnipotence – it felt as though he was galloping on horseback. The combined action of the oars breaking against the water and the sails swelling with wind drove the vessel forward at a frenetic pace. The captain informed him that they had reached the impressive speed of almost ten knots, well over the eight and a half a trireme could normally achieve.

For this reason, the announcement that the flotilla had reached Brindisi surprised him. He squinted, and seemed to recognise the outline of the coast, identifying the dual port of the city. He knew it quite well because he had done service there when he had been cast out of the sect, collaborating with Maecenas to undermine the cohesion of Mark Antony's legions camped nearby. He gave orders to turn and head for the right side of the port. Soon he could see the silhouettes of ships halfway between his fleet and the mainland. They could not be the vanguard of those of Mark Antony, whose vessels were spread out near the port, though. Murcus, then, was already there. Probably busy observing the movements of the transport ships in front of him, he had not even realised that other vessels were approaching from behind. Excellent. Now was the moment for them to go hard at it. Agrippa ordered the oarsmen to row at their fastest rhythm, because they no longer had the wind in their favour, and some time passed before Murcus noticed his presence. Now he could overtake him.

The enemy triremes began to spread out. There were thirty of them, perfectly capable of constituting a barrier, had Agrippa had given them time to do so, but his ships were close together and continued to move swiftly, heading for the right side of the enemy line. Murcus had finally realised his intentions and manoeuvred his ships to cover the exposed side. Agrippa was still in the lead, and – his ships in a wedge formation – he continued his mad rush forward while the enemy moved sideways at a slower pace. They risked colliding.

His flagship, at the head, crossed the line along which the enemy fleet proceeded, unhindered. Agrippa turned and watched the movements of the ships. Murcus's ships approached while his slipped by one after the other. But though the flagship was now safe, he could not be sure that those behind it were – some risked being cut off. He wished he had left at least one turret on board so that he could observe them from above, and finally, impatiently, he pounced on the rigging of the mainmast and began to climb it until he had almost reached the summit. Some might criticise him, thinking it undignified for a commander to climb like a monkey, but he couldn't just stand there doing nothing.

From up there he saw that Mark Antony's fleet had begun to move, although with maddening slowness. He observed the progress of his own ships, while observing the advance of Murcus's. Five of his were still behind the line of the attackers and were now close at hand. The first managed to pass, followed by two triremes almost side by side. One of the prows passed that of Murcus's nearby ship and went in front of its ram, which, however, made contact with the rear part of the stern. There was a glancing collision, which sent up a high wave, hiding the scene for a moment from Agrippa's eyes. The ship was knocked off course and brushed against the trireme which flanked it, breaking its oars and forcing it to proceed almost in a zigzag.

The damaged ship managed to continue on its course, but in the meantime Murcus cut off the penultimate ship and battle became inevitable. Travelling at speed, the trireme from Agrippa's flotilla rammed violently into the enemy ship, smashing through the hull until it reached the main mast. The sails collapsed and covered what remained of the deck, imprisoning the men in a carcass destined to sink quickly beneath the waves. Meanwhile, Murcus's other ships arrived, forcing the last of Agrippa's column to stop or meet the same fate.

Their commander felt a stabbing pain in his chest when he saw his men surrendering to the enemy and others jumping into the sea, clinging to flotsam, but above all he felt mounting desperation when he saw figures imprisoned by the ropes, struggling under the sails, trying in vain to avoid sinking with their doomed ship. He had to remind himself that he had a job to do. He climbed down from the mast and checked that the ships which were still intact were moving perpendicular to the coast, creating a wall to favour the safe departure of Mark Antony's vessels.

It was time to launch the second phase of the operation.

He ordered his thirty archers to line up along the bulwark and nock their arrows. When he saw that they were ready, he checked that there were enough enemy ships within range and gave the order to fire. In an instant, thirty arrows flew simultaneously in a low arc across the short stretch of sea between the two fleets, sowing havoc on the enemy decks. Immediately afterwards, the archers in his other vessels fired, their arrows striking the enemy ships and sending men falling to the ground or into the sea.

Meanwhile, Mark Antony's convoy was passing. Agrippa had calculated that he would have to hold out for at least an hour.

He ordered them to continue firing. The one thing they had plenty of were arrows. Enemy arrows began to rain down on them, but they were few and far between. Murcus had not based his tactics on archers and had brought few of them along. He could not now attempt to ram him, as he was too close to use his momentum. Nor could he board them. Agrippa's ships were so agile that he could forget about that.

The second part of the plan was working, and already the mind of the young commander was focused upon the third.

XVI

Rufus gave the helmsman the order to pull to the left but the man didn't seem to hear him so he climbed down from the tower on the prow – from whence he had been watching the depressing spectacle of the failure of his strategy – and rushed to the stern, where the helmsman was standing. Why wasn't the idiot moving? What was he waiting for? The quadrireme on their right flank to be pushed against them by the waves and the enemy triremes? He had already seen that happen more than once to his own fleet: the ships smashed into one another, knocking them out of action and leaving them at the mercy of their opponents, who could then ram and board them at their leisure.

He dodged the men he encountered, green-faced ghosts who were feeling their way around the deck, some spewing into the sea and others grasping the rigging. Hardly any of them seemed able to cope with the swell of the ocean, and he too was assailed by a sense of nausea that blurred his vision, but he had no intention of letting them see that: what would they think if they saw their commander was suffering from seasickness?

He had to grab hold of the ropes several times in order to make it along the full length of the ship, and at every step he heard arrows flying overhead and was sprayed with water, sometimes powerfully enough to throw him to the deck. He was drenched by the time he reached the helmsman, who he discovered in even worse shape than himself: the man had an arrow lodged in his shin, but continued to remain standing in the stern, giving directions to the two men in charge of the steering oars they manoeuvred on the sides.

"Why aren't you steering left?" he shouted, as soon as he was within earshot. "Can't you see that we're about to ram our own ships?"

The helmsman seemed to barely recognize him. "I can't turn left, sir!" he said. "The current is already pushing us against those two galleys, and I can't get the ship round enough to get the prow facing them!"

"It doesn't matter!" Rufus shouted. "We can risk colliding with the triremes but not the quadriremes! Do as I say!"

"But it'll be our flank that hits them!" protested the helmsman.

"And it'll expose their flank to us! Come on!" he ordered, in an even more peremptory tone, and the man had no choice but to obey, passing on the order to his two subordinates. For a few moments the ship remained at the mercy of the waves, but then slowly began to veer to the left, though not turning sufficiently to complete the manoeuvre. The helmsman shouted at one of the men on the steering oars, but the man just stood with his head bowed and his shoulders hunched, and when Rufus grabbed his hair and lifted his head, he saw that the man's face was contorted with nausea. The helmsman pushed him aside and took hold of the great oar which governed the ship's course. The two galleys, though, were now side by side.

Fortunately, neither of them had its ram facing the other, but impact was clearly unavoidable. Rufus shouted to the helmsman to pull up the steering oars and he didn't need to be told twice. The collision of the triremes against the quadrireme shook the latter, knocking all on board to the floor. Rufus slipped on the decking, banging his back and head against the bulwark, and it was only his helmet that saved him from being knocked unconscious. Clutching the wet railings, he attempted to pull himself to his feet, but the lurching of the ship prevented him and he continued to slide back and forth across the width of the deck.

Suddenly, there was a devastating thud that jolted the very beams of the ship. When he finally managed to get a decent grip on the bulwark, he sat up and saw that the side of one of the galleys had been destroyed by the impact, while the other, with which they had collided only laterally, had dropped its boarding ramp and its ram had penetrated them between the bow and the mast. Underneath the boarding bridge was a man who had the misfortune of being pinned directly underneath it when it had been dropped, and he lay there crushed, arms and limbs akimbo and showing no sign of life.

They were about to be boarded.

In an instant, the gangway was filled with armed men, and Rufus feared that enemy soldiers were also arriving from the other trireme. A quick glance showed, though, that it was taking on water from the side which had been smashed open and that the occupants were throwing themselves into the sea. If nothing else, he would face only one ship's soldiers, and there were less men in a trireme than in a quadrireme. He looked at his own men and saw the poor state they were in: some were not even aware they were under attack, and those that were did not look prepared for combat.

"Men, to me!" he shouted, calling them to get into formation and drawing his sword. However, only a few obeyed his order. He went over to the helmsman. "Come on, gather the soldiers! I'll try and hold off the enemy as well as I can, but hurry!"

The man nodded and disappeared behind the others who had responded to the call: fifteen of them, counted Rufus, with which to hold off at least twice as many of the enemy.

Cursing himself for not having taken the opportunity to throw the boarders into the sea while they were still precariously balanced on the *corvus*, he decided to deploy his ranks in two wide rows, blocking the deck across its width to avoid being surrounded. He felt his head throbbing and spinning, and imagined that his subordinates must be feeling much the same. They weren't used to being at sea, they were legionaries who had been taken from the units under his command. Pompey's men, on the other hand, seemed confident, to judge from the determined expressions he saw on their faces as they approached.

It was he who exchanged the first blows with the enemy. The man had launched himself against one of Rufus's troops, but Rufus had cut him off to prevent a defeat in a one-on-one battle that might demoralise his already dazed men. Their blades clanged, and soon Rufus felt again the familiar sensations of close combat, despite the rolling deck underfoot constantly reminding him of where he was, the elation he felt in dealing with an opponent excited him and allowed him to master his nausea: suddenly, the soldier he was fighting became a clear, sharp target, moving slowly, and he had no trouble running him through his neck, savouring the feeling of triumph that he tasted whenever he was sprayed with the blood of an adversary.

Meanwhile the entire line that had formed were engaged in combat. Their opponents had taken advantage of the rough conditions of his men to force a way through their lines, and two of them were lying on the ground, while the others were fighting overwhelming numbers of opponents. Things looked bad. He tackled another soldier, duelling with him until he managed to catch him with his guard down on the left and buried his blade in his ribs. Struggling to free his weapon from the man's shattered bones, he found himself under attack from another opponent, but managed to dodge the blow by using the body as a shield. The man's blade struck the corpse, and Rufus hurled it at him to throw him off balance, pulled out his sword and skewered him through the armpit.

With relief, he saw the helmsman return with other men who rushed to replenish the now thinned ranks of the defenders, knots of whom were fighting scattered battles about the deck. Momentarily freed from the need to defend himself, Rufus ran between his men and their opponents, shouting at them to get back in line and close ranks, but he saw that almost all of them had sluggish reflexes and moved with difficulty, and they seemed unsteady on their feet. He managed to get only ten behind him, while the others continued to retreat under the relentless blows of Pompey's men, who were balanced and more energetic.

At this rate, the enemy would take the ship and the battle would be lost. He saw one of his men leap into the sea to escape an opponent's sword, while another ended up entangled in the rigging, where he was stabbed in the abdomen before he could defend himself. If they had been on dry land, he would have called for a tactical retreat, but there was nowhere to fall back to. Suddenly, the deck was lit by a flash of fire, followed immediately by a thump which testified that a projectile had landed on the nearby trireme. Immediately the combatants on the deck froze, their attention seized by this new light: the ship next to them had caught fire, and the few remaining men on deck were unable to put it out. Rufus heard an order to retreat, followed by an attempt by some of their opponents to fight their way back to the *corvus*. Some found no opposition and managed to get to the boarding bridge right away while others continued to fight to free themselves.

Rufus shouted to his men to take advantage of their numerical superiority to eliminate those who were still on the deck, but they looked exhausted and just stepped aside to let them pass. He shouted and yelled, then he tackled one of the last to escape, killing him with ease, but it was pointless: his men were struggling just to stay on their feet. He watched their opponents crowd onto the deck of their trireme and throw themselves into putting out the fire, and consoled himself by thinking that at least from them they had no more to fear. He took the opportunity to go to the bow and climb the tower. Once at the top, he realised that his ships were having to defend themselves not only from the enemy, but also from their fellows: the waters were even more crowded than before, and there was no room to manoeuvre. Pompey's men could carry on boarding them, and had just discovered that his own men were too sick to fight.

He had to get out of there before it was too late. He

ordered his navarch to sound the retreat, then glanced up at the fortress on the promontory of Scilla. He knew that Octavian was watching, and cursed having to let him see the spectacle of his retreat.

*

Rufus had given the order to retreat. Which made him the loser.

Which made *him* – Octavian, the supreme commander – the loser too.

To tell the truth, he would have done the same in Rufus's place. And perhaps even sooner. In the situation in which he found himself, to continue the confrontation would only lead to a hopeless defeat, whereas if he managed to break free immediately, with the help of some of that positive propaganda of which Maecenas was capable of orchestrating, they could pass it off as a draw. But even as they withdrew, with the deliberation that characterized Rufus's quadriremes, there was always the risk of it ending in disaster. It was necessary to prevent those clumsy ships, moving like elephants in a forest, from being trapped in the narrow stretch of sea and offering themselves as sacrificial victims to the galleys of Sextus Pompey.

Fires were already visible. Vessels were burning everywhere, men engulfed in flames were throwing themselves into the water screaming, burning flotsam floated on the surface of the sea amongst half-submerged debris, and sparks danced through the air, setting light to the few sails still unfurled. The flames enveloped the triremes and quadriremes, but the latter moved slowly, which exposed them more to the risk of fire from the burning projectiles launched by the catapults on Pompey's ships.

Rufus wasn't going to make it. Even though his remaining ships were sailing toward the entrance to the strait, attempting to reach the bay where Octavian's forces were assembled, the galleys were at his heels and would soon be able to get alongside or ram them. In short, despite his decision, the battle was not over. Unless he intervened from the fortress. Octavian didn't have many throwing weapons available, but he intended to use them to the full. "Centurion!" he shouted to the head of the defence. "Load the catapults with boulders and the scorpios with incendiary projectiles."

The officer gave the order, and the soldiers in the battlements immediately crowded around the machines in small groups while others used tongs to take rags soaked in burning pitch and wrap them round the scorpio darts.

"Fire at the galleys closest to our own, and the ones behind them!" he shouted, and the centurion ordered the machines to be aimed in the direction the triumvir had commanded.

"Keep loading and firing until they are right below. Don't wait for them to get out of range!" Octavian shouted. If the chase continued, he wouldn't have another chance to prevent it. He waited with trepidation for the first launch, anxious to see what effect his orders would produce. Immediately afterwards, there were violent bangs followed by trails of light streaming across the sky in front of him. Faster than the rocks, the incendiary darts hissed through the air and fell onto the rear of Pompey's ships a moment before the rocks rained down just ahead of them, smashing the deck of at least one of the closest triremes. A projectile struck a sail, setting fire to it, and in a moment the flames had enveloped the mast and the stays, sending the ship off course. But it was at the rear of the formation, and caused little damage.

"Move the scorpios! Target further ahead!" cried Octavian, and the men obeyed. There was another launch of rocks, which again almost all fell in the water, sending up high waves. One rock struck a glancing blow to a trireme, smashing the handrail and sending two men to a watery grave. Then it was the scorpios' turn, the flaming arrows rained down more or less where the boulders had fallen, triggering two more fires. One ship was hit simultaneously by a stone and a dart, and began to take on water whilst fire spread across the deck, forcing the crew to jump overboard.

Meanwhile, the remaining galleys were alongside Rufus's ships, they too not hesitating to use their scorpios. One shot found its mark, hitting the sail of a quadrireme, which inevitably slowed, making it easy prey for the ram of its nearest enemy. It was struck in the stern, and Pompey's trireme attempted to throw down its *corvus*, but the grappling hook missed the handrail by a whisker and the archers on the quadrireme began firing at the men who were trying to pull the boarding ramp back up, preventing them from making another attempt.

Pompey, however, did not want to sound the signal of retreat. Apparently, even that pirate – who had given shelter to many outlaws fleeing from Rome – knew the propaganda value of defeating a triumvir, and was holding out in the hope of finishing off Rufus's fleet. And he would certainly be successful if the fire from the promontory of

Scilla eased.

"Fire! Fire faster!" shouted Octavian. He was beginning to panic, and started to worry that he might have one of his coughing fits. The soldiers strove to intensify the pace of operations, and the projectiles continued to rain down on Pompey's galleys. The problem was that most of them missed their targets and did not deter the determined pirate.

Another trireme was hit by two boulders, and the ship immediately took on water and began to sink. A little further along the same line, a ship's deck caught fire and the helmsman lost control, and soon a sort of bottleneck had formed behind the two wrecks: triremes began to pile up and collide with one another. It was exactly what they needed.

"Concentrate the firing in that area!" shouted Octavian, with all the breath he had left in his lungs. After a few moments for targeting, dozens of projectiles flew over the battlements, converging on the tangle of ships just as some of them were starting to break away. This time, inevitably, many more projectiles struck home, and horns began to blow the signal to retreat on Pompey's galleys. They veered toward the coast of Sicily, moving out of the range of Octavian's weapons, but no longer in pursuit of Rufus. Even the few remaining triremes diverted their course and sailed towards Charybdis.

It was done. He had inflicted enough damage upon the fleet of Sextus Pompey to pass the battle off as a draw. After all, in his first clash with Pompey the Great, even Caesar had suffered a defeat which he had painted as a kind of stalemate in his memoirs. But in reality, the cult of Mars Ultor had simply wasted time, and would not have another opportunity to take on Sextus Pompey in combat before leaving for Macedonia.

He had failed.

*

And another legion had left in turn for Macedonia. Agrippa had managed to engage the blockade of Staius Murcus and allow Antony's ships through. Thanks to the constant work of the archers he had been able to keep the enemies away from his ally's fleet as well as from his own. Yes, he had lost two ships when he had slipped between Murcus and Antony, but the damage to the others was limited: they were all seaworthy, although some were in pretty bad shape.

However, it was not over yet. Two other convoys were due to depart for Macedonia, and they had to make sure that Murcus no longer caused trouble along the coastal route around the Adriatic. For this reason, as soon as he saw Antony's ships reach the open sea, where they were now safely out of the blockade's reach, he had ordered the hoisting of the flagship's sails and headed for Murcus's base, where he had already sent an advance guard to take control of the port. On his return, the enemy commander would have an unpleasant surprise, and would be forced to find another place to dock, far from Brindisi.

Agrippa would have felt safer if he had part of his fleet with him, but he would still have had Murcus behind him in any case. He sailed fast, keeping a constant lookout for any ships behind them, and soon came in sight of the port. As they approached, he noticed that there were two galleys docked in the little harbour: he could only hope that his men had already taken control.

He slowed down considerably as he entered the harbour and studied the few buildings arranged along the three sides which enclosed it, the boats docked on the wharf and the two warships. It was unusually calm, even for a little port like that. It was usually full of people, or at least fishermen, but he could see no one. The oarsmen slowed their pace until they were barely moving and the ship came in under its own momentum and coasted slowly toward the quay. In the prow, Agrippa was still unable to detect any movement.

Suddenly, a cry from the bulwark called his attention. One of his men pointed to the side pier, and the young man briefly saw two figures running between buildings before disappearing.

Another shout made him look the other way. This time he saw three men running along the pier, one of whom was being chased by the other two. In an instant they reached their prey, ran him through with their swords and threw him into the water. The ship was now almost behind the docked galleys, and Agrippa distinctly heard the sound of blades clanging from the deck. He peered at the two ships until he could make out armed men fighting. One jumped down from the boat onto the quayside and fled among the buildings.

And suddenly it was clear what was happening: his men were still struggling to take the port. There were no people around because all the civilians had fled after the start of the battle.

Things, therefore, were not going to plan. And if Murcus arrived, they would lose the opportunity to take the base and would be forced to repeat the same risky manoeuvre with the next convoy, but with less chance of success, because now the enemy would know their tactics.

They had to take that port at any cost.

Agrippa was unsure of the situation on the ground as well as that aboard the triremes, though, and had no idea how many of his advance guard had survived and how many of the defenders were still able to fight. But he had no time to find out: he had to take the chance, go ashore and back up his men. There was a possibility they would fall into a trap and waste all the good work he had done at the port of Brindisi, yet if didn't act, he and Octavian's fleet would continue to run huge risks over the following weeks.

He decided to dock, and ordered the navarch to bring them alongside the trireme aboard which there was fighting. The men on the deck noticed his presence and there were shouts for help, while some enemy soldiers threw themselves overboard and swam to the shore, quickly climbing onto the quayside. Agrippa ordered his archers to shoot them, and soon all those who had escaped from the ship were floating in the sea with arrows in their backs. On the deck of the moored ship there were cries of triumph and the fighting began anew, this time with renewed vigour.

Before ordering his men onto the wharf, Agrippa asked one of the fighters for information. "What's the situation on the ground?" he shouted to him.

"There were more of them than we expected, sir!" replied the other man, breathing heavily from the effort of fighting. "But we're hunting them down one by one. Just when we thought we had the port under control, others arrived from the village behind. They must have been on leave, and were enjoying themselves with the local women.

They jumped us when we had just attacked the ships: we managed to take control of one right away, but the men in the other had time to react."

Agrippa nodded and gave the order to disembark. By now, the success of his men seemed a foregone conclusion. They had to weaken any resistance on land immediately, to avoid being caught between two adversaries when Murcus arrived. He reached the pier with twenty-five of his thirty men, but at that precise moment the watchman shouted that there were ships on the horizon.

It could only be Murcus, curse him! Agrippa ordered ten men back on board to help the captain find a way to move all the galleys so that they blocked the mouth of the harbour, and then divided the remaining men into three squads. He scanned the horizon, attempting to estimate how long it would take Murcus to reach the port, and then said, "Each squad take one part of the dwellings and provide assistance to our men, but be back here with the men you find in half an hour – I want you deployed on the pier!"

Then he set off at a run, ordering his squad to follow him, and they entered the narrow streets between the buildings. Once past the warehouses, they reached the houses of the small village and went straight towards the sounds of a struggle. In a small square, Agrippa saw two of his men trapped against the wall of a building, defending themselves against the same number of enemies. Agrippa rushed over, and the six of them swooped down on the two assailants, who found themselves surrounded with no time to flee, then impaled on more swords than their bodies could accommodate.

The two survivors thanked Agrippa for his

providential appearance, and told him that they knew where another group of enemies were holed up. They took him to the edge of the little town where, outside a circular temple dedicated to Hercules and surrounded by a garden of olive trees, Agrippa found eight of his men.

"There are fifteen of them inside, sir," said a soldier. "And there are too few of us to flush them out."

There was no time to lose, and now there were fifteen of them too. Two went to take oil lamps from the nearest houses, others to pull branches from the trees to make torches. Hercules and his father Jupiter would forgive them for that sacrilege: killing Caesar – the divine Caesar – was a far worse outrage, and he was only doing it in order to punish the killers.

He motioned to the men with torches to advance with him and burn the trees around the building while he and another man headed for the entrance. Crouched behind his shield, he passed his torch to one of his men and lunged at the door in an attempt to break it down. After three violent impacts he felt the hinges give. He took back his torch and kicked at the door, which finally gave way, then immediately threw the burning brand inside before backing off through the burning trees. They paused at the edge of the garden and waited. It was only a few moments before the men in the temple came out in a disorderly rush. One was on fire, and another was trying to put out the flames on the hem of his robe.

Agrippa blocked their escape route, forcing them to fight. They were outnumbered now, and their eyes were filled with tears. Some fell immediately, while others stood firm. From the position of the sun Agrippa deduced that half an hour had already passed, so he intensified his action, cleanly slicing off the arm of one opponent without bothering to kill him, then the leg of another, who fell to the ground and was finished off by one of his men. The survivors, at that point, dropped their swords and surrendered. Agrippa ordered everyone to follow him and bring the prisoners with them.

When they returned to the dock, they found many of their men and some prisoners awaiting them.

The young man looked at the harbour mouth. His ships were obstructing it, but just beyond them Murcus's triremes, with their pointed rams, were preparing to break through. Agrippa ran the length and breadth of the harbour, posting his men along all three sides: there were around two hundred of them, but if they spread out, it might look as though there were more.

They waited.

For a long time, nothing happened and there was silence, apart from the odd shout from behind him and the echoes of the fighting in the village. Murcus was clearly assessing the situation from aboard his ship. If he entered, he had easy game: his fleet, with all those armed men, was more powerful than the slim forces Agrippa had at his disposal, and Agrippa's control of the port and of the town was not yet complete.

Agrippa realised that he was sweating. A cold sweat. He tried not to betray his anxiety so as not to further unnerve his men, who were already trembling with fear. He heard some commenting on his plan, saying it was crazy. Perhaps it was, he thought, but Caesar had had many crazy plans, like that of crossing the Rubicon with a single legion.

And after a wait that seemed endless, he saw Murcus's

flagship turn and leave, followed by the others.

He had won. For the second time that day, he had won.

XVII

In the distance, a great cloud of dust was rising in the middle of the plain. Soon afterwards another cloud appeared to its side, and yet another appeared along the ridge of the adjacent hill. Salvidienus Rufus looked at Mark Antony, then at Maecenas, and shook his head: the scene presaged the same outcome as that of the previous day.

Before long they were able to make out the shapes of the riders out on patrol, and along with them they could also distinguish two enemy squads who were converging on the column and about to trap it in a pincer movement.

"Send out the Velites, now!" cried Antony, addressing the tribunes with himself, Rufus and Maecenas in the battlements of the fortified camp. He should have done that yesterday, Rufus said to himself, but he had acted too late, and his scouts had mourned many losses. They watched the movements of the column, which suddenly swerved to the left, seeking an escape route towards the sea.

One of the two squads following them turned in the same direction, while the other continued as it was. In the background were the two hills upon which Marcus Brutus and Cassius Longinus had built their camps, and in the middle the trenches which connected the two forts until they seemed to be one, vast stronghold

Inside those fortifications there were nineteen legions, and their commanders had been able to comfortably choose the best position possible for an army as powerful and fierce as that of Caesar's killers. If Brutus and Cassius decided to do battle now, Antony's forces, outnumbered and in an infelicitous position, would risk ending up like his scouts.

Antony's horsemen were not far from their fort. The triumvir had arrived a few days earlier on the plain of Philippi, just in time to reinforce the eight vanguard legions led by Norbanus and Decidius Saxa, before they were attacked by the enemy. If he had taken any longer to arrive, Caesar's avengers would have been forced to confront their opponents with at least forty thousand less men: the legates were, in fact, starving and stuck in the plain, at the mercy of the enemy, who would easily have had the best of them.

And because Brutus and Cassius had taken the best positions, Antony had decided he could put pressure on by occupying the hill closest to them, fortifying it right under their noses, and challenging them to stop him. But his arrogance exposed him to great risks, and Rufus had been in a cold sweat since he had arrived in Macedonia with Octavian's vanguard. Until the camp was completely fortified, their tactical inferiority was absolutely intolerable: Antony seemed to want to provoke the enemy into battle even before the other triumvir arrived to support them.

Suddenly, a realisation struck him: Antony wanted to cheat them, even if it meant being surprised by his opponents. Rufus looked over at Maecenas and was about to open his mouth when the Etruscan motioned him to be silent, indicating the battle taking shape before their eyes. Rufus made a gesture of annoyance: he could have seen what Antony was up to by himself, but instead Octavian, whom ill health had forced to remain on the coast of

Epirus, had decided to send him there with that damn fop. As though that weakling understood anything about military tactics...

But he couldn't help seeing what was happening beyond the fortifications. The manoeuvre Antony's horsemen were executing to escape the pincer had forced them into the swamp that separated the coast from the land, and their movements had abruptly slowed. Perhaps they hoped that the marshes would dissuade their opponents from following them, but it did not seem to have that effect. Indeed, they too had entered the marshland. Rufus saw the first spears flying against Antony's men just as the light infantry emerged from the fort to reinforce them. Two fell from the saddle and their bodies sank into the mud, disappearing instantly. The fugitives spurred their tired horses on, trying to get them back to solid ground, but their progress was painfully slow as they lurched and struggled through the swamp. One horse lost his footing and rolled over into the mud, trapping his rider beneath him. Two of the enemy approached them, the scout did not even have time to grab his shield: he drew his sword and tried to defend himself, but his opponents possessed spears and, after a few defensive swings, he succumbed to their lunges.

Meanwhile, the group were breaking up. The better mounted had managed to advance relatively quickly while others had been left behind, and it was upon them that the action of the pursuers was concentrated. The back of the column, now flanked on both sides, had resigned themselves to fighting: they turned their horses and began swinging their swords in turn, as they prepared for battle. But then they saw the slingers and spear throwers approaching on foot and paused, awaiting their arrival before counterattacking. Meanwhile, however, they were outnumbered, and Rufus saw many fall.

The slingers and spear throwers began hurling their projectiles at their opponents, many of whom were forced to slacken their pressure on Antony's horsemen. Some of the enemy horsemen, however, charged them in an attempt to break their ranks: Rufus saw one knocked off his horse by a stone just as he was about to reach the line of slingers. His companions hesitated, giving way to Antony's horsemen, who had finally joined the light infantry, to fight back.

At that point, the enemy were getting too close to Antony's fortifications, and decided their work was done. Their decurion shouted the order to retreat, and the horsemen headed off quickly, but some were hit from behind by further projectiles, fell from their horses and were finished off by the spears of those who, moments before, had been at their mercy. A dejected Rufus was contemplating the backs of the enemy horsemen: their retreat could not hide from the eyes of an experienced soldier that they had nonetheless achieved their purpose and prevailed in the battle.

Just like the previous day.

He could no longer contain himself. "What kind of position is this, triumvir?" he shouted to Antony. "They can do whatever they like to us. I thought you were supposed to be a talented leader?"

Maecenas tried to shut him up, but Antony was already responding. "What, must I even be taken to task by that brat's minions now? As though he himself weren't enough! What is it that you want, boy?"

Rufus saw red with rage, especially after being called that name. "Even a 'boy', triumvir, would have adopted a more astute tactic," he said, bluntly. "You knew that for the moment you had less men than Brutus and Cassius, but you decided to make camp practically right next to them. And if we don't hurry up and finish fortifying all the sectors, starting with the one along the marsh, our enemies will come as and when they want. It amazes me, in fact, that they have not yet done so!"

"You idiot! Our strategic situation is complicated, and we can't hold off doing battle just because your master has a tummy ache..." quipped Antony. "We must fight now, I cannot wait until it is convenient for Octavian. I told him that he wasn't up to facing the demands of a campaign. And now I have to fight without his troops! If he would at least send them to me, but no – he holds onto them and doesn't allow us to use them! By the gods, why didn't Lepidus come, instead of that useless creature?"

"It's you who's trying to cause trouble, triumvir!" insisted Rufus, not at all intimidated. "All they need to do is rush down the slope – which favours them – and they can do for us as though we were unarmed, inside or outside the fortifications. And then, they can get firewood in the wooded hills on their side, while we have only the marsh available: we will never fortify it properly. And they can also draw water from the river, while we have to dig wells. And if that's not enough, they get their supplies from Thasos, which is right here, while we get ours from Amphipolis, which is three hundred and fifty stadions away..."

At that point Maecenas took him by the arm and dragged him away from the battlements before Antony, who was the larger of the two, could lay a hand on him.

"I understand, triumvir, that your choice was dictated by necessity," said the Etruscan in a conciliatory tone. "The hill upon which you set the camp is the only one on the plain, and you could not place yourself any further away as the rains are likely to turn the whole area into a swamp. You were wise."

Antony's expression grew less grim. "That's right. Explain it to that idiot," he said, and turned to look away, once again ignoring Octavian's two emissaries as they climbed down from the battlements.

"What's wrong with you?" protested Rufus, when he and Maecenas were alone. "Don't you see that he wants to win without us? What if he loses? Why didn't you say anything? What damn use are you?"

"For reasoning." his friend answered, with ostentatious condescension. "That is why I'm here. Let us go straight back to Octavian, as soon as we can."

*

When the slave came to announce that Gaius Chaerea was at the door, Octavia was pleasantly surprised. She would never have expected the centurion to come and visit her on his own. And while her husband Marcellus was out, moreover. Then it occurred to her: he must have some news on behalf of the sect, for that was the only thing which could have induced him to overcome his resistance. She felt disappointed, and at the same time curious. What was so important that it could have induced him to come personally, without delivering the message via some courier? She had the little Marcella taken into another room and prepared to welcome him.

She spent more time putting on her makeup and coiffing her hair than she would have for any other guest, realising only when she was ready that perhaps Gaius had urgent news to report to her and that further delay was not appropriate. Although the centurion had already chosen his own family over her and had practically left the sect in order to avoid coming into contact with her, Octavia still had the unreasonable belief that she exercised a powerful influence on him, and she would not give up the opportunity to test him even in these circumstances. She knew it was wrong – that she shouldn't do it and that it caused him great suffering, but she couldn't help it: that was her battle, and she would fight it all her life for the only man she had loved.

She had always dedicated herself to others. Well, in this, at least, she would put herself first. She and Gaius had saved each other's lives only a short time before: if that was not a sign that the gods blessed their union, she could not see what would be.

When he was brought into the *tablinum* where she was awaiting him, the usual clutch in her stomach confirmed that she would never give up trying to win him back. He bowed his head deferentially, trying to maintain a respectful and aloof attitude, but said nothing.

Even Octavia was silent for a few moments. Then, seeing that he was waiting for her to speak first, she decided to break the ice. "News from Greece, dear Gaius?" she said, getting up from her couch and taking a step toward him.

Just one step, for the moment.

"It's still too early for that, my lady," he replied evenly.

"But, we can at least say that Octavian and our ministers have managed to pass our enemies' blockade of the Adriatic unscathed. We know only that they landed without major difficulties on the coast of Epirus, despite your brother falling ill during the journey. But it is nothing serious. Now there are only two legions stationed in Brindisi awaiting boarding and we will have the numerical superiority over Caesar's murderers."

She moved imperceptibly closer to him. "I hope that everything goes well. Antony is certainly a commander of higher quality than Brutus or Cassius. But you..." she said. "I see that you still speak of 'we': you still feel yourself part of this sect, then?"

"Of course," he said, looking away as she approached. "I no longer agree with its methods, but its goals are still mine."

"I thought you had withdrawn because of me. And instead it is because you dislike the methods?" she said innocently, close enough now for him to feel her breath on his face. She sensed confusion in his eyes.

"I... There were many things that led me to leave..." said Gaius hesitantly, visibly uncomfortable.

She maintained her composure. If she really wanted him she would have to force the situation unscrupulously, overcoming the feelings of guilt which always oppressed her.

"But you are not convinced, are you?" she pressed him.

"I am, yes." But the tone of his voice said otherwise.

"Why do you repress what you feel?" Octavia hardly recognised herself – she hadn't realised that she was capable of being so shameless. "Why suffer so much? I know you are not happy."

"But I wouldn't be happy even if..."

She put a finger to his lips to shush him, and moved her face close to his, removed her hand and kissed him. He stepped back a little but didn't pull away. She took advantage of their nearness, and when she put her lips to his for the second time, Gaius did not flinch. Octavia was the first to open hers, and he followed suit, docile at first, then with growing enthusiasm, until he finally put his hands round her waist.

Happily, she threw her arms around him and jumped up onto on him, putting her legs around him like a child. Large as he was, the centurion could more than cope with her weight.

Octavia began to kiss his face – breathless, enthusiastic kisses, from forehead to chin, running her fingers through his hair as he shifted his hands to her thighs and then to her waist and breasts.

Panting, she broke away for a moment to say, "I'm so happy that you finally decided to come here to me. Don't you see that we belong together?"

He looked at her quizzically. "But it was you who called me ... " he said, his breathing equally laboured.

"No, I didn't call you. Didn't you come here to announce our arrival in Greece? Or was it just an excuse to see me?"

"No... I... I was not going to come here. But I was told that you wished to speak to me and..."

They looked at each other questioningly, both undecided as to whether to continue in their effusions or investigate the causes behind their meeting.

At that moment, a glint behind Gaius caught Octavia's eye. She screamed instinctively, the centurion spun round, and she saw her husband emerge from the door that connected the *tablinum* to the library brandishing a dagger. The blade swung a palm's width from the officer's chest, before Gaius managed to seize the attacker's wrist. Octavia watched the brief scuffle and its predictable outcome: Gaius was so strong and experienced that he easily overcame Marcellus. He twisted her husband's arm, causing him to emit a strangled cry, before realising with whom he was dealing and standing paralysed by shock. He let go of Marcellus's arm, but only after taking his knife from him.

Octavia was appalled. Gaius stepped between her and the senator, putting himself in front of the door to the hallway to prevent him from leaving. "This explains why I'm here..." said the centurion finally, addressing both of them.

Only then did Octavia realise that it had been her husband who had drawn Gaius into a trap. Marcellus, in the meantime, looked away, his face full of resentment and shame.

"Why did you want to kill him, my husband?" she asked.

The senator paused again, then looked into her eyes. He was bullish as always, only more listless. "Do you need to ask? I have had enough of you two... Do you think I do not know about your son?"

Octavia flinched. "How... how did you know?"

"I did some investigating. I had you followed to the Suburra when you went to see him, months ago, and forced the companion of Gaius to tell me the truth, on threat of the child's life. I knew that you had never loved or respected me, but that discovery removed any scruple..."

Octavia saw Gaius wince at learning that Fabia had been threatened. The centurion seemed about to attack him, but he managed to contain himself. "You spoke to my wife?" was all he said, albeit in a threatening tone.

"Yes, but it doesn't matter – she wasn't harmed in the slightest," Marcellus said, with a shrug. "I only forbade her to inform you."

"You wanted to kill us both?" asked Octavia, who had an unpleasant feeling.

Marcellus said nothing and looked away, and his attitude was eloquent. As much as it hurt her, she decided to press him. "And perhaps this isn't the first time you've tried, is it?"

More silence.

Gaius realised what she was implying. "So you have the deaths of Atia and Etain on your conscience."

Marcellus took a few moments too long to answer, and when it came, his denial was unconvincing: it was practically a confession. The man, thought Octavia, was not even capable of lying. Gaius was trembling with indignation, and she felt her eyes filling with tears for her mother and her maid. And for the fate that Marcellus would have had in store for her, if Veleda and Agrippa had not saved her. She had to wait for the lump in her throat to pass before she was able to utter a word again. But Gaius got there first.

"You caused a massacre... out of revenge?" he said.

"I... I did not want all those deaths," blurted out Marcellus, whose voice had grown querulous. "It was the Republicans' fault..." He, too, began to cry.

"Explain. And you had better talk now," urged Gaius. "You'll pay for this, you know that?"

"That will depend if you co-operate," intervened Octavia. "My brother does not want a scandal in the family, nor more deaths. Not unless you force him. Co-operate and perhaps you will be safe," she said, conscious of the need to not scare him too much if they wanted to obtain any information.

"Your brother?" Marcellus said, defiantly. "Your brother is in Greece, and might lose at any moment..."

"And he might also win. Indeed, that is the most likely thing. But if he does lose, I will kill you," said Gaius. "Speak," he added, and this time drew his sword and pointed it at the man's throat.

The senator hesitated, then decided. "Well... the supporters of the liberators knew how I felt, and had been trying to persuade me to do something for them. After discovering your child... I was furious, and I decided to collaborate. They put me in touch with Quintus Labienus, and he got me to tell him where you would be..."

"And to get back at me, you had all those people killed?" asked Octavia, her face now bathed in tears. "Even your mother-in-law? What had my mother to do with all this?"

Marcellus looked down. "I... They had assured me that they would eliminate only you. It was to serve as another warning to your brother, after the assassination of Quintus Pedius."

Octavia could contain herself no longer, and slapped her husband with all her strength, releasing a cry of despair as she did so. It occurred to her that Octavian had left without being able to find out who in the sect had revealed the hiding place of his family to his enemies, and despite having him appointed consul to replace Quintus

Pedius, had marginalised Lucius Pinarius, assuming that it must be him. Her brother had confided in her before going to Sicily, and her cousin had come to visit her often to complain of being sidelined, despite his institutional role and their relationship.

Well, there *was* a traitor in the sect. It was her own husband, who did not even know of the association's existence, but had plotted against his own family. Octavian had gone to war undermined by doubt, feeling little confidence in his closest collaborators and putting to one side a resource which could be valuable in this moment, when they had already lost two recruits. She had to let him know what was going on. Her brother could not face a decisive pitched battle without the knowledge that the cult was firmly under his command. That would be the most active contribution that she could give the Mars Ultor. Even if it meant making a gesture that, for her, was the greatest of sacrifices.

She took Chaerea by the arm and pulled him aside so that her husband could not hear. "Gaius, I must ask you a favour," she whispered.

*

Octavian would have given anything not to be feeling ill just then. He cursed himself, and cursed the frailness which would never allow him to emulate Caesar and become the most important leader in the history of Rome. He didn't often feel sorry for himself: there were Agrippa and Rufus, and their victories were his, because they were a group that had him as its banner, its heart and its reason for existing.

But in that moment he would have gladly have given up

their help for a little bit of good health. He could not bear to admit that Antony, who would love nothing more than to shout from the rooftops that he was unfit for military campaigns, was right. Certainly the triumvir was gratified by his illness, considering as he did Octavian's presence in Greece counter productive. Octavian hated helping Antony discredit him and he wanted to reach the field of Philippi, where the bulk of the army was quartered, as soon as possible, but in the condition he was in, it would provide Antony with further opportunities to mock and humiliate him. Nor did he want to send his troops on ahead, which would mean risking total exclusion from any victory.

No. Antony would have to wait until he recovered, he told himself as he drank the infusion of herbs that his new doctor Astorius had given him. The other triumvirs had to wait for him, even if it meant losing the army of Caesar's killers. In any case, it all depended on Antony: for all he knew, his opponents were in no hurry to fight – indeed, it was in their interest to delay. Since his landing on the coast of Epirus, Octavian had been informed of the plight of the troops, short of supplies and cut off from communications with Italy by Staius Murcus and Domitius Ahenobarbus's fleets in the Adriatic. Not to mention the need to put an early end to the campaign and take part of the legions back to Italy, thus preventing Sextus Pompey from taking advantage of its poor defences to invade and take control of it.

As soon as he recovered, he and his ministers would claim the credit for the final victory over the murderers of his father, whoever had actually been responsible for it. Even if it was Antony. That was part of the reason he had made peace with him: to be able to use him as a battering ram with which to break down the resistance of his opponents and as an unknowing assistant in his revenge and his rise to power. And then, once the campaign was successful, Maecenas would find a way to downplay his period of ill health. Because nothing is stronger than a victory, and no one ever questioned the words of a winner.

Light filtered suddenly through the flap of the tent, dazzling his half-closed eyes. The silhouettes of three figures were outlined against the light, and gradually took on the appearance of Agrippa, Maecenas and Rufus. For some reason, the presence of all the ministers of Mars Ultor comforted him: after excluding Lucius Pinarius from any future meetings, he liked to think that the demands of war were bringing closer together what remained of the sect after the last, painful losses. Including the partial defection of Gaius Chaerea: he had made a compromise with the centurion that he would remain at the service of Mars Ultor with the sole task of watching over his relatives back in Italy.

But when he was finally able to see the faces of his friends, he knew immediately that there was nothing to rejoice over.

"Things are looking bad, Octavian," began Rufus, who seemed particularly agitated.

"We came here as fast as we could – we nearly killed the horses," added Maecenas. "But I cannot guarantee that all hell hasn't broken loose in the meantime."

"What do you mean?" asked Octavian, feeling a sweat break out in addition to the one he already had because of the fever. The doctor hastily laid a wet cloth on his forehead, but he threw it aside. He did not like looking frail in front of his subordinates, except for Agrippa, who had seen him in his most embarrassing moments as a child.

"Antony wants to fight before you arrive, there's no doubt of it," continued the Etruscan.

"He intends to take all the credit for the victory," said Rufus, "and, moreover, make you look ridiculous by showing that you have been completely useless."

"Is he mad?" cried Agrippa. "He's outnumbered! He hasn't got our troops yet!"

"For that matter, he is also at a disadvantage from a tactical point of view," said Rufus. "The slope of the land goes against him and he has problems with supplies. And he can't even find the wood to complete the construction of the trenches."

"I doubt that will stop him," objected Agrippa. "He has great confidence in his own abilities…"

"What do you know about it'" said Rufus, sounding increasingly irked. "You've never faced serious enemies and you've never faced important tactical problems. But that doesn't mean that other people haven't…"

Octavian wanted to kick Rufus. In that moment the stakes were high, and he was griping about the recent battles he and Agrippa had fought. He had tried to stop his friend's defeat from weighing upon him, but Agrippa's success hung like an indelible disgrace upon Rufus's head.

"Staius Murcus is no idiot, as he is proving now that no ship can sail the Adriatic without being intercepted by him and Domitius Ahenobarbus," said Agrippa, resentment audible, for once, in his voice.

"Do you want to compare him with Sextus Pompey? He is of the same calibre as his father as an admiral – indeed, perhaps even better! And I had the tactical disadvantage of having to operate in a very narrow stretch of sea!" protested Rufus, unwittingly admitting that Agrippa had been right when he had warned him against using quadriremes in the Strait.

"Silence!" muttered Octavian with the little strength that remained to him, before immediately being overcome by a fit of coughing. "We are not here to waste time bickering!" he continued, when he was again able to express himself. "I want to know the situation on the ground. Speak, Maecenas."

The other two were silent. The Etruscan cleared his throat and said, "It is with his apparent tactical and strategic, as well as numerical, inferiority that Antony hopes to lure Brutus and Cassius to attack. He is camped almost beneath them and his fortifications are still in a precarious state: it is clear that he is trying to provoke an immediate clash, and not simply because he is worried about the lack of supplies. He wants to cut you out, even if it means fighting with less legions and less chance of winning."

"So if he loses, he will claim he was forced to take the field without us so as not to let the enemy escape and avoid running out of supplies. And he will blame you, Octavian, for the defeat..." added Agrippa. "In any case, we will probably lose any chance of avenging Caesar. I am sure that, after having discredited us, he will eventually come to some agreement with Caesar's murderers."

"And if he wins, he will take all the credit and, with the prestige gained, will do everything possible to force you out of the triumvirate, blaming your inadequacies," echoed Rufus.

Octavian nodded. It was clear to all what was

happening.

"So I'm done for," he was forced to admit, "whether Antony wins or loses."

"Exactly," echoed Maecenas. "Unless…"

"Unless?"

"Unless you set off immediately for Philippi with the whole army."

Octavian looked at him in amazement. "But… Can't you see the state I'm in?" he mumbled.

"I can see it all too well. But you have no choice. He will not wait for you, and now you must risk. We are at the reckoning – it is what we wanted and we cannot throw everything away now, you must see that."

Astorius, the doctor, broke in: "He is absolutely not fit to travel, let alone to stand at the head of the legions."

"I… I'm also afraid to let myself be seen like this. What would the troops think of me?" hesitated Octavian. Yet he knew that Maecenas was right: he had no choice. Better death on the field than ending up being shamed by Antony and deprived of his revenge.

"We shall make sure that they do not see you," said the Etruscan. "And you will not be present at the battle. On the other hand, you *cannot allow yourself* to die, Octavian: you have too much to do, as I have said many times. There is no need for you to risk your life on the battlefield. Antony will take care of that for you, you'll see: I have an idea…" he concluded cryptically, before urging Agrippa and Rufus to give instructions to the troops for their immediate departure.

XVIII

Agrippa could have sworn that, for a moment, an expression of annoyance crossed Antony's face at the sight of Octavian and his staff appearing with the praetorian cohort. But then the triumvir gave a forced smile and strode off to greet his colleague and take his hands.

"So you've come at last!" said Antony, as he approached. He was on foot, but looked in any case more impressive than Octavian on horseback. "But you still look unwell, my friend. Was it wise to rush here? Were you afraid that I would take all the glory for myself? Is that what your errand boys told you?" he concluded, looking at Rufus and Maecenas, who were walking by their leader's side.

"Or perhaps I... came to save your arse. If you had... attacked, you would have... cut an embarrassing figure... and ruined everything, even... my chances for revenge..." shot back Octavian, but his broken voice, slurred words, hunched shoulders and foggy gaze demonstrated beyond a doubt that he was in no position to play the braggart.

In fact, Antony gave him such a contemptuously superior smile that Rufus bridled, putting his hand to the pommel of his sword. "In your condition, I doubt that you're much use for anything, boy," snapped the consul. "In fact, you might even make things worse. The best thing for you would be to get yourself off to your tent: if the soldiers see you in this state they'll start asking themselves who they are fighting for and lose heart. Unless you've come to give me your legions... In that case, I'll be happy to accommodate your lieutenants in my staff and put them under my orders."

"I've no intention of giving you anything," said the young man. "My men obey my orders alone. And do not dare take any initiatives without consulting me, as I am certain you were planning to do."

"So what exactly would you like me to do?" asked Antony. "I had almost managed to flush them out, but with the arrival of your troops, they'll head back to their holes and sooner or later we'll have to retreat to avoid starvation, without having achieved anything."

Agrippa allowed himself to step in before his leader at that point. On the basis of the information he had received from Maecenas and Rufus, he had developed an idea of the situation, and when the Etruscan had asked him to draw up a strategy to buy them some time and let Octavian recover, an idea had begun to take shape in his mind. On the way there and while Octavian and Antony had been speaking, he had been studying the battlefield. Brutus and Cassius's positions were unassailable, situated as they were in a high, well defended position, and, joined by the causeway that linked them, they made up a fortress the size and width of which made it impossible to besiege without the risk of being attacked from behind in one sector of the battlefield while you were trying to attack in another. On the other hand, the plain was all slime and mud, a slippery and treacherous terrain that did not allow anyone – infantry *or* cavalry – to get up enough momentum to climb the slope where the enemy were perched.

But if Brutus and Cassius were unassailable, they could perhaps still be flushed out, and in a less reckless way than that adopted hitherto by Antony. A quick glance over the plain of Philippi had, in fact, confirmed Agrippa's assumptions: the presence of marshes along the southern side of the two fronts could be an advantage for them. Over there, just on the other side of them, there was the sea, with all the most immediate supply routes. "So let's make sure that they suffer from hunger too, and have to come down to the plains to fight a way through for their supplies," he said, suddenly.

Everyone looked at him, but it was again Antony who spoke.

"Bravo! You are a *genius*! Why, nobody had thought of that!" Then he turned to his legate Norbanus "Does it seem reasonable to you that I have to play nurse to these children? It's like being at military school with know-it-all students who think they know more than the teacher."

"You've already thought about blocking the swamp, then..." said Agrippa, not at all abashed.

"The swamp? Why should I block the swamp?" growled Antony. "It's no use to us – and anyway, how do you intend to do it?"

"No use? If we cut off their access to the sea we could starve them out."

"Oh really? To do that we would need to get over to Cassius's camp, which is practically impossible: he would do everything in his power to stop us as soon as we began! Not to mention that we have no wood available for fortifications. And anyway, they would just withdraw and go round us..."

"No, he wouldn't: from what I know, there are gorges behind them. It would be difficult to get to the sea that way, and he would be forced to come down and fight."

Antony sighed dismissively, and said, "The fact remains

that we cannot build fortifications along the marsh. We are too close to their field and their archers and spears." But Agrippa was ready with the idea that Maecenas had come up with when he had suggested closing off access to the sea. He too had encountered the same problem as Antony, and now that he had made an inspection of the ground he realised that his plan was feasible, thanks to the Etruscan's suggestion. They really were a good team, and Octavian had been a genius to put them together. "The marsh is full of canes, Triumvir. We will cut only those necessary to create a road which will gradually lead us to the enemy camp with a parallel fence which we will man with many soldiers, adding fortifications as we go. The work and the presence of the soldiers will be hidden by the tall canes, and the enemy will notice only when it is too late to prevent us from closing off its access to the sea."

Antony and his lieutenants looked at one another. The triumvir was visibly uncomfortable: you could see he wanted to oppose the idea with all his power, but could find no valid reason to do so. Finally he turned back to Agrippa and said, "It won't work. It would cost us a lot of men. And anyway, I've already told you – we have no timber."

Agrippa had an answer ready for this too. "Well," he pointed out, "during the work each day, you deploy your troops on the plain ready for battle, with all the emblems in sight so the enemy thinks you have the whole army on the field. Instead, a portion of each cohort will be devoted to the work."

The gleam in his eyes that showed that Antony did not scorn the idea, but neither was he willing to endorse it openly. "Even if we did... What about the wood for the fortifications? You don't want to make them out of canes, surely?"

Agrippa hesitated a moment, then looked around himself, hoping to see something that would give him an idea for solving that problem. But Rufus intervened. "We'll use those stones sticking out of the ground. There's plenty of them. We'll make dry stone walls instead of a fence. Anyway, we can always get to the woods on the hills on the other side and deploy the army to protect the transport of the wood. They wouldn't be able to see what we were doing until the forts were already built."

The silence that followed was a clear agreement. Agrippa was pleased again, and felt no discomfort that it had been Rufus who had found the solution to the problem: he was the first to rejoice when the cult of Mars Ultor proved itself to be a cohesive team.

"But we'll use half of my men and half of yours," said Antony. "I don't want to lose all my soldiers if something goes wrong."

"So be it," said Octavian.

"And there's no room on the hill for your camp," the triumvir added, "so you will have to build it on the slopes or on the plain."

"That's nasty, and dangerous," thought Agrippa. There was a bit of space on the hill, but it was clear that Antony wanted to expose them, perhaps to use them as bait, or perhaps in the hope that in an eventual battle their opponents would concentrate on Octavian's camp and leave his in peace. If he won and at the same time Octavian fell ill, that would be cause for great celebration for Antony...

He was about to reply when he saw his friend Maecenas

323

give him a nod of assent. He hesitated, and the Etruscan said, "Very well. We'll set up along the slight elevation of the land further north," he said, pointing to an area of the plain just beyond the hill which housed Antony's camp. Agrippa asked himself what Maecenas was thinking, but decided that he must undoubtedly be following one of his convoluted and tortuous plans...

*

When Gaius Chaerea had agreed to carry out the task which Octavia had assigned him, he had known very well what awaited him. He knew that he would run the risk of dying and never seeing her or his own family again, and also that he would have to face danger from the moment he set sail from Brindisi.

But he had accepted it just the same. To please Octavia, not to prove himself worthy of the vow he had made before Mars Ultor, and to have the courage to look his son Marcus in the face in the future. Now, however, after seeing Staius Murcus's impressive fleet of warships surrounding the transport ships on which he was traveling, he had grave doubts about being able to complete the task that – and on this he was in agreement with Octavia – could prove crucial for the survival of the sect. He hadn't known that Octavian suspected any of his followers after the massacre that had involved her mother and Etain, but realised now what a fool he had been not to have: it was only logical. Perhaps the triumvir had even suspected him, and perhaps that was why he had not insisted upon taking him along on the campaign. When Octavia had told him, he realised that nothing was more vital than that his leader knew the truth. Not only would that give them back their unity, on the eve of his most important ordeal, but it would also restore his honour, which bore the stain of a reasonable suspicion.

In any case, it looked as though an unavoidable catastrophe was now on the cards. Two legions, including his own, the Martia, a praetorian cohort and four squadrons of cavalry – all intended for Octavian and perhaps decisive in the confrontation with Caesar's killers – were likely to disappear somewhere in the Adriatic without ever having managed to even set foot on the shores of Epirus. He looked in the direction of the flagship, wondering what the intentions of their commander, Domitius Calvinus, were. Calvinus, unfortunately, had never been a great general: he had been rapidly defeated by Pharnaces of Pontus, who Caesar had soon after eliminated in the blink of an eye. If Agrippa had been in his place, he would have known what to do despite his young age. In Calvinus, however, Gaius had little confidence: the fact alone of not having brought along a sufficient number of galleys to protect the transport fleet spoke volumes about his inadequacy as an admiral.

And there was not a breath of wind. Even assuming that the commander gave the order to escape before the blockade closed its grip and that the heavy transport barges managed to escape Murcus's agile triremes, their vessels would be going nowhere with only oars and without the assistance of sails.

They had to fight.

The number, ability and training of the soldiers of the two legions distributed on the transport ships would have re-assured any commander faced with an enemy fleet:

more than ten thousand men, mostly veterans, made up an army which was hard to defeat in any circumstances. Unless they were loaded onto practically immobile transport ships, at the mercy of warships which could ram and destroy them before the legionaries had the opportunity to board the enemy vessels. It was as though they were on a series of islands with no defences, surrounded and under attack from all sides, targeted by dozens of throwing machines and archers.

The triremes began to move, converging on the area of the sea occupied by the transport fleet, and Gaius realised that they could take advantage of their manoeuvrability to dart between one barge and the next, ripping open their sides, breaking their oars, firing at them from close range and sending them crashing against each other, until in no time at all they would be just a collection of wrecks.

Unless…

Unless Calvinus gave orders to all the oarsmen to move the ships side by side and form a single line, like the wall of shields of a phalanx. A tactic which, if nothing else, would protect the sides of the ships and give the decks enough stability to provide the soldiers with a solid platform from which to execute their boardings before their opponents did.

But Calvinus was not equipped with enough imagination to come up with such a tactic. Gaius had to find a way of suggesting it to him.

And of achieving it. It was no easy feat to line up a fleet which was already under pressure and without the propulsion required to perform manoeuvres. Gaius knew nothing about seamanship, but even he knew enough to realise that they were in deep trouble, and the first impact confirmed this: two of Murcus's triremes attacked a barge a short distance from his, ramming it from both sides, and the trireme protecting that part of the convoy, which was obliged to cover too wide an area, just sat there watching, too far away to intervene and helpless in the face of the threats looming on all sides.

Gaius saw his fellow soldiers rolling across the deck and being thrown into the water, while the more determined attempted to hoist themselves up on the bulwark and throw themselves on the trireme's deck. He could only admire their courage: if they were to die, then they would do it fighting and taking with them as many opponents as possible. He decided that he would do the same, when it was his turn. Which, by the looks of things, would be soon enough.

Especially as no signal was forthcoming from the admiral.

The ship which had been rammed was already sinking, its stern submerged and its bow much higher than the enemy's deck, and the men who had sought safety in the part of the ship furthest from the water clung desperately to the bulwark until the bucking of the sinking vessel forced them to let go, when they slid across the deck and disappeared beneath the waves, some re-emerging in the midst of the debris, though more often disappearing without a trace.

The god Aeolus had it in for Caesar's avengers, it seemed. With a gust of wind, they would have had a chance, but as things stood they were virtually prisoners of the enemy. You could not even place all the blame on the shoulders of Calvinus, whose options had been limited from the start: there were no other routes he could take without running into the fleet led by Domitius Ahenobarbus, and he could not wait for a more propitious time to set sail without the risk of reaching Octavian too late or of running into an autumn storm and an inevitable shipwreck.

The two galleys responsible for the ramming freed themselves and set off to find new prey. It was easy for them – the barges were sitting targets, and the warships assigned to their defence could protect only a few, so their enemies threw themselves on the ships lacking protection.

And his was one of them.

He had only just realised this when he noticed that the prows of the two enemy triremes were pointed toward his ship. The captain ordered the oarsmen to pull harder and move them out of the way, and the helmsman to turn the bow towards the enemy boats to offer their rams a smaller target, but the two triremes began swinging outwards, preparing a converging manoeuvre, and there was no way of avoiding at least one of them ramming them in the side.

Gaius turned his gaze back to the flagship, and saw that it had veered towards Brindisi. More than half of the transport fleet was still in front of it, and its manoeuvre had broken up the convoy. What was happening was all too clear now.

Domitius Calvinus had decided to cut his losses and take home all the ships that were not yet within range of the enemy triremes. Sacrificing all those who were already at the mercy of Murcus.

Including him.

*

And so here he was, back in Macedonia and about to take part in a great and decisive battle between his commander and his rival, Ortwin said to himself while he cut yet another bundle of canes to clear the way for the engineers in charge of building the road through the swamp. Six years ago at Pharsalus he had been one of the protagonists in one of the greatest internecine battles – between Julius Caesar and Pompey the Great – and had believed that the victory of the future dictator would end the civil wars. But then there were the campaigns in Africa and Spain, the great battles of Thapsus and Munda, which gave only the illusion of renewed stability to the city state. When Caesar died it had all started again, and the war of Modena had begun. And now there was this battle looming at Philippi: there, where it had all started.

And he, Ortwin, had profited not at all from all those Romans slaughtering one another: at Pharsalus he had been Caesar's chief bodyguard, but now, at Philippi, he was just one of Octavian's lackeys and in no way indispensable. He knew that was what Veleda, who was by his side and busy, like him, cutting down canes, thought. And whilst at Pharsalus the supreme commander had given him decision making autonomy and a subordinate command, he was now forced to endure the company and authority of an individual as unpleasant as Popillius Laenas, nominally his equal in the sect but superior to him in the field thanks to his rank of centurion.

A fact of which Laenas never tired of reminding him.

The officer, as always, was barking insults at them. "Come on you barbarians, get a move on! It takes more than knowing how to fight to be like a Roman soldier – you have to know how to build too! And seeing how uncivilised you lot are, you'll never manage it, so we might as well use you as labourers! Come, get those canes piled up on the wall." He enjoyed humiliating them. But not only them: he tormented anyone under his command, from foot soldiers to *optiones*. With his superiors, on the other hand, from centurions to tribunes, Laenas was fawning. Caesar would not have put up with him, Ortwin said to himself, but Octavian was more pragmatic and valued people more for what they could offer than for their human qualities.

"He's the newest member of the sect and yet he treats you like a slave," whispered Veleda.

Ortwin shrugged, playing it down. "He's just another arrogant centurion. Do you know how many of them I've had to deal with since the days of Caesar?"

"But he is not just a centurion," she replied, "he is a follower of the sect – and he does not respect you."

"But he is useful to the sect, and therefore even if he is slow witted we will all put up with him. Even me."

"You're just repeating Octavian's words. You don't really believe that..."

"Stop your grunting, you two!" shouted Laenas. "There'll be time for that tonight in your grimy lair! Get to work. And I'll tell you what, to give you animals a sense of responsibility, I'm moving you to the final stretch of the road over there, under the enemy camp. That way maybe you'll work a bit harder. You too, stump face – hurry up!" He turned to the legionaries in the front line. "Go to the rear, you lot. You're changing places with the barbarians!"

Ortwin had promised himself that he wouldn't react, but the offensive reference to Veleda's impairment angered him. He walked towards the centurion with great strides until they were face to face, removed the cloth covering his missing eye to make his appearance even more brutal than it already was, and hissed, "I'm used to much worse than this, Laenas, and I can put up with the rantings and insults even of one like you. But speak disrespectfully of my wife again and they will be forced to expel me from the sect for having sliced one of its members open from his balls to the top of his head." He said it in a calm, flat tone, with the assurance of those who have seen it all.

For the first time, Laenas looked worried. The centurion looked away and instinctively stepped back, intimidated by his attitude. Ortwin was certain: all you needed to do with people like that was raise your voice. And if he had not done so until then it was because he feared the reaction of Octavian, who probably considered a one-eyed barbarian the most expendable of the members of the sect, in spite of all that Ortwin had done for him so far. Caesar had treated him very differently, but they were in no position to pick and choose: the dictator's young heir was all that Ortwin and Veleda had, after all.

The German gestured to his men to follow him and moved to the front line, aware of the danger that they would face: for the last ten days the men – mainly those of Antony, but those of Octavian too – had been working in the swamp, building the road as well as the fortifications. If the tall canes had hidden their operations from the enemy for the first week, as they approached the heights occupied by Cassius's camp their presence had become more visible, and for the last two days it had no longer been possible to conceal it at all. During the night, in fact, their enemies had hurriedly built counter-fortifications to prevent Antony's soldiers from going any further, leaving

Caesar's murderers a wide corridor allowing free access to the sea. Moreover, since the previous day, the easternmost end of the road and the fortifications in the marshes had been subjected to a continuous rain of bolts and projectiles of all sorts which their improvised canopies and screens could only partially block.

"You'd better hope for the best now, boys." The exhortation of the *optio* who commanded the retreating team confirmed his fears. The soldiers were carrying on their shoulders a legionary with an arrow in his armpit and holding up another with a mangled leg, the victim of a boulder thrown from a ballista. In Ortwin's opinion, Octavian would not be pleased to learn that the members of the sect had been so freely exposed to danger, but it would never have crossed his mind to go and complain to his lieutenants.

He reached the place where the road ended. To the sides and in front, as well as the canes still waiting to be cut, there were mobile siege engines and screens covered with fireproof material which bristled with enemy projectiles. He estimated the distance that separated them from the slopes of the hill occupied by Cassius. It was not far, but those last few steps would cost far more time and effort than had been needed for everything that had been achieved so far.

And now, because of Laenas, it was his, Veleda and his men's turn to pay that price.

He felt a thud followed by a vibration. An arrow had lodged in the screen in front of him. He looked at the canopy over his head and noticed that parts of it had been smashed by the boulders at his feet and that no one had dared repair it. He took a deep breath and ordered his men to move it slightly forward, thus freeing some space to extend the road at least up to the enemy's fortifications. He decided to use the stones hurled by their opponents to give the road some consistency, and began to dig around one of them to drive it in deeper. Meanwhile, his companions brought wheelbarrows full of earth which they emptied out next to him while others hastily shored up and compacted the edge of the road with other rocks, and further back, some auxiliaries threw bundles of canes into a dip in the road to fill it up. Ortwin imagined that a road built like that would cause many twisted ankles among the soldiers who could not always watch where they put their feet, and hoped he wouldn't have to use it to retreat. The purpose of the construction, as Agrippa had explained, was to frighten their opponents and force them down onto the plains for battle. It was unlikely that these fortifications would ever be put to the test.

"Fortunately," he thought, "because I doubt they would withstand an attack."

"I hope he dies," said Veleda, when she was next to him, gesturing behind them with her head. The reference to Laenas was clear. "In fact, one day I'll kill him myself."

"We will do *nothing* that might upset our leader," said Ortwin, slowly and emphatically, as he continued to dig.

Then he felt another impact, and then another. The screen in front of him shuddered violently, and the sound echoed throughout the protective structure around them. Another shot, this time over their heads, preceded by an instant the fall of a boulder that almost hit Veleda. Instinctively, she jumped back and Ortwin stood up and peered around the edge of the screen to see what was happening.

And saw something he never thought he would witness.

Dozens of men, racing like lunatics towards their position, preceded by the launch of projectiles and followed by hundreds, perhaps thousands, of their fellow soldiers.

The battle had begun. But not in the sector of the battlefield the leaders had envisaged. And he and Veleda were on the front line.

XIX

Within moments, the calm that had reigned around Veleda turned into chaos. From the slope of the hill above the earthworks swarms of soldiers were hurtling down towards them, and projectiles of every type rained down onto the swamp. Around her, the legionaries and auxiliaries who were almost at the foot of the rise threw down their tools, and in some cases even their shields, and abandoned their posts in a desperate attempt to reach the rest of the army.

She stood there in shock: could their leaders have not foreseen the possibility of the troops of Caesar's killers attacking from that side? But then she noticed that there were senior officers at the head of the enemy columns, and that they were not even organised into units – it seemed to be a spontaneous attack, with the legionaries in no particular order. Perhaps it was just a sudden attempt to stop the works to isolate the hill from the sea.

No one attempted to fight them off. Ortwin himself urged her to fall back, and together they ran along the road they had just been building, which was full of more and more fugitives as they raced towards the rear. It soon became almost impossible to advance along the embankment: people stumbled over the boulders used to hold it together, or, hit in the back by an arrow, fell, tripping up those behind them, while others elbowed their way past those in front of them and used the bodies of their fellow soldiers behind them as protection from projectiles, while others still wallowed in the mud, struggling desperately to climb out to safety and grasping at the arms and legs of their fellows to pull themselves out.

"To the fort! Run to the fort!" yelled Ortwin, grabbing her hand to try and prevent her from being overwhelmed by those more robust, heavily-armoured and crazed than her. He dragged her along, gesturing with his head to the nearest of the four forts that the soldiers had built along the road in the swamp, but a violent collision with a legionary made Veleda let go of his hand – she lost her balance and, buffeted by other fugitives, was hurled into the swamp. As she lay face down in the mud, she felt a soldier tread upon her back, and then another trample her thigh. She tried to rise but the pain of the blows and the density of the mud would not allow her. A hand grabbed her arm, and as soon as he felt herself being lifted up she instinctively reacted with her nails, scratching her aggressor's hand.

"Do you want to scratch out my other eye?" asked Ortwin, pulling her to her feet and even finding the strength to smile.

She shook her head, stepped back onto the road and set off again in the crowd. They were close to the first fort, but Veleda realised that it was already full of people and the entrance barred even before Ortwin pointed it out to her. They had to continue to the next one. Meanwhile, however, the enemy was approaching, and there was no guarantee that they would get there. Arrows continued to hiss through the air, though less frequently now: as their opponents grew closer, their archers were increasingly hesitant about firing.

The two Germans, followed by their men, circled the fort and continued along the embankment. The crowd was less dense, now, but they still had to fight to stay on their feet. Ortwin's companions managed to create a cordon around Veleda, obeying an unspoken order from their leader. She saw the profile of the second fort, but the legionaries in front of them were crowding into it, and she was afraid they would have to go even further. She turned for a moment, and from the corner of her eye saw their pursuers, or at least some of them, surrounding the first fort and attacking it from all sides. The defensive wall was only a little taller than two men one above the other, and the attackers were trying to climb it by piling stones from the embankment at the base and forming into tortoises.

She saw nothing more: her companions pushed her past and onwards towards the second fort. The doors were still open, but the flow of people trying to get in made it inaccessible. Some were punching their fellow soldiers to try and get in, and even the Germans had to fight to stop themselves from being pushed back, but the crowd that thronged the door allowed them to make little progress. Veleda turned and saw that the enemy were drawing nearer. She looked back towards the door that they would never be able to enter now. They were advancing one step at a time, while their enemies were running.

They had to fight. She drew her sword before her companions who, seeing her, followed suit. Ortwin did the same: it was pointless to continue to push at the soldiers in front of them and risk getting stabbed in the back by the enemy when they reached them. They were the last in the line, and they would be the first to face the column of men arriving. And just to allow the Romans to find shelter in the fort, she said to herself. She, saving Romans – utter madness! The Germans fanned out, some on the

337

embankment and others in the marshes, while she and Ortwin found themselves side by side in the centre of the road, and positioned themselves to face the first group of assailants, who were advancing toward them brandishing their swords.

The first swing was directed at her. Veleda raised her shield but Ortwin was faster, stopping the blow with the blade of his sword. He pushed the enemy's sword back, opening the Roman's guard and promptly piercing his chest with a powerful jab that ripped through the chain mail and penetrated the flesh.

Veleda gave her man an offended look. "Do you think I do not know how to take care of myself?" she shouted, before using her sword to block the lunge of another opponent. She tried to imitate Ortwin, swinging her blade to push aside the guard of the enemy, but he was strong and resisted, holding his sword hard against her shield. The woman screamed in frustration and threw another jab. The soldier blocked it with his shield, and she darted suddenly to her right, throwing herself towards the marsh. Swinging out over the edge, she stepped around her opponent just enough to flank him, then swung her blade, which fell on his shoulder with all its momentum.

Veleda fell to the ground at the very moment the shield of her enemy did the same. With the man's arm still attached to it. Ortwin found time to issue a whistle of approval, drowned out immediately by cries of pain from his adversary, from whose chest spurted copious amounts of blood. Veleda got up, covered from head to toe in mud and blood, and was immediately faced with another opponent, whose spear missed her by a whisker. She was still unsteady on her feet, and for a moment hoped that the other warriors of her squad would help her – but each of her companions was busy with their own battles.

As was Ortwin. She would have to take care of herself. The man jabbed at her again, without giving her time to recover her footing, and she fell again. The tip of the spear passed a finger's width from her side and rammed into the ground as she tried to get up. Suddenly an idea came to her, and she threw herself onto the shaft, using her weight to force it down and lever it out of the Roman's hand, then, rolling beneath him, she stabbed him between the legs before he could pull his sword from its scabbard. The man collapsed on top of her, but Veleda sprang out of his way and finally managed to regain her feet, ready to fight again.

But there was no enemy, for the moment. Before her, she saw other soldiers arriving from the first fort, which had fallen into their assailants' hands. To her side, the last members of the group they had faced were falling under the blows of the Germans. She noticed that their easy victory had been propitiated by the contribution of some legionaries who, instead of entering the fort, had stayed with them to offer them assistance.

Ortwin got rid of his opponent, assessed the situation, and then turned to the fort behind him. The last soldiers were passing through the narrow gap between the half closed doors, and even those who had been helping the Germans followed suit. The group of assailants advancing was larger than the one they had just defeated, and they would have no chance this time. Ortwin motioned to Veleda and his men to follow him; there was no longer a crowd in front of the entrance, and it seemed easily accessible. They approached the door while, behind them, the enemy column swelled and swiftly closed on them.

Veleda saw Popillius Laenas peer through the doors, and let out a sigh of relief. They could count on the assistance of another member of the sect to help them, at least for the moment. She increased her pace, hearing the steps of the enemy behind her, but at that moment the centurion pushed the doors shut.

They slammed closed in the Germans' faces.

*

"The ropes! Grab the ropes!" cried Gaius, seeing the two galleys that had targeted his ship approaching. He had been trying to find a way to create a barrier against the enemy attacks, and hoped that his idea was the right one: circumstances would give him no opportunity for another. The captain looked at him blankly, then ran over to him and shouted, "What are you doing, centurion? You're not in command here!"

"There's no time to respect rank," he replied. "You know that I am part of the General Staff of the triumvirate – we have to try to form a kind of fortress with the ships beside us so they can't hit our sides, and then together we can board them and take advantage of our numerical superiority."

"And how exactly do you reckon you're going to form this fortress?" said the other, sceptically.

"We throw ropes to the other ships and pull them together until we're side by side, forming a single row!" he explained.

The man shook his head. "Where do you think you are, on a battlefield? It'll never work: even if we do manage to pull them together, we run the risk of doing the enemy's work for him and smashing our own ships up before they do it with their rams!"

"So?" asked Gaius, angrily. "Do you have a better idea than sitting here waiting to be sunk, wasting the potential we have on these ships, with all the veterans we have aboard?"

"We just have to hope we survive the ramming. After that, we send our soldiers to attack for as long as the ship remains afloat... We have no choice."

Gaius had no time to lose, and interrupted the captain with a punch to the jaw that sent him sprawling, unconscious, to the ground. The crew looked at him suspiciously, but the legionaries nodded and some even managed a smirk of approval – the soldiers did not hold the sailors in particularly high regard. The centurion repeated his plan out loud, and all immediately accepted him as leader. In any case, he was not only the highest ranking officer aboard, but also one of the men most trusted by the triumvirate, and that conferred upon him authority over all those Domitius Calvinus had abandoned to the mercies of the enemy.

Gaius distributed ropes and split the soldiers into two teams, lining them up along the sides of the barge. He was the first to throw a rope, but missed the side of the nearest ship. Meanwhile, the triremes continued to approach, their threatening bows growing larger and larger, like two sea monsters about to seize them in their jaws. Others threw too, and some managed to reach the handrail. It had taken those on the other ship a while to understand Gaius's intentions, but the centurion saw that they were starting to busily grab the ropes and, in turn, other soldiers were rushing to the opposite side to do the same.

The legionaries on the decks began to pull, and very slowly the ships started to move closer to each other. Too slowly, given the speed at which the galleys were advancing. The gap next to Gaius's ship was still quite large, and the nearest enemy vessel would have no difficulty ramming their side.

"The poles! Get the poles!" shouted the centurion, and some men immediately rushed to grab the long poles used for docking. They pushed them out horizontally through the handrail until they reached the parapet of the other ship, and the new connection gave stability to the two vessels and speeded up the operation with the ropes, but now the trireme was too close and Gaius doubted they would be able to close the gap. He glanced at the opposite side of his ship, and saw that they were having the same problem. It would be difficult, if not impossible, to avoid being rammed.

He pulled the ropes with all his strength, and urged the others to follow suit, scraping the skin off his hands regardless of the fact that, if his manoeuvre was successful, he would soon need to wield a sword. The sides were closer now, but the bow of the trireme jutted towards that of his ship. "Come on! Pull! If you don't want to end up in the sea!" he shouted, bracing himself in anticipation of the imminent impact.

He continued to pull, but with his eyes on the trireme, like all the others. The gap was almost closed and the sides of the two vessels almost adjacent, but they were still some distance apart when the rising and falling bow of the trireme reached those of the two barges. It slipped between them, and immediately afterwards the deck of Gaius's ship was shaken by the impact, and then again. But it remained stable. The centurion tried to work out what had happened. He watched the trireme, and, seeing that it was sinking, realised that the narrow space had forced it to go straight, missing the rostrum of both barges and ending up being crushed between them, its light build unable to withstand the pressure from the heavy cargo ships.

The legionaries shouted with joy, and Gaius looked over to the opposite side. Over there, his manoeuvre was going even better: the trireme had found its way blocked and had to stop before reaching the barges. And they hadn't lowered their boarding bridge: the ships of Caesar's avengers carried a far greater number of soldiers, and boarding them would be suicidal for Murcus's men. They had to take advantage of that, decided Gaius. He waited for the momentum of the trireme to bring it close to his barge, then ordered the counter attack. The legionaries didn't need telling twice, for many were already climbing up on the bulwark, taking advantage of the higher deck of their ship to attack their opponent's deck below. Gaius jumped down too: he wanted to fight, and in that moment forgot that he was supposed to preserve his own life for the task that had been entrusted to him. And for Octavia, Fabia and Marcus.

He fell onto another legionary, almost impaling himself on the man's sword. He parried the blow with his shield, then swung one himself that connected with his opponent's forearm, tearing tendons and muscles up to below the shoulder, leaving it inert and dangling at his side, then moved on to another, while behind him more of his men jumped aboard. Yes, he felt that they were his now, and that it was he who was making the decisions for once, not the ministers of the sect for whom he had fought for the past two years.

His hand was burning from the abrasion caused by the rope and his arms ached from the effort, but he continued to swing his sword tirelessly and accurately, shouting out to give himself energy and momentum. He shot a glance at the sea and saw other triremes approaching what remained of the convoy. However, the transport ships were increasingly following his example and creating groups of boats which were anchored to each other. He hoped that Murcus would be discouraged and give the order to retreat, but then he saw that the few triremes of Caesar's avengers – a tiny group compared to that of the enemy – were about to be encircled, and were in no position to provide support to the rest of the fleet.

He judged that the enemy commander must have well over a hundred boats: too many for them to hope to prevail in the clash. They could only hope to resist, deploying closer to one another and letting the soldiers do what they did best: fight one-on-one. Then, night would come to put an end the conflict and, perhaps, even the wind, which would allow the slow cargo ships to break free and head for the coast of Epirus which was now nearby.

Suddenly, a flash of light caught his eye. A flaming projectile streaked across the sky just above his head, falling right onto his vessel. The deck immediately caught fire, and many of the sailors still on board jumped into the sea. But it was what he saw on the adjacent boat which shocked him most: the crew on the deck were rushing along the handrail pulling out the poles and cutting the ropes to break away from the burning ship.

So he couldn't even get back onto the barge from which he had come.

Popillius Laenas assessed the situation carefully, as a true commander should. It was just a question of holding out – sooner or later Antony's troops would come to the rescue of the men surprised by the enemy in the swamp. Until then, it would be he, and he alone, who co-ordinated defence operations.

He felt that he had developed a good plan. Those Germans out there had proven to be skilled fighters, and would form a bulwark against the enemy tide until Antony's troops had organised themselves. In the meantime, he would be able to prepare the resistance inside the fort.

He knew he should have let them in. They were followers of the Sect of Mars Ultor, and he was supposed to help them before all others. Octavian would certainly have demanded it. But once they had fallen, they would just be two more deaths in the battle, and none of the other members would ever know how.

And anyway, they were barbarians.

He would not have said so to Octavian, but he could not bear the idea of savages being part of such an exclusive sect. He had concluded that his supreme leader must have chosen them as labourers, and that they were expendable. Well, he was sacrificing them, to save the Romans of the sacred bond, who were much more important for implementing the projects of the ministers of Mars Ultor. The sect that he had in mind, and the perfect society that it would create at the end of its work, was to be composed exclusively of Romans, the only ones with a divine right to dominate other people.

He went up to the battlements and began to issue orders to all the *optiones* who had taken refuge inside the fort. "How many scorpios have we got? Distribute them evenly along the four sides. Actually, no: only put one on the side towards the marsh!" he shouted. "All on the battlements, come on! *Optiones*, distribute the men equally! Are there any archers? Slingers? Come forward! Get a move on with those scorpios, I still can't see them in the battlements! The door! Bar the door! You there, you're not doing anything – get some shovels, start digging in the centre and pile the earth in front of the doors."

Yes, he felt like a god, able to do to with the men what he pleased. He liked being a centurion, but he liked being in the sect even more – it was a position that would give him more opportunity to influence, or even determine, the fates of others, than that of an officer. He was no aristocrat, and would never be able to command great armies or take important political decisions like the senators, but through the sect he could say his piece and make history. It was so exhilarating that he had never before faced a battle with such excitement.

Having issued his first commands, he turned his attention to the situation outside the fort. The Germans were about to be overrun by the enemy. As brave as they were, they couldn't hold out for long, and it was good that his men were rapidly preparing for the assault. But then he saw the Germans spreading out and falling back along the two sides. He had been wrong, then – they were not brave, they were damned cowards who were of no use at all! And in fact they were now trying to save themselves by sacrificing the Romans, and even an adherent of the sect!

He felt a wave of panic grip his stomach, and his

exultation of a second before gave way to agitation. He grabbed the closest legionary by his scarf and unleashed all his frustration in the man's face. "What are you doing standing there like an idiot? Get a spear and prepare to throw it at the first enemy who dares touch this wall!"

The soldier looked terrified, but Laenas was already shouting at another. They needed scorpios to sow disarray in the ranks of their opponents. And they were not yet ready. If they left it any longer they would be useless, like any similar machine against targets which were too close or too low. "Slingers! Archers! I want you here, by me, damn you!" he shouted, cursing those Germans who had abandoned them, to himself. But he would make them pay.

He was soon joined by all the available archers and slingers, and looked at them in dismay. "Is that all?" he asked, regarding the twenty men. Nothing compared to the tide rushing towards the fort. He looked down for a moment, and saw that the soldiers were working hard to reinforce the doors with an embankment. "More legionaries with spears, here, come on!" he shouted. And while two teams put the available scorpios into place, he deployed fighters along the side that would be attacked first – the east.

"Scorpios ready, centurion!" shouted one of the operators.

"Ready, over here!" shouted another, near the second machine in the stands.

"So what are you waiting for?" he cried, hysterically. "The enemy to climb over the parapet? Fire! Fire!"

Immediately afterwards he heard two thuds almost in unison and the bolts flew over the battlements. He followed their trajectories into the mob before them. He had no way of knowing whether or not they hit their target, but the density of the fighters was such that there was little doubt about it. His men launched other projectiles, and this time he saw a man collapse, knocking over several of his fellow soldiers. "Shooters, wait until they are closer!" he ordered, leaving only the scorpios in action for the moment. But it seemed that the enemy tide had grown even denser and that the entire army of Cassius had descended upon the battlefield. He hoped with all his heart that Antony, who was responsible for the sector along the marsh, would intervene promptly.

The third scorpio arrived at the front of the fort, and set to work, but they were drops of water against a human sea. "Slingers! Fire!" shouted Laenas, and his men began to twirl their slings, launching the deadly projectiles which could pierce a helmet at a great distance.

"Archers! Your turn!" the centurion shouted now, and immediately arrows joined the stones flying from the stands. More drops in the ocean. The more enterprising of their enemies ran under the walls, where they were safe from the projectiles, so Laenas ordered his men to throw their javelins down on them, and some legionaries leaned out over the parapet to obey him. The spears struck the first to arrive, surprising those who had not been sufficiently prepared to protect themselves with their shields, while others were unbalanced by the impact, falling and ending up at the mercy of new projectiles. But there were marksmen in the enemy ranks too, and Laenas saw a legionary by his side, who had leaned out over the parapet, fall into space, his neck pierced neck by a *pilum*.

A second fell, plunging down after being stunned by an object the centurion was unable to identify, and at that

348

point the others became more cautious and stopped leaning out. "Cowards! You damn cowards!" cried Laenas. "Throw! Throw, like me!" and so saying he snatched a spear from a legionary, leaned out over the parapet and threw it down at two soldiers who were beginning to form a tortoise. His throw was so violent that, with the help of gravity, it pierced a shield and slipped into the shoulder of one of the enemy soldiers, sending him sprawling to the ground. Laenas remained standing there ostentatiously, holding out his hand for his men to pass him another spear.

They brought him two, but in the meanwhile his men had started throwing spears at the base of the fort again. "Good," he thought. "Nothing better than an example to inspire courage in the soldiers." And to hell with all the shit that their commanders had told them: that lot always made sure they were far from the front. But there were now so many assailants under the walls that it was impossible to stop them. Their efforts to establish a tortoise were starting to take shape and, using the bodies of their dead comrades and those fallen from the battlements to increase the height of their base, a canopy of shields had formed which was increasingly resistant to the projectiles from above.

The slingers continued to fire, stopping some enemies from climbing onto the shields of their fellow soldiers to form the second layer of the structure, but for each man who lost his balance and fell, two more took his place, and in a short time the second level was ready. Laenas saw it forming before his eyes: the soldiers climbed from the rear onto the backs and the shields of their companions, then began to advance precariously towards him on that improvised canopy. They were thus able to gain access to the battlements where, in the meantime, the supply of spears had run out. There was nothing for it: they would just have to wait for their opponents to be close enough to force them back with their swords. Blades out, moments later they were fighting what was practically a standard pitched battle.

Laenas defended himself doggedly, as did his men, but each time a legionary fell on the battlements it became more difficult to replace him and at the same time fill the gap that had been created, while their opponents had an endless number of replacements swarming up over the tortoise. The centurion slashed tirelessly, mowing down anyone who came within range, but he soon began to despair of maintaining their defences: he realised that he was having to cover a larger area than at the beginning of the assault, and increasingly feared that he would not manage to prevent them from taking the fort.

A few steps away from him, where two legionaries had collapsed under the blows of their assailants, a breach was created: Laenas shouted for others to converge on it, but nobody obeyed, so he went himself. He pounced on the fastest of their enemies and sliced open his neck. The man fell to the ground inside the fort, and Laenas pushed the next soldier into the railing, swinging wildly at him until he managed to strike him in the groin, freeing himself soon after. He turned to another soldier, who was preparing to swing at him and just about to cross the battlements when he saw him suddenly disappear behind the parapet. After a moment of waiting, he dared take a look below. The tortoise had dissolved, and its components were moving away. He glanced around him in bafflement and then looked towards the plain.

Antony's men were arriving in force.

XX

The trouble with war was that it was the politicians who made it. If the decisions were left to professional soldiers, they would fight on the battlefield, fairly and with no tricks, and the strongest, as opposed to the most cunning, would win. This was what Salvidienus Rufus was thinking as he observed his troops deployed just outside the gates of Octavian's camp, ready to assist those of Antony.

But the triumvir, unexpectedly, did not need any help.

Maecenas's bizarre plan was not having the desired effect. The Etruscan, using the strategy devised by Agrippa, had hoped to force Antony to threaten Cassius and induce him to act. As expected, though, a battle had broken out along the causeway and the enemy's defensive fortifications, and the triumvir had taken advantage of it to unleash an attack on the camp of Caesar's killers. And after having blocked the enemy assault on the forts along the marsh, Antony had set off to conquer the enemy camp – and it was at that point that Maecenas's plans had gone up in smoke.

In fact, in spite of all their predictions, Antony's men had actually managed to overcome the fortifications and climb the slope leading to the camp, and now had a good chance of taking possession of the assassins' most important stronghold without requiring any help from Octavian's troops. The convoluted plans of that damned Etruscan risked actually backfiring against the sect, giving Antony a victory as resounding as it was unexpected.

Helplessly, he watched the columns of Antony's

soldiers flow towards the fortifications around Cassius's camp, keeping an eye on what was happening in Brutus's fortress, where the battlements were packed with soldiers watching the battle. The triumvir was fairly close to the front row, surrounded by a swarm of squires acting almost as his personal tortoise to protect him from projectiles arriving almost continuously from the battlements. His presence among the soldiers highlighted the absence of Octavian, even from his own camp, and on the very day that battle had broken out.

That was another of Maecenas's brilliant ideas. Why didn't he go back to Rome and be a politician instead of playing at strategist? The Etruscan, aware of how weak the still convalescent Octavian was, had put about a rumour saying that the new Caesar had seen in a dream that he must leave the battlefield. And incidentally, he had it the night his spies had seen Cassius's men building the counter-fortifications which would make a battle inevitable. His idea was to pass off this dream as a warning from the gods to stay out of the battle until things had settled down, attesting to a divine predilection for the son of Caesar, and with the simultaneous action of his troops in favour of Antony and the subsequent victory, people would think that, as the favourite of the gods, Octavian was able to exert a powerful influence on events even in his absence. Only the ministers of the sect knew that, in fact, his presence on the battlefield would be irrelevant, because he was anything but a warrior.

Too bad then that Octavian would now simply look like a coward. Rufus wondered what he could do to save the situation. He and Agrippa had split the tasks, he taking command of the legions deployed outside the camp and the other the command of those inside. In the original plan, it would have been for him to decide when it was time to march in support of Antony. And now? Should he send them off all the same? In all probability, Antony would be offended and accuse Octavian of trying to appropriate a victory achieved with his own strength, and it might result in a diplomatic incident for which he would be held responsible. On the other hand, if he didn't mobilise, Octavian could accuse him of having scuppered the plan: there was always the chance of something going wrong and it would be good to have any excuse for claiming to have got Antony off the hook. With the propaganda that Maecenas was able to orchestrate, it should be possible to pass off his contribution as decisive even if it actually had been only chaining up the prisoners. But only if some of Octavian's soldiers were present in Cassius's camp.

Rufus looked at Brutus's fort again. The men there looked to be champing at the bit, but showed no intention of leaving the camp – they had not done even so to provide assistance to Cassius, as Maecenas had expected, perhaps out of fear that, in the meantime, Octavian's troops would attack the camp they had left defenceless. And this detail too, made the question of rushing to Antony's aid a sticky one. If Rufus moved, there was a real danger that they too would enter the battlefield...

It was the hardest decision he had had to make as a commander but, considering all the possibilities, he concluded that mobilising was the least risky option. The chances of their own camp being attacked were, after all, minimal: there were more than enough of Agrippa's troops to fight off any attempts at attack.

He gave the order. The trumpets sounded across the

valley of the Philippi and the units marched off, cutting diagonally across the plain. As they passed under Brutus's camp, it occurred to Rufus that parading like this before the eyes of the enemy troops might seem a deliberate insult, a provocation. But he did not care: their commander, that coward Marcus Brutus, was afraid, and if he had not already emerged to assist his accomplice in his difficulties, he would not do so now either.

He continued to march at the head of the long line which bisected the plain, studying what was going around Cassius's camp. There was still fighting along the battlements, and some groups of soldiers were taking turns to break through the front door with long poles taken from the fortifications along the marshes. Perhaps there *was* still a chance of influencing the outcome of the battle, then. He had made the right decision.

He was at least two-thirds of the way towards Cassius's camp when he heard shouts from the rear of the column. He turned, and saw a sight that stunned him into immobility: Brutus's legions were pouring out of their stronghold, taking advantage of the slope to rush down on the flank of his army.

Which was straggling, and in marching, not battle, formation.

*

It was all going wrong. No one on Octavian's general staff had imagined that Brutus's entire army would have poured down out of its camp without finding any opposition outside. In fact, Agrippa said to himself as he tried to keep the men lined up, no one had imagined that

355

Brutus would pay any attention to Octavian's camp: at worst – they had said in the tactical meetings – the opponents would leave their stronghold only to provide assistance to Cassius or to join the battle. And in any case, all the ministers of the sect had been convinced that the troops deployed outside of the fortifications and led by Rufus would have stopped any attempt at penetration.

Instead, his column had not only failed to give support to Antony's army, it had even failed to stop the entrance onto the plain of Brutus's men. Rufus had allowed himself to be surprised from his flank, with his legions in marching order and the units separated from one another, without adequate lateral cover from the cavalry and light infantry. And for Brutus's legionaries it was like crushing flies.

From the battlements, Agrippa had been forced to observe Rufus's legionaries overrun by a human tornado that swept them away one by one. The soldiers had ended up under their enemies' shields and feet without having had a chance to pull their swords from their scabbards and defend themselves. Others had fled immediately, only to offer their backs to the enemy swords. The few units that had tried to maintain formation and oppose the raging torrent had fallen apart in an instant, while still others tried unsuccessfully to return to their camp.

And that was the most serious problem of all, because it threatened to turn a retreat into a total debacle.

The men who were escaping wanted to find shelter in the camp, but Agrippa knew that letting them enter would mean letting their pursuers, who were advancing without any opposition, enter too. Yet he could not risk condemning thousands of legionaries to death by slamming the gates in their faces. There was an actual risk of losing half of Octavian's troops in one fell swoop, and it would be a fatal blow to the prestige of his friend and to the aspirations of the sect. Especially if Antony managed to win the battle he was fighting.

He had to save them, he decided when the first soldiers reached the still open gates of the fort. But there was practically no break between the fugitives and their pursuers. The plain between the two camps was teeming with armed men without a real battle.

"Centurion! Line up your *centuria* next to the door, in columns! Only allow entry to our men and stop the others! And you, tribune, do the same with your units on the opposite side!" he shouted to the officers who were watching the retreat with him from the battlements.

His two subordinates acted promptly, and soon the praetorian gate was surrounded by legionaries arrayed on either side, behind whom the first of their fellow soldiers to arrive hurried to find shelter. Many were even without their shields, panting desperately, unsteady on their legs, and could contribute little to the defence, on the contrary, their presence – Agrippa sensed immediately – was a hindrance to their comrades. Chaos was threatening. He called Maecenas, who was nearby.

"Go down to the gate and get those who are no use out of the way – they'll cause us nothing but trouble!" he shouted, and the Etruscan nodded, climbed down from the battlements and raced into the throng. Agrippa saw him shouting and dragging the weakest ones, some of whom were injured, too confused and afraid to play any part in the fighting and too proud to accept being sidelined. He had given Maecenas a hard job, and saw that for every man the Etruscan managed to shift there were at least another three who refused to move: they were probably ashamed for running away and wanted to redeem themselves.

Meanwhile, outside the fortifications, soldiers of both armies were starting to pile up, and the difficulty of entering the fort forced the fugitives at the rear to defend themselves from the attacks of their enemies. But the others had room to manoeuvre behind them and were better organised, with their respective officers alongside the soldiers issuing orders and co-ordinating the movements of the squadrons. Octavian's men lacked cohesion and leadership, and their centurions and *optiones* were separated from their units. Agrippa wondered if Rufus had fallen or had ended up with the part of the column that had managed to reach Antony.

Inside, the fleeing legionaries burst through the entrance in an increasingly chaotic flood, disrupting the ranks of the two lines on either side of the gate. The few opponents who managed to get in took advantage of the confusion and the difficulty of distinguishing them from Octavian's men and immediately pounced on the defenders, managing to stab a few before being put out of action.

Agrippa looked back outside. The fighting was mostly going in favour of Brutus's men, because Rufus's were crammed too close together to be able to move their swords freely or evade enemy blows, and with each of Rufus's men who fell, Brutus's soldiers moved a few steps closer to the wall. Octavian's legionaries who could not get through the gate were pushed by the crowd along the ramparts, and some lost their balance and ended up in the ditch with broken necks. Agrippa noticed that the enemy were taking the opportunity to push other soldiers or corpses in. Their intention was clear.

They wanted to fill up the gap with the bodies and then climb up the embankment.

In fact, some had already started to do it, while the two armies on either side of the gate had become an indistinct mass of armed men moving this way and that. Agrippa summoned a dozen legionaries and rushed along the battlements to the most critical point. He arrived just as an enemy soldier, hoisted up by some comrades, showed his face over the top. He chopped the man's head off completely, and the rest of his body fell backwards, though he was soon replaced by another enemy, who managed to avoid the young tribune's swing, but not that of a legionary at his side, and his head too, rolled down the embankment.

Meanwhile, the bridge of bodies in the ditch was allowing an increasing number of Brutus's legionaries to climb up the battlements, and the area Agrippa had to defend was too large for the few soldiers he had brought with him. Furthermore, many of their opponents were busy forcing their way through elsewhere, and it was almost impossible now, to oversee all the threatened areas of the walls. From the entrance too, enemies flocked in increasing numbers, while outside, Octavian's men, unable to prevail in combat or get over the battlements, began to lay down their arms and surrender, freeing the way for Brutus's soldiers.

It was no longer possible to hold them off along the battlements. Agrippa decided to organize a last line of defence around the praetorian tent, Octavian's headquarters when the triumvir was present. He came down from the stands and ran toward the entrance, giving orders to each officer he met to pull back the men and assemble them in the middle of the camp. He also told Maecenas, who had by now given up attempting to create a semblance of order around the gate and sought only to form little pockets of resistance to oppose the increasingly overwhelming tide.

The only hope was that Rufus would return and attack the enemy from behind while they were trying to break through the last line of defence, or that Antony would quickly prevail over Cassius and send them reinforcements. Otherwise, the number of opponents was too high to hope to resist. But from a glance at the fighting on the plain there was no sign of Rufus, and it was probably too far away for the commander – if he was still alive – to be able to reorganize the ranks and lead a counter attack.

Their chances of getting out of this alive had been cut to the bone by Rufus's recklessness.

*

Isolated on an enemy ship and surrounded by burning vessels, Gaius Chaerea tried to remember when he had been in a worse situation, but none came to mind. If nothing else, though, they had taken the trireme they had boarded, and the last of their enemies, now outnumbered, were throwing themselves into the sea to escape their swords. But it was pointless if they could not free themselves from the ring of fire surrounding them.

Gaius looked around him. Not all the cargo vessels had

managed to get away from those in flames, and the fire had spread from deck to deck, enveloping sailors and soldiers, sails and rigging, planking and masts. The air was full of smoke and heat from the other blazing ships, and those which had not caught fire were clumsily seeking an exit, but ended up crashing into one another and becoming wrecks in turn, blocking even more thoroughly any possible – although increasingly elusive – escape route.

And yet, said Gaius to himself, if any of what had once been the fleet of Calvinus could get away, it would be they, who had seized a trireme. It was a smaller and more agile ship than the cargo vessels, and could slip through the fire and debris, with a little luck. Or with a lot of luck. The soldiers crowded around him, asking what to do. They all had the same horrible visions in their eyes: men stumbling, running, crawling all fours, rolling around on the deck, enveloped in flames, or leaving behind them a trail of fire before jumping into the water. The piercing screams of pain of the soldiers who had been turned into human torches were a gloomy funeral anthem for the survivors, for whom Gaius was now responsible.

The ship closest to them suddenly practically collapsed in on itself, and the burning wreckage disappeared rapidly from sight, as if the hand of some great god had seized it and smashed it into matchwood, and a moment later, on the surface of the sea, flat and calm in spite of the many ships that had been there so recently, there was only scattered debris and men floundering in the water. Many struggled to grab pieces of flotsam to stay afloat, but sometimes the wood was still so hot they were forced to abandon them and look for another piece, if they still had the strength to swim at all.

Yet in that way salvation might lie, thought Gaius. There was a gap between Murcus's fleet and the wrecked ships of Calvinus, and at that moment, several enemy ships were concentrating their attentions on the triremes escorting the cargo fleet. He had to try. Gaius ordered the helmsman to turn in that direction, and the chief rower to demand maximum effort from the oarsmen. The ship began to rotate and move forwards amidst a landscape composed of ghostly immobile shipwrecks, the air thick and dark with smoke and the approaching dusk, the crackle of flames merging with the sighing of the sea and the moans and cries for help of those in the water. Gradually they gained speed, while Gaius watched the movements of the enemy fleet. For now, thanks to the thick blanket of smoke, their opponents seemed not to have noticed anything – or perhaps, ignorant of the boarding, still thought it was one of their ships, and were waiting for it to re-join them.

Gaius looked down the sides of the ship and saw men in the waves stretching out their arms for help, and others disappearing under the water as they were submerged by the passage of the vessel. No, he could not stop to pick any of them up: he tried to convince himself that he had a delicate mission to accomplish, and that his safety was a priority. He looked away, and his eyes returned to the battle. On the deck, all were silent, their expressions tense and their faces contracted in dread that Murcus's galleys would catch up with them. Without wind, the strength of the oarsmen would soon wane, but they only needed to get out of the sight of the enemy, who were probably already satisfied with their success.

The centurion held his breath when he saw a trireme

pull away from Murcus's fleet. It seemed to be heading in their direction and instinctively he gripped the pommel of his sword, but the ship veered off again and headed towards a cargo vessel that had surrendered. Immediately afterwards, another moved away, and once again proceeded toward them. Gaius commanded the chief oarsman to intensify the effort, but the rowers were already doing their best, under the threat of the soldiers' swords. The trireme was approaching and the centurion resigned himself to fighting – hopelessly, because his men would have to defend themselves not only from their enemies but also from the oarsmen. It reached two transport vessels and stopped alongside another vessel of its fleet to rescue the men who were abandoning the deck to escape the fire.

Gaius breathed a deep sigh of relief. Perhaps they had managed to escape the battle.

But reaching the coasts of Epirus in that dead calm was another matter.

*

Maecenas was appalled. The circumstances and the unpredictable behaviour of Marcus Brutus's men, not to mention the recklessness of Rufus, had turned his sophisticated plan upside down, and now all they could do was cut their losses. There was no question: Rufus could only be a follower, never a leader. If Agrippa had been commanding the troops outside and he those in the camp, Maecenas was sure things would have been different. And now they would probably have been attacking Brutus's camp instead of defending Octavian's.

As he was dressed as a tribune, the men gathered around, waiting for his orders, but the idea of having to fight a pitched battle without the protection of fortifications still terrified him, despite the baptism of fire he had endured in Modena, and he was struggling to think clearly. Now the camp would become the battlefield, and he would have to defend himself against people who were more robust, athletic, trained, experienced and courageous than he. A horrible prospect and one which, as part of Octavian's General Staff, he had hoped to be able to avoid.

Soldiers raced between the tents, appearing fleetingly between them as they ran towards the *praetorium*. Whenever Maecenas saw the huge silhouette of some legionary appear round a corner, he jumped in fear that it was an enemy soldier. He hoped his soldiers wouldn't notice. He tried to avoid the praetorian way, down which the enemy were pouring, and passed through the barricades to reach the square between the praetorian tent and the *Principia*. There he found Agrippa, who had deployed the men at his disposal in a semi-circle.

"Fill out the ranks, come on!" he shouted. "We need to create a barrier from one side of the battlements to the other."

Maecenas was happy to be obeying orders again instead of giving them. He trusted Agrippa blindly, and was sure that his friend knew what he was doing. He went to post his men where he saw the line was weak and received into his ranks the fugitives that arrived, placing them in several rows, as though they were a unit deployed on the battlefield. He knew that the men expected him to be with them on the front line, and after some hesitation he resigned himself to the fact and took up the position to which he was entitled as a senior officer.

Not far away he noticed several groups of enemy soldiers who, seeing the defenders arranged in formation, stopped throwing themselves against them and paused to wait for reinforcements. Meanwhile, however, they slaughtered some of Octavian's men who were trying to reach the centre of the camp to join their comrades. Some of the fugitives managed to hide themselves amongst the tents to avoid being intercepted.

The Etruscan and his men found themselves impotent observers of the desperate flight of many of their comrades, who were trying to escape the enemy at their heels. Slowly, shouts of encouragement rose from the line of Octavian's men, and the cheering grew louder when a comrade managed to slip through the enemy's grip and, breathless, reach his fellow soldiers, where he was greeted with congratulations and thumps on the back, before Maecenas ordered him into line.

But they were also forced to witness summary executions: one legionary was stabbed in the back by a spear just when he seemed to have escaped the closest group of enemy soldiers, and another, who had valiantly swung his sword to fight a way through, earning himself loud applause from his fellow soldiers, was set upon by three other soldiers and fell under their swords. Two fugitives emerging suddenly from a tent found themselves surrounded, and their deaths were obvious from the number of swords they could see rising and falling at the point where they were intercepted. Another was dragged out of a tent and his severed head thrown towards the line of Octavian's men.

After a while no more appeared. Maecenas shuddered

at the sight of the enemy ranks growing greater by the moment, and as the seconds passed, he considered it increasingly unlikely that they would be able to hold them off.

The attack began almost immediately, with the enemy advancing close enough to be able to throw their spears, and then stopping.

"Close ranks! All behind your shields!" cried the Etruscan. "Let's throw some spears ourselves!" shouted a centurion. "No!" he answered. "The only hope is to maintain position. We'll try to withstand their throw and then await the assault! They are among the tents, they won't be able to build up much momentum." At least he *thought* that was this tactic decided upon by Agrippa.

Soon after, projectiles were thrown from the enemy ranks. It was worse than if the line of shields had been hit by a hail of stones. A series of violent impacts rocked the soldiers, and many were forced to take a step back, banging into those behind them, while others found themselves with their shields pierced and the tip of a spear in the shoulder or chest and fell to the ground, creating gaps in the line. Still others were unhurt, but without a shield, theirs having been rendered unusable after being penetrated by a spear.

The throwing of spears could only be the prelude to the assault, which began shortly after, accompanied by the roared chorus of their slogan: "Freedom!"

Maecenas saw among the enemy ranks armour of gold and silver which, it was said, Brutus and Cassius had made for their most deserving men by melting down the precious metals they had plundered from the occupied cities of Asia. Those must be the best warriors, and he hoped to avoid encountering any of them.

He noticed, however, that one of those legionaries with the golden armour seemed to have targeted him, and it struck him that, as a tribune, he was prestigious prey for any particularly belligerent soldier. He saw the man coming closer and was at a loss as to what to do. Looking impressive in his shiny outfit, the legionary swung his sword about, and the Etruscan felt the emptiness around him: none of his men was going to stand up to a warrior like that, obviously. He realised that he was at the man's mercy, and gave himself up for lost, but then, at his side, he saw on the ground one of the shields, with a spear still attached. He moved so that it was near his foot and, when his opponent was almost on him and ready to throw his first thrust, Maecenas kicked it up at him. The soldier stumbled and fell forward, right at the feet of the Etruscan, who hurriedly raised his sword and sank it into the gap between the bottom of his helmet and the edge of his armour before the man had a chance to get up, and the golden armour was instantly covered with a torrent of blood.

His victory had been noticed by the nearest soldiers, who gave a cry of triumph, but they too were struggling with their opponents, and the line of defenders, already thinned out by the spears, was struggling. Using his shield and sword, Maecenas defended himself with a new aggression as he tried to assess the situation. The pressure of the enemy was overwhelming thanks to their superior numbers, and the gaps opened up by the spears had already allowed the first of them through. They would not last long. There was only one thing to do.

He had to go and speak to Agrippa.

XXI

"Are you joking?"

Agrippa could not believe his ears when Maecenas, who arrived breathless at his side, explained his idea. The young man blocked the sword of his closest opponent and with his shield pushed him towards a fellow soldier who finished him off, and then turned back to his friend. "It would be like admitting defeat," he said, his breathing only slightly heavier than normal.

"But don't you see that we have already *been* defeated?" said Maecenas, keeping an eye on the battlefront, which was fluctuating ever more worryingly. The enemy had increased their pressure on the parts where several defenders had fallen, and Octavian's men were being pushed back, leaving the flanks of those who resisted, exposed. The dam, therefore, was breaking and splitting into a series of pockets of resistance, and Agrippa had to admit that they would soon find themselves with enemies in front of, beside and behind them.

"Pulling back and leaving by the *decumana* gate would allow us to save much of the army. This isn't the decisive battle. And anyway," said Maecenas, "even if Antony does defeat Cassius it will only be a tentative victory – it will take another battle to determine who will rule the Roman world."

"They'll jump on us," objected Agrippa. "They'll never let us fall back in order. They'll force us to crowd against the battlements and massacre us as we try to go through the *decumana* gate!"

"I think not," said Maecenas, more and more convinced. "Let me take the furnishings and Octavian's property out of the *praetorium*, as though we were going to take them away. But then we will leave them there, as though we hadn't managed to get it done in time. You'll see that the first to break through will rush over to take possession of them, and the others will try to get the booty in the tents, especially in those of the officers, and won't bother chasing us."

"Their commanders will call them to order. They're Romans, not barbarians!"

"Brutus won't. He's never been much of a commander."

Agrippa was baffled. His heart cried out at having to hand over to the enemy – to the men who fought for the killers of his friend's father – many of the objects of which Octavian was most fond. It felt like a betrayal.

"I understand your hesitation," said Maecenas, sensing his thoughts, "but Octavian will be happier to save the soldiers with which to avenge his father and recover his reputation than his personal effects. And he will lose some men either way. Neither Rufus nor Antony are going to come to our aid, I am afraid, and sooner or later we'll be forced to give in."

Agrippa thought. Even if he tried, Rufus did not have enough troops to help them, and Antony... Antony was probably was enjoying the situation his colleague had got himself into. It was only Octavian's goading that had stopped him from making a deal with Caesar's killers...

He looked at his men. They were fighting with valour, battling to defend each tiny piece of the camp, but it was inevitable that more and more of the enemy would arrive from behind them, turning the camp into a cage from which they would never escape. Or at least, not alive.

Yes, they had to break free while they still could.

He looked at Maecenas and nodded. "Take some legionaries and empty Octavian's tent," he said. "I'll pull back the line but keep a garrison around the *praetorium* to protect your retreat. See you at the *decumana* gate!"

Maecenas rushed off with his characteristically awkward gait, immediately asserting his rank as tribune and dragging four legionaries off towards Octavian's lodgings, where they disappeared rapidly behind the leather flaps of the entrance.

Agrippa lunged forward and made his way past some soldiers until he reached a centurion. "Take your units over to the *praetorium* and cover Maecenas's retreat when he leaves!" he cried, then, without waiting for an answer, he went over to the *bucinator* and ordered him to sound the retreat. After a moment's disorientation, the men began to fall back, harried by the enemy as they went. Agrippa was in the front line, swinging his sword relentlessly to ward off their opponents and glancing occasionally towards the triumvir's tent, around which the *centuria* who had been ordered to protect the Etruscan were taking up position.

As his men gave ground, he saw that the enemies were increasing the pressure. Some were already beginning to rush inside the tents of the officers and the Principia, abandoning the battle, but there were still many of Octavian's men who were in danger of being cut off, and on the far flank, towards the side rampart, several enemy legionaries were marching along the perimeter to form a barrier in front of the *decumana* gate. He took with him a *half-centuria* and rushed over to force them back. He was the first there, reaching the enemy column before they could get into formation and ramming his sword between the neck and shoulder of his nearest opponent. A moment later, the legionary's head was dangling onto his chest, before his now inert body collapsed to the ground.

The soldier just behind the victim was intimidated by the violence of the young man's attack, and surprised in turn by a jab which struck him between the legs. Agrippa lifted him off the ground and threw him at his companions, who drew back in horror. Encouraged by their leader's determination, Agrippa's subordinates flung themselves as one upon their enemies, pushing them towards the rampart, and in the meantime, the groups of legionaries following them were able to proceed relatively undisturbed towards the *decumana* gate. The young man gave chase to the opponents who tried to escape his attack by climbing the stairs leading to the battlements. He stabbed one, pinning him to the wood, and with his shield parried another as he pulled his sword from the corpse, climbed a few steps and severed the other man's ankle. Seeing that there was no one at the top, he turned and went back down the stairs, falling upon a soldier who had been forced to fight with his back against the fence. He chopped into his shoulder with a vertical stroke, and saw that the few survivors of the enemy column were, by now, interested only in getting away from them.

He ordered his men to resume their retreat before other groups of opponents arrived, forcing him to continue to fight. Passing between the tents, he reached the rear fence and fell in behind the line that was funnelling through the door. He was among the last, and turned to look back at the camp, expecting to have to defend himself from an attack from the rear. But behind him he saw no one. And observing the camp, he noticed that most of Brutus's men were busy looting the tents.

All the tents.

Maecenas had been right. The prospect of booty had made them give up the chase.

After he had eventually managed to cross the threshold, his attendant handed him the reins of his horse and, once in the saddle, Agrippa walked along the entire column, evaluating the number of soldiers he had managed to save. He soon realised that it was most of them and that the officers were gradually re-grouping cohorts and centurie. He went back up to the front looking for Maecenas, but saw no sign of him anywhere. He spent the next hour looking for him and asking around for him, until he met a centurion, who said, "Those around the *praetorium* didn't make it, tribune. I saw them surrounded almost immediately."

Agrippa was appalled, and had to stifle the urge to cry in front of his men. He had not only lost a friend, but also the principal brain of the Sect of Mars Ultor. Octavian would never forgive him, but in any case, he would never be able to forgive himself. With the loss of the Etruscan, he told himself, as he rode towards his lifelong friend, the defeat, already serious, began to take on the proportions of a debacle.

*

Ortwin surveyed the desolation that reigned in Cassius's camp. The banners of Antony's legions were raised to the heavens by the victors who, uncaring about what was happening only a few stadions away in Octavian's camp or about chasing the fugitives in the gorges behind the camp, celebrated their victory by tormenting and teasing the prisoners, and continuing to scour one tent after another. They hadn't bothered looking for the commander, who had time to escape the raid of Antony's men inside the fortifications and who must have sought refuge in the surrounding mountains. The German would have liked Antony to give him a squad with which to go and flush him out, and was certain that this was what Octavian – and his staff – desired, but he couldn't find the triumvir. And above all, he was extremely worried about what had happened to his comrades on the other side of the plain, and was angered that he had been part of the contingent lent to Antony for the work along the marshes. Even though things seemed to have gone very badly over in Octavian's sector, he wanted to be there, helping his comrades. Instead, he was there with Antony's men, in the company of the hateful Popillius Laenas. As he had expected, Laenas had simply given him a contemptuous look before unhesitatingly joining the other soldiers in search of plunder.

Antony's men had piled up the prisoners' weapons and the worthless booty they had found in the soldier's quarters and had made it into a trophy, around which many were busy getting drunk on stocks of wine found in the tents of the officers and the warehouses. Many legionaries clung to their loot, to the point where they looked more like porters than soldiers, and instead of maintaining discipline, the officers followed suit. As always, Antony did not bother to take advantage of his victories: the same old failing, ever since Ortwin had fought alongside him in Gaul during Caesar's proconsulate and at the great rebellion of Vercingetorix.

He almost hoped that Brutus's men would surprise them in that state and massacre them, but he knew it wouldn't happen: their enemies were probably behaving in the same way in Octavian's camp. Each winner was content with his own partial victory, and perhaps the commanders were already considering some agreement where they would not be thorns in one another's sides too much in the future. He had to find a way to break up that festive atmosphere – Octavian was definitely still alive, part of his troops were still intact, and Caesar's heir would certainly have wanted to get revenge.

But to do that, he needed to track down Rufus. He and Veleda had separated in the hope that at least one of them would find him: he was wandering around Cassius's camp among Antony's men while she was searching the units which had escaped Brutus's attack and were bivouacked, demoralised, outside the fort, and it was she who eventually found him and called Ortwin to come and speak to him – no minister of the sect would have gone to confer with, or justify himself to, a mere follower, much less Rufus. When Ortwin arrived, he found him in the midst of his men – who were ignoring him – sitting with his head in his hands and his elbows on his knees, vexed by the shouts of joy and festive atmosphere in Cassius's camp.

Rufus looked distraught. And he had every reason to: if Octavian's forces had been defeated, he had a share of the blame. He didn't even raise his head – Ortwin had to solicit his attention. "Commander," he asked, "do you know what the situation is in our camp?"

Rufus slowly raised his head and took a moment to recognize him. Or maybe just gather his thoughts. "You can see for yourself. Or can't you even see out of the one eye you've got left, you damned barbarian?" he mumbled, talking like a drunk, and it was only then that Ortwin realised that he actually was. He must have knocked back a bellyful of wine to console himself after the rout of his column.

"I see the men Brutus defeated. And I wonder how many of our men were saved. Here with us we still have so many, and we could try to continue the battle and take back the camp," he said, cautiously.

Rufus looked at him as though he though he were insane. "Oh yes? You want to risk losing the troops that are left after Agrippa got all those others killed because of his incompetence as well? I have to save what's left, if anything, and hand it over to Antony…"

Ortwin found this criticism of Agrippa ungenerous. After all, Rufus had offered no support with his own troops, and anyone would have struggled to defend the area against superior forces. But he couldn't afford to argue. In any case, Rufus did have a point: an attempt to regain the camp would very likely fail. But they couldn't make themselves available to Antony, not that…

"Well then let's wait for Brutus's men to leave the camp and see what's left and what we can take back to Octavian," was all he said.

Rufus nodded absently, saying only "Yes, let's wait…"

He was apathetic – a broken man, even though in his mind he continued to blame others for the defeat. Ortwin felt compelled to press him. If Rufus did not intend to make decisions, he at least was ready to keep the objectives of the sect in sight. "Tribune, Cassius Longinus has fled. You know what I did with Decimus Brutus," he reminded

375

him. "I am ready to do the same to him, before he can join Brutus…"

Rufus looked at him blankly and without speaking, so he went on. "I mean, if you think it right, I can take my Germans and some other soldiers and look for him in the mountains. We must not allow him to survive, don't you think?"

The tribune did not answer. He was too depressed to take responsibility upon himself, so Ortwin decided that – in the absence of the supreme leader, with the army in disarray, the fate of the other ministers of the sect uncertain, and Antony triumphant – no one would blame him for taking the initiative.

He gathered his few Germans and Veleda, and headed to the mountains.

*

"Tell me where I can find Cassius Longinus or we will kill you all, one by one," said Ortwin, positioning his horse between the small group of escaping enemy soldiers and the top of the hill.

The legionaries moved into combat formation, crouching behind their shields with their swords held out before them. No one answered. Veleda joined Ortwin and the other Germans moved to their sides, blocking any possible escape route for their opponents.

"Do not let yourselves be massacred," said Ortwin. "There are more of us than there are of you, and there is a reward for the one who tells me where your commander is." One of the soldiers spat towards the German. "Get lost or fight, you barbarian bastard!" he shouted, and the others followed suit. Ortwin spurred his horse toward the man who had insulted him, forcing the other soldiers to move out of the way, and his target was knocked down and fell under his horse's hooves, just before the German's spear went through his ribs, pinning him to the ground. Ortwin reined in his horse and drew his sword from its scabbard, while the legionaries around him stood there cautiously, not daring to attack for fear that the other horsemen would go for them. But the Germans were not moving: their leader had expressly ordered them to avoid aggression to encourage the legionaries to talk. "Anyone else want to go the same way? Is it worth it, for a man who killed your commander, and who you only served because he paid you well?" continued Ortwin. "If you speak, not only will you survive, not only will you return to fighting for Caesar's son, but you will be rewarded even better than you were by Cassius."

"That's shit! You're going to kill us all!" cried another legionary, hurling himself toward the German. Veleda could stay immobile no longer. She spurred her horse and threw herself between her man and the soldier, blocking his sword with her own. The two blades collided, throwing off sparks, and the clang rang out among the sparse trees of the gentle slope. She hoped that Ortwin would not come to her assistance, and in fact her companion, knowing how proud she was, remained where he was: Veleda knew his every muscle was taut and ready to intervene in the case of her needing help, but for the moment he was letting her deal with it.

The soldier, annoyed by her intrusion, started swinging at her, and she parried his blows with her shield. Two more legionaries started to move forward, but the spears of as many warriors dissuaded them from approaching further: they all knew that Veleda liked proving that she was just as skilled in combat as her comrades.

She had the advantage over her opponent of being on horseback, but could not exploit this to its full for she had no spear. The legionary slashed at the animal's hocks, but Veleda spurred her horse forward so that he missed, then she turned round, now with the soldier on her right side – the one where she held her sword – and unleashed a torrent of swings at his head. It was all the man could do to defend himself, raising his shield over his helmet without being able to approach the animal's flank, and when he did manage, a kick from Veleda sent him stumbling backwards. The man threw himself to the ground and rolled under the horse's legs, almost being crushed. She resolved to throw herself on him before she lost her horse. She jumped down from the saddle and threw herself onto his back, and immediately had her blade to his throat which she slit with a horizontal gesture. She stood up, panting...

And found herself surrounded by enemy soldiers.

Without her horse.

Before she had time to assume the defensive position, Ortwin appeared between her and the Romans and mowed down the nearest one with a single blow. For a moment the others stood there, hesitating, then, seemingly having given up hope, they screamed wildly and threw themselves on the nearest German. By now they had no way out: the Romans were outnumbered, their opponents were on horseback and most of Ortwin's men still had their spears. Veleda saw the legionaries fall one after another, pierced by a spear or trampled under hooves.

One stepped back to avoid one opponent's blade, only to end up being stabbed from behind by that of another. A second leapt backwards, dodging a couple of spear jabs but accidentally making himself into an easy target for Veleda. She didn't want to kill him from behind, though, so she grabbed his arm and turned him round with a jerk, ready to stick her sword in his stomach, but as soon as he saw that he was done for, he shouted, "No! Please spare me! I'll tell you what I know!"

Veleda paused, but remained cautious. The soldier threw down his sword and then his shield, and soon had several spears pointing at his back and Ortwin's sword resting against the nape of his neck. The woman looked at him: he was young, probably one of the many new recruits in the army of Caesar's killers, and he did not want to die. He had held out until then so as not to look like a weakling to his more experienced comrades, but there was no longer anyone left to keep up a bold front for. They were surrounded by a pile of corpses.

"So?" said Veleda finally, anticipating Ortwin's words. "Where is Cassius Longinus holed up? Speak, if you want to live!"

"I... I saw him not long ago. He was ahead of us... higher up on this plain, together with his henchman and his attendant. That's all I know," the boy murmured, in a trembling voice.

"Henchman? What henchman?" asked Veleda. That definition was well suited to a name which she both feared and longed to hear.

"You know, that Labienus – the one who follows him around like a puppy..." said the soldier.

Veleda winced, then looked over at Ortwin and saw his

one eye narrow and his face transform into a grimace of hate. "Come on, up the hill, follow me!" cried the German immediately, urging on his horse, but she had another idea and grabbed his reins, stopping him from setting off. It wasn't easy: Ortwin seemed possessed, and glared at her with hatred. But the woman did not appear intimidated – Quintus had always shown a remarkable ability, ever since she had first met him, to get himself out of any situation and to take advantage of their emotions. They must not risk letting him escape this time too.

"Do not underestimate Labienus. We have already done that too many times," she said, stroking his leg in an attempt to calm him. "If he sees a group of Germans chasing him, he will surely find a way to evade capture."

Ortwin took a deep breath, closed his eye and snapped impatiently, "So, what do you propose?" He was making a great effort to accommodate her.

"I propose stripping the corpses of the soldiers and putting on their armour. The shields will attest we are in one of Cassius's legions and the Romans will let us get closer. Then we can do what we want with them."

Ortwin looked at her. "And what do you want to do with them?" he asked, once again putting her feelings to the test.

But she had no doubt. Whatever the cord was which bound her to Quintus, it was time to cut it. Forever. "We will treat him like any of Caesar's murderers. For him there is only death," she replied, in a tone which she hoped Ortwin would find sufficiently determined.

Her man seemed to relax. "So be it. Quick, take their equipment," he said to his men, nodding at the corpses around them, then he turned to the surviving soldier.

"You're coming with us. If you behave yourself, you will enter one of the legions of Caesar Octavian."

They worked fast, and in no time at all, the group of barbarians had become a squadron of Roman cavalry, though equipped as heavy infantry, and had begun to climb the slope, where the trees grew more densely. The prisoner was riding alongside Ortwin, seated behind one of his men, and pointing out the direction in which he had seen Cassius and Labienus fleeing. Veleda realised she no longer cared about finding Cassius – or at least, cared less about it than she did about capturing her ex-lover, and she was certain that Ortwin felt the same way. At that moment, her desire for personal revenge was stronger than her commitment to the sect.

Dense woodland alternated with clearings, while below them, the victory songs and cries of joy from the armies of Brutus and Antony on the plain below could be heard over the sound of hooves on soft grass. Behind the group of Germans dressed as Romans, a pall of smoke rose from the camps, slowly climbing the slope behind them.

Finally, Veleda heard movement in front of them, and saw that Ortwin had too: her man froze like a statue. She feared he would set off at a gallop and ruin everything, and was moving towards him when she noticed a man approaching. Ortwin stopped. She saw that behind the soldier, who was quite a way off and amongst the trees, she could see another two. The man approaching had a conciliatory demeanour: he must be Cassius's steward. It was clear that he thought they were friends. He called out a greeting, to which they responded cautiously.

Veleda saw that behind him there was a small gully, which they would have to go round to reach the two fugitives. As they drew closer to the steward, she was able to make out the features of the other two. Both were without their helmets, and although she wasn't sure that she recognised Cassius, she had no difficulty in identifying the other.

Quintus Labienus was only a few steps away from her. She looked at Ortwin. He, too, knew with whom he was dealing.

And that small gully represented an unforeseen difficulty.

"Friends, come around and join us!" cried the attendant. "Our enemies will never find us here and we can join Brutus." It occurred to Veleda that, just as they had recognized Labienus, he might recognize them, in spite of their disguises, and she tried to move further back in the line, but then she distinctly heard her former lover's voice. "Careful, those are Octavian's Germans! I know them well, that one-eyed one and the woman without a hand!"

The aide appeared disorientated, and Ortwin urged his horse forward and ran him down, before cantering to the edge of the gully. He paused there for a moment considering whether to risk breaking his horse's legs by riding through it, and in the meantime Veleda saw Labienus push Cassius Longinus down into it. The man rolled down the slope, and Quintus, with the mocking laugh which Veleda knew all too well, jumped into the saddle of a horse tethered nearby and raced away, disappearing between the trees. Ortwin froze, trying to follow with his one eye both Labienus and Cassius, who was now at the bottom of the small gorge. Cassius got up awkwardly, eyeing the Germans and looking for an escape route.

Ortwin gave a gesture of annoyance. He ordered his men to split into two groups and go round the gully – whether to surround Caesar's murderer or to Labienus, Veleda could not say, nor did she find the courage to ask. But just then, Cassius cried out, "I acted as a free man and I will die as a free man!" He grabbed the handle of his sword with both hands, placed the point against his stomach and pushed, collapsing to his knees. Veleda and Ortwin watched him sink face down onto the earth while his sword, held firm by the contact with the ground, emerged almost in its entirety from his back.

The Germans looked dismayed, and Veleda was sure that she knew what her man was thinking.

The leader of Caesar's murderers had just died in front of their eyes. But Labienus had escaped again.

XXII

Never in his life would Gaius Chaerea have imagined being reduced to licking tar to assuage his hunger. The problem now was that he did not know if the cramps he felt in his stomach were caused by the hunger itself or by having ingested something harmful. And even had he wanted to, he wouldn't have had the strength or the opportunity to procure more, after going to seek the last piece in the gaps between the planking. Weakened by five days of hardship, he merely lay motionless on the deck of the ship which had escaped Staius Murcus, from which he had already torn out all the wood which he could deprive the ship of without sinking.

The others were no better off. Indeed, looking carefully at one of his comrades who lay nearby, he realised that he was no longer breathing. He tried to remember how long it had been since he had last heard him moan, but could not bring the images of the previous days, nor even the long, endless hours of that day itself, into focus. Blurred and indistinct, images of soldiers and oarsmen diving into the sea in despair and drowning in the waves, or gnawing on the ropes and sails of the wreck upon which they floated to give themselves the illusion of sustenance flashed before his eyes. He recalled that one, or maybe two, or more likely, three days before, a man had lowered a bucket into the sea to draw water which he had started drinking before Gaius, his reflexes already groggy, had been able to stop him. Within hours, the soldier had begun to show signs of madness, gesticulating and ranting with a new energy before eventually throwing himself upon a fellow soldier and slicing him open with a dagger, biting at chunks of flesh he tore from his body. Gaius had wounded his hand trying to stop him, and had been forced to kill the man with his sword before he could harm the other survivors.

But that had been days ago, and it seemed to that an eternity had passed since then. Now, he would not have even had the strength to shout at him to stop, let alone overpower him. If one of his companions had gone mad, all he would be able to do now would be to let him kill himself. He looked at the seven other survivors, but saw that they were all in a semi-comatose state, and he decided they were not the danger he needed to protect himself from now.

Anyway, he had plenty of other things to worry about. He hadn't eaten or drunk for days, and didn't think he could hold out much longer. The boat was adrift without sails and none of them had the strength to use the few oars that had not been broken during the naval battle. Sometimes, though indistinctly, he seemed to see land – the outline of the coast of Epirus, or of Italy, or of one of the many other islands of the Adriatic, he couldn't tell. And at any moment he expected to hear the ship run up against a rock and drag its occupants down to the seabed with it.

And then there had been the rain. The day before they had been surprised by violent storms with thunder and lightning which had shaken the boat, and a tempest which had made her sway dangerously until he feared that she would capsize. It seemed to him too, though he was not sure, that he had lost two men when the elements had unleashed their fury, one washed away by a wave and another, who had failed to grasp the guardrail in time, and been thrown into the sea by one of the most violent swells. There were even those who, at the end of the storm, had rejoiced over the deaths of their fellow soldiers because it meant there was more for the survivors to put into their stomachs, notwithstanding which, fights had broken out over some frayed ropes and torn sails, dirty with the excrement scattered over the deck by men who could no longer control their bodily functions. Gaius had given up early on attempting to intervene to quell the bickering, surrendering to the evidence of being no longer able to impose his authority on those who were reduced to little more than animals.

With great difficulty, he dragged the body of the man he believed to be dead over to check that he actually was. Wearily he leaned his head on his chest to listen for a heartbeat, and realised that another soldier was looking at him. He heard him whisper something and realised that the man was asking him if he was dead. He nodded, and the other man turned to his neighbour, who pulled out a knife from his belt. Together, the two legionaries began to crawl towards the body and towards Gaius.

"What... what are you doing?" murmured Chaerea, with barely the strength to speak.

"You know very well, Centurion," said one of them, when he was closer. "And you won't try to stop us."

"No, not that," said Gaius. He would not allow it, not as long as he was nominally in charge of that small group of legionaries. Under his command, no one would feed upon a fellow soldier. He had said so right after the battle: no one would lose his dignity as a Roman soldier, whatever the conditions events forced upon them. But those who survived with him on that ship were now neither soldiers nor citizens. They were no longer even human beings, and he wondered how he could prevent the atrocity that they were now preparing to commit upon the corpse.

He watched them as they approached, their faces deformed by hardship but also by the anticipation of their meal. Their eyes were popping out of their sockets, their cheekbones protruded, their hair was plastered on their foreheads and their lips were ravaged by thirst and by biting themselves in hunger. He wondered if he was in the same state, and thought it likely: if he looked in a mirror, he would see a ghost.

"You... You won't do it," he said, without the authority or strength necessary to deter them.

"Yes, we will," replied one. "And there's some for you too, Centurion."

"...or we'll be feasting on your flesh too," added the other.

*

If nothing else, all was not yet lost, Maecenas said to himself after having listened carefully to the guards who surrounded the section of the camp Brutus had reserved for the prisoners Caesar's murderers had taken after the battle. Wandering casually amongst the soldiers who had been captured with him, he heard the guards saying that the victors had ripped Octavian's litter to pieces with arrows and had plundered his tent of everything of value it contained, but of Caesar's heir there was no trace. Many said that the triumvir must have disguised himself as a

387

soldier to avoid recognition, and there had been a manhunt. Some had actually boasted of killing him and had brought his body before Brutus, but it had turned out only to be a lad, a recruit, who happened to look like him.

Was there still any hope? Maecenas attempted to analyse the situation objectively. Brutus's soldiers boasted of having taken three eagles and having destroyed three of Octavian's legions, but those of Antony were still intact, and the heir of Caesar had enough left to still be decisive in a new battle, as long as it was Agrippa leading them and not Rufus. On the other hand, Cassius too had suffered heavy losses, and the news that he had committed suicide provided some comfort to the Etruscan, who knew that he had been the best commander Caesar's killers possessed. Of course, the numbers the sentries gave them were not encouraging: they spoke of sixteen thousand dead among those supporting Caesar's cause and half of their own comrades, but it might merely be Brutus's propaganda to console the soldiers for the half-defeat of their opposite numbers and to keep them motivated in view of the inevitable confrontation.

A confrontation – as he well knew – in which their opponents started from a position of great advantage. If the numbers going around the camp were true, in addition to their strategic and tactical superiority, they also had numerical superiority. Especially if the news that had been circulating in the camp for the last few hours, passing from mouth to mouth until it reached the pens holding the prisoners, was reliable. It seemed that the two legions Octavian had been expecting from Italy had run into Staius Murcus's blockade at sea and that had been the end of them. The enemy admiral had captured thirty-five of

Calvinus's galleys and sunk many cargo ships, scattering the fleet and making it impossible for the legionaries to reach the eastern shores. If this was true, they had no way of making up the losses they had suffered in the battle.

It was not at all in Brutus's interest, then, to do battle. He occupied an enviable location, on high ground and near sources of fresh water, and the attempts of Caesar's avengers to block his supply routes had failed miserably. Conversely, the alleged victory of Murcus on the Adriatic prevented Octavian and Antony not only from obtaining supplies from Italy, but even from returning to the Peninsula if events took a turn for the worse. And he would have bet that they would get worse soon, what with the bad weather now on its way. Even before the battle, Maecenas had encountered difficulty in obtaining provisions in the surrounding areas, which had now been exhausted by the long bivouacking of the troops and the increasingly unhealthy autumn weather, which had forced the soldiers on the plain to wade through mud, swamps and marshes. And things were only going to get worse.

All in all, he admitted sadly to himself, there was nothing to be optimistic about. The situation was desperate and the only positive thing was the survival of Octavian, who had escaped thanks to his providential idea of sending him away before the battle. But then everything had gone wrong, and now he had ended up a prisoner of the enemy, able to do nothing except watch events play out. In all probability, Caesar's avengers would have no choice but to attack, before hunger and hardship did Brutus's work for him, and for an army forced to attack an opponent because it had no alternatives, there was no hope. Even he, who knew little of military tactics, realised that Brutus would simply have to wait, or at most repel any attempts to take his camp, to win a final victory with minimal effort.

Moreover, the internal situation of the Sect of Mars Ultor had already been extremely delicate when they had set off on the Greek campaign thanks to the disagreements, defections, fights, deaths, murders, the defeat of Rufus in Sicily... And since their initial confrontation with Caesar's killers things had not improved at all, and had, in fact, gone as badly as they could have. Even he, who had great respect for his own resourcefulness, could think of no way to stop what appeared to be the inevitable decline of the group. He had believed in it, and had invested his time and his wealth in it, but now it seemed that all was lost.

When a guard called him over and escorted him out of the pen holding the prisoners, Maecenas realised that he had been thinking about the fate of the sect and of Octavian, but not about his own. Right now it was he, of all the members of the Sect of Mars Ultor, who was in the worst position and whose fate hung by a thread, and he grew even more convinced of this when he saw that they were taking him before Marcus Junius Brutus: as soon as he saw him, Maecenas knew that the man held his life in his hand.

He felt that he was being scrutinised and evaluated, but didn't allow himself to feel intimidated: he knew that Brutus didn't have the steely personality of Octavian, nor the intimidating one of Cassius or Antony, and had it not been for the situation he would not have been in the least awed.

"So *you* are the new tyrant's most trusted lieutenant..." began Brutus, after studying him for a long time. He was surrounded by a dozen bodyguards and stood on the edge of the area reserved for prisoners. He was unprepossessing and uncharismatic to look at, and the fact that he had bothered to come to the prisoners rather than summon him to his tent spoke volumes about his lack of authority. His elusive gaze was testament to his shyness and, for a moment, the Etruscan had the impression of being before a man who had taken on more responsibility than he could manage. On the other hand, it was no secret that Cassius had struggled to convince him to lead the conspiracy against Caesar.

"Disappointed?" he said, smiling slightly. "Did you expect a brute like Agrippa, perhaps?" He knew the human soul well, and was certain that it would take much more than some silly provocation to make someone as composed as Brutus lose his calm.

In fact, he didn't react. "And why ever would I?" he answered quietly. "I am very well aware that your mind is your greatest asset, and I'm glad to know that among the soldiers who have fallen into my hands there is one whose ideas would have been more damaging to me than his sword."

"I don't know if I should be flattered or worried…" said the Etruscan.

"All that need worry you is that you will not be able to provide assistance to your leader, if that re-assures you," said Brutus, and his words cheered Maecenas a little. But only a little.

"Assuming that this time he actually appears on the battlefield," continued the murderer of Caesar. "If he had been where he should have been, like a real commander, instead of fleeing the fighting, the reasons for contention between Antony and myself would vanish too, I'm sure. And you would be free. Free also not to submit yourself to the monarchy that your leader aims to establish."

Maecenas, too, was certain that, were it not for Octavian, Brutus and Antony would already have come to some arrangement. That, above all, was why he had wanted to keep his friend away from the battle. Without his presence, however, he feared that the young triumvir might not be as wise next time. "As a representative of the descendants of Venus and defender of justice in Rome, Octavian has the gods on his side, and they warned him in a dream to stay away from the fighting until he had recovered," he specified. "And anyway, it appears to me that you have little to brag about – everybody knows that your men went into battle of their own accord, which means you can claim no credit for the victory that you attribute yourself. It was coincidence, nothing more."

"A coincidence? Perhaps this too is a sign from the gods, then!" said Brutus. "At least for those who do not want Rome ruled by tyrants. The same gods who have cut off your route for retreat and supplies, allowing Staius Murcus to prevail over Domitius Calvinus. You'll see when the survivors of your army and your friends eventually die of starvation. And the first to go will be Octavian, whose health, I think, must be rather poor, especially in such trying conditions."

"So you didn't win six days ago and won't win in the future either, but plan to simply reap the benefits of favourable circumstances..." said Maecenas, continuing to provoke him.

"I won't send my men to die, if I can avoid it. You who have such a refined brain should know that. You'd do the same thing…"

Maecenas agreed, but he could not admit that to Brutus. Quite the opposite. An idea was forming in his mind. "Thank you for the compliment," he replied. "But because I *do* have a mind capable of understanding the human soul, I know that soldiers, in the long run, do not respect a commander who does not win them victories in the field. Especially if they have served in the past under the command of one such as Julius Caesar, the greatest leader who ever lived. And most of your men served under him. I doubt that you can afford to evade combat."

Brutus finally lost his temper. Maecenas had hit the mark, he noted with satisfaction: the murderer was aware of his lack of total authority over his men. "And I will do it. I am their commander," he replied testily. "Take him back to his quarters," he said curtly, addressing the guards who had brought Maecenas before him.

Pleased, the Etruscan bade him farewell. He had identified the weakness of Brutus's seemingly unassailable position. It was a small crack, but it might work, especially as the enemy commander was planning to let time pass. All in all, he could still be useful to the sect, he thought. Provided that the sect still existed.

There was one thing he was still curious about. As they led him away, he stopped for a moment, turned round and asked Brutus point blank, "You do not seem the type to nourish envy, jealousy, frustration or resentment, unlike the others who killed Caesar for their petty personal reasons. Why did you do it?"

For the first time, Brutus looked him in the eye. He remained silent a long time, and the guards remained immobile until he had responded. "You wouldn't understand," he said finally, "because you do not bear a name like mine, nor a rank which obliges you to do certain things. I am not proud of what I did to the person," he concluded, turning and walking away, "but I am proud of what I did for myself and for Rome."

*

Gaius Chaerea scrutinized the two soldiers dragging themselves toward him, drew his sword from its scabbard and looked around. The ship was enveloped in a dense fog, which made it impossible to understand where they were, and on the deck the other survivors watched the scene with lifeless, absent eyes. They would have liked to help, but he knew he could not count on them: the only ones who had the strength to move were those who were determined to get their hands on food. Whatever the cost.

"If you even attempt to violate your comrade, you will die," he whispered.

"We will die anyway, just more slowly," was the inevitable response.

Gaius remained crouched on his knees behind the body and waited for the attack. They didn't have the strength to stand either, and that comforted him, but the two managed to proceed on all fours, sometimes with the help of their elbows when they lost their balance, and soon they were almost over their dead comrade. The first swung his dagger in the direction of Gaius, who dodged behind the corpse. The dagger sank into the rigid flesh, blocking for a moment the arm of the attacker. Chaerea was torn between the desire to strike his opponent or simply disarm him: he did not want to kill a man who had been entrusted to him and who he had not been able to save.

The other took advantage of his hesitation to free the blade with a movement which in other circumstances Gaius would have found ridiculously slow. He decided to try to knock him out, even though it occurred to him that he would then have to watch out for him all the time. For as long as they remained alive. The soldier lunged at him again, but his jab was predictable and Gaius managed to avoid it by moving a few feet. But then he saw the sword of the other coming at him. His survival instinct enabled him to block it with his own blade, metal against metal. His opponent was so weak that the impact knocked the weapon out of his grip, and Chaerea immediately dealt him a blow to the face with the pommel of his sword. He watched him out of the corner of his eye as he fell backwards, and decided he would have to tie him up as soon as he had dealt with the other assailant, who was moving forward, ready to strike.

In that moment, Gaius heard a roaring noise, and the ship rose and then fell back into the water with a mighty splash.

The centurion and his opponents were tossed across the deck, and Gaius was so devoid of strength that he was unable to seize hold of anything that would allow him to avoid smashing into the railing or being thrown into the sea. He heard a gurgling in the hold and the sound of splintering wood, and he realised that the ship was taking on water. They had struck something that he was unable to see, and were sinking.

In that moment, the boat tilted worryingly and then ground to a halt. He looked around him and saw only two soldiers on the deck with enough strength left to moan but not to react. They were destined to drown if he didn't help them to get hold of something to cling to, quickly. But the ship had stopped, and, for the moment at least, wasn't sinking. He dragged himself to the railing and looked overboard, where he made out a huge rock, behind which he seemed to see other rock formations through the thick fog. If the ship had run aground, that meant that the seabed was not far below them. He looked over the railing but saw only water: all the other survivors, apart from the two lying on the deck, must have fallen into the ocean and drowned.

He couldn't stay on the ship. He felt the deck vibrating and creaking, and sooner or later it would split open, catapulting him into the water. He must be very close to the land, and so he decided to swim ashore. He gathered what was left of his strength and, dragging himself across the deck, went to urge the two legionaries to go into the water with him. One of them only shook his head and mumbled something unintelligible, however: he was done for. The other nodded weakly, although Gaius was not sure he understood, and let himself be pulled to his feet and heaved onto the railing. Chaerea threw a piece of broken planking into the water and told him to cling to it, pushed the soldier into the water, then dived in himself. The contact with the cold of the sea gave him a boost of energy, so he plunged beneath the surface to see how far down the seabed was and his feet touched something. He rose immediately, and drew in a lungful of air, looking around him for the planking he had thrown overboard. Seeing it was only a few strokes away, he began looking for the soldier, and saw him thrashing about just beyond the piece of wood, which the man had not even noticed. Gaius ordered himself to reach the man, and began to swim towards him. It was only a few strokes, but each one cost him a tremendous effort.

Exhausted, he arrived by the legionary who, semiconscious, was spending more time under the surface of the water than he was above it – and just as Gaius was about to grab him, he disappeared beneath the surface again. Gaius forced himself to dive down and grope about for him, seeing nothing even though he kept his eyes open. He thought he brushed against him once, but couldn't get a grip on him. He touched him again, then lost him again, and, conscious that he was at the very limits of his strength now, tried to push even deeper towards the bottom, until finally he slammed against his comrade. He quickly wrapped an arm around him and pulled him back up to the surface, then began to swim, dragging the man's dead weight behind him and deciding he would check on the condition of the soldier when he arrived at the piece of wreckage.

In a few strenuous strokes he reached his goal, seized it and pushed the legionary onto it, making sure that he was secure and supporting him with one arm. He examined him, and, seeing that the man was on the verge of drowning, hoisted him up onto the small piece of planking, climbed on himself and began to pump his chest until the man vomited sea water. He was unconscious but alive, at least, so Gaius focused on his next move. He peered into the mist, and seemed to sense that the shore was not far away, so he threw himself back into the water and began to push the makeshift raft with flailing legs, careful to avoid the rocks that occasionally reared up out of the sea.

Thanks to the assistance of the waves, they reached the

coast just before his strength abandoned him altogether, and he made for a small cove where he could land without danger from the rocks. Gaius dragged himself up onto the shore, and pulled his still-unconscious companion up after him. The moment he was out of the water he was overcome by exhaustion, and he sank immediately into the warm embrace of the sand, drifting into unconsciousness almost without realizing it.

He could not say how long he had slept or had been unconscious when he opened his eyes, realising that a man had shaken him awake. He looked at the individual and decided he was harmless. The man, for his part, simply stared back at him curiously. Gaius looked around and noticed that there were nets piled up next to him. He must be a fisherman.

"You're Romans, aren't you?" said the man, smiling a little. He spoke Greek, and this comforted Gaius: he had ended up on the right side of the sea.

"We are Romans," he replied in Greek, checking that his partner was still alive. He was, but he was either unconscious or asleep. "Where are we?" he asked the fisherman.

"You're in Aetolia, opposite the island of Lefkada." Gaius tried to remember. It was located about halfway along the western coast of the Hellenic peninsula. The front was on the other side, beyond Macedonia, at the height of the Thracian Sea.

Far, far away.

"Were you trying to get to Thrace? You're late," said the fisherman. "The battle between the Romans has already taken place. The news reached my village just this morning."

Gaius stood up, in spite of his weakness, and instantly felt an icy hand grip his stomach. "A battle? Where? Who won?" he asked, unable to conceal his agitation.

"At Philippi. And nobody won."

"What do you mean, nobody won?"

"Nobody. I know that Mark Antony defeated Cassius, while Marcus Brutus took Octavian's camp. But the two armies were still fighting when the messenger departed from Philippi, six days ago."

"Are any of the commanders dead?" urged Gaius.

"Only Cassius for now, they say." So Octavian was still alive. That was comforting news for the centurion.

Six days. So that was at least how long it would take to reach the front. What had become of Octavian and his followers? There had been defeats, and Gaius knew that he had abandoned his duties and his friends, walking out on them at the very moment of greatest need, he thought. He felt deeply ashamed and terrified at the thought of never seeing them again. He had to find out if the defeat was irreparable for Octavian, and communicate not only that there were no traitors in the sect, but that Octavian could still count on him, especially if he had to fight Caesar's murderers.

"Quickly, take me to your village, give me something to eat and two horses. And look after my comrade," he ordered the fisherman in an authoritarian tone, exercising his role as a Roman soldier who never had to ask something of a subject people, only demand it. Then he went over to the other soldier and set about waking him up.

*

"You lot are just a bunch of cowards, my friend!"

"Yeah – you've got everything in your favour and you daren't even go into battle... you milksops!"

"It's easy to win if you do it like that! Even my four year old son could!"

"And you fought for Caesar in the past! You're cowards, as well as traitors!"

"How much did Brutus pay you to change sides?"

"You're afraid of taking on real soldiers in combat, aren't you?"

The sentries were starting to get jumpy, noticed Maecenas with satisfaction: the prisoners' goading was beginning to produce the desired effect. Brutus would never allow a massacre of other Roman soldiers, so the Etruscan was certain that this teasing was more dangerous for Caesar's killers than it was for Octavian's soldiers, and he exhorted the legionaries to continue. His plan had taken shape three days before, immediately after he had spoken to Brutus, when he had started telling his soldiers about the inaction of the enemy army and encouraging them to deride their captors.

As he had expected, the taunts of the hostages had come to the ears of the guards: at first, some had reacted angrily, prodding those responsible with their spears, but then those same sentries had started talking with their fellow soldiers during their break, and in the later shifts some had even started nodding in agreement with the prisoners' insults. One guard had even begun to talk to one of them, and that man had, in turn, told Maecenas about the man's complaints regarding their forced inaction. Since then, there had been growing consensus among Brutus's soldiers – so much so that the hostages could now get away with any taunt, in the knowledge that the sentries were inclined to agree with them. By now, in fact, they had lost the furious expressions that they had worn at the beginning, and their faces bore a shadow of shame that made it look as though *they* were the prisoners...

Maecenas decided to approach a guard to gauge the mood of the camp. He chose the watchman who had seemed more sympathetic to the considerations of the captured legionnaires. "Soldier, I'm sure you'd rather earn the prize that Brutus will give you for fighting instead of playing nursemaid for Roman citizens..." he began.

"You can say that again, by the gods!" the other replied, bluntly. "That's the trouble with being commanded by senators who've never been professional soldiers... They're always trying to get a political result, not a military one. And I just don't like it."

"I understand," nodded the Etruscan. "He never fought for Caesar, as you did, I imagine. Caesar was used to taking risks, and that is something that you would understand. But this stalling... it would not be Caesar's way, nor that of those who fought for him."

"And it's not even a risk!" the other complained. "That soldier of yours is right, the tribune, when he says that we have all the advantages on our side: numbers, terrain, provisions... Why hesitate, then? There's no honour in obtaining a victory by waiting for your opponent to die of starvation. I know that the commander pays me, but this isn't what I signed up for."

"Yes," admitted Maecenas, seriously. "It is not very edifying, for a veteran, to tell his sons that he won like that. I think that children eager to hear war stories from their father or grandfather would be a bit disappointed to learn how things went at Philippi: watching Roman citizens who, in other circumstances, would have been friends, starve to death. No, they would not be proud of their father."

"You're right, by Jove! But it's not my fault! It's not the soldiers' fault! You can see yourself that we want to fight," he protested, turning to the nearest sentry, "isn't that right Pescennius?"

"Of course it's not our fault! We are the hostages of the politicians," agreed the other. "But we were even before the battle that we won! If it wasn't for us taking the initiative, the commander would never have given the order to attack and we would never have taken Octavian's camp. And now we would be talking about a defeat, not a half victory. Which, as far as our work goes, was a complete victory..."

Maecenas's interlocutor looked at the Etruscan. "What did I tell you?" he winked. "He's right. It's *us* who are the real winners of the fighting, not our commanders."

"Well, that means that you'll have to do it again..." said Maecenas. He knew that what Antony and Octavian wanted more than anything else was a fight: he was not sure who would win, but at least there was no certainty they would lose, which was what would certainly happen if Brutus was able to keep his soldiers on a leash. It was down to him to prevent that, by exploiting the fact that the enemy commander was not an individual able to impose his will on the soldiery.

It was time to investigate the aspect that interested him most. "But... What about your officers? The tribunes, the centurions, the *optiones*... What do they think of all this?" he asked with apparent nonchalance.

"The centurions are all with us, of course. They're real

soldiers, that lot, even if they're often complete bastards!" said the legionary. "As for the tribunes... The *laticlavius* tribunes all lick Brutus's arse, obviously. They're senators like him. The *angusticlavius* tribunes think like us, but they cannot declare it openly."

"And who told you that, soldier? I for one do not think like you – quite the opposite." A voice interrupted the soldier, and sent a quiver through the stomach of Maecenas, who spun around in its direction.

Horace was standing there.

The Etruscan could think of nothing intelligent to say, and thus preferred to keep quiet, awaiting the next words of the man who had made such an impression on him months before. When he had last seen him he was an *optio*, but now he found him a tribune, like himself.

Horace took him by the arm and led him into a secluded corner of the prisoner's camp. He was carrying a sack, which he deposited on the ground as soon as he decided they were safe from prying eyes. "Are you planning to make the entire army mutiny?"

"I-I'm just doing my... my job," stammered Maecenas, overcome by emotion and immediately chiding himself for not managing a wittier retort.

"Then go and do it in the camps of Antony and Octavian. You are doing too much damage here. In there," he said, pointing to the bag, "is the uniform and equipment of one of our legionaries. When it's time for the changing of the guard on the praetorian gate, I will come to get you. Once out of the prisoner's section, you will put it on, and then I'll take you to the exit, where you will say today's watchword – 'Three eagles' – before declaring that you're going out for the evening patrol. After that, I don't want to see you around here again."

Maecenas was silent for a while. Seeing that he did not react, Horace was about to leave, but Maecenas grabbed his arm. "Why are you doing this for me?"

"Because you are causing problems... and because Brutus has figured out what you're up to and might forget about his proverbial good manners and get rid of you."

Maecenas swallowed, feeling an even more intense wave of emotion wash over him. His temples were throbbing wildly and his vision was blurred. He felt like a little boy. "Then you are not wholly indifferent to me after all..." he said in a strangled voice.

Horace pulled away abruptly and walked off. "Remember. I will be here at nightfall," he repeated, before leaving once and for all. The Etruscan stared at him as he walked away, thinking that he had obtained two great victories that day. No, all was not lost. Soon he would see his friends again.

Soon, the battle of revenge would take place. And soon, he hoped, one way or another, he would meet Horace again.

XXIII

The taller legionary snatched the biscuit from his shorter, stockier comrade, and pushed him to the ground. "We made a bet and you lost," he shouted in his face. "You owe me your ration!"

But the other wasn't having it. He got up and gave him a surly stare. "*You* say I lost the bet, but it's not over yet, so for now *I'm* eating my ration!" he retorted, and so saying, started trying to get the piece of hardtack back. The tall man dodged, and the pudgy one swung a punch at him which went wide, upon which the other responded with a kick between his legs. The shorter legionary fell to his knees while his fellow soldier burst out laughing, but he recovered quickly and grabbed the man's legs, pulling him off balance. The biscuit fell into the mud the two were rolling in. In any other circumstances it would have been inedible, but Octavian, who was watching the scene from nearby, was in no doubt that they would continue to fight over that lump of mud. Soon afterwards, in fact, that stocky one found himself within reach of the biscuit, grabbed it and put it in his mouth, sinking his teeth into it like an animal. The tall one tried to hit him in the stomach with one hand while snatching the food from his mouth with the other, and in the meantime they continued to roll around on the ground, looking more and more like two clay statues.

The triumvir decided that enough was enough. He saw an *optio* a few steps away and called to him, and the officer hurried over. "You! Don't you see your subordinates fighting? How can you tolerate such a lack of discipline in your unit?" he said scornfully. "Separate them immediately and see that they are given appropriate punishment."

The officer looked confused. "Forgive me, Triumvir... I was putting down a brawl behind those tents and I didn't notice anything. The centurion died in the battle and I'm the only one in charge of the whole unit, and in these conditions..." he stammered.

"I am not interested in your excuses," interrupted Octavian, peremptorily. "Stop them, or I shall do so myself – and then you will receive punishment with them!"

The other nodded and rushed over to separate the two, who were fighting so savagely for the biscuit that it was all he could do not to end up not covered with mud himself.

"That *optio* has a point, unfortunately," said Agrippa, who was walking next to Octavian. "We no longer have enough officers to keep the men in line, and Antony has no intention of lending us any..."

"He has his work cut out controlling his own men," replied Octavian, bitterly. "After all, they're starving too. I know very well that there's nothing more that *optio* can do, but we have to maintain a semblance of discipline and authority over the troops, otherwise Brutus will have won without even touching his sword."

The young man was extremely dejected. He had returned to the camp immediately after the battle, and had found it devastated. He had lost three legions and then the news had arrived that he would not even be able to count on the two that Domitius Calvinus was supposed to be bringing him. From the heights of his victory, Antony had begun to ignore him openly, just as he had when Octavian had first appeared on the political scene: he didn't bother to summon him to councils of war and made his decisions regardless of him, or merely sent messages requesting his co-operation. The men were dying of hunger, supplies could no longer reach them from Thessaly and the intermittent autumn rains had made the plain they inhabited intolerable and unhealthy – the water soaked the tents, wrapping the soldiers in its icy grip at night, while during the day they waded through a sea of mud.

And to make matters worse, the condition of the Sect of Mars Ultor was increasingly critical. Octavian had been thinking about the reasons that had led to the debacle of the battle a few days before, and had not yet managed to reach a firm conclusion regarding individual responsibility. Was Rufus or Agrippa to blame? At first, on the basis of the junior officers reports, he had got the idea that it had been Rufus who had made the defence of the camp impossible by marching his column with its flank exposed to a counter attack from Brutus's camp, but then Rufus himself, in a private interview, had come out with a flood of justifications and excuses which shifted all the blame onto Agrippa. Octavian had confronted the latter, and as was his wont, Agrippa had neither thought it necessary to justify himself, nor had attributed the responsibility to his fellow minister. The result, however, was that Octavian was now more confused than ever.

And he had lost Maecenas. But the biggest problem as regarded the Etruscan was that he did not know if the loss was a blessing or a curse.

Was he dead, had he been captured or had he voluntarily handed himself over to the enemy? With his disappearance, he had in fact become the most likely culprit for the betrayal that had cost the lives of his mother and of Etain. And perhaps the real reason he had convinced Octavian to leave the battlefield at the decisive moment, claiming it was for his own good, had been to discredit him in the eyes of the troops. Yes, that must be it – Octavian was more convinced than ever. Maecenas and all that rubbish about the need to stay out of the fray, that a general should observe the battle from above, without taking risks... It was just a way of making him look ridiculous – of making him look like the least able of the commanders involved in that great battle for the destiny of Rome. One of the many subtle plans of that damned Etruscan. Who knew for whom he worked... For Antony, perhaps, or for Caesar's murderers, or simply for himself? Octavian could not know the extent of the man's ambition – apparently so interested in gratifying others and willing to serve him, but perhaps simply to guarantee himself the greatest advantage.

He had mentioned this to Agrippa, but his friend was too pure of mind to think the worst of one who had helped him on several occasions and he considered him almost a brother, so Octavian, therefore, had to keep his thoughts to himself and continue to agonise over how to drive forward the sect and get himself out of the thorny situation the defeat had put him in. His only consolation – having got Cassius Longinus, the real leader of the conspiracy against Caesar, out of the way – had ended up being of little importance in the face of the bleak prospects awaiting him and the survival of all the other murderers in Brutus's army.

"Caesar Octavian, this man here was caught while trying to escape. What shall we do with him?" Rufus suddenly appeared before him, dragging with him yet another defector. He seemed to take particular pleasure from the unpleasant task, which he had undertaken to deal with in person, aided by a group of assistants. It was useful, certainly, and contributed to preventing the dissolution of an army which seemed on the verge of collapse... but Octavian would have preferred him to carry out more edifying tasks, such as the development of a winning strategy, something in which he no longer seemed interested.

"Do what you feel is appropriate. You are responsible for the deserters, aren't you?" he replied peevishly, knowing that, in this way, he was condemning the soldier to death. Rufus seemed to want to take out all his frustrations on what he considered the scum of the army. His friend nodded in satisfaction and dragged the deserter off by his arm. When they had disappeared behind the tents, Octavian imagined what would now be happening: they would make him kneel down and with a clean, decisive blow, would sever his head, giving it then to one of his lieutenants who would place it on a pole and set it on the battlements, where it was clearly visible to both the occupants of the camp and their opponents. There were already many heads along the battlements, but the dismal vision of them had not deterred other soldiers from attempting to flee. The conditions in which his army found itself were so desperate that the men felt they had little to lose by risking death to get away.

"Triumvir, we have problems with propaganda." A breathless centurion stood before him.

Octavian could not stop himself from holding out his arms wide in a gesture of exasperation. He urged the officer to follow him and they walked towards the fence. It was not the first time that this had happened. A few days ago, he had decided to use Maecenas's old idea and start launching propaganda leaflets into the enemy camp, hoping that it would create defections in Brutus's ranks. But once under the enemy's fence, their men let themselves get carried away by their desire to fight, to avenge the defeat and to escape a desperate situation, and provoked their opponents in the battlements, exposing themselves to greater risks and to fights in which they inevitably came off worse. Nor could it be otherwise: they were fighting uphill against enemies who outnumbered them and who were protected by their ditch, embankment and fence, and who could limit themselves to simply bombarding them with all kinds of projectile. And they too, like the deserters, felt they had nothing to lose, and would rather die fighting than of starvation.

Octavian climbed up to the battlements with Agrippa, only to witness a scene that he had already seen in the previous days. A group of legionaries was trying to form a tortoise close to the moat of Brutus's camp to shelter from the objects that the archers and scorpios were hurling at them while another was falling back in disarray, apparently driven by the survival instinct to give up their suicidal undertaking.

But then he noticed something new. The gate to the enemy camp had opened and a group of horsemen were setting off. For the first time, Brutus's men were putting their noses outside the walls. He was tempted to send out a contingent of cavalry to seize a small consolatory victory in a skirmish, when he noticed a figure whose unmistakeable form he knew all too well heading for the

410

fence of his fort.

Maecenas. Maecenas the traitor.

*

Agrippa saw Octavian stiffen as soon as Maecenas became identifiable on the plain that separated them from the enemy camp. And considering how he had heard his leader speak of him in the previous days, he knew that there would be trouble. As if the troubles they already had were not enough. For his part, he was convinced that Maecenas had nothing to do with the betrayal of which Etain had been victim, especially since during the battle he had shown a spirit of sacrifice as well as plenty of courage. He had tried to explain all this to Octavian, but his friend, just as he had done when Agrippa had acted impulsively after Etain had been raped, wouldn't listen to reason and refused to change his mind. Agrippa, however, had no reservations and was overjoyed to see the Etruscan alive and back with them, so he raced down from the battlements to meet him, ordering the gate opened after he had checked that there were no enemies nearby.

He met him at the threshold, his joy visible in his face. "By the gods, Maecenas, I never thought to see you again so soon! Indeed, I didn't think I'd *ever* see you again! How did you escape? Or did Brutus release you?" he asked breathlessly, patting his fragile shoulders powerfully.

Meanwhile, from above Octavian called to a centurion to send out a contingent of cavalry to reinforce the retreating legionaries.

"No time for that now," said Maecenas, panting and out of breath, "I need to talk to Octavian, straightaway!"

411

And practically dodging around him, he headed for the battlements where the triumvir was standing, Agrippa at his heels.

"Don't send anyone out, Octavian. You'll need the cavalry soon enough for battle!" cried Maecenas, to the young commander as soon as he was within hearing distance.

But Octavian's hard expression didn't change. He turned to the *primus pilus* centurion to whom he had given the order, and who, baffled, was now hesitating, and repeated, "Did not you hear what I said? Hurry up!"

But Maecenas grasped the officer's arm and said, "Don't do it, I tell you! We'll defend the retreating infantry with the scorpios! They are going to attack all together. There's going to be a battle! Brutus can no longer control his men!"

"Why should I believe you?" hissed Octavian, in an icy voice. "You re-appear out of nowhere after fifteen days – spent who knows where, and with who knows who – and you expect me to believe you?"

Dumbfounded, Maecenas stopped. It was clear, thought Agrippa, that he had not expected such a reaction from the one he considered his dearest friend. Even the nearby soldiers looked shocked by the intransigence of Octavian, who should have been jumping for joy at the re-appearance of one of his closest lieutenants.

Agrippa stepped between the two, trying to ease the tension.

"Octavian, perhaps Maecenas has good reasons for his suggestion," he ventured. "Perhaps we should listen to him…"

"Oh, I'm sure he has…" replied the triumvir

412

sarcastically. "Good reasons for him and his friends, whoever they are."

Maecenas began to press him once more. "I don't understand what you mean, but I know what I saw and what I managed to stir up in Brutus's camp. We will have the battle we need, and I think it will happen at any moment: did not you see the enemy soldiers making sorties? Their commander is no longer able to keep them under control... Rather like yourself, I see," he added, peering at those who were near the enemy camp, although the tortoise was now retreating.

"Or *perhaps* you are simply passing on to us what Brutus has told you to say. Why would he have allowed you to come here otherwise? Soldiers, arrest this man! And you, *primus pilus*, send out those damn cavalry!" spat Octavian, purple in the face, making those around him flinch. But no one moved – his behaviour would have seemed absurd in any context. Agrippa moved closer and tried to reason with him, whispering, "Octavian, please, don't let your anxiety overwhelm you. Not in front of the soldiers, at least... Let's hear what he has to say before making a decision."

But Octavian was beside himself. He had not yet recovered fully from his relapse of a few weeks before, and the fatigue of the campaign was putting him almost as much to the test as was his frustration at seeing all of his hopes dashed. He had become a shadow of the brilliant and determined young man that Agrippa had come to know and appreciate over the years – even more so since he had learned he was Caesar's heir and had become increasingly aware of his qualities. He was losing control, and this was the most obvious sign of how much he was struggling.

Not surprisingly, the triumvir made a dismissive gesture with his hand and did not deign to reply. At that moment the *primus pilus* centurion called to him, announcing the arrival of a messenger from Antony, and the scorpios went into action to curb the momentum of the pursuers, who were now approaching the fortifications, without Octavian having given the word. The young commander noticed, and walked toward the nearest scorpio, shouting, "Who told you to pull?"

"But, triumvir..." said the soldier, afraid of his reaction, "our men need cover."

Octavian's reaction was immediate. He launched a slap at the man, and shouted for all the others to stop, then began coughing convulsively. It was a full-blown attack, Agrippa realised, and he rushed over to support him before he passed out. He imagined that his friend's nerves, rather than his health, had succumbed, and that his body no longer had the support of that powerful mind: there were too many problems to deal with, and the collapse of confidence inside the sect had undermined his resistance. The tragic loss of his mother and his cousin had clouded his judgment, and now Maecenas was paying the price.

"Antony needs you to deploy immediately. They are attacking!" The messenger sent by the other triumvir, who everyone had forgotten about, had decided to speak without being invited to.

"What do you mean?" asked Agrippa, turning to him while still supporting a staggering Octavian, who was coughing and cursing everything and everyone.

"Yes, tribune. You know that hill along the swamp we seized days ago when Marcus Brutus left it?" said the

414

envoy, excitedly. "Until yesterday we couldn't defend it: the enemy was throwing everything they had at us, and there was no way to maintain a garrison. Then the triumvir had the idea of building screens with animal skins, and tonight he sent four legions to occupy it. And the screens worked! At that point, the enemy must have got scared that we were going to cut off their lines of communication with the sea and reacted. An hour ago Brutus began to send out units for battle, but only on our side. On your side he just sent out a few troublemaker units to make them split up their deployment. Well, Antony asks that you deploy quickly, otherwise Brutus will be able to attack not only to the front, but also at the side."

Agrippa looked at Maecenas. The Etruscan had been right. The prayers of Caesar's avengers had been answered and the only chance of survival – a pitched battle – was materializing. The soldiers had forced Brutus to attack but, once again, Octavian's legions were unprepared, and the triumvir himself was in no condition to encourage the legionaries. Indeed, in that moment the physical collapse he had suffered many times before had been joined, for the first time, by a nervous one: a spectacle that occurred under the eyes of the soldiers, inevitably undermining the already low morale.

It was a complete disaster. He did not see how it could be worse.

Agrippa turned to Octavian to try and encourage him to give some sensible orders, but his friend ignored him and turned to Maecenas, who was standing a few feet away from him. "We're doomed... They're attacking us... And it's your fault, you damned Etruscan!" he said, brandishing his sword and advancing on him with the tip pointing to his throat. He swung before Agrippa could stop him, cutting through the wire mail with which the Etruscan's torso was covered. Maecenas moaned softly and sank to his knees, while in the distance the trumpets of Brutus's legions about to leave their camp were audible.

Agrippa rushed to support Maecenas before he fell from the battlements, at a complete loss as to what to do.

*

The second horse he had requisitioned on the shores of Aetolia was exhausted. Gaius Chaerea had been riding for six days, alternating between the two, but a day and a half ago, one of them had collapsed to the ground with a broken leg, and he had to abandon it on the plains of Thessaly, and was forced to take frequent breaks so as not to ride the other to death. But once he was in view of his goal, once he had entered Thrace, he could wait no longer. For all he knew, the battle might have already taken place, but there was still a chance of participating and of providing the sect with new motivation and cohesion – he did not want to leave anything to chance, so he began spurring on his horse even more frequently, drawing from him all the strength he had left.

By now, however, the poor animal could take no more. His breathing was increasingly laboured, and he was stumbling with fatigue as his hooves dragged in the mud that covered the road, which was in an atrocious state thanks to the autumn weather and poor maintenance. Gaius tried to work out how far he was from Philippi. The night before, at the last village where he had stopped to take refreshment, they had told him it was a few hundred stadions away, so it couldn't be far: he had only to continue to follow the coastline and soon he would come upon the two armies.

If they were still there, facing one another.

He couldn't help spurring his horse on even more, although his legs seemed increasingly glued to the muddy ground, and when he saw in the distance the unmistakable silhouettes of Roman camps he knew he had arrived. He banged his heels yet again against the belly of his horse and tried to throw himself towards that familiar image, but the animal was struggling in the increasingly thick mud and moved with excruciating slowness. The crushing feelings of guilt which had been growing in Gaius throughout the weeks in which he had distanced himself from the sect and from military life had him in a state of intolerable frenzy.

His desire to take part in what was happening grew by the second, and it comforted him see that the camps were still there. Moving closer, he noticed other fortifications on higher ground in the background and, still further behind, the profile of a city, which must be Philippi. But just then his horse stopped, exhausted, and all efforts to make him move proved fruitless. And when the poor animal crumpled to the ground, sinking into the mud, Gaius realised that he would have to walk. He tried to run, and quickly saw what an immense effort he had forced his steed to make: for after just a few steps he already felt tired, and the marsh seemed to be trying to pull off his boots, as though some infernal demon wanted to prevent him from doing what he must.

He trudged on and on, and as he grew closer began to make out a mass of people just beyond the camps. They were clearly troops who were lining up. Could he possibly have arrived after the battle had started? He tried to hasten his pace, but his frustration and sense of helplessness increased with every step. When he saw that the right flank had already started fighting, he cried out in despair and began to crawl through the mud.

He arrived at the gates of the camp in the plains completely bedraggled. The gates were closed, and he deduced that the soldiers involved in the fighting must have come from the other camp. He asked himself why, while waving to attract the attention of the sentries on the towers.

They opened up after he had stated his name and rank, and he soon ascertained that this was Octavian's camp. He immediately asked for the commander and was escorted to the battlements, where he saw a scene which he almost took for a vision caused by his exhaustion: there was Octavian, staggering as though during one of his attacks, while next to him Agrippa held up Maecenas, who was slumped against the fence in a pool of blood. Rufus tried to climb the ramp, pushing his way past the cordon of Germans commanded by Ortwin and Veleda. There in the stands, close to Octavian, was that detestable Popillius Laenas.

The sect were all there, apart from Pinarius, who was confined to the rear, at Amphipolis.

But it was not a pretty picture.

When Ortwin saw Gaius, he widened his one eye in surprise. "Let me pass. I have urgent news for Octavian," said Chaerea.

"Does he look in any state to hear it?" replied the German.

"It doesn't matter. It might help him get better." With a gesture of resignation, Ortwin ordered his Germans to let the muddy centurion pass. Gaius climbed the ramp and found himself behind Rufus, who was trying to attract the attention of Octavian, and alongside Agrippa, who looked even more surprised than Ortwin. He was holding Maecenas in his arms and calling for a doctor, and the Etruscan appeared to be unconscious.

"What are you doing here?" the young man asked him.

"Octavian, we have to attack!" cried Rufus to the triumvir, who briefly appeared not to recognise him.

"I... I'm afraid. I no longer have the support of the gods," muttered a trembling Octavian, between one cough and the next.

"Yes, you do!" ventured Gaius, stepping forward alongside Rufus. "Listen to what I have to tell you, Caesar!"

"Well look who's here..." said Rufus, icily. "And how come *you've* deigned to join us?"

Gaius ignored him, even though, being a minister of the sect, he should not have. All the more so with Rufus, rancorous and vindictive as he was.

"Caesar, please, your sister sends me. I have to tell you something in private," he insisted, and dared to grab Octavian's arm.

Octavian looked at him with rage, then shouted, "How dare you? Get out, traitor! You are not worthy to stand with us, you who have spent months away from your duties! Begone, unless you want me to have you whipped!"

"Did you hear what he said?" asked Rufus, turning to Chaerea. "I will whip you, and personally." Then he pushed him away, almost sending him falling from the battlements. As soon as he recovered his balance, Gaius turned desperately to Agrippa, who had finally found a doctor for Maecenas. "Tribune, you will listen to me, at least," he whispered. "I came from Italy and I survived the disaster of the fleet, of which you have heard, only because Octavia asked me to give this news to her brother – the person behind the treachery which cost the lives of his mother, as well as Etain, is her husband. I was present when the senator confessed and I can confirm it. The *domina* believed that the information was important, and that is why I am here. For this, and to do my duty in the battle."

"Still here?" shouted Rufus, taking him by the edge of his filthy tunic and trying to throw him down to the ground below, but Agrippa blocked his arm. "Stop. He absolutely must speak to Octavian," he said, addressing his friend with an expression more determined than any Gaius had ever seen on his face.

Even Rufus noticed, and remained silent for a moment before saying: "Try it, then. Though I doubt he'll be able to understand anything at the moment."

Agrippa left Gaius where he was and approached Octavian, who was looking out over the parapet at the plain where the armies were getting into formation. He grasped his belt and whispered at length into his ear. At first, the triumvir, still wracked with coughing, shook his head, and even tried to push him away, but gradually his expression grew thoughtful and pensive and his coughing began to abate until it had disappeared almost completely. Eventually, he turned his gaze upon Gaius, then upon Maecenas, and then back to Gaius.

Octavian approached the centurion, placed a hand on

his shoulder and said, "Gaius Chaerea, I can only thank you for the heroism and dedication that you have shown in coming here. I can barely begin to imagine what you have been through to get here and to do your duty to the end. Have no fear, you will be given the chance to show all of your qualities, which are immense."

The triumvir then went over to Maecenas, whose wound the doctor was industriously dabbing. "My friend, I hope that I can earn your forgiveness, whatever it requires. I am unworthy of you, who has shown me the most total devotion. But now I intend to earn your esteem, and if you will excuse me, this time I will not listen to your advice." He stroked the cheek of Etruscan, then said to the doctor: "Save him, at any cost. If he dies, it is though I had killed myself too."

Then he stood up and turned towards the interior of the fort, where to the sides of the praetorian gate were massed hundreds of soldiers and officers, looking perturbed by what was happening outside the camp and intrigued by what was going on up in the battlements. He stood at the top of the access ramp and waved his arms to the soldiers to stop their murmuring and let him speak.

"Legionaries of Rome!" he began. "Tribunes! Centurions! *Optiones*… The time has come! The battle we have been awaiting is finally here. We have the opportunity of proving our superiority over those who have taken advantage of our confusion and of my absence to seize an interim victory. Our fate will be decided today, and this time *I* will lead you into battle! The gods have sent me a signal that has convinced me I can dare anything without the risk of falling under an enemy sword – a sign of our victory, just as they had previously warned me to stay away from the battlefield! The gods are with us, and therefore we cannot lose. There are less of us than there are of our foe, it is true, and we are more hungry and desperate. But it is exactly with this illusion that the gods have bewitched our enemy, convincing him that he will be able to swallow us up in a single mouthful and urging him to go into battle carelessly. We, however, are motivated by our despair, and by the knowledge that we are risking everything, and this will triple our strength, you will see! Even mine! Did you not see that only a few moments ago I was sick? And now, after having received a divine message, I feel like a lion who can lead you to victory! We are in a position of inferiority, but so was Caesar when he went against Pompey at Pharsalus, and he won a clear victory. I too, am the son of Caesar, descended from Venus like him, and the goddess wants to avenge him, using me as her tool! And you, choose not to fight against hunger, against which we have no hope, but against the walls and the bodies of our enemies! Officers, prepare your men and let us go out to assist Mark Antony, who is already committed on the other flank. And let us ensure that posterity judges our action as decisive!"

A cheer rose from the ranks of the soldiers even before he had finished. Gaius Chaerea felt a wave of exaltation wash over him that he had not experienced in a long time, and he knew that his greatest desire at that moment was to avenge Caesar. Octavian descended the stands and waved to him and to the other members of the Sect of Mars Ultor to follow him. All – except for Maecenas, of course – joined him in a secluded area away from the legionaries who were darting everywhere, making last minute preparations and getting into formation for leaving the camp.

"That was the speech for the troops, my friends," declared the young commander, who seemed to display no outward sign of his earlier crisis. "As for us, especially Mars Ultor requires above all the blood of Caesar's murderers. And this time we *are* going to find them, one by one. I want each of you to use all possible means to flush them out of the ranks of the enemy and kill them. We will let Antony win the battle for us; our greatest concern must be to not let the murderers escape. And in any case, by killing them – who are the leaders – we will provoke disarray in the ranks of the enemy, leaving soldiers without commanders, and will obtain victory in any case. For Mars Ultor!" he cried, at last. "For Caesar!"

Agrippa, Rufus, Ortwin, Veleda, Popillius Laenas and Gaius Chaerea echoed his words with conviction.

XXIV

"There he is – Servilius Casca! It was he who was the first to stab Caesar! I want him dead – now!" shouted Octavian, pointing at a tribune fighting at the head of an enemy unit in front of them. Ortwin hesitated, wondering whether it was wise to abandon the protection of the triumvir in the midst of the battle, but the young commander gave him a gesture of assent, and urged him to deal with the murderer, from whom they were now separated only by a few steps and a horde of men fighting hand-to-hand.

Ortwin gathered his strength for another run. He had already run all the way over here from their own camp when they had engaged with their opponents – Brutus's army, in fact, had been waiting immobile under their battlements so that they could retreat behind them should things go badly. The advance had been hard on Octavian's men, but they had been able to exploit their momentum to compensate for the disadvantage of the counter-slope and break up the unity of the enemy ranks. There had been no throwing of spears or firing of arrows, just immediate, brutal hand-to-hand combat with the heavy infantry, and the area outside Brutus's camp quickly turned into a battlefield, with men fighting individually or in groups with no clearly-defined front line and the two sides soon merging into a single, swarming mass.

Over the course of his long career, Ortwin had participated in countless battles, first between Germans, then between Romans and barbarians, and finally between

Romans, and he was able to assess and sense the mood of the warriors on both sides and evaluate the most effective tools for victory. And at the moment, he saw that the desperation of Octavian and Antony's armies gave his fellow soldiers an advantage. He could see the determination in their eyes, more ferocious than those of their opponents, and in their movements, which were more incisive, and he could hear it in the cries they gave to encourage themselves, which were feral. And he realised that, despite the adverse conditions, they actually had a chance of victory.

This knowledge motivated him to launch himself upon Casca. He would have to dodge many obstacles and climb a muddy slope, but he now genuinely believed Octavian's speech to the troops, and was convinced that he too enjoyed the support of the gods. He broke into a run, and seemed almost to hover in the air with each leap over the mud, feeling powerful enough to hurl aside any other fighter in his path. He gave a wild scream, well aware that his intimidating appearance – with the bandage over his missing eye, the thousand scars that crowded every visible inch of flesh and his majestic physique – would intimidate any opponent. He even scared his own comrades, who leapt out of his way before he knocked them over, while his enemies took occasional swings at him before giving up, preferring to go back to facing legionaries who seemed more reasonable opponents than this crazed fury.

But as he approached Casca, the cordon of soldiers became denser. Octavian's men had not yet got that far, and now he would have to open up his own way through. He did not hesitate, and barged forward with a swinging blow that cut the head of one of his enemies clean off, and as his blade swung back it slammed into the helmet of another of Brutus's men, knocking him to the ground unconscious. Ortwin stood on him, crushing his face, then used his shield to ram another soldier onto the sword of one of his comrades, before, with a final swing of his weapon, transforming the face of yet another antagonist into a bloody mask.

He saw that only two legionaries remained between him and his target, who at that point noticed his presence.

"It's the one-eyed assassin who killed Decimus Brutus and Trebonius!" shouted Casca, urging the soldiers around him to attack Ortwin. "Get him! *Get him!*" But the German had opened up the way for his fellow soldiers, who had forced the enemy to fan out to tackle them, and now they were fighting one-on-one. Casca looked behind him for a moment, obviously considering making a run for it, but some of his own soldiers blocked his way, and began pushing him forward. He turned to face Ortwin, shielding himself behind two of his own men.

It was him, though, that the German wanted. With his shield, he parried the blow of the man to his left, which meant lowering his guard to Casca's sword. He blocked his blade, but found the sword of the legionary to his right pointed at his chest. He spun round on himself, knocking the weapon away with his shield while his own sword tore the enemy's chest open. Casca stood frozen to the spot, and Ortwin shouted proudly, "I am no hired killer, Casca! I am a warrior!" Then he cut open the throat of the other legionary, who, thinking that the barbarian's attack was concentrated on his leader, had allowed himself to relax.

Casca tried to hide his fear but Ortwin knew that he was terrified. It would be easy, he told himself as he prepared to swing the final blow, knowing that it could not miss – the other man was in such a state of panic that he did not even attempt to hold up his shield.

"No, Ortwin, no!" Veleda's voice stayed his arm. Ortwin turned and saw Octavian with a sword pointed at his throat. Veleda was near him, together with some of the Germans he had left with the triumvir. But closest of all to Octavian was an enemy tribune.

"Let him go!" shouted Veleda, "It's Casca's brother!" Octavian's face bore an expression which seemed both inscrutable and unafraid.

It must be Gaius Servilius Casca, then. He had found the most effective way to save his brother Publius.

They had two of Julius Caesar's murderers at hand, and yet could not kill them.

Mars Ultor would not stand for it.

*

Tillius Cimber. One of the more important names on the list. Agrippa had identified him in the early stages of the battle, but had not managed to reach him. As tribune, he was also responsible for the legion Octavian had entrusted to him, and could not risk sending thousands of men to their doom to ensure the death of only one, and therefore he had to balance managing the general progress of the battle with his own goals – as well, unfortunately, as reining in the excesses of Popillius Laenas, who had made no attempt to hide his aspirations to earn himself a promotion to *Primus Pilus* on the battlefield.

The centurion had got it into his head to reach the enemy battlements and force their adversaries back against them using only his *centuria*. At the risk, however, of being cut off from the rest of the legion. He had not asked permission, the idiot, but had simply sent a runner to inform him immediately after setting off at the head of a unit on the opposite flank in an attempt to penetrate the defence which, for the moment, seemed unlikely to succeed.

Unless he, Agrippa, put some pressure on from his own side.

And he had to, if he didn't want to lose an entire *centuria*.

That meant putting aside, for the moment, Tillius Cimber. He left the line and ordered the standard bearer of the first cohort to signal the outflanking attack on their wing. The officer waved his banner, the trumpeter sounded, and the approximately eight hundred men who made up the main unit began pulling back from their individual battles to gather around the signifer. Agrippa ordered them into a column, set himself at their head and began to march along the side of the enemy formation, which for the moment was being kept busy on the other front by the rest of the legion. But the tribune was careful not to expose his flank to the other enemy legion, which was in front of the unit of which Octavian had taken direct command.

But others noticed his attempt to bypass them. Both on the right side and on the left, centurions started rallying their troops and tried to cut them off in a pincer movement as they headed towards the fort. This meant that the pressure on Laenas slackened, but also that he was in danger of being surrounded.

To save a *centuria*, he was risking a cohort, but if the pincer movement worked, they would cut the enemy off from their own battlefield. He called a runner and told him to tell Laenas to persist at all costs, then extended the cohort's line, entrusting the legionaries on the sides with the task of providing a defensive screen for those in the centre, who would deal with breaking through and penetrating the enemy forces. He ordered them thus into three columns, placing himself at the head of the central one and leading them off diagonally.

He was the first to meet the enemy, bearing down upon a group of legionaries who offered little resistance to their co-ordinated attack. Agrippa swung at their shields, driven on by the men to either side and just behind him and a breach was opened, but a denser enemy front line was revealed behind it. He began slashing away at the blockade, prompting his men to do the same, as though they were hacking their way through rock. He split shields, dented helmets, tore open throats, and slashed calves and hands with his sword until the second line gave too. And with each step forward his men praised his name, chanting it as they hurled themselves against their opponents.

A centurion stood before them, urging his men to group around him, and the new obstacle slowed Agrippa, who began to feel the pressure on his flanks too. He realised that the legion in front of Octavian had broken through the protective cordon he had set up. The soldiers began to crowd together in a crush that barely left them room to swing their swords, and each fighter found himself stuck, shoulder to shoulder with comrades and opponents, leaving many no choice but to head butt their enemy. Some were able to push an enemy to the ground and then stamp on him or finish him off with the bottom edge of their shield, while others even started biting, and

Agrippa saw one soldier spit out a nose while the face of the man in front of him turned into a mask of blood.

Suddenly, the soldiers in front of him disappeared, and Agrippa realised that he and his men had driven them into the ditch of their own camp with their attack. This gave them more space to free themselves of the enemy pressure on their flank, so the tribune ordered several legionaries to attend to it, and they soon began to recover ground, pushing their opponents back towards the main body of their units. He peered more closely into the ditch and saw that the survivors were attempting to escape from the trench by climbing up over the bodies of their dead comrades, many of whom had broken their necks in the fall.

Agrippa urged his men to follow him and they immediately set about finishing off the soldiers who were forming a sort of human ladder in an attempt to climb back out. At the head of his column, he ran along the bottom of the embankment, holding his shield over his head for shelter from the projectiles fired from the battlements and tried to find Laenas, whom he hoped had broken through too, so that he could thus re-unite the two contingents and attack the enemy from behind while the rest of his legion continued to attack the front line, pushing them into the ditch. But Laenas was nowhere to be seen in the crowd of battling soldiers. Passing along the rear of the enemy formation, Agrippa noticed Tillius Cimber and set off to cross the moat, where there were now dozens of soldiers, and attack him, but at that moment he finally saw Laenas, his crest protruding from the centre of a group of legionaries carrying shields that bore his unit's coat of arms.

They were standing in a circle and attempting to hold off the enemy who were attacking them from all sides.

They were surrounded and doomed.

Unless he once again gave up Tillius Cimber and went to help them.

*

Rufus intended to prove to Octavian and the rest of the sect for once and for all that he was a better man than Agrippa. He couldn't stand the idea that in the previous battle – when it had so obviously been his friend who had failed in his defence of the camp – the triumvir had actually considered the possibility that the fault had been his for having led his men down onto the plain, and not Agrippa's. Octavian had pronounced no judgements, but the mere fact that he had speculated upon his eventual responsibility was offensive.

This time there would be no complaints, and it was for that reason that he wanted to be the member of the sect who had the highest number of Caesar's killers' heads to his name, as well as the first commander to take the enemy camp.

He wanted to kill them himself, one by one, but there was one in whom he was more interested than the others: Marcus Junius Brutus. Killing him would also put an end to the battle.

It wouldn't be easy, and he knew it. Brutus had remained outside the fray and was surrounded by a swarm of bodyguards, and to get to him Rufus would have to attempt to break through the right flank where the enemy general was. It was for that reason, knowing full well where he would be positioned, that he had requested and obtained the command of the left flank of Octavian's legions. And he could barely wait to come face to face with Brutus.

"Chaerea! Your turn!" he shouted, feeling that the moment to implement his plan had come. His legion had engaged with its opposite number and was now fighting man to man, but Rufus had kept the first cohort of reserves in the rear to use when he needed to strike the decisive blow for the breakthrough. The manoeuvre would open the way for them to set off against the position occupied by Brutus with a second reserve which consisted of two squadrons of cavalry at his direct command.

A double reserve, as Caesar had used at Pharsalus. Brutus would never expect to see yet another contingent appear after the column which came to the rescue of the front line, and that would take him by surprise.

But Gaius Chaerea did not move.

Rufus rode up to join him in the head of the column. "What's the matter? Why aren't you setting off?" he asked, in a surly voice.

"Don't you see, Tribune? Our men are few, and are under pressure from the enemy. They are falling back and we are too far away from Brutus's camp – we risk encirclement. If I attack now we risk causing further confusion: in my opinion, it would be better to simply reinforce our ranks and hold out until we have the strength to resume our advance."

Rufus looked incredulously at the deployment before them. Chaerea was telling him nothing he didn't know already: he had reckoned that by weakening their lines, the enemy would advance, albeit slightly. But there had been no breach, and that was what was important for the success of his plan.

"I know what I'm doing, centurion," he said coldly. "Obey – that is all."

"As you wish, Tribune," replied Chaerea, in the same tone. He signalled to the trumpeters to sound the attack and ordered his men to follow him, then began to march quickly toward his fellow soldiers. At the sound of the trumpets, these should have moved aside to let them pass, but they were already partially out of formation, and their centurions could not get them back in place in time for them to manoeuvre, so many therefore remained isolated or in small groups along the route of the column headed by Chaerea who, upon reaching the front line, was forced to slow down.

Rufus shouted repeatedly, calling the slower legionaries – who were still struggling with the enemy and, lacking the assistance of their comrades, falling more frequently – fools, and he also raged against the centurion to whom he had entrusted the manoeuvre but who lacked the courage to get rid of a few fellow soldiers in order to accomplish his task: the sacrifice of a handful of legionaries, he was convinced, would have been a small price to pay for the death of Brutus.

However, Chaerea's initiative seemed to have been successful anyway. At least at that point, his column had brought the front line forward, and the concentration of enemy troops in that narrow sector had forced their opponents to retreat to the sides of the camp, where their ranks had even been broken in some places. Rufus observed the area where Brutus was on horseback, flanked by his bodyguards and encouraging his men to fight. He wondered for a few moments whether it was actually wise to undertake this personal manhunt himself, then decided he would try: there were still breaches open, and if he waited they would probably close. He had to exploit them now.

He raised his arm and ordered the cavalry column, of which had assumed command, to charge, then headed straight for the breach closest to the area occupied by Brutus. When he met the first infantrymen, he raced through and over them at a gallop, uncaring as to whether they belonged to his unit or the enemy. He could barely make out the features of his target beneath his helmet. Brutus was his. There was only one final cordon of legionaries to get past, an unbroken line of shields.

The wall of men withstood the impact, and the horses slowed to a halt. Some of them managed to get past the barricade of shields, but at least two horsemen were knocked off balance and fell to the ground, where they were rapidly finished off by the infantry. Rufus's steed reared and brought down his hooves on the skull of a soldier, who fell to the ground, knocking down the man next to him and opening up a further breach. Rufus was about to spur him on at a gallop towards Brutus, but when he looked round to see how many men were following him he saw that some riders were falling back while others lay on the ground and others trotted about in front of a still intact wall of shields.

Even further back, the infantry were retreating quickly under the pressure of the enemy legionaries.

He was alone.

*

Veleda cursed herself for not having stopped Octavian's bodyguards from focusing solely on the frontal area. In their conviction that the enemy would never manage to get past their line and that the legionaries of the other units would stay close to their commander, no one had thought they needed to guard their flanks, but in reality the simultaneous pressure of the two enemy armies was creating breaches, and the tribune who held his blade at the throat of Octavian had taken advantage of one which had opened up there to break through and surprise him from behind.

"Tell him to release my brother, I said!" repeated Gaius Servilius Casca as he pressed the sword against the young commander's throat. Octavian looked like a statue carved from ice, and despite the situation, his glacial gaze did not fail him even now. Veleda had to admit that, despite what she thought of the sect's leader, he had guts.

"If you kill me, your brother dies too," hissed Octavian.

"And the same holds true for you if *he* dies," said Casca. "So what are we going to do?"

Veleda had the impression that the scene she was watching remained frozen in time, while all around them soldiers were leaping into the air, collapsing to the ground, screaming, swinging their swords and lunging, waving their shields and fighting with all the strength they possessed. She turned back towards Ortwin and saw that he too was immobile, one arm firmly gripping the other Casca brother, no opponent daring to touch him lest he kill the tribune. It was a surreal situation – as though they, the actors upon that stage, inhabited some separate world.

She wondered what Octavian would have done. And what she would soon have to do. She was worried about

Ortwin, isolated there behind enemy lines, and wanted to keep an eye on him, but she had to concentrate on the nearest Casca.

"Veleda, call Ortwin off," said Octavian, turning to her. "I don't want him to end up in a sector occupied mainly by enemies. He will bring Casca with him, of course, and once they are here, the two murderers may go back among their own soldiers."

"Of course," replied Gaius Casca, contemptuously. "And once we're both here, in the midst of your men, you can do with us what you will!"

"No," said Octavian, quietly, "I will go with you. Until you are safely behind your own lines."

The words of the triumvir left the man momentarily disorientated, and even Veleda asked herself if Octavian had gone mad to thus surrender himself to his enemies. But the triumvir stared at her, a determined expression on his face, and she read in his eyes a peremptory order to do as he commanded. His eyes flicked down to her waist for a moment and then back up to her face. Was he trying to tell her something? Once again, Veleda did not understand. She looked down and saw her dagger. Was that what he was referring to?

"So be it then. Have my brother brought over," said Casca to Octavian, and Veleda was forced to move closer to her man and tell him with sweeping gestures to bring the hostage over. Ortwin didn't bat an eyelid and began to approach, no one daring to hinder him – the soldiers around him either ignored him, if they were engaged with an enemy, or impotently watched him pass. The German arrived near his men and Octavian, and looked carefully at all present, especially the triumvir, who nodded to him to release the murderer of Caesar.

Veleda, meanwhile, was trying to work out how to carry out the tacit order given to her by her supreme commander. Ortwin released Casca who, in disbelief, walked toward his brother. Veleda moved over to Ortwin and whispered, "Caesar Octavian was staring at my dagger. What do you think he wanted me to do?"

"He has a plan. Clearly he wants you to throw at one of the two brothers when they start to walk away."

"Me?" Veleda was incredulous. And above all, she was incredulous that Octavian would entrust his safety to her. Yes, to her, who he had accused of failing to prevent the death of his mother.

"You," confirmed Ortwin. "He wants to prove to you that he trusts you."

"But I'll only kill one, even if I do manage to hit him, and the other will kill him."

"No, he won't, because I will take care of the other," replied the German, firmly.

Meanwhile, the bodyguards had moved aside, allowing the two brothers to re-unite. The Cascas stood alongside Octavian, removed his sword, and gestured to him to march towards their lines, squeezing him between their larger bodies and holding their blades to his stomach.

Veleda watched the three men walking side by side away from her, and instinctively grasped the handle of the knife in her belt and pulled it out – but she hesitated before throwing. Octavian was too close to her targets and, above all, the Cascas had him at sword point: even if she managed to hit one of them and not him, any sudden move on her part could cause the triumvir's death.

"I'll take the one on the right, you take the one on the

left," whispered Ortwin, who did not seem worried. With a deep sigh, she prepared to throw. Her man did the same. At that moment, Octavian, with a quick movement of the arm, seemed to hit the Casca to the right of him, who slumped even as the dagger left Ortwin's hand. The knife flew over the tribune's head, missing him. The other Casca stood bewildered for a moment, then took half a step away from Octavian – and it was at that moment that she threw.

Hitting him in the neck, just above the edge of his armour.

A moment later, both of the murderers were on the ground and Octavian, in a fit of rage, had recovered his dagger and was stabbing them frantically and repeatedly, doing to them what they had done to Caesar.

Eventually, the triumvir's fury seemed to be spent. He walked over to Veleda and Ortwin and, looking at the woman, said, "I knew I could count on you, Veleda. You did exactly what I expected."

"But, sir," stammered the woman, still not quite understanding what had happened, "I did not know that you…"

"That I had a dagger and intended to use it? Sometimes wearing four tunics under your armour against the cold is an advantage: you can hide a weapon in them," he said, with a broad smile. The first that Veleda had seen him give in a long time.

XXV

Agrippa made a gesture of annoyance and once again gave up his hopes of killing Tillius Cimber. He could not afford to lose Popillius Laenas nor his *centuria*, so he therefore put the murderer out of his mind and continued along the ditch until he reached him, by which time the officer was surrounded by enemy legionaries. Laenas was screaming wildly at his men to resist, but large gaps had opened up in the circle of shields his unit had formed and the centurion was forced to close the line continuously.

Agrippa took advantage of those who had fallen into the ditch to provide him with a way of getting across it, and, still at the head of his column, he threw himself upon the soldiers fighting Laenas. The enemy, who were putting increasing pressure upon the cult member's men, found themselves in turn under pressure, and Laenas's men started fighting them off with fresh courage, crushing in a pincer movement the opponents who a moment before had been crushing them. At the same moment Agrippa stabbed one in the back the tip of another sword emerged beside the hilt of his own, almost running him through, and when his victim fell to the ground, the figure of Popillius Laenas appeared behind him: he pulled his sword from the same body Agrippa was extracting his own from and gave a coarse laugh as he realised the identity of the man he had almost crossed blades with.

Agrippa could see nothing funny about the situation, though he realised that if he had found himself in front of Gaius Chaerea and not Popillius Laenas he might have laughed at the absurdity of it. He turned and began to swing his sword, making sure in the meantime that the rest of the cohort managed to get over to this side of the moat.

"When you kill someone or see a corpse on the ground, throw it in there!" he shouted to them. Meanwhile, his sword held out towards his opponents, he pushed the body of the man he and Laenas had killed towards the ditch with his foot. He broke free of his nearest enemy, thrusting his sword into his neck until it slid out of the back, knocking his helmet off his head as it did so, then crouched down and pushed the body into the hole. The soldiers had been obeying his orders, and now the ditch could be crossed – in fact, almost all of his units had already done so, and their enemies were now between two fires. Agrippa had re-joined Laenas's column and could now force their opponents onto the front line of his own legion. But first there was one thing that needed be done.

"Laenas!" he called to the centurion. "Take your men and guard the praetorian gate of Brutus's camp! They will try to get back inside to escape being encircled and we have to stop them!"

The centurion frowned, visibly displeased at having to obey an order that brought him no glory, but Agrippa ignored him: after all, Laenas had set off on the attack without respecting orders.

As for him, now that things seemed to be going well in his part of the battlefield he could resume the hunt for Tillius Cimber, and together with a column of his men, he returned to where he had last seen him. He wandered through the fighting, ignoring the individual battles and clashes between small groups, seeking only the detachment of a tribune. When he finally located him, Cimber was facing in the other direction. Unwilling to stab an opponent in the back in a duel, Agrippa ran at him, shouting at him to turn round. And when he was almost upon him, the man did, and Agrippa saw that he was not Caesar's killer. But he had to take him down, even though the real Tillius Cimber was only a few steps away, had noticed his hunter and was attempting to make his way through the crush to escape the confrontation.

Agrippa swung blow after blow at the man, upon whom he could ill afford to waste time, but the man seemed to know his stuff – he nether retreated nor let him pass, blocking him blow for blow. Agrippa began to grow impatient. Tullius Cimber was getting further and further away. He pressed his opponent but in his haste lowered his guard, and the other man slashed his thigh, creating a deep cut. Agrippa reacted to the burning in his leg with a roar, followed by a tremendous number of blows into which he put all his strength. He realised that he had broken the enemy's shield, which the man now cast away, and was ready to deliver the decisive thrust when his injury made him trip, and he fell to his knees in the mud. The enemy soldier could hardly believe his luck at finding his opponent at his mercy, and made a jab at him which the young man parried with his shield before swinging an upwards blow that cut cleanly through the tribune's arm.

He wasted no time finishing him off, then climbed to his feet with great effort and limped off as fast as he was able towards Tullius Cimber. Cimber was fleeing, but when he saw Agrippa hobbling towards him he gave an evil smile, paused, and turned to face him, encouraged by his enemy's wound. Agrippa was immediately subjected to a hail of blows that forced him to retreat, until his leg gave way and he collapsed again into the mire. Cimber shouted in joy and attacked, but Agrippa dodged, rolling out of the way in the mud, and Cimber's sword struck the ground where he had lain a moment earlier. Agrippa pulled his shield from his arm and hurled it along the ground at the tribune's shins. Cimber collapsed forward and Agrippa threw himself at him, holding his arms down with his own body weight.

Cimber squirmed and kicked, like a wrestler pinned to the floor, but was unable to get to his feet. With his right hand, Agrippa grasped Cimber's sword hand. The men's two blades were touching now, and moving now towards Cimber's face, now towards Agrippa's ribs. Agrippa decided to risk letting go and striking a blow, hoping he would be quick enough to pre-empt his opponent, who would certainly try to stab him.

He released the other man's arm and swung his sword to the left, in the direction of Cimber's face, and the blade entered the tribune's mouth. Cimber's eyes widened and he stiffened, then vomited blood onto the mud and lay still. But not before his sword had pricked Agrippa's side.

The young man lay there for a few moments on the lifeless body of the murderer, trying to catch his breath, and then with great difficulty rose to his knees and, eventually, to his feet, forcing himself to ignore the pain in his thigh. He had lost a lot of blood but could not afford to stop. He looked around him, and saw that the situation had changed. The enemy were retreating from his legion and moving towards the sector occupied by Rufus's units. He asked one of his soldiers what had happened and the man informed him that the men of his fellow member of Mars Ultor had succumbed and that now all of Brutus's

442

men nearby were pursuing them.

Losing any residual cohesion, from what he could see.

Perhaps the battle could be won there. They needed men, though, and they didn't have enough. But then he remembered what Octavian had said: "We'll let Antony win for us."

And it was clear what would be the next move. Involuntarily, Rufus would act as bait.

*

Gaius Chaerea was struggling but he saw that Rufus was struggling even more. The legion was broken up, with some parts retreating, and they were isolated behind enemy lines. It had been easy to predict that this would have happened, but the tribune had not wanted to listen to reason. And now he was more exposed than anyone else to a counter attack from Brutus.

He had to help him.

The enemy were dispersing in pursuit of his fellow soldiers further back, and this allowed him to manoeuvre his column diagonally without attracting enemy pressure on their flanks. They only had to deal with a few isolated group of soldiers who had been tardy setting off, and his men stayed in formation. On the other hand, their opponents were more interested in attacking those with their backs to them than a solid unit ready to resist: if they met opposition they didn't insist too much and simply took another direction. Only a few of the units in front of Brutus maintained their positions, but Chaerea, unlike Rufus, had no intention of attacking the enemy commander for the moment. It would have been suicide.

Rufus was trying to wriggle his way out of the forest of legionaries in which he found himself, but his steed, like those of many of the horsemen who had accompanied him, could find no space to move. The tribune was swinging his sword to keep off the soldiers around him, but there were too many of them and, sooner or later, he would be done for. Some of his subordinates had already seen their horses killed beneath them and had fallen to the ground, only to find themselves struck by a dozen swords moments later. Which was what would happen to Rufus too, unless Gaius intervened quickly. He led the column straight towards Rufus as the tribune was knocked from his horse and fell to the ground.

Chaerea immediately commanded his men to break through, bearing down upon the soldiers who were about to finish off his comrade. Some noticed his arrival and turned in time to face him and his men, but others, busy with Rufus, let themselves be surprised from behind. The column arrived solid and compact, and even those who had prepared for them were unable to resist – Chaerea and his men engulfed them, slamming the enemy legionaries to the ground and slaughtering them with their swords. Some fell onto Rufus, who found himself buried beneath more than one corpse. When he eventually managed to regain his feet, he gave Gaius a fleeting nod of thanks and turned to look in the direction of Brutus.

At that very moment, the enemy commander was urging his horse on, and, along with his bodyguards and some of the units closest to him, was leaving that part of the battlefield. Where he was going, Gaius had no idea, but then he noticed several enemy contingents appearing from the sector entrusted to Agrippa, and knew that Brutus was running away. He saw their tribune leading the newcomers and, along with Rufus, went over to meet him.

"What happened?" asked Rufus, as soon as they met. "Why are you here?"

"I could say that I have come to give you a hand because I saw that you were in trouble," said Agrippa. "But the truth is that I noticed the enemy were busy pursuing you so I thought I'd take the opportunity to attack them from the side and from behind. I convinced Antony to take advantage of the situation, and he sent a contingent with my unit and I rushed over here."

Rufus didn't attempt to hide his annoyance. "You needn't have bothered," he said bitterly, "everything was under control here." But Chaerea knew that the front there had collapsed, and that it took one as brazen as Rufus not to admit it. Agrippa's appearance was providential.

"If you say so… Let's say that we are working to inflict a decisive blow upon the enemy," said Agrippa, philosophically.

Rufus muttered something unintelligible and went off to round up his horsemen and get himself a horse from among those who had survived.

"You did right to come, Agrippa" said Gaius, once the tribune had left. "Shall I come after them with you?"

"No. I'd prefer you to supplement my sector, I had to leave it undefended," said the tribune. "We weren't in trouble. In fact, we'd virtually surrounded the enemy. But I took a cohort with my legion when I came to your aid, and wouldn't want there not to be enough men to force them to surrender."

Chaerea nodded, then motioned to his unit, which in the meantime had reconstituted its ranks, and went where

Agrippa had ordered him. He passed the enemy ramparts and saw that the encirclement manoeuvre had almost been successful. Some of the enemy had actually already laid down their arms in surrender. Others, however, resisted and, in some cases, had proven themselves capable of breaking through the blockade.

He was distributing his own men over the sectors most at risk when he heard his name being called. He turned and saw Popillius Laenas gesturing for his attention, and went to him. Laenas was just below the embankment, near the praetorian gate, along with other soldiers, and together they were forming a sort of tortoise for protection against the projectiles arriving from the stands.

"What do you want?" he asked, as soon as he was within earshot.

"Change places with me! I've been here for ages now stopping enemy troops from getting back in, and I've already lost three men!"

Gaius was puzzled for a moment. Why should he oblige him?

"Come on, Chaerea!" insisted the other. "Do a favour for a man who's more than just a comrade, if you know what I mean…" he added. "I've been here long enough!"

Gaius threw open his arms in resignation. Laenas was quite capable of making himself a pain in the arse unless he kept him happy, and it made little difference to him whether he was under the battlements or involved in encircling the enemy. He motioned to his remaining men to follow him and ordered them to form a tortoise in the same place as Laenas's men. The centurion gave up his position and hurried off, vanishing into the crowd, apparently eager to fight.

Shortly afterwards, a squad of enemy legionaries who had escaped encirclement and were headed for the door tried to break through the blockade. Their fellows in the battlements noticed, and unleashed upon the tortoise a hail of arrows and small and large stones that the roof of shields deflected easily. But now they had to fight too, to foil the attempt at retreat. Gaius ordered his men to advance towards the squad with shields together and led them to counterattack. A few seconds later there was the impact, which sparked a melee where he immediately realised they were outnumbered. Nevertheless, availing himself of the slope, they managed to repel their opponents at the price of only two soldiers and inflicted heavy losses on the enemy.

He was about to resume their position and reform the tortoise when he suddenly saw a boulder flying towards him from the battlements. He just had time to shift his torso but not his right leg, which was hit by the projectile, sending a wave of pain through him that felt like being stabbed simultaneously with dozens of swords. He heard his bones shattering into a thousand pieces then rolled over and fell backwards into the ditch, hitting his head and losing consciousness.

*

As incredible it might seem, the battle was won. Ortwin knew how to recognise the signs. The enemy army still had several units intact, and Brutus's camp had not yet fallen, but the beginning of the dissolution of the enemy ranks was more than evident to a trained eye like his. Mark Antony had wiped out all resistance in his sector of the field and was gradually advancing towards the centre, pressing against the flanks of the legions engaged against Octavian who, for his part, had been facilitating the task of routing the enemy. The enemy cohorts were no longer either united nor in formation, and rather than fighting they were tending to retreat and take refuge in the gorges and mountains bordering the battlefield. The legionaries were no longer listening to their officers, busy as they were saving their own skins, no one was gathering around the standard bearers nor did anyone attempt to force the blockades that prevented access to the camps. Some soldiers threw down their arms and surrendered as soon as they saw the approaching army of Caesar's avengers while others sent messages to talk terms.

But of Brutus there was no sign.

Octavian, of course, had entrusted to Ortwin the task of finding him at all costs, and thus the barbarian had climbed into the saddle, taking with him a squadron of Germanic and Roman horsemen – but not Veleda, who had remained with the triumvir – and had set off on the trail of the enemy commander, starting from the last position where he had been sighted, near Rufus's sector of the battlefield. Every time he had the opportunity to talk to a fleeing enemy soldier, he asked him where the general was, promising him a rich reward or, alternatively, a quick death. But even the most talkative and co-operative had no idea of Brutus's eventual goals and intentions, and could only say where they last saw him.

If nothing else, they could follow his trail. He had now come to steeper, wooded ground that forced him to dismount and climb the slope on foot. The silhouettes of fugitives could be seen amongst the trees up above them. If what the prisoners had told him was true, that was where Brutus might be. He quickened his pace, making his way through the bush and leaving behind the others, until he reached a clearing where he saw a wounded man.

He approached him and asked, "Were you with Brutus?"

The soldier spat blood. He had a gash on his side. "No, I was with that animal Labienus," he said, with difficulty. There was a flutter of rage deep inside Ortwin's soul. "They were together until a moment ago, then they split up when they left this clearing. I was stupid enough to decide to stay with Labienus, thinking that they'd be all over Brutus in no time... But the damn tribune dumped me here when he saw that I was hurt and might slow him down..."

Ortwin knelt down and seized him by the edge of his armour. "Where? Where did Labienus go?" he hissed at the man.

The soldier had only a breath of life remaining but did not hesitate to answer. "He went that way," he whispered, with the little strength he had left, pointing ahead. "And Brutus went that way," he added, pointing behind him. Then he closed his eyes and died.

At that moment, Ortwin's men appeared. They looked at the German and peered around the clearing quizzically, then asked, "Now what?"

There was no doubt in Ortwin's mind. "This soldier told me that Brutus went that way and is close by," he said, pointing in the direction Labienus had taken. "Quickly!"

He set off even faster than before and, the others behind him, raced off into the bush, all feelings of fatigue now vanished. The idea of facing his rival put wings upon his feet, and soon the others could no longer keep up. The

German realised that he was supposed to be waiting for them to back him up, but he was afraid of losing track of Labienus, and did not slow down until, eventually, he spotted a few soldiers and, among them, an officer with a crest on his helmet. It could only be him.

"Quintus! Stop and face me man to man, scum!" he cried. "I assure you that it will be just you and me!"

The commanding officer halted suddenly at his words. He turned slowly and stared at him. It was Quintus Labienus. The other soldiers with him stood awaiting orders, and in the meantime Ortwin's men appeared. Ortwin took a step forward and so did Labienus. Again, the German moved closer and the Roman followed suit, one step at a time, until they were face to face, only a few paces apart. All around, the soldiers of both factions, panting with fatigue, stood watching the duel as though frozen, the only sound the distant echoes of the battle on the plain.

"Why not? It's about time we put an end to all this," said Labienus, with a grin. "I won't run away this time, Ortwin."

"Oh really? How strange…" replied the other defiantly. His words provoked an attack from the Roman, whose blade smashed into his shield with a clang that echoed in the ears of those present. The German reacted with a swinging downward blow which went wide, hitting the ground next to the enemy. Labienus tried a lunge, which Ortwin, twisting his torso, avoided only by a whisker, before striking a blow in return which caught Quintus in the thigh, opening a gash in his flesh. The Roman glanced at his opponent with hatred and resumed his attack with renewed fury, raining blows upon him which went wide or crashed against his shield. His rage stoked that of Ortwin, who became equally disorientated, and the duel rapidly turned into a brawl. Whenever Ortwin's eyes met the mad stare of the Roman, he remembered all the suffering that the man had caused Veleda, and his strength was renewed.

"Tribune, more of the enemy are coming!" shouted a voice from the bushes, warning Labienus to disengage. "No, not that," thought Ortwin. "I must be the one to capture or to kill him," and he intensified his fighting, lowering his own guard in order to encourage his opponent to do the same. But he had underestimated the reflexes of Labienus, who immediately took advantage of the fact and sank his blade into the chest of his eternal enemy. The German felt it penetrate deeply into the muscles and tendons of his shoulder, and the searing pain was renewed when the tribune withdrew it, took a deep breath, and prepared to strike the final blow.

"This is the end, it would appear…" said Labienus with an evil grin, while Ortwin fell to his knees, his vision growing foggy as he held his shoulder injury. "One day I will return to Rome to take Veleda. And you will be able to do nothing about it, because you will be dead!"

The Roman raised his arm but a soldier stopped him.

"Forget about him! They're here, they're here!" he shouted, and his comrades began to flee. Labienus looked down the slope, from whence even Ortwin could hear the trampling of hundreds of feet, then made a gesture of irritation, and disappeared into the trees in an instant.

Ortwin slumped to the ground, and his men rushed to his aid. He had failed. He had disobeyed Octavian's order and gone in search of personal vengeance, and now he could not even bring the triumvir the head of the man who had killed his mother.

And even less prove once and for all to Veleda whether it was he or Quintus who was worth loving.

Epilogue

Octavia felt as though she was losing her mind. Her fate had never been as uncertain as at was in that moment, and she had never been so alone. Her mother was dead, as was her maid, and her brother was away on a demanding military campaign which would put huge strains upon his delicate physique. Her husband had become a threat since she had discovered he was willing to kill anyone just to take his revenge upon her... And Gaius Chaerea... Gaius Chaerea was probably already dead too.

The latest news to arrive from the front had made her more and more downcast. In Rome they had learned that there had been an initial battle between Octavian and the assassins of Julius Caesar, and that Octavian had lost. Antony had won in his part of the battleground, however, so the situation was not entirely compromised, although food and supplies were scarce, which was causing serious problems for her brother's army.

And then there was the disaster in the Adriatic. Domitius Calvinus had been forced to return to Italy without much of his fleet – the fleet in which Gaius had been travelling. By now, the only man Octavia had ever loved might well be at the bottom of the sea, or, at best, a prisoner of the enemy.

In Rome, all were awaiting the decisive battle, and no one dared to take sides before they knew who would win. With the proscriptions and the dominance of the triumvirate, it had appeared that all were now supporters of Caesar – but when news had started arriving of the triumvirate's difficulties overseas, many Republicans had started making their voices heard once more, and no one dared silence them, for fear of falling victim to persecution in the event of Brutus being victorious.

She took care not to be seen in public, and while she awaited news from the front lived a reclusive life, locked up inside her house and receiving no visitors, as all those who had dealings with Octavian's family now feared compromising themselves. She spent the days playing with her little daughter Marcella and wondering what would happen to them if Caesar's murderers prevailed: she would probably end up in exile, if she was lucky – otherwise, some hothead might send them to join her mother.

And not a day went by that she didn't feel guilty for having sent Gaius Chaerea to his death, depriving his son Marcus of a loving father. She had forced him to compromise his principles, and the fate of the child tormented her too.

If only she hadn't had that ridiculous idea of sending Gaius to Macedonia… now he would have been near her, and would have defended her and his own family from the tumult that would undoubtedly arise in Rome in the increasingly likely event of an enemy victory. Gaius had agreed for her sake, but inside he must have known that it was a hopeless undertaking. Still, he had attempted it just the same. Octavia had thought she was making herself useful to the sect by tearing him from the warmth of his family and using him as a messenger, but instead she had delivered the mortal blow to the sacred brotherhood by sending the only one of them who had a real chance of saving himself, off to die.

Rarely was there a knock on the door of her *domus* in those days, and when there was, Octavia always started in fear: it might be news from the front, of which there had been none for almost a month. She started again when she heard the door open, and motioned for Marcella to be quiet when she heard the heavy footsteps of the caretaker and his voice telling a slave to take a letter to the *domina*. She felt an icy grip in her stomach and her temples began to throb, and when the door of the *tablinum* opened and the man handed her the package containing the wax tablet, she wished that the duty of reading it fell on another.

But she forced herself to take it and dismissed the slave. With trembling hands she opened the little parcel and, after taking a deep breath, began to read the letter.

> Philippi, v day before the *Nonae* of October
>
> Dear sister, we have won. The Mars Ultor sect has triumphed and avenged our father after a hard campaign and a battle we had to fight twice. Of course, not all the murderers are dead. Cassius Longinus committed suicide in the first battle, as you may have already heard. Marcus Brutus did the same after the second defeat, when he saw that his soldiers preferred to surrender rather than continue to fight for him. I personally killed one of the Casca brothers, Veleda killed the other. Agrippa eliminated Tullius Cimber. Others fell in combat and only a few remain on the loose, but we will hunt them down, and sooner or later they

will pay for their crimes. Quintus Labienus, the murderer of our mother and Etain, also escaped because Ortwin did not manage to stop him. Luckily, all our followers survived, but Ortwin, Maecenas and Gaius Chaerea were wounded. Chaerea got it worse: he lost a leg, but I will never cease to be grateful to him for showing his attachment to the sect by crossing Italy, the sea, Greece and Macedonia. He survived a shipwreck to fight for us and to inform me of your husband's betrayal.

Just as I will never cease to be grateful to you, my sister, for having had the initiative to send him to me. You have no idea how vital it was to strengthen our resolve and our unity, which, under the weight of a thousand difficulties, had threatened to fall apart. You are truly a valuable member of the sect, and I owe you an apology for not having realised this earlier.

I will soon be back in Italy, where it is vital that I remind all who the victor of Philippi was. Antony, for his part, is about to set off for Egypt, where he will meet Queen Cleopatra, who helped us by ignoring Cassius's demands for assistance. Antony and I have decided that Lepidus has become superfluous and, at the appropriate time, we will remove his authority. Why govern in three when we can do it in two? We have defeated the murderers of Julius Caesar, we have the support of the army, and there is no reason for him too to benefit from our power. It will be another step, my sister, towards the realisation of all the goals we set ourselves when we swore to avenge Caesar and to complete his work of reforming the empire of Rome. Once again, we have proven ourselves to be invincible.

Take care and give my love to my niece Marcella. We will see each other soon, and when I return we will decide what to do with your husband.

Yours,

Gaius Julius Caesar Octavian

We hope you enjoyed this book!

More addictive fiction from Aria:

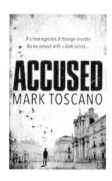
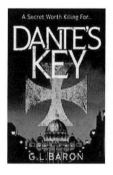

Find out more
http://headofzeus.com/books/isbn/9781784978907

Find out more
http://headofzeus.com/books/isbn/9781784977511

Find out more
http://headofzeus.com/books/isbn/9781786690692

About Andrew Frediani

ANDREW FREDIANI is an Italian author and academic. He has published several non-fiction books as well as historical novels including the *Invincible* series and the *Dictator* trilogy. His works have been translated into five languages.

Find me on Facebook
https://www.facebook.com/andreafredianipaginaufficiale/a
tab=page_info

Visit my website
http://www.andreafrediani.it/

About the Rome's Invincibles Series

Find out more
http://headofzeus.com/books/isbn/9781784978884

Find out more
http://headofzeus.com/books/isbn/9781784978938

Visit Aria now
http://www.ariafiction.com

Become an Aria Addict

Aria is the new digital-first fiction imprint from Head of Zeus.

It's Aria's ambition to discover and publish tomorrow's superstars, targeting fiction addicts and readers keen to discover new and exciting authors.

Aria will publish a variety of genres under the commercial fiction umbrella such as women's fiction, crime, thrillers, historical fiction, saga and erotica.

So, whether you're a budding writer looking for a publisher or an avid reader looking for something to escape with – Aria will have something for you.

Get in touch: aria@headofzeus.com

Become an Aria Addict
http://www.ariafiction.com

Find us on Twitter
https://twitter.com/Aria_Fiction

Find us on Facebook
http://www.facebook.com/ariafiction

Find us on BookGrail
http://www.bookgrail.com/store/aria/

Addictive Fiction

First published in Italy in 2016 by Newton Compton

First published in the UK in 2016 by Aria, an imprint of Head of Zeus Ltd

Copyright © Andrew Frediani, 2015

The moral right of Andrew Frediani to be identified as the author of this work
has been asserted in accordance with the Copyright, Designs and Patents Act of
1988.

All rights reserved. No part of this publication may be reproduced, stored in a
retrieval system, or transmitted, in any form or by any means, electronic,
mechanical, photocopying, recording, or otherwise, without the prior
permission of both the copyright owner and the above publisher of this book.

This is a work of fiction. All characters, organizations, and events portrayed in
this novel are either products of the author's imagination or are used fictitiously.

975312468

A CIP catalogue record for this book is available from the British Library.

ISBN (E) 9781784978938

Aria
Clerkenwell House
45-47 Clerkenwell Green
London EC1R 0HT

www.ariafiction.com

19910856R00258

Printed in Great Britain
by Amazon